The Days of Noah

Virginia Smith

The Days of Noah

© 2013, 2017 by Virginia Smith

Published by Next Step Books LLC, P.O. Box 70271, West Valley City, Utah 84170

Cover design by Nick Delliskave

ISBN-13: 978-1-937671-11-2
ISBN-10: 1937671119

A Note from Virginia Smith

The book of Genesis doesn't have much to say about the society in which Noah and his family lived. What a delight to an author with a vivid imagination, because the framework for stories set during that time period is wide open. All we are told is that in Noah's day mankind had become evil and corrupt. Many have assumed the culture to be primitive–but what if that assumption is wrong? What if civilization had progressed to the point of cultivating technology? What if Noah's society had developed some of the alarming elements of our own society?

As it was in the days of Noah, so it will be at the coming of the Son of Man.

Matthew 24:37

Part One

City of the God

Chapter 1

Behind a well-bloodied altar, the high priestess stood ramrod straight, a razor-sharp blade poised above her head. Eliana matched the rigid posture, her gaze riveted on the glistening knife gripped in her mother's hands. A lamb lay bleating in terror on the altar, held in place by two blue-robed priestesses. Knots formed in Eliana's stomach, and she averted her gaze from the struggling animal. Gathered in the courtyard before the open-air dais, the mesmerized crowd drew an audible breath, anticipating the moment of the knife's descent.

From her position on the rear of the dais, deep beneath the shade of the golden canopy, Eliana watched her mother's slender back, taut cords of muscle plainly visible beneath the filmy white gown. Her gaze shifted to the opposite side of the platform where another dark-haired priestess waited. The woman's hand rested gently, almost lovingly, on the shoulder of a child.

The last of the morning's sacrifices stood motionless, watching the ritual through drug-laden eyes.

The crowd roared approval as the knife fell, and Eliana's stomach lurched. By sheer force of will she remained outwardly passive, though her throat convulsed with the effort of keeping her breakfast in place. Why did the blood still disturb her so? Sacrifices had been part of her daily routine for years, since she ascended from the temple's nursery to dwell in the upper halls. High Priestess Liadan made no secret of the fact that she despised this weakness in her daughter, and that Eliana must master her squeamishness. She had no choice. For in only a few years, Eliana would be called to take her mother's place at the altar.

A movement among the masses caught her eye. A man dressed in farmer's trousers and a loose-fitting shirt turned away to push through the crowd. Before the people closed in and hid him from view, he looked once more toward the dais where the high priestess stood. Even from the distance, his distaste at the spectacle showed clearly on his face. He shook his head sadly before disappearing into the crowd.

As the attendant priestesses removed the lamb's carcass, Eliana's gaze traveled once again to the opposite end of the dais. All hair had been shaved from the child's head, making the gender impossible to determine. A white linen robe hung loosely from thin shoulders, and as Eliana watched, the priestess gently nudged the child toward the stairs leading to the altar. For one moment, dark, dull eyes locked onto Eliana's in an unfocused stare.

With the speed of a lion attacking its prey, repugnance struck her like a physical assault. Burning acid surged into her throat, and her knees threatened to buckle. She shrank against the heavy gold curtain behind her. One urgent thought pummeled her brain: escape, before she vomited. If forced to watch one more sacrifice this morning, she would shame herself, her mother, and worst of all, the mighty god, Cain.

Though she would certainly be called to task later, Eliana slipped behind the curtain into the temple, and ran.

Breath burning in her lungs, Eliana catapulted through a side door that led from the temple into a secluded corner of the public gardens. Bright sunlight assaulted her eyes after the dim lighting of the temple corridors. She stopped on the cobbled walkway to recover her breath, inhaling deep draughts of rose-scented air to clear the stench of sacrificial blood from her nostrils. In the distance she heard the roar of a hundred exhilarated voices and knew the final sacrifice of the morning had been performed. An image rose unbidden in her mind: sightless eyes, dark and dull, stared skyward as the child's life dripped into the high priestess's chalice to appease the hungry god.

Huge gulps of cool morning air tasted sweet against the bitter bile that again threatened to choke her.

No! She pressed fists against her eyes. *Think of something else.*

"Alms, lady?"

Startled, she opened her eyes to see a filthy urchin before her. He must have been hiding behind the hedge that lined the cobbled path. Beggars were unusual in the secluded cluster of shops and taverns that surrounded the temple gardens. In the unlikely event one decided to try his luck inside the ornamental iron gates separating the private marketplace from the press of Cainlan's city streets, dozens of uniformed guardsman were normally on hand to point out his error. This child had somehow escaped notice. The bones in his wrist protruded beneath thin, dirt-encrusted skin as he thrust his palm toward her, gazing up with liquid brown eyes.

Eyes that flickered with life.

Eliana reached for the bag that hung at her side
when she shopped. Then she remembered. She hadn't
needed a bag for the morning sacrifice. It was back in
her rooms in the temple's resident hall.

"I'm sorry. I've nothing to give."

Disbelief flashed across the child's features. His
gaze dropped to take in her silk gown, followed by a
smirk of disgust. He spat, barely missing her embroi-
dered slippers, and ran off. She watched as he ducked
under the cover of a thick, flowering bush.

At least he was alive to run away.

When the urchin was out of sight, Eliana hesitated. Duty demanded that she return to the temple.
Girta would be waiting in her rooms with something
cool and calming to drink. But this morning the thick
stone walls of the only home she'd ever known threatened to press the breath right out of her body.

With a guilty backward glance, Eliana turned away
from the temple and hurried down the walkway, her
silken gown whispering around her feet. The gardens
lay inside the high hedge to her right. At the center a
statue of Cain towered above the greenery, his back to
the temple dedicated to his service. Sometimes that
ever-watchful presence comforted her, but in recent
days, with her official entry into the priesthood drawing nearer, the god's regard presented a menacing
force that haunted her dreams. She kept her head
turned away.

At the far end of the stone and wood shops that
comprised the market square rose the imposing building that housed the Cabinet of Energy. She avoided
looking in that direction as well. The smooth, polished
walls, so different from the rough hewn stone of the
temple, stirred feelings of disquiet deep in her stomach. The sun's rays reflected off glass panels, blinding
her and hiding the actions of those who worked within
doing ... what? The workings of Cainlan's government
were largely a mystery, at least to a fledgling priestess.
Each morning men and women filed inside clutching

satchels and moving with quick, hurried steps that gave the impression of important activities awaiting them inside the shining walls. At the end of the day, those same men and women filed out carrying the same satchels. At night the energy-powered lights lining the roof cast a harsh glow into the sky and blotted out the twinkling stars. In daylight, the building stood as a gleaming symbol of progress, staring defiance across the gardens toward the ancient temple and the statue of the god the temple served.

When the building was erected ten years before, Liadan's voice had snapped with irritation whenever it was mentioned. But in recent years the High Priestess's attitude had undergone a change. Though Eliana still heard the occasional grumble about 'that monstrosity' blocking her view of the city that sprawled to the south, her mother had ceased grumbling about the government. The reason, Eliana suspected, had little to do with politics and everything to do with Captor, the handsome governor whose first official project after his appointment was to champion the building project.

Eliana jumped when a loud blast from a horn signaled the end of the sacrifice ceremony. Within moments the walkway filled with people intent on their own errands. Shopkeepers threw open their shutters and attempted to coax customers through their doorways with promises of bargains and temple-blessed wares. Eliana allowed herself to be swept along toward the far end of the market square, where she turned into the relative peace of a narrow alleyway.

The scent of freshly baked bread carried from the corner bakery, so like the kitchen near the temple nursery. She missed those peaceful years, when she'd been too young to attract her mother's attention beyond the obligatory monthly visits to the high priestess's chambers.

A movement ahead caught her eye. The pet shop owner wrestled a heavy iron cage through the doorway of his store. Inside, a colorful bird squawked in protest at the rough handling. Another man emerged from the shop in the owner's wake, his quiet voice easily heard in the narrow confines of the alley.

"I'm quite sure my father would be interested in a pair, if you could manage to find a female."

At a glimpse of his profile, her breath caught in her throat. He was the man she had seen in the crowd, the farmer who had turned away before the end of the sacrificial ritual.

The shop owner placed the cage near the window and faced his customer, hands on his hips. "Your father has quite a collection by now, I'd say."

A warm laugh rumbled toward her. "That he does, but none like this."

Collection? Was the stranger's father a bird handler, then? A pair of women entered the alley, chatting with one another as they headed toward the fabric shop at the far end. Curious, Eliana crept closer to the men, her eyes averted but her ears tuned to their conversation.

"My supplier can find a female, but they're expensive. They come all the way from Enoch, and the roads are dangerous these days." The shop owner shook his head. "I'll need payment in advance."

A shadow fell across Eliana, accompanied by the stench of rotten breath. She whirled and lifted her eyes to a face much closer than she liked. A man, tall and broad-shouldered, towered over her. His companion, whose clothes bore evidence of much wear and little washing, stepped behind her to successfully box her in. Narrowed eyes glinted down at her as cracked lips parted in a grin.

Alarm plunged into her belly.

"What do we have here? A lady in fancy clothes."

He fingered the gold-embroidered silk of her gown where it draped across her collarbone, and Eliana drew breath to voice an outraged protest. His rough hand brushed against her breast. Her words died unspoken while icy fear froze the blood in her veins. She shrank away, but the man behind her formed an immovable barrier. Twisting sideways, she pressed her back against the stone wall. Why had she run off without a cloak to cover her gown? She might as well have strung gold coins from her ears and invited thieves to take them. Hadn't Girta warned her over and over? She cast about frantically for a means of escape, but could not tear her gaze from the menacing grin blocking her view. Could she outrun them, make a dash for the alley entrance?

As though he heard her thought, the man raised a meaty arm and planted his hand against the stone beside her, entrapping her in a cage of sweaty flesh.

The second man lifted a fat finger to point at her face. "Hey, I know her. She was up by the altar."

The first man's grin deepened. "A priestess, eh?" He put his other hand on the wall beside her head and leaned closer. "I've heard some of them priestesses can be mighty friendly to a working man when they're asked real nice."

The man's hand dropped to her shoulder and slid down her arm. A trail of fire seared her skin where his fingers touched, and a fierce trembling in her knees threatened to drop her to the cobbled ground. She had to get away, to run to the safety of the temple, and of Girta's arms.

"I—" Her voice failed her. She gulped and tried again. "I must get back. I'm...I'm expected."

The second man's low chuckle resonated in her ears. "What's the hurry? We've got a nice place out in the city where—"

"Pardon my intrusion."

Eliana jerked her gaze to the man who suddenly appeared behind her captors. The farmer who'd been bargaining for the colorful bird. Anger erupted on the faces of the ruffians as they turned toward him, shoulder-to-shoulder. Their backs formed a wall of muscle and flesh in front of Eliana.

Courtesy and steel blended in the farmer's soft

voice. "I'm concluding my business here, and then I can accompany the lady back to the temple."

The backs of her captors swelled until they seemed to double in size. "Mind your business. This lady don't need no dirt digger to take her anywhere."

The farmer's soft voice did not change. "I think she does."

As one, they took a menacing step toward him. With a quick sideways movement, Eliana slid out of their reach. Without a backward glance, she dashed blindly down the alley. Half a breath later she realized her mistake. She should have run the other way, toward the alley's entrance and the safety of the wide-open gardens where the marketplace guards would see her. There was no place to go in this direction except into one of the shops in this tiny alley. She skidded to a halt behind the dubious protection of the metal bird-cage, just as the animal keeper emerged from the open doorway of his shop. In one hand he carried a short but sturdy club, which he slapped rhythmically into the palm of the other as he stalked toward the place where the farmer stood his ground before the pair of brutes.

"Here now, we'll have none of this. Be on your way."

The larger of the thugs glanced toward Eliana, clearly considering whether or not she was worth pursuing. She huddled behind the cage, fear coursing down her spine. Though the farmer stood half a head taller, they both possessed arms nearly the width of Eliana's waist, and were decades younger than the shopkeeper. If they decided to fight, could she scream loud enough to attract the attention of the temple guards? Were there any guards near enough to come to their aid?

The first ruffian turned his head and spat. "Let's go." Apparently he didn't mind the odds of two men against one petite woman, but didn't relish the idea of pairing off against other men.

His companion hesitated, and then joined him. Eliana's rescuers did not move until the thugs had left the alley.

When her would-be attackers were out of sight, she sagged against the shop's doorway, eyes closed, and willed her heartbeat to slow. Footsteps approached.

"Are you hurt, lady?"

She shook her head and looked up into the kind gray eyes of the farmer. "I'm fine, thanks to you." She slid her gaze to include the shopkeeper. "Thanks to you both."

The man slapped his club once more into his palm. "I'll have a word with the guards, I will. We don't need their kind in here. The temple marketplace should be safe for priestesses." He peered at her. "Seen you here before, I have. You won't warn your friends not to come?"

Eliana's smile trembled nearly as much as her knees. She saw no need to correct his assumption that she was a priestess. "I'll tell everyone I know of your bravery and how you rescued me from..." She shuddered, unable to contemplate exactly what she'd been rescued from at the hands of those crude men. Something terrible, for certain.

He jerked a satisfied nod. "That's alright, then."

The farmer smiled, tiny lines deepening around his kind eyes. He was tall and trim with muscular arms evident beneath a loose-fitting shirt the color of mature wheat. A plain strip of leather at the base of his neck secured dark hair sprinkled lightly with silver.

She looked toward the alley's entrance. "Thank you again. I should go." The thought of leaving the safety these men provided set her pulse racing once again. Were the two ruffians out of sight, waiting for her to leave her rescuers' company?

The man followed her gaze. "If you're returning to the temple, I'll go with you."

Relief flooded her. She didn't trust her voice, but accepted his offer with a nod.

He turned to the animal keeper and gestured toward the cage. "About that bird. I'll need to check with my father concerning the expense."

"My supplier leaves in six days. I don't know when he'll make another trip."

The farmer dipped his forehead. "Then I will return in five."

The shop owner waved a hand in dismissal, and with a final smile in her direction, disappeared into his shop. When he was out of sight, the handsome stranger watched the bird smooth the colorful feathers that covered its wing, an unreadable expression on his face. Wistful, maybe? Or merely secretive?

His expression cleared, and he gestured toward the market square's main walkway. "Shall we?"

Eliana fell in step beside him. His arms swung at his sides with an easy grace as he walked. She had to hurry to keep up with his long-legged gait.

"I heard you mention that your father is a bird collector." Her mouth snapped shut on the last word. She'd just given herself away as an eavesdropper.

He seemed not to notice. "Not really, though he is keenly interested in animals of all kinds, especially those from distant lands."

"Is he a breeder, then?"

"Not exactly." For one moment, his lips twitched with a secret. "My father is a simple farmer, as are I and my two brothers. He's also something of a carpenter." He pulled up short as they approached the end of the alley, and turned to face her. "I've not introduced myself. Forgive me. I am Shem de Noah, eldest son of Noah and Midian."

He executed a formal half-bow and gave her an expectant look.

Eliana tore her gaze from his face. How should she identify herself, her parentage? Hadn't Girta warned her more than once against telling anyone who she was? She avoided his eyes. The crowd on the marketplace walkways had dwindled to a handful of shoppers who hurried past. The two men she feared were not in sight. Maybe she should forgo the introduction and make a hasty exit.

One look into his warm gray eyes and her desire to part this man's company dissolved. Her father's name was a common one. Perhaps Shem wouldn't make the connection to the famous man who was, after all, a complete stranger to her.

She mimicked Shem's bow. "I am Eliana de Ashbel." She left off the traditional identification of her maternal parent. There was, after all, only one Liadan. The name was recognized the world over.

His features did not change as he nodded. "I thought so. You're the primogenitor, the heiress to the high priestess. I saw you on the dais this morning, behind your mother."

A quick breath hissed as it entered her lungs. She hadn't needed to identify her mother. Of course he would recognize the name of the former governor of Cainlan, and make the connection. She'd been foolish to think otherwise. Girta would be beyond furious that she had revealed her identity to a stranger after promising faithfully never to do so.

"I—I shouldn't have stayed so long." She edged sideways, toward the temple. "Thank you for helping me."

"Why are you frightened?" Shem's outstretched hand hovered in the air between them. "You have nothing to fear from me. I promised to see you safely home, and I will keep my word."

The entreaty in his voice stopped her. Unlike the two who had frightened her in the alley, no hidden intentions lurked in Shem's face. He would not harm her. She relented and allowed him to walk beside her.

In silence they traveled the wide path toward the temple. A pair of uniformed guardsmen appeared on the walkway in front of them, their faces lighting with recognition when they caught sight of her. One straightened, his shoulders back in an almost-salute,

but the other merely dipped his head in a silent greeting as they passed. Eliana did not acknowledge them,
but Shem returned the gesture with a pleasant nod of
his own.

When the side entryway through which Eliana had
escaped earlier came into view, Shem's step slowed.

"Can you stay a moment and talk?" He gestured
toward an empty bench near the tall hedge that bordered the temple gardens. "I've some time before I meet
my friend."

Eliana glanced at the position of the sun. She really should return to her rooms. Yet something about
this man intrigued her. What harm was there in a
moment or two's delay?

"Girta won't raise the alarm quite this soon." She
crossed the cobbled path and perched on the iron seat.

Shem joined her. "I never expected to see the primogenitor alone in the marketplace. With a flock of
protective priestesses or temple guards in tow, perhaps, but not alone."

"No one knows I'm here." Their immediate sur-
roundings were vacant, with no one to overhear her
confession. "I slipped away just before the end of the
morning ceremony." She almost added, *as you did.*

"And is Girta a priestess, then?"

"Oh no, she's my nursemaid. Or—" She fought a
blush, embarrassed to have him think she still needed
nursing. "—she *was* my nursemaid, from the day I was
born. Now she's my maid, but she still treats me like I
crawled out of the cradle yesterday. She worries that
someone will try to steal me away."

The moment the words were spoken, an ugly realization struck her. Apparently Girta's fears were not
unfounded. That is exactly what nearly happened.

Shem nodded, his expression solemn. "The heir to
the high priestess of Cain could command a high price
in some quarters. That aside, the city is full of unscru-
pulous men who would take advantage of a beautiful
young woman, no matter what her position may be.

You should be more cautious."

Eliana hid her delight in his compliment by brushing a piece of dried grass from the hem of her silky gown. Did he find her beautiful? When she'd regained her composure, she settled against the back of the bench. In the distance, from the direction of the temple stables, the clang of metal played a rhythmic accompaniment to the low murmur of barely audible shoppers' voices. "Tell me of your father's farm. Is it near the city?"

"No, we live to the west of here."

The temple rested on the northern edge of Cainlan, with the city sprawling outward from its protected gates on three sides. The window of Eliana's room looked westward upon the city's narrow streets, crowded with dwellings and packed with people and animals. No farmland lay beyond the city's edge in that direction, only a barren ribbon of land, and beyond that, a deep canopy of green. "Your farm is in the forest?"

"Just beyond, a half-day's journey by wagon."

"Wagon?" She gave a small laugh. "Not many people travel by wagon these days."

Secrets appeared again in the smoky eyes. "No doubt we're a little backward by modern standards. My father isn't fond of landriders, or the energy that runs them."

Eliana looked away, embarrassed. Perhaps Shem's family was poor, and couldn't afford a rider, or the energy cartridges to power it.

She searched for a topic to distract him from her ill-mannered comment. "Tell me of your home. I've never seen a real farm, only the lands that surround Cainlan. Girta tells me they're not proper farms, like the ones where her people used to live in the south."

Shem extended his long legs and folded his arms behind his head as he described his home. He spoke of working the fields and harvesting produce, of his love for animals, and his favorite exotic birds. He possessed a passion for feathered creatures that surpassed his father's. Enthralled, she listened as he detailed the ways to care for captive birds, of their strict dietary requirements and the importance of providing an atmosphere free from stress.

Long before Eliana tired of listening, a piercing signal blasted from the Cabinet of Energy building to mark the hour.

He straightened abruptly. "I am late. I've delayed you much longer than I realized."

Disappointment sank through her, but Girta must have noticed her absence by now, and begun to worry. Even worse, what if the high priestess had summoned her daughter to reprimand her for leaving the morning ceremony early, and no one knew where to find her?

That thought sent Eliana scrambling to her feet. "I've enjoyed meeting you, Shem de Noah. Perhaps we can talk again sometime."

He shaded his eyes with a hand as he stood. "I hope so. Sometimes my wife comes to the city with me, and I think she would enjoy talking with you as well."

His wife? She struggled to school her features against a wash of disappointment. The term told her much. Followers of the One God joined in marriage for life instead of forming normal marital alliances. For some reason, she found his admission that he practiced this old-fashioned custom oddly embarrassing. "Of course. I'd... like to meet her."

The proper thing to say, though untrue.

He ducked his head in an invitation to force her to look up, into his face. Smiling gray eyes peered deeply into hers. "I hope we meet again, Eliana. I will add you to my daily prayers, and ask the One God to watch over you."

Blood surged through her veins to roar in her ears. What daring, to mention the One God to the daughter of the high priestess of Cain. Was this man a fanatic, then?

With a final sideways grin, as though fully aware of

the lapse he'd just committed, his fingers touched his forehead and he strode away.

Eliana cracked the door wide enough to slip through. Just before she pulled the heavy iron latch closed, she glanced at his retreating back. Amazing that she, the primogenitor, would meet a follower of the One God in the very shadow of the temple dedicated to the service of Cain.

Now she knew two who practiced that outdated religion.

Chapter 2

Shem hurried along the walkway until he reached a crowded tavern near the gates that separated the exclusive temple marketplace from Cainlan's common masses. Liberal application of his elbows gained him entrance through the people blocking the doorway. Once inside, his gaze swept the clutter of tables until he caught sight of Jarrell. His friend was halfway out of his seat, waving in his direction. Shem threaded through the mass of people and furniture, to where Jarrell clasped his forearm and clapped him soundly on the back.

"I thought you'd forgotten me."

"I never forget." Shem slid into the chair on the opposite side of the small table.

Jarrell gestured to get the attention of the server. A grim, red-faced woman appeared beside them to take their order. When she had gone, Shem took in his friend's appearance. Years ago Jarrell had shed the trousers of a farmer, opting instead for the more modern breeches and colorful jerkins frequently chosen by businessmen. Today he had twisted his hair into a contemporary rope down his back, a long, beaded thread intertwined throughout. The style was very feminine on one so slight, but Shem didn't voice the thought.

Jarrell eyed him through narrowed lids. "We meet in this same tavern every four weeks, and you've never been late. Why have you kept me waiting half the morning?"

"You've not waited that long." Shem clouted his friend on the shoulder. "But I do owe you an explanation. I have been talking with a girl."

"A girl!" Jarrell assumed a look of mock outrage. "Who is this girl, and does Mara know you spend your time in the city preying on other women?"

"You attribute your own sinful ways to me, I see." Shem joked, and then became serious. "A pair of thugs tried to molest her in an alley. I hate to think what would have happened if the shopkeeper and I hadn't been on hand. Afterward, she was understandably upset, so I sat with her until she calmed."

Jarrell shook his head. "The city is becoming more unsafe every day." He leaned against the back of his chair. "I forgive your tardiness, given your reason. But now, give me news of your family. And of Methuselah. How is the old man?"

"Remarkably well for someone who has seen 964 summers. He asked after you when I last made the trip up the mountain. Between us, I am not sure how much longer he will live. He confessed that he did not expect to see my children born." Sorrow tugged at him. He loved the old man, but common sense decreed that his great-grandfather would not live forever.

"I expect one day you'll tell me he's simply disappeared, that God has taken him away, like Enoch in the stories he used to tell us." Jarrell laughed.

Shem nodded. "Truthfully, I expect the same

thing."

The laughter faded from Jarrell's face. "Surely you don't still believe those tales."

"Don't you?"

"No." He voiced his denial with a firm jerk of his head. "They were stories. Entertaining for young boys, but we're men now."

Shem schooled his expression. His childhood friend had changed since he left the farm of Noah and moved to the city to find his fortune. This change disturbed Shem more than most. "Do you still worship the One God, Jarrell, or have you turned to Cain?"

Jarrell leaned forward over the table. "Of course I still believe in the One God." He glanced toward those who occupied tables nearby. "But some things are too much to ask of a rational man. Can you honestly say you believe in Adam and Eve, as Methuselah used to tell us?"

"Yes," Shem said with no hesitation. "Methuselah even met Adam once, so how could I not believe?"

"Of course he met a man named Adam. But the first man, formed by the One God's hands?" Jarrell shook his head. "The One God doesn't have hands, so how could he form a man's body? No, I fully believe that the One God created us, but He used the laws of this world to do it."

Shem planted his elbows on the wooden surface before him. "Suppose you are right, which I do not concede for a moment. If He did create us through worldly means, there still had to be a first man. Mankind did not suddenly appear in multitudes, as we are now. Why could that first man not be the same Adam my grandfather Methuselah met?"

Shem grinned as he presented his argument, and Jarrell threw his hands up in mock disgust. They'd debated the same topic many times in their adult lives.

The attendant arrived. Fragrant ribbons of steam rose from the bowls she placed before them, and set Shem's mouth to watering. He attacked his meal with gusto, savoring the thick broth. Breakfast at the farm had been a long time ago.

As they ate, Shem turned the subject to one he knew he would be questioned about when he returned home. "Speaking of women." He grinned over his spoon. "Have any caught your attention?"

Jarrell shook his head. "I don't have time for that sort of thing."

"How about your fellow businessmen? Do none of them have daughters?"

"Plenty." Jarrell shuddered, then lowered his voice to a conspiratorial whisper. "Seriously, they are so pious I want to laugh in their faces every time they extol the virtues of their false god. I can't marry into a family like that. Besides, if I get close enough that anyone suspects I'm not a devotee of Cain, I might find myself without a job."

Shem grew serious. "Has it come to that?"

Jarrell pursed his lips. "If you don't worship the god, you don't work for the government, and especially the cabinet of Social Action. The rule is unwritten, but those who don't follow Cain will soon find themselves without viable employment." He cast a cautious glance at the table nearest them. "I never hear of anyone who believes in the One God anymore, Shem. He simply isn't discussed." He leaned forward, lowering his voice even more. Shem bent his head closer to hear his friend. "The funny part is that most of the men I know don't believe in Cain any more than I do. Cain's religion is self-serving, so it suits their purposes."

"Then why do you stay? Why not quit, come to the farm for a while? We can use your help."

Jarrell gave his friend a pitying look, and Shem swallowed a sigh. He had lived with the ridicule of his neighbors long enough to recognize the expression, but he had not expected to see it on the face of his childhood friend.

"Your way is not my way." Jarrell looked into his eyes. "I applaud Father Noah for following the direc-

tives of the One God as he hears them, but..." He
paused. "I can't believe in his vision, Shem."
    Disappointment formed a knot in Shem's throat.
He swallowed past it and leaned forward to squeeze his
friend's shoulder. "Remember that you have a place to
go, come what may." He scraped the last bite of stew
from his bowl and set down his spoon. "A traveler
stopped by the farm some weeks ago with news. In the
mountain villages north of Enoch worship of Cain
gains strength. Devotees attack followers of rival gods
with single-minded vengeance, especially worshipers of
the One God. Entire families are being slaughtered as
sacrificial offerings to Cain."
    Jarrell's brows drew together. "How can they justify
that? There are no precedents, no traditions for wiping
out an entire bloodline."
    "The precedent is being set. A similar practice in
Cainlan is not hard to imagine, especially if it serves to
wipe out an opposing religion." He leveled a sober look
on his friend. "Take care, Jarrell."
    Jarrell lifted his mug. "Have no worries on my be-
half."
    Lowering his gaze, Shem hesitated before asking
his next question. He wasn't sure he wanted to hear
the answer. "Jarrell, do you do obeisance to Cain?"
    "Sometimes." Jarrell sipped from the mug. "But on-
ly when I'm with others who do, and I can't avoid it."
    "So." Sharp disappointment kept Shem's eyes fixed
on his bowl. "No one knows that you are a worshiper of
the One God."
    "Probably not." Jarrell stuffed bread into his mouth
and chewed for a minute. "As I said, if that became
public knowledge I would soon find myself begging on
the streets, not to mention guarding my life, if what
you've said is true."
    Shem made an attempt to filter the disappointment
from his voice. "But to compromise your beliefs?" He
shook his head.
    Jarrell grew serious. "I don't compromise my be-

liefs. And I have never denied the One God. So what if I bob my head in front of a statue once in a while? It is merely a piece of stone." He used his final crust of bread to emphasize his point. "But if I cooperate with them, I have a chance for a promotion into the Cabinet of Energy. Then I will be positioned to accomplish good for the people of this city."

"At what cost? There may not be a god named Cain, but your own God is watching."

Jarrell threw the bread abruptly on the table, and Shem knew the time had come for another subject. He valued his friendship with Jarrell, loved him like a brother, in fact. Who would influence him if he stopped talking to Shem?

"Tell me about this promotion," he said.

Obviously relieved at Shem's retreat, Jarrell launched into an enthusiastic description of his professional opportunity. "Councilor Asquith of the Cabinet of Energy is not well. His health is failing, and he's expected to relinquish his seat on the Council within the next few years. There is talk that Virden de Marathi will be elected."

"And you are friendly with Virden?"

"Not friendly, exactly." Jarrell grimaced. "The man is pompous and we argue constantly. But he does have the occasional idea of which I approve. I have publicly supported him on several issues."

"And you expect this Virden to promote you, when you argue with him constantly?"

"Shem, Shem." Jarrell gave him a pitying look. "You have no understanding of the workings of politics. Virden doesn't mind that I argue with him. It shows him that I am not afraid to speak my mind."

Shem tried to follow the logic. "And he will promote you because of this respect?"

Jarrell cocked his head and grinned. "Not exactly. It happens that Virden's assistant, Roblin de Yibin, is a friend of mine."

Ah. The situation became clearer. "When Virden

becomes councilor, he will need to build his own staff. This Roblin will speak on your behalf."

Jarrell sat back and gave a satisfied nod. "Exactly."

Shem's mind reeled with the thought of trying to maneuver the intricate dance of politics. "I appreciate more deeply the monotony of life as a lowly farmer."

The blast from a horn outside marked the passage of another hour. Jarrell scooted his chair back from the table. "I must go. I spent half my free time waiting while you picked up girls in the marketplace."

Shem responded with an elbow to the ribs. "Next time I shall find one for you."

They each tossed a few coins on the table. The stout woman quickly made her way to retrieve them before the other customers helped themselves. Jarrell and Shem walked outside, where they clasped right forearms, clapping each other's shoulders with their left hands in farewell.

"I will see you again in four weeks." Shem released Jarrell's arm.

"Try to be on time." Jarrell accompanied his parting jibe with a grin, then joined the crowd on the cobbled walkway.

Shem watched his friend stroll toward the guarded gates at the south end of the market square. The building that housed the Cabinet of Social Action lay just outside them. An uneasy feeling settled over him, darkening his mood even as the sunlight dazzled his eyes. He could not imagine bowing before a false god for any reason. Jarrell had chosen a career in the city over the uncomplicated life of a farmer. He seemed to thrive on the writhing nest of politics that existed within Cainlan's government buildings. But what did his compromise indicate about his relationship with the One God?

As he joined the crowd on the walkway, Shem determined to renew his prayers on Jarrell's behalf. He had to convince his childhood friend of the truth before it was too late.

Chapter 3

Eliana eased her way through the door to her rooms without a sound. Fortune had been with her, and she'd managed to slip through the halls of the temple's residential wing without encountering anyone except a couple of uninterested priestesses. She inched the door closed with agonizing slowness, the sound of the *click* as it shut no louder than a heartbeat.

But loud enough.

"Where have you been?" Girta snorted through the doorway from an adjoining room like a bull released from his stall.

She grasped Eliana's shoulders in rough, work-reddened hands, and gave a pair of firm shakes that rattled Eliana's teeth like a click beetle.

Throat dry, Eliana's voice cracked. "I went to the marketplace after the ritual."

"The marketplace?" A third shake followed the first two. "I've paced a groove in the stone, afraid to alert the guard for fear of inviting the high priestess's anger. And all the while you've been casually sauntering through the shops in the square?"

Deep worry lines creased the nursemaid's forehead beneath her cap of steel-gray hair. Guilt rushed over Eliana. Nothing could coax an admission of her terrifying experience with the ruffians from her now.

"I'm sorry, Girta, truly. I lost track of time. I didn't mean for you to worry."

"Not worry?" With a final shake, Girta's hands dropped to wring at each other with white-knuckled intensity. "A page told me he saw you running from the ritual. When I received no word, I imagined all sorts of terrible things."

Eliana winced. If a page had already reported her flight from the ceremony to Girta, word of her transgression must have spread through the temple. If her mother didn't notice her absence this morning, she'd certainly heard of it since.

"I'm truly sorry," she repeated. She moved toward the room's single window to look westward, beyond the city, where the forest filled the horizon. "I ... I wanted to get away before the final sacrifice was performed."

Girta came up behind her. "I thought that might be the case. I'm sorry, lamb."

Easy to keep her composure in the face of fury, but the tenderness in Girta's voice brought the sting of tears to her eyes. The morning's trauma and her failure on the dais knotted together and lodged in her throat. Whirling, Eliana threw her arms around Girta and buried her face in a plump shoulder. "What is wrong with me? Why can't I be like her?"

Strong arms encircled her, and rough hands patted her back, the same hands that had soothed her hurts from infancy. "Things will be different when you enter the priesthood officially. You'll learn the ways, the secrets, and they won't frighten you anymore."

Eliana did not answer. Had her mother been reluctant to enter the priesthood as her twenty-first birth-

day loomed? Eliana could not imagine it. No doubt
Liadan had embraced her destiny with the same enthusiasm she exhibited now, twenty-three years later.
And she fully expected her only daughter and heir to
do the same.

But the blood. How would she ever grow accustomed to the blood?

Eliana stepped away from Girta's embrace and
brushed moisture from her cheeks with impatient fingers. She must shrug off this dismal attitude, lest it
overpower her. Better to think happier thoughts.
Thoughts of farms, and birds, and smiling gray eyes.

"I met someone who worships your God this morning." She crossed to the small table beside her bed and
poured a cup of water from the pitcher there. "At least,
I'm fairly sure he does."

She lowered herself to the edge of her bed and lifted the cup to her lips before noticing that Girta's face
had gone pale.

"You met someone? You actually spoke to someone
in the marketplace, after all my warnings?"

Eliana took a deep drink to hide for a moment behind the cup. She would never mention her frightening
encounter with the ruffians. But Shem? An irresistible
urge to talk about him would not go away. "He was
friendly. He told me about his work with birds. He's
even trained one to speak a few words."

A smile tugged at her lips at the memory of Shem's
stories. She wiped it away when she saw Girta's eyelids narrow.

"He?"

With a shake, she tossed her hair over her shoulder. "His name is Shem. When I left he said he would
ask the One God to watch over me."

Girta became suddenly still. "Did he know who you
were?"

"Y...yes." Eliana refused to meet her nursemaid's
gaze.

"Then he's a fool, if he speaks of the One God to

the daughter of Liadan." Her voice dripped scorn.

Anger flared at the insult to her new friend. Eliana thrust her chin into the air. "He was not a fool. He was _"

A quiet rap interrupted her, followed immediately by the opening of the door. Such an entrance to Eliana's private rooms, uninvited and unannounced, heralded only one possible visitor. Girta rushed to the vanity, where she began straightening pots of scents and tints with quick, nervous motions. Eliana rose and jerked the bedcovers free of wrinkles. Her eyes swept the room for anything that would draw the high priestess's displeasure.

A page entered first. The child stepped to the left of the door and took his post as his mistress followed across the threshold.

High Priestess Liadan looked regal in deep green robes that emphasized her fair skin. Dark hair cascaded down her back, the curls falling to a tiny waist that belied any evidence of the birth that had resulted in Eliana's existence. She strode into the room, ignoring the presence of both her page and Girta, who escaped silently through the doorway into the adjoining dressing room. Liadan's eyes rested briefly on Eliana before she crossed to stand before the cold hearth.

"You left the ceremony early."

Eliana ignored the urge to quail beneath the accusation and returned her mother's gaze steadily. "I felt unwell."

Liadan accepted the excuse with a slight nod. "I intended to speak with you afterward. I have news. Caphtor has formally requested a marital alliance." She fixed Eliana with a hard stare. "With you."

Eliana's jaw went slack. Governor Caphtor, leader of Cainlan's ruling Council, wanted an alliance with *her*? No wonder Liadan's eyes stabbed angry fire across the room. By longstanding tradition, the governor of Cainlan formed a formal alliance with the head of the dominant religion – the high priestess of Cain.

Liadan had been allied with Eliana's father, Governor Ashbel, until his death a few weeks before Eliana's birth. She then entered into an alliance with Governor Poshen, who succeeded him. Eliana knew that her mother had impatiently awaited a similar offer during the year since Caphtor became governor.

Now Caphtor had requested an alliance with *her* instead of her mother? Stunned, Eliana tore her gaze from the barely suppressed fury in her mother's face.

"I see you recognize the honor being done you. Though I can't comprehend his motives, I must assume that youth appeals to him. I have heard rumors of..." Her red-tinted lips snapped together. She strode with quick steps to the window and stood with her hands clasped at the small of her back. "You would have had to form an alliance next year regardless, after the onset of your formal induction into the priesthood. I explained this to Caphtor, but he prefers not to wait."

He refused to wait a few seasons? *Why?* The question pressed against her lips, but she didn't dare interrupt the high priestess.

Liadan turned to face her. "These are uncertain times. I need Caphtor's support on the Council." One dainty nostril curled with disdain. "Commoners have become more demanding. A group of ore miners has actually threatened a labor strike if their request for a wage increase is refused. Their petition was presented at yesterday's Council session."

Liadan had never discussed Council business with her before. Stunned, Eliana closed her mouth on the questions whirling in her mind.

After a pause, the high priestess continued. "Caphtor and I have not always agreed on key Council decisions. A disagreement between the government and religious leaders is dangerous in the best of times. Granting his request will create a bond between us."

Granting his request. The terrifying thought of sharing a home, a *bed,* with the powerful governor of

Cainlan robbed Eliana of breath. Many women found
the man attractive, and she was not blind to his rug-
ged good looks and muscular build. But those near-
black eyes held a coldness that sent a shiver rippling
through Eliana the few times they had turned her way.

And why her? Why not form an alliance with
Liadan, as everyone expected? Eliana would not believe that Caphtor desired her for herself. The shrewd
governor had earned a reputation for doing nothing
that wouldn't further his personal goals. How did she
fit in with those goals? A sudden desperation nearly
overpowered her. She did not want to find out.

Suppressing the impulse to wipe her sweating
palms on her gown, she took a fortifying breath. "I
want nothing more than to be of service to my high
priestess and to my city, but I wish to refuse the governor's request."

Eliana felt her mother's shock even as she watched
the blood drain from her face. She had never voiced an
opinion to her mother in all her twenty years, especially one that opposed her.

"You stupid child." The high priestess's voice oozed
contempt. Her stare hardened, and she looked through
narrowed lids as though at a particularly loathsome
insect. "He is the governor of Cainlan's Council, and
you—you are nothing but an ill-bred child. What idiocy
would make you refuse such an offer? I would doubt a
drop of my blood runs through your veins if I had not
pulled you from my body with my own hands."

Liadan's words fell on her like blows. She had never heard such scorn in her mother's voice. Did Liadan
hate her, then? She must, to speak to her so. The
pounding of Eliana's heart echoed like drums in her
ears.

The high priestess glared green fire, then drew a
long, slow breath before speaking with a visible effort
to keep her tone even. "Consider your decision carefully, daughter. You've been sheltered." Her head dipped
forward. "My fault, perhaps. I've left your education to

others. But surely even you are aware of the power you will one day wield. Power is the only thing in this world worth having."

She crossed the room in three smooth strides, and held her face so close her breath warmed Eliana's cheek. "I am the most powerful woman in Cainlan, the mightiest city in the world. And one day you will stand in my place." Her arm lifted, and her hand formed a tight fist. "You *must* learn to grab power wherever you can, and to fight off all who would wrest it from you. With that power, you will play a part in forging Cainlan's future. Imagine the dominance within your grasp."

Shoulders rigid, Eliana returned Liadan's gaze, proud that she did not flinch.

"What Caphtor offers is power. Take it. Use it wisely, and you can control him."

Her, control the forceful governor? Breathless, Eliana lowered her gaze, unwilling to let her mother see the fear that must surely show in her eyes.

Because no one ever defied the high priestess for long, Liadan took the gesture as a sign of submission. "Good. I will arrange the ceremony with the governor. He has requested a three-year contract, and you may wish to allow a child. One day you will be high priestess in my stead, so you must produce a daughter before you are twenty-five in any case. A child will give you a bond with Caphtor that could prove most useful."

A child? Eliana's head snapped up, but Liadan swept through the doorway. The page left his post to scurry after her, and the door closed with a solid thump.

For one moment, silence pressed on Eliana's ears. Then she threw herself onto the bed, the terror that had closed her throat erupting in loud sobs. Girta rushed into the room, slipped onto the bed and pulled Eliana's head onto her lap. A comforting hand moved across her back in a circular motion.

"There, there, my lamb. It's not so bad, is it? I've seen the governor. He's a handsome man. No need to cry so."

Eliana sniffed, her breath coming in ragged heaves. "I don't w...w...want an alliance with him, Girta."

Girta's soothing hand continued. "This is an honorable offer, one that any girl in your position would dream of. What more could you want?"

Eliana sat up, brushing the hair away from her damp cheeks. "I don't want to be in my position." She refused to look into her nursemaid's face. "I don't want to be the most powerful woman in the world. I don't even want to be a priestess."

Shocked, Girta raised a finger to her lips. "Hush, child, you shouldn't say that."

"You don't worship Cain, and neither does Shem. I would rather be like him than have all the power in the world." There. She'd said it. Her chin rose. "I'd rather *marry* someone I care about, like your people do, than enter into an alliance to help forge Cainlan's future."

Girta's forehead creased. "I never hid my background from you, though maybe I shouldn't have spoken so freely of my people's traditions. But those ways are not yours, lamb. You are a child of Cainlan, and you must follow the ways of your own people."

Tears welled again to blur Eliana's vision. Girta spoke the truth. What choice did she have? She was a child of Cainlan, and of the god who gave that city its name. She must serve that god with her life as surely as the young child on the dais had served.

She flung herself across the bed again and gave in to sobs. If she cried loud enough, perhaps she might blot out the gentle voice that echoed in her ears.

Would the One God heed Shem's request? Could he watch over her, even in his rival's temple?

Mara lifted the storage barrel above her head. She

tilted it so the raw grain poured into the grinder's top chute. When the receptacle was full she lowered the barrel and secured the lid before stowing it beside the others. Then she took an energy cartridge from the pocket of her apron and snapped it into place in the back of the grinder. At the press of a button the machine hummed to life. In a few seconds, powdery flour began to flow into a small container.

As the machine performed its task, Mara let her gaze stray out the window, across the field to the huge structure where her father-in-marriage and two of his sons worked. She could just make out a tiny figure on top and recognized Ham by the color of his shirt. Father Noah and Japheth were inside then, working on the stalls. The men poured over sketches each night while they discussed the day's progress and planned the morrow's. She herself could not make the connection between the lines and scrawled notes they studied, and the mammoth boat taking form before her eyes.

The last time she visited the construction site the boat had resembled the skeleton of a huge animal. She'd had an eerie feeling, like it was a living thing waiting to have life breathed into it. The structure rose helpless into the sky, dependent on the frail hands of the men who labored over it. Now the outer hull was being applied so the bones of the skeleton would begin to disappear. Soon, Father Noah assured her, it would look less like a skeleton and more like a boat.

As always, Mara's stomach fluttered at the thought. Timna confided some time ago that she was not sure Father Noah really heard the voice of God. Mara had no doubts at all. The first time Father Noah spoke with her, confiding his message from the One God, she felt the truth of his vision deep in her soul. She knew that water would fall from the sky and rise from the seas just as Father Noah prophesied. Shuddering, she pictured the terror that would grip all people when the heavens opened and the One God's wrath poured out. Would they remember the old man and his warnings when the destruction began?

For once there were no spectators around the boat, or *ark* as Father Noah called it. In the past few months, word of the project spread, and the curious had begun to gather and gawk. Father Noah always took time to talk to them, convinced that if the world repented, the heart of the One God would soften. Too often his entreaties were met with laughter and even contempt.

The hum of the grinder changed pitch, and Mara turned from the window to her chore. With a wooden rod, she tapped the container to loosen any stray grain clinging to the sides and then switched the machine off. Pocketing the energy cartridge, she covered the carton with a waxed cloth and, settling it comfortably in one arm, left the shed.

The rear door of the family home entered into the kitchen. Midian, her mother-in-marriage, sat at the rough wooden table chopping vegetables. For once there was no sign of her sisters.

"Here's the flour." Mara set the container on the table. "Shall I begin the bread?"

"That would be fine. Use the older flour first."

Mara smiled as she retrieved the appropriate carton. Mother Midian said the same thing every time a new supply entered the house, and Mara knew she would continue to give such advice until the day she died. When Mara first joined the household as Shem's wife almost twenty years ago, the two women had become fast friends. Despite the fact that she'd been cooking in her own mother's kitchen since she could first creep into the room, Mara had learned a lot from Midian during the first years of her marriage. Now she hardly remembered the style of cooking her own folk of the hills practiced.

"Soup tonight?" she asked as she assembled the ingredients for bread.

"No, I thought a mixture of these roots, and maybe

you could mash some of the yellow bulbs. You have such a way with seasoning that dish."

"Of course." Mara glanced toward the doorway, wondering at the silence in the house.

Midian saw her unspoken question. "I've set the girls to mending. I think they've taken their work outside to enjoy the day. Perhaps you'd rather join them and let me cook the meal."

"I'd rather help you."

Midian smiled, and reached for another vegetable to chop. "Will Shem be home in time to eat with us?"

Mara shook her head. "He was to meet Jarrell before shopping for the supplies we requested, and then he had to have the energy cartridges recharged. I look for him late, maybe even after dark."

"That Jarrell." A grin stole across the older woman's lips. "Always the slyboots. Did I ever tell you about the time he convinced Shem to leave his chores and spend the day in the forest?"

Mara had heard the story many times, but she loved tales of Shem's childhood. She flashed a broad smile across the table. "Tell me."

"They stayed in the forest all day and came home in time for the meal. They didn't realize that Noah had gone to check on them in the far field. When he asked how their day's labor had gone, they tried to deceive him with tales of how hard they'd worked. It was the only time Noah ever took a rod to Shem. It was enough." She shook her head at the memory, the edges of her lips tugging upward. "Jarrell was always getting Shem into trouble when they were young. Though Shem did his share, too. Once, he convinced Jarrell to ride a wild ram that had been hanging around the farm. They caught the thing, old and cantankerous as it was, and Shem held it in place while Jarrell straddled its back. It took off running, and Jarrell was so frightened he froze. It bumped him into trees and branches trying to throw him off, but he held on to its horns for life. Shem ran after it, shouting and waving, yelling for Jarrell to jump off, and when Ham and Japheth heard the commotion they joined in. I came out of the house in time to see Noah join the race, the four of them chasing the terrified ram. When Jarrell finally came to his senses and let go of the horns, he fell to the ground and lay there, rolling and moaning. I never saw such a raw backside in all my days!"

The two women laughed, and Mara's ended with a wistful sigh. "Children provide such wonderful memories."

Midian's gaze became soft and full of understanding. "God chooses his times carefully, daughter. He has special plans for the wives of my sons. You must be patient, and trust Him."

Mara nodded. "I do."

That evening as the women readied the table for dinner, Japheth's wife Abiri rushed into the kitchen, her cheeks flushed.

"The men are coming, and they're bringing someone with them!" Waves of her honey-oak hair bounced with a life of their own.

"Who is it?" asked Timna.

"I don't know. I can see four figures and one of them is small, like a child."

"A child?" Timna exchanged a glance with Mara.

"Timna, another plate," said Midian, her voice steady as always.

After what seemed an eternity the door opened and Father Noah entered, followed by Japheth, Ham and a boy. Though his skin showed deep creases of age, Father Noah still stood straight, his arms firm and his muscles strong with years of use. His sons were both powerful men of the same build as their father, though Mara spared a proud thought that Shem stood taller than them all. The men hung their tool belts on wall hooks while the boy hung back, his gaze darting around the room.

Noah greeted his wife with a kiss and then put a hand on the boy's back. "Young Devon is passing through these lands on his way to seek work in the ore mines. Can we spare him dinner and a bed?"

Mara examined the boy. He looked about eight summers, and covered in dirt. Far too young to be seeking work of any kind, much less the dangerous job of a miner. His clothes, made for someone larger than he, had collected an assortment of burrs and thistles during his travels. Peering at his unkempt hair, she couldn't decide on the natural color beneath a thick layer of dirt. His chin protruded sharply below hollow cheeks.

"Of course," replied Midian cheerfully. "Dinner is almost ready. Girls, help your men prepare. Since Shem is away perhaps you would allow our guest to use your rooms, Mara?"

"Certainly." The boy looked fearfully up at Mara, and she greeted him with a wide smile. "Come this way."

She gestured for him to follow her down the long hallway that lead to the rooms occupied by each of Father Noah's sons and their wives. Mara opened the door to the rooms she shared with Shem. The boy paused, casting a fearful look toward Japheth as he passed. "This way, child. Father Noah said your name is Devon?" He nodded and did not meet her eyes. "I'm Mara. Welcome to our home. I would be honored if you treat these rooms as your own while you are our guest."

The child entered and stopped just inside to look around. Mara examined her home through fresh eyes. Shem had built this wing when he brought Mara here as his wife, just as Ham and Japheth built their own when they were wed. They stood in a small public room, furnished primarily with things Mara brought from her family in the hills when she wed. The couch frames were of a red wood, layered deep with cushions stuffed with fluffy lamb's wool. They sat angled to the hearth, side tables within easy reach of both. One wall held shelves displaying decorative pottery and a few inexpensive pieces of art. A small table with two chairs lined the other wall, an inviting bowl of fruit placed in the center. Not, Mara realized, a very exciting place to a young boy's eyes, but Devon's shoulders relaxed.

Mara turned a smile on him. "We'd better get cleaned up and ready for the evening meal. Now let's see." She examined the boy with her hands on her hips. "How long have you been traveling, young guest?"

"Ten days."

Mara's heart lurched at the sound of his soft northern accent. The way he pronounced *days* sounded like the burr of her people.

Devon looked down at his clothes, and held out his hands, turning them in front of him. "Been a while since I cleaned. Had to dig into the brush once or twice. Hiding. Guess I could use a bath."

Mara held her tongue, though she wanted desperately to ask from whom he had hidden. Instead she smiled into his solemn face. "That's easily taken care of."

She led him through a second door into the bathing room. The boy's eyes widened, and Mara guessed he'd never seen a private bathing room. If she was right about his accent, he came from one of the northern villages where luxuries like this were unknown and unimagined. She remembered her own fascination with the bathing room when she first married.

She pumped water into the tub, indicating that Devon was to remove his clothes and place them by the door. He did so, displaying no embarrassment. Mara helped him step over the high rim to settle into the clean water, then handed him a slab of cleanser and a brush. She left the room with his clothes.

Midian and Father Noah were still in the kitchen, Noah sharpening the bread knife while his wife pulled

Mara's freshly baked loaves from the oven.

"Mother Midian, do you happen to have any clothes from when Japheth was y—oh." She paused as Midian bent to pick up a neat stack of clothing.

"How is he doing?" Midian asked, handing her the bundle.

"Fine, I think. By the sound of his voice, he's from the north."

"I thought the same." Noah stared in the direction of Mara and Shem's rooms. "He showed up at the ark this morning. Never seen such a hungry-looking boy." Father Noah shook his head. "We shared our midday meal with him, and he ate everything we gave him without chewing."

Mother Midian set the loaves on the table in front of her husband. "Did he say why he was out there alone?"

"He mentioned joining a brother who left to find work in the mines, but there is more behind his journey than he claims."

"He told me he has been digging into the brush to hide," Mara told them.

"We must convince him to stay with us for a while." Midian gave a decisive nod.

Mara returned to find Devon sitting in muddy brown water scrubbing his elbows.

"I was dirtier than I thought." He gave her a shy grin.

She showed him how to open the trap in the floor below the tub, and then removed the drain stop. The dirty water ran out of the tub and down a chute through the floor. Then she pumped in clean water and scrubbed his hair with cleanser.

When he finally stood dry and dressed, he looked like a different child.

"You're very handsome when you're clean," she told him.

"Thank you." A blush stained his fair cheeks. "For the clothes, too. They feel better than mine."

"I think yours are a little large."

"They belonged to my brother. I'm smaller than him."

He hung his head in shame, and the child's dejected posture stung Mara.

"I always had the opposite problem," she confessed. "Girls are supposed to be small and dainty, and I was always bigger and stronger than my brothers. I used to feel like a great big oaf, so much taller than everyone."

"Do you still feel that way?" asked Devon, his expression serious.

Mara thought of Abiri's dainty figure. "Sometimes."

Devon nodded in sympathy, and a look of understanding passed between them.

"But now, young guest, I think we've kept the others waiting long enough. Are you hungry?"

Devon nodded again, this time with vigor.

"Then let's join my family. In my husband's absence, I will serve you tonight."

Shem brought the wagon to a halt in its accustomed place behind the shed. As he unhitched the horse and led it to a well-deserved dinner waiting in the stall, he spared a wish that Father would let him buy one of the new landriders that ran on energy cartridges. The horse, as though sensing his thoughts, turned a mournful gaze his way.

Shem laughed and awarded the animal a playful slap on the neck. "You have no need to worry. Father won't sanction spending any portion of our savings on what he considers a temporary indulgence."

The thought sobered Shem. His glance stole across the field to the giant structure he could just make out in the waning light. The nearer the ark came to completion, the more closely they must examine every action they took. Each planting season brought questions of necessity – would they be here to harvest the produce of this planting? Or would the seed be destroyed in the One God's wrath, along with the rest of the earth?

Shaking off thoughts of the coming judgment, Shem finished unloading the wagon and secured the locks on the storage shed. Though vandals rarely traveled this far from the city, the ark had attracted a lot of attention lately. No sense taking chances.

The evening was mild, and he stood a moment, cartons in his arms, listening to the night's song. In the distance, a bird called from within the forest, and a small animal scuttled through the grass off to his left. Crickets played symphonies all around him, creating a peaceful background to the rest of the nighttime sounds. He drew clean air deep into his chest. How could Jarrell tolerate the constant bustle and commotion of the city after having grown up in the quiet of nature? Only a few hours left Shem feeling drained, all his tranquility used up.

Serenity returned, and he approached the rear entrance of the house. The windows were dark on this side, though a dim, flickering light shone through small cracks in the shutters of the kitchen window. He lifted the latch to the door. Unbolted. Shem's jaw clenched. No one else worried about security. Of course, he was the one who most often ventured off the farm, the one who sold their produce, bought supplies, recharged the few energy cartridges they owned, and heard the news of violence and damage. He had tried to make his family understand the need for caution, but Father would only say, "God will protect us."

Shem did believe in the One God's protection. He had only to look toward the construction site to see evidence of that. The means of God's ultimate protection showed in silhouette in the distance. But he also believed that the One God had given him brains and the ability to do things for himself.

Inside the house, Shem pulled the door closed behind him. He set his cartons on the table before turning to drop the bolt into place.

"Father? Mother? Mara, I'm home." He aimed his voice toward the entrance to the large public room in which the family usually gathered in the evenings.

His mother and Mara came into the kitchen, both wearing smiles of welcome. Mother began unpacking the largest carton, placing energy cartridges and packages on the table. Mara reached for the other, but was shooed away.

"Feed your husband, girl." Mother accompanied her scold with a gentle shove. "I can handle the unpacking."

Mara grinned and nodded toward the basin for him to wash. When he had finished, he turned to find a plate of hot food waiting for him at the table. A spicy aroma reached his nostrils, sending a flood of anticipation into his mouth. The stew he'd shared with Jarrell was a distant memory to his empty stomach.

"How was your trip?" Mara asked as she pushed aside the heavy curtain and descended the rough steps to the cool room. A moment later she returned with a pitcher of fruit juice. "Good." Shem tore off a thick portion of bread. "The shops weren't crowded, and I got a good price on recharging the cartridges. I also got some fresh fruit. Redberries, all the way from Manessah."

"Timna will love that."

Shem scooped succulent tubers into his mouth with his bread. "Oh, does she like redberries?"

Both women rounded on him in disbelief.

Mother planted her hands on her hips. "Shem, you've lived in the same house with Timna for more than ten years. How could you not know redberries are her favorite food in the world?"

Shem gave her a puzzled look. "Was I supposed to know that? I don't remember anyone mentioning it."

Mara shook her head, lifting her eyes to the heavens. "I suppose we should be glad you remember her name."

Shem took another bite of bread as Mother took an armload of cartridges and disappeared through another doorway, into the dry storage room. Mara reached for a cup from the high shelf above the basin. A mane of brown hair, with no evidence yet of silver, swung below her waist. She was taller than his mother, and her hands were stronger than most women—just the thing for massaging muscles stiff from a long day at harvest. Her strength came from years of hard work, the work of a farmer's wife. Many times she labored in the field alongside him from early morning until dark.

How different from Eliana. The primogenitor's hands had been soft and delicate, and had probably never seen a full day's work. She was at least a head shorter than Mara, even smaller than petite Abiri, Japheth's wife.

"We had an interesting day here." Mara interrupted his thoughts.

"Oh?" He forced his thoughts away from Eliana to focus on his wife.

"Yes. We have a guest, a young boy."

Faint spots of color rode high on each sun-darkened cheek as she recounted the tale of the child's arrival. She looked happy, excited even. He hadn't seen that light in her eyes in a long time. His heart stirred to see her joy.

"You like this boy, this... what is his name?"

"Devon." She flashed a quick smile. "And yes, I do. He's small and rather frail, but I've a feeling there's strength in him."

Mara's longing for a child of her own was no secret. In fact, all three wives of Noah's sons prayed unceasingly for the One God to bless them with babes to suckle and love, but as eldest, Mara seemed to feel the lack most keenly. In over twenty years of marriage, Shem had wondered, privately of course, if Mara might be barren. But when years passed with neither Timna nor Abiri conceiving either, his private musings had turned in another direction. He had never discussed the matter with Father, but was it possible that the One God had stopped their wombs in light of the coming judgment?

"I can't wait to meet him," Shem said.

His wife's face lit with a quiet joy that caused his misgiving to swell.

When he drained his mug and pushed his empty plate away, they joined the rest of the family in the other room. Father sat in his usual chair near the fireplace, his feet extended to the flames, discussing the day's progress on the ark with Ham. Near the door, Ham's wife, Timna, stitched with steady fingers on a bundle of brightly colored fabric in her lap. A boy sat opposite Father, his chair slightly outside the family circle, staring at the flames as though captivated by their dance.

Noah looked up at their entry. "Shem, come and meet our guest." He nodded toward the child. "Young Devon is passing through these lands on his way to seek work in the ore mines."

Shem examined the boy. Reddened skin showed signs of a recent scrubbing. Thin and slightly built, he appeared too young to work in the mines. In fact, he was not much older than the drugged child who had lost his life on the temple dais this morning. Shem swallowed against the threat of rising bile, and nodded a greeting at Devon. The boy gave a shy nod before returning to his study of the flames.

Shem took the empty chair near the fire and addressed his father. "I found a male Contragrey in the animal shop. The keeper thinks he can get a female as well."

Father's shoulders moved in a silent laugh. "Son, the One God has promised to send animals to us to be kept alive. He gave no instructions to gather them."

"I know, but these birds come from so far away I don't see how they can get here on their own."

Father's white brows arched over his blue eyes.

"Do you think that is a barrier our God cannot overcome?"

Shem jutted out his chin. "Of course not. But if the One God did not want our help, would He not have built the ark Himself?"

"We have plenty to do in gathering all the food that will be needed to feed the animals, and ourselves."

Shem suppressed an impatient sigh. "I know, Father, but we can't begin until the ark is closer to completion—the food will go bad. And I am able to find a few animals and birds here and there along the way." He leaned forward in his chair, elbows on his knees. "Do you believe the One God does not want me to buy the bird?"

Noah's eyes grew distant, and Shem knew he was weighing the question in his heart.

Finally, the old man shook his head, an indulgent smile playing about his lips. "No, Shem, I don't think the One God minds if you help Him. In fact, He may very well have guided you to that shop today to see that particular bird. Buy the bird, and its mate if you can."

The door opened and Abiri entered, followed by Japheth with an arm full of fluffy wool.

"Ho, brother!" Japheth called as he entered. Mara jumped up to take an armload of wool from him and gestured for Abiri to follow her down the hallway. Fixing a bed for the child, no doubt.

Japheth hooked a chair with a hand and set it close to Shem's. "How was the city today?"

"Crowded. Smelly." Shem didn't bother to suppress a shudder. "Corrupt. Three different people approached me selling something called hetaera, which I assume is a drug. The last was no more than twelve years old."

Father shook his head, sadness heavy in his eyes. "When we witness the corruption of our children, who can question why God regrets His creation?"

Shem watched the firelight play on the wall behind

his father's head for a moment. "Speaking of corruption, I met someone in the market square near the temple gardens today."

"Someone more corrupt than youthful drug sellers?" Ham laughed. "It must have been a priestess of Cain, then."

Mara and Abiri returned from their errand as Shem answered. "Close. I met the primogenitor, the daughter of the high priestess."

Jaws around the room went slack. Timna lowered her sewing to her lap mid-stitch.

"And how in all the heavens did that come about?" Japheth asked.

Shem's teeth clenched at the memory of the encounter. "She was being harassed by a pair of thugs." He shrugged. "The owner of the pet shop and I helped her."

"What was she like, Shem?" Abiri asked.

A vision of Eliana swam into focus in his mind, dark hair curling past her shoulders and green eyes twinkling above full lips. How to describe the delicate innocence that had tugged at his memory throughout the long ride home? "Pretty. Young. She wanted to hear about our farm. I felt..."

He let the sentence hang. With her face etched into the front of his mind, he didn't know how to describe what he felt — not to himself, and especially not to his family.

"You felt what, Shem?" Mara asked.

Shem straightened in his chair. "Sorry for her." His tone ended that discussion.

"And how did you find Jarrell?" asked Father after a moment's pause. "He is well?"

"Well, yes. He sends his greetings, and disturbing news. He says that worship of the One God is cause for dismissal from government work. Not formally, but enforced nevertheless."

Japheth leaned forward, his strong carpenter's arms resting on his legs. "And how is it that Jarrell still has his job?"

Shem hesitated. His news would upset them all. "He doesn't acknowledge his beliefs." There was nothing to be gained from withholding the truth. "He told me he is even forced to do obeisance to Cain at times, in order to keep his secret."

Mara gasped. "What kind of man is he, that he could forsake the One God for a job?"

Father smiled in her direction, his blue eyes kind. "A weak man, like his fathers before him. Like us all." He turned his head toward Shem. "Did you encourage Jarrell to join us here?"

"I did. But his ambitions lay in his government work, and besides..." Shem paused, then gentled his voice. "He doesn't believe in your vision, Father."

Father leaned forward, his voice full of earnest. "We must convince him, and any who will listen. There is no other way to forestall the great destruction about to befall the world."

"It's an awkward subject." Guilt was a heavy burden to bear. Shem's shoulders sagged beneath the weight of it. "Jarrell has never said so, but I know he wonders *why you and not me*?" He swept the room with a glance. "The question plagues me as well. Why us? What have we done to set us apart from the rest of the One God's people? You are a pious man, Father, but not perfect, nor any better than a dozen others I can name." His gaze circled back to the hearth, and the blazing fire. "When I looked Jarrell in the face I was ashamed. God has chosen us over him, and we don't deserve it."

"None of you have ever bowed to another god." The anger in Mother's sharp voice made him look up at her. "Nor would you, no matter the circumstances."

"Does that make Jarrell worthy of death? And what of the others, the many who don't bow to Cain, or anyone but the One God?"

He glanced at Mara. A worried frown drew lines in her forehead. Was she thinking of her own father, who was a righteous man?

Father rose and placed a hand upon Shem's shoulder. "It is not easy to follow our God. Why have we been selected? I've asked, and He chooses not to enlighten me. Perhaps the One God's reasons will be clear someday. Perhaps not. But I know this." Father straightened, his face lifted upward, his eyes alight with a faraway memory. When he spoke, his deep voice filled the room. "The God of Adam, the God of Seth, called to me. He asked me to play a part in His great plan. I trust Him. He is just, and righteous. I may never understand His reasons, but I will follow the One God until I die."

The power in Father's words resonated in the room. Shame washed over Shem. If only he possessed a tiny portion of his father's faith. A movement drew his gaze to Mara. She stared toward the boy, Devon, and Shem had no answers for the questions he saw in her face. Would children such as this one also be swept away in the One God's judgment?

Another face loomed in his mind. Bright, guileless eyes. A delicate blush riding high on curved cheeks. A weight dragged at Shem's heart. He covered his face with a hand and dug at his eyes with a thumb and forefinger. Eliana's image would not be banished. Like Devon, the beautiful young woman would suffer the wrath of the One God.

Chapter 4

Caphtor paused outside the Council chamber doors, motioning to the man behind him to wait. His gaze swept the faces of the five senior councilors inside before they noticed his arrival. What was their mood? A collection of emotions were evident around the oblong table, ranging from irritation to concern. He had summoned them for a special closed session, something that hadn't happened in recent memory. Closed sessions were always scheduled at least a week in advance.

His jaw clenched as he realized the high priestess had not yet arrived. He hoped to make his entrance after they were all in place.

At the sound of swishing silk, he turned. Liadan swept toward him trailing several lengths of fabric, her musky perfume permeating the air. He fought to keep his nose from curling at the nearly overpowering scent.

"Who do we have here?" she asked in her deliber-
ate husky voice as she scanned the man standing beside Caphtor from toe to head.

Her words alerted those inside the Council chamber to their presence, and they all turned.

"What's the meaning of this summons, Caphtor?"
Councilor Feren demanded, half-rising out of his seat.

Councilor Asquith's gray-spattered eyebrows rose
as he caught sight of the yellow-bearded man standing
behind Caphtor. The others inspected him through
narrowed lids, their distrust apparent. Caphtor set his
teeth. This all-important meeting was not beginning as
he planned. The Council *must* accept and support his
authority without question, or he would not be able to
move forward as he wanted. Fighting a wave of irritation, he motioned for the high priestess to precede him
into the room. He swept in after her, and crossed to
the head of the table as she took her accustomed seat
near the door. His guest trailed behind him, and stood
to one side where Caphtor indicated with a nod.

"Gentlemen, and High Priestess," he began, "pardon the interruption of your duties. I appreciate that
all of you could come with so little notice."

"We weren't given a choice." Limpopo's scowl announced that he may have presented himself, but not
happily.

"Yes, this is quite an imposition, Governor," put in
Asquith with every bit as much irritation as Limpopo.
The rest of the councilors nodded.

"My apologies to you all," Caphtor replied, "but I'm
certain you'll agree soon enough that this meeting was
necessary. I've had some important news from the
east."

Caphtor gestured to the visitor, who stepped forward. He had a full head of thick, black hair, though
his beard was stained yellow in the Manessite tradition. He was tall, fully as tall as Caphtor, with a muscular frame that Caphtor envied. "This had better be
important." Liadan managed to glare at Caphtor while

giving the stranger's physique an appreciative stare. "It is highly irregular to invite a foreigner into the Council chamber."

"Ah, but this is no foreigner, High Priestess. This is an associate of mine, an employee if you will. He's been living for a number of years in Manessah, and has for his own safety adopted the dress and habits of a Manessite."

"A spy?" Asquith's bushy eyebrows rose in interest. "I'd no idea you employed agents, Caphtor." A gleam of grudging respect lit his eyes.

Caphtor suppressed a smile. "Several years before I became Governor, I decided to keep an eye some of our closest neighbors. The aggressive tendencies of the cities of Enoch and Manessah have worried me for some time. When Manessah increased their level of import a few months ago-"

"What?" Asquith straightened in his chair.

Caphtor gritted his teeth. "The information is in the reports your department circulates." He allowed a touch of condescension to creep into his tight smile. "In the past several months our export to Manessah has tripled, and their latest order is their largest yet."

Asquith sank in his chair, tendons flexing along his jaw. Glancing around the table, Caphtor noted that the information was new to all of the councilors. He wanted to snort with disgust. How men who didn't bother to look beyond next week came to positions of leadership was beyond him.

"So what?" With a delicate hand Liadan covered a yawn. "We have plenty of energy now, and we can produce any amount we need at will. Let's take their money, all of it they want to give."

"Haven't you heard of the trouble Manessite tourists have caused in Cainlan recently?" Caphtor steeled his voice to patience, as with a child. "They're congregating around energy outposts, trying to get inside. They almost caused a riot at a storage facility the other day."

"That's right." Seneset's nod was aimed around the table at his fellow councilors. "The Department of Energy called in Behavior Control troops, and also at the southeast processing plant a few days before."

"But why today's summons?" Limpopo set his square jaw. "So far I've heard nothing that couldn't have waited for the next regular Council meeting."

"Because of what I learned this morning." Caphtor indicated the yellow-beard. "Tell them what you told me."

"Manessah is training a new branch within their army." The man spoke in a voice so low the councilors had to strain forward to hear him. "They've been recruiting for two seasons. This branch is limited to the physically elite. Membership is coveted. I applied, thinking my best access to information would be there. I was accepted, and I've been in training since."

Seneset leaned forward over the table. "What kind of training?"

"Weapons, and tactical aggression. We spent the first season learning to use a series of hand-held weapons, including bows, swords and a new weapon, one that uses a regular household energy cartridge to propel an explosive missile over a great distance. I've seen others, big ones that are mounted on top of a landrider and the missile is much larger."

Caphtor glanced around the table. The councilors, including Liadan, all leaned forward in their seats, their attention riveted on the stranger.

"I've never heard of anything like that," murmured Feren.

"Nor had I," the yellow-beard responded, "nor any of the other soldiers. But the hand-held weapon is amazingly accurate, much more than a bow, and deadly. Depending on the range, the missile can penetrate a body. I assume the bigger ones could blow a hole through a building."

Liadan shuddered.

"How long have you known about this?" Tomsk

fixed Caphtor with an accusing gaze.

"I've had reports." Caphtor clasped his hands calmly on the table in front of him. "Though I didn't know the extent of their operation."

"What are they going to do with this army?" Seneset asked the spy.

"I have not heard, but I saw something recently that I knew I must report in person."

He paused, and Limpopo prodded with an irritated, "Well?"

"The Manessites built a new training facility out-side the eastern edge of their city, a large barracks along with an exercise field. When my squad arrived, I participated in a mock battle within a newly con-structed exercise field. A field with a layout I recog-nized." He glanced at Caphtor, who nodded for him to continue. "The Manessite soldiers are being trained to attack Cainlan."

After a moment of shocked silence, the councilors began shouting, both at the spy and at one another. Caphtor let them rage a moment, then held out his hands and gestured for silence.

"Fellow Councilors, High Priestess," he nodded to Liadan, "we have been warned. If the Manessites have a two-season gain on us, Cainlan still has the ad-vantage."

"What advantage?" Feren's voice held a snarl. "Our army is trained at crowd control, not at resisting a full-blown attack with weapons such as this man de-scribes." He glared at Seneset, director over the de-partment in charge of the army.

Seneset returned the glare. "My army can defend Cainlan."

"Perhaps it can," Caphtor said, "but it is not enough. Our advantage is that we have a monopoly on energy."

"But they've been importing an excessive amount, as you pointed out," said Asquith. "It's obvious they've been hoarding it in preparation for this campaign."

"I agree." Caphtor hid a smile. Finally, the conversation was going exactly as he'd hoped. "But don't forget they've also been using it for these new weapons. We don't know yet how much the weapons use, but this man was able to bring his personal firearm with him. I'll turn it over to you, Feren. Let Manufacturing take it apart, see if we can duplicate it."

Feren nodded, appeased by the unexpected gift of responsibility.

"Before we say anything else," put in Liadan, "shouldn't we dismiss your spy? Not that we aren't grateful for his information," she directed a sly smile at the yellow-beard, "but after all, this is a closed Council session."

Caphtor nodded. "She's right, my friend. You have Cainlan's thanks for your efforts. My assistant will find you rooms where you can rest. I'm sure we'll have further need of your services in the near future."

The man bowed and made his exit, pulling the giant bronzed doors closed behind him with a smooth click. Caphtor lowered himself into in his seat at the opposite end of the table from the High Priestess.

"Now, we must make some plans," he said.

"You have a suggestion?" asked Tomsk.

"I do. I believe we should begin to assemble our own special branch, as Manessah has done."

"Impossible!" Limpopo glared around the table. "Where will we get the funds?"

"Funds? You imbecile!" Seneset's shout filled the chamber. "Where will your precious funds be if we are overrun by yellow-beards and murdered within the city walls? We have no choice but to build an army bigger and better than Manessah's."

Several shouts of agreement joined with Seneset, and Limpopo fell silent, his face red and eyes seething.

"Won't Manessah hear of it? And attack earlier, before we're able to prepare ourselves?" asked Feren.

"That is a risk," Caphtor agreed. "But I think it likelier that our action will cause them to pause, espe-

cially if they learn we have developed energy-powered
weapons too. If they're only two seasons into their invasion plan, they aren't that far ahead of us. And don't
forget, if we go to war all exports stop. I doubt they've
had enough time to stockpile the energy to last them
through a war, even if we are less prepared than they.
We'll know more about that after Feren's group has
had a chance to examine that weapon and do some
projections on power consumption."

Several heads nodded. Caphtor leaned against the
back of his chair and infused his smile with calm as-
surance. As Governor of Cainlan and leader of this
Council, he felt a responsibility to project an attitude
of confidence.

"Has our energy export level increased to Enoch as
well?" asked Liadan.

He looked at her in surprise. An astute question for
one who usually thought no further than her own in-
terests.

"No, not noticeably. We've seen a steady rise for a
long time now, but that can be attributed to increased
populations and advancing technologies."

"Then wouldn't Enoch come to our aid? Surely they
wouldn't stand by and watch us destroyed, and their
energy supply cut off."

"More likely they'd join in with the Manessites to
overrun us," answered Councilor Tomsk.

Liadan glared at him, but Caphtor nodded his
head.

"Tomsk is right. It's a good thought, and they
might surprise us, but Enoch, too, has begun to
grumble about our monopoly on energy production.
They would like to force us to share our production
technology."

"Which proves that our decision to keep energy
production under the government's control was wise."
Seneset sat back in his chair with a satisfied smirk.
"Otherwise the secrecy of the true nature of its manu-
facture would have become impossible."

Caphtor's jaw tightened as the counselors exchanged congratulatory nods. Had they forgotten that he had been instrumental in that decision? When the break-through in energy production occurred, the rest had merely followed along with his suggestions like a herd of sheep, without a shred of foresight of their own.

"In addition to the creation of our special branch," he said, watching their faces to judge their reaction, "I think we should take steps now to increase the size of Cainlan's army."

"That makes sense." Seneset nodded agreement. "This may even solve the recent problems we've had with the miners. Some of them will surely apply. A bigger army will help the unemployment problem."

"It will *alleviate* the unemployment problem," Tomsk said. "But Limpopo has made a point. Funds. How will we pay for this new army?"

They all looked to Caphtor. When he spoke, he kept his tone even. "You won't like the answer, but we have to fund the army from the city's treasury."

Limpopo, who controlled that branch of government, exploded. Rising out of his seat, he pounded a fist on the table while glaring at Caphtor. "You'll reduce us all to poverty level."

"Listen, Limpopo." Caphtor schooled his voice to a reasonable tone. "If we don't raise an army we will be overrun by the Manessites. Cainlan will be destroyed. That isn't a possibility, it is a fact. Besides, foreign energy sales have fattened Cainlan's purse. We'll reduce the unemployment allotments, and that will pay for some of it. The treasury can well afford to cover the rest.

"I have two more suggestions," Caphtor went on before Limpopo could think of another argument. "First, we should take immediate action to make the city walls more defensible. Seneset, that's your department."

Seneset gave a decisive nod.

"Good. Then the last suggestion I have concerns export." He looked at Limpopo again, for Import/Export fell under the direction of Economic Resources. "We need to immediately reduce the amount of energy exported to Manessah."

This time Limpopo simply closed his eyes, apparently resigned to defeat before he began the argument. "Is there no other way?" he questioned in a longsuffering voice.

"Of course not, you idiot," Tomsk replied nastily, "if we continue to give them three times what they need, they'll soon have enough stockpiled to overrun us."

Limpopo's suppressed rage at the insult turned his face a bright purply-red.

"That's part of it." Caphtor exercised iron control to keep from snapping at them. Grown men who spatted with each other like children annoyed him more than he could say. "We'll also be retarding their weapons research. They'll have to reduce the amount distributed to their population in order to continue to supply their weapons. That's going to cause unrest within their city. If we can introduce a little chaos in Manessah, the government will have to deal with it. That buys time, and any time, even a little, will only help us."

Everyone around the table nodded, and Caphtor allowed himself to relax against the back of his chair. Despite a rough beginning, this meeting had gone according to plan. They were sufficiently frightened by this development with Manessah, and looked to him to provide the solution. The next time he called a Council session, they'd comply without grousing. Whether they realized it or not, he'd gained a measure of power over them today.

"Speaking of unrest," said Tomsk, "some of our people may applaud increasing the army, but I think the majority will respond to the news with fear. We'd better be prepared to handle that."

"You're right," agreed Caphtor. "Any ideas?"

Limpopo broke the brief silence. "The approach is everything. If the announcement is worded correctly, the news will create excitement instead of fear."

Caphtor bit back a smile. Even the surly councilor had resigned himself to cooperating under Capthor's leadership.

"True," Feren agreed. "We should concentrate on the number of jobs this move will create."

At the other end of the table, Liadan frowned. "If the people hear the whole story about the Manessite army, I don't care how pretty the speech is, we'll have panic on our hands."

Asquith spoke up. "I can have young Roblin draft the announcement. He can be trusted to impart only what's necessary, and he has a way with words."

Nods around the table. Caphtor could think of several ways Roblin might come in useful. This would be a good test. He stood. "Do that, and send the draft around for our approval. Thank you, councilors and High Priestess."

Caphtor left the room as the others were still gathering their possessions. He pretended not to see Liadan's wave, and hurried away before she could ask him yet another inane question about his upcoming alliance with her daughter. He had no time for that today. Excitement tensed his stomach as he strode from the chamber. A war was exactly what he needed to propel those lazy councilors into action. And he intended to keep a firm grip on Cainlan's army.

Eliana chose her position with care, selecting a bench just opposite the alley leading to the pet shop. From that seat she could see the door and easily recognize anyone entering. She intended to stay all morning if necessary.

The shop was not a busy one, and she soon grew bored watching the antics of the colorful bird in its iron cage outside the door. The bakery enjoyed more business. Eliana had never been here this early, and so had never seen the city women hurry about their morning tasks, small children in tow. She caught snatches of their conversations as they passed.

"He's raised his prices again. The nerve of that..."

"...how I'm going to make this stretch..."

"...could buy five for the same price this time last season."

Though she planned this morning's activity carefully, doubt nagged at her. Was she acting like a fool, lying in wait for Shem? He had a *wife*. Her plan to feign a chance encounter when he arrived at the pet shop seemed suddenly childish; he was sure to see through her scheme. The last thing she wanted was for him to think her a child. Perhaps she should leave after all.

Yes, that's what she should do. Leave. This was a fool's errand. She stood and turned toward the temple.

"Hello," said a deep voice.

Eliana's heart leapt in her chest, pounding like a carpenter's hammer. "H-hello. I ... you're here!"

Fine lines around Shem's gray eyes crinkled with humor. "So I am. As are you, I see."

"Yes, well, I was just leaving." She edged a step sideways toward the temple. "So ... goodbye."

She meant to turn and leave, to walk regally and gracefully away, but her legs did not obey.

"Must you go so soon?" he asked. "I have a little time. Maybe we could talk over a mug of cider." His smile was just as she remembered, warm and welcoming and a little crooked. Though she tried hard to read more into his offer, she saw only friendliness in his expression. Before she could stop herself, she nodded.

"There's a place over here I know." He led her down the cobbled walkway to a stone tavern. "Since it's not yet meal time we're sure to find a table."

Inside, Eliana followed Shem toward a round table by the wall. Dozens of tables crowded the room, and a

wide counter along the back held high stacks of pottery. A door beside the counter swung on hinges. Customers seated at two of the tables looked up as the
newcomers entered, then returned to their own conversations.

She settled into a chair across from Shem and giggled. "I've never been in a tavern before."

"No? Then allow me to make your selections. Are
you hungry?"

She nodded as a man approached, wiping his
hands on a stained apron. Shem smiled up at him, but
he remained straight-lipped.

"Soup's not ready yet," he said in a loud voice that
dared them to order soup.

"How about a couple of fresh pastries and maybe a
slice of melon? And two redberry ices to drink."

The man nodded as he left.

Shem smiled across the table at her. "Have you ever had a redberry ice?"

"Oh yes, we have ices in the temple."

"I guarantee you've never had one like this man
makes. I have yet to figure out what he puts in them,
but I keep trying. Cooling tanks are one of the better
energy-powered inventions to spring up in the past few
years, if you ask me."

Eliana looked around the room. Smooth pieces of
wood hung on the walls with pictures etched into their
surfaces. The one directly above her head was of a
man with curly hair and merry eyes watching over a
flock of sheep.

"That's one of my favorites," Shem said, noticing
her study of the etching. "I like to pretend he's Abel,
though I'm certain the artist never intended him to
be."

"Abel?" questioned Eliana. "Is he a friend of
yours?"

Shem snorted laughter. "Not a friend. A relative,
sort of. Distant."

"Ah." Eliana nodded as though she understood.

"Have you never heard of Abel?" asked Shem, and then continued, as if to himself. "Of course not. They certainly would not have told you that bit of history."

"History?"

"Well, yes, but perhaps it isn't appropriate..." Shem's voice trailed off.

"I love history," she prompted, wanting to keep him talking so she could go on watching those expressive eyes as long as possible.

"Yes, but... well no matter. First I must confess something." He lowered his voice and leaned toward her. "Can I trust you?"

"You can trust me with your life," she replied with mock drama.

"You say that lightly, but it may come to that. You see, I am not a worshiper of Cain."

Eliana almost laughed out loud at his grave expression. She could not suppress a giggle, and Shem frowned.

"I'm sorry," she whispered. "But you look so serious."

"The matter *is* serious."

Eliana managed to force the smile from her lips. "I'm sorry, but you're not telling me anything new. You gave yourself away when you spoke of a wife, and when you promised to ask God to watch over me. I only know one other person who talks like that, and she does not bow knee to Cain."

Comprehension cleared his features. "Ah, the nursemaid."

Eliana nodded. "She knows of the One God, and she's taught me some of His ways."

At that moment the server returned with a laden tray. He placed the food between them, and hovered while she tried the frothy redberry ice. When she declared that she had never tasted anything so wonderful, the man grunted with satisfaction. Eliana pronounced the pastries delicious too, light, crispy and filled with a sweet mixture of fruit. Shem waited until the satisfied man had retreated before continuing his story.

"Have you heard of Adam?"

Eliana nodded. "Yes. Girta told me he was the first man, the one created by the One God. He sinned and was forced out of his garden paradise."

"That's right. And do you know what happened to him afterward?" Eliana shook her head, her mouth full of pastry. "He and his wife had a child, a son. The child's name was Cain."

Eliana's eyes widened. "Cain? Like the god?"

Shem nodded. "The same. Cain grew, and the One God loved him. Then Adam and Eve had another son, and this one they named Abel."

As Eliana listened to his story, a feeling of unease spread through her. When he described Cain's murder of his brother, she put down her pastry, her appetite gone. Then Shem told her of the One God's curse, that the ground would never yield its fruit for Cain. Her throat constricted.

"And this is the same Cain that Cainlan is named for?"

Shem nodded. "He settled in the East, where he established the city of Enoch, which is named for his son. This city was founded after his death by one of his descendants, a woman named Jaline."

"Jaline, my ancestress."

Shem shrugged, and looked awkwardly down at his pastry. Eliana toyed with her cup. Of course she knew of Jaline, the first high priestess in Cainlan. As Liadan's heir, Eliana was required to study the history of the world. She never questioned the legend which told of the founding of Cainlan, how the mighty god Cain came to aid a group of men and women in danger of being annihilated by an overwhelming enemy army; how that god then returned to the heavenly realm, leaving instructions for the establishment of a religion to honor him; how the warrior Jaline earned her place as the first high priestess by her bravery on the battlefield.

As she considered Shem's version of the story, a horrifying thought occurred to her. If what Shem said was true, then Cain was not a god at all. What if he was nothing more than a man? Jaline descended from Cain, and she descended from Jaline. That meant that she was directly descended from a murderer.

Numbness crept over her limbs. Had she been lied to all these years? Her mother had faults aplenty, but surely she wouldn't lie about the god she had dedicated her life to serve.

Aware that Shem's gaze was once again fixed on her, she thrust the thought from her mind. She would consider this later, when she had time. For now, she wanted nothing to spoil her morning.

Taking a determined sip of the frothy drink, she studied the etching on the wall above her head. "You're right. I think it is Abel."

Cocking his head sideways, Shem asked, "And how did he find his way into the city of Cainlan?"

"Destiny," replied Eliana with a nod. "He's come to watch over the goings-on of his brother's descendants. Either that," she lowered her voice to a conspiratorial whisper, "or the tavern owner is a believer in the One God."

Shem laughed out loud, and Eliana joined him. When the laughter subsided, they were left smiling at one another.

"Tell me about your family."

Shem leaned back in his chair, sipping from his cup. "I am the eldest of three brothers. You already know we are farmers. That means we are of the line of Seth, Father Adam's third son. I run the farm for my family."

"In the tradition of your ancestors?" Eliana allowed a tease to creep into her tone.

"Because your ancestors could not!" He grinned as he returned the jibe.

"And what of your father and brothers? Do they

help you on the farm?"

Shem examined his fingers, which fiddled with the remains of his pastry.

"No," he replied slowly. "Father has taken up carpentry, and my brothers help him with his project. He is building a boat."

"A boat."

"A very big one. An ark, actually. Three hundred cubits long, to be exact."

"Three hundred cubits?" Eliana leaned back in her chair. "That's far too big for a stream or river, and there's no ocean within twenty days of here."

"Sounds crazy, I know. Do you have time for another story?"

Eliana glanced around the room. More tables had filled while they talked. A quick glance at the sun outside told her the morning was nearly half over.

"A little."

"Shall we walk in the gardens?"

She nodded, and Shem signaled the shopkeeper. He handed the man a few coins and received a nod of thanks in return.

The sunshine outside dazzled Eliana's eyes. Shem guided her across the cobbled walkway and through an opening in the garden hedge. Then he slowed, walking at her side as he talked.

"For a long time, my father ran the farm with my brothers as his helpers. As the eldest, I handled the trading. One day while my father worked in the far field, he heard a voice call his name. He recognized the voice of God, for he is no stranger to the One God. He fell to his knees there in the field, and-"

"Wait." Eliana stopped on the path and held up a hand. "Your God talks to you? Just talks, in plain speech, as I would?"

The very idea of a god, any god, speaking to an ordinary person without a priestess to interpret was almost too much to believe. She peered up into Shem's face, but could detect no sign that he was toying with her.

"Certainly. At least, He talks to my father, and to my grandfather. He has not spoken to me yet, but I have hopes that He will someday, if I am worthy."

Shem's expression grew distant. Embarrassed, Eliana looked away from the open longing apparent on his face. Though she barely knew him, she could not imagine anyone worthier than Shem de Noah to hear from his God. With a start, he seemed to remember she walked beside him. "He told my father that He regretted His creation, because the earth is evil and corrupt and violent. He said He planned to destroy the earth and every living thing upon it."

Eliana gasped, and he nodded. "I know. It is a frightening thought. But He told my father to build an ark, and even specified the dimensions. The ark will hold a pair of every kind of living animal to keep them safe during the flood so that the earth can be repopulated afterward."

"Flood?"

"Yes, God will send floodwaters to cover the entire earth, destroying all creation except those within the ark."

Eliana's gaze swept the area around her. Impossible to believe that one day water would cover these gardens, these buildings. The ocean was so far away, and that was the biggest water anyone had ever heard of. How could such a thing happen? And what of the people who lived here?

"Will He do this, Shem? Will your God really kill us all?"

Shem sighed. "My father says He will, unless people give up their corrupt ways and turn to Him. He hopes to convince enough people to turn to the One God, and soften His heart."

The councilors, her teachers, Caphtor and her mother—there was no chance they would ever change. They would laugh at the idea. Some might believe, but not many. Girta, for instance...

She stopped on the rose-scented path, turning angrily toward Shem. "I don't believe that. Girta says the One God is kind and loving, not bloodthirsty. If the whole world was evil, I suppose He might do something like that. But there are good people, people who worship Him. He'd be killing them too."

"I know." Shem's expression clouded. "I myself know good people who are true to the One God. Father says only that he must obey God even when he does not understand His purpose. God remains silent to my questions."

They wound their way through the maze of flowering hedges as they talked, through the many smaller gardens and blooming alcoves. They stepped into the central garden, the one that held the giant statue of Cain. Shem guided Eliana to an empty bench away from the few people who milled about, and behind the oppressive regard of the god.

Troubled lines carved crevices into Shem's forehead. Her anger fled. He truly cared for the people his God wanted to destroy. Like her, he marched toward a future that held pain and heartache, and could only obey.

"Will there be any people saved with the animals?" she asked in a quiet voice.

"Yes." He sounded more wretched than before. "My father and mother, their sons and their sons' wives."

He looked up at the sky, his eyes distant as though he fought an inner battle. "I've asked not to be included. I've asked it of my father, and of the One God. I told them both that I would give up my place in the ark to someone more deserving." His gaze dropped to the rich soil around the base of the statue. "My brothers feel the same way, even my father, I suspect. But he said the choice is not ours to make. Obedience to God is never easy."

Eliana sat quietly, looking anywhere but at the private pain on Shem's face.

The perfume of blooming roses in the hedge clung

to the air like dew to the morning grass. From the garden paths, over several rows of hedges, floated the distant murmur of voices that somehow added to the silence instead of breaking it. A gentle stillness grew between them, washing over them as softly as the breeze that stirred the rose petals.

Presently Shem turned on the bench. "What of you? Tell me of your life in the temple."

"There's nothing very interesting about my life." She gave him a sideways grin. "Certainly nothing as dramatic as the end of the world."

Shem laughed, and she warmed at the sound. "Thank goodness! But really, the daughter of the high priestess has nothing interesting to talk about?"

"Truly. I'm sure there are great things going on in the temple, but none within my hearing. I don't see my mother much. When I was a child she hardly noticed me. I see Girta more than anyone, and she knows less than I."

"Ah, Girta who watches over you and does not bow knee to Cain. I've been wondering about her."

"Wondering what?"

"How could a believer in the One God attain such an important position inside the temple of Cain? And once there, how has she escaped notice all this time?"

Eliana shrugged. "Easy. My mother never paid much attention to me, as I said. As long as I looked presentable and didn't embarrass her during the few formal ceremonies that required my attendance, she was satisfied with my upbringing."

"But surely her background was investigated before she was selected to be your nursemaid."

Eliana cocked her head. "I've never thought about it." She shrugged. "I'll ask her. Anyway, until recently my life has been dull. But that will change soon."

"Because you've reached the age when priestesses begin their training?"

Eliana shook her head. "No. I can't enter the training for another year. But something's about to happen that will surely remind my mother that I need to take on more responsibilities."

"What is that?"

She looked away. She hated to spoil the morning by thinking of the changes that loomed in her life. But ignoring them would not make them go away.

She drew a deep breath. "I am about to enter into a formal alliance with Governor Caphtor."

Shem said nothing. She tilted her head sideways to look up at him, and he wasn't even looking at her. He studied the flowers blooming in the hedge in front of him. His throat moved, the knob in its center bobbing up and down.

When he finally spoke, he kept his gaze fixed on the hedge. "That will cause some excitement. The talk, of course, is that the governor will form an alliance with the high priestess."

"Yes, that's what my mother expected, too. We're all surprised."

Shem did look down at her then. "How can that surprise you? Doubtless there are many eager to partner with someone as beautiful as you."

Eliana's pulse beat faster as she gazed into his eyes.

Suddenly he jumped up. "Once again I lost track of time. You probably have something to do, and I must go to the pet shop."

"Are you going to buy something?"

"Yes, a rare bird not often seen this far west."

"And you want it for the ark." Eliana couldn't stop a grin of excitement as she realized the reason for his errand.

Shem nodded.

"May I go with you? Please?"

He studied her a moment, then shrugged a shoulder. "Maybe I will get a better price with a pretty girl along." He gestured for her to precede him out of the garden.

Inside the pet shop, Eliana wandered from cage to

cage, stopping to chuckle at the antics of a monkey and poke a finger at a playful kitten as Shem arranged to purchase a yellow and scarlet bird. He gave the man a deposit in the event a female could be found.

When he finished his deal, he joined Eliana before a small cage. Inside, a tiny bird with bright red wings fixed a black eye on Eliana. The dainty creature extended its throat to warble a song, a lacy crest atop its head dancing with the effort.

"Oh, how beautiful!"

"That's a crested pisidia," Shem told her. "Be careful of this one."

She looked up at him. "Why?"

"This little beauty has a dark reputation." Shem's lips drew into a mock-serious frown. "Legend has it that he sings the most beautiful songs in the world, so beautiful they ensnare the hearts of all who hear. Then he flies away, carrying with him the heart and soul of his listeners."

Eliana turned back to the cage. "Little bird, I'd gladly give you my heart if you'd sing your special songs for me. Go ahead, sing."

But the bird, perhaps frightened by their voices, closed its tiny beak and refused to utter a sound. Eliana and Shem laughed, and were still smiling when they left the shop and returned to the bright sunshine outside.

"I must leave now, my friend," said Shem. "Thank you for spending your morning with me.

She stood still beneath a wash of sudden sorrow. Would she ever see Shem again? She swallowed hard against a throat gone suddenly dry. When or where, she couldn't imagine.

"Thank you for the ice and pastries."

Eliana took a backward step. Shem stood where he was, his arms wrapped around the large birdcage he had purchased.

"Good luck on your alliance."

"Thank you. And you on your... venture."

He nodded, unsmiling, and they turned to walk in opposite directions. Eliana took great pride in the fact that she did not once look back.

Chapter 5

Jarrell looked up to see Roblin de Yibin threading his way through the maze of desks between him and the door. He leaned back in his chair and tossed the pen away, rubbing the feeling back into numb fingers as he awaited his friend's approach.

Acquaintance, Jarrell corrected himself. *Business associate.* Shem was a friend, probably the only true friend he had. Roblin was far too self-centered and politically motivated to be considered a friend. A good man to know, given Jarrell's professional aspirations, but to assume anything like familiarity with the shrewd Roblin could prove dangerous.

Moving like an athlete, Roblin flashed his handsome smile at everyone he passed, a true politician. He paused to speak with one of the women analysts, and she practically swooned.

Jarrell suppressed a grin. One day Roblin would run for office, and would probably give some of the more sour-faced councilors a tough time maintaining their seats.

Roblin arrived at Jarrell's desk and leaned gracefully against the edge. "What are your plans for the afternoon?"

With a snort, Jarrell waved at the stack of documents littering the surface in front of him. "What does it look like? I've got three reports due by the end of the week, and a speech to write."

Roblin dismissed those tasks with a flick of his fingers. "You can do that later. Join me for the afternoon instead."

Jarrell laughed at the absurdity of Roblin's suggestion. "You in the Cabinet of Energy might be able to ditch the office on a whim, but here in Social Action we work for a living."

A conspiratorial grin took Roblin's lips as he leaned toward Jarrell to whisper. "You've got a date with a priestess." His eyebrows arched. "A *foreign* priestess."

"I do?"

Roblin nodded. "As do I. I met the pair in the temple gardens the other day and arranged to show them around Cainlan this afternoon."

Jarrell's gaze dropped to his desk, and he waved at the piles there. "You could have given me some time to prepare, you know."

Roblin crossed his arms, his grin widening. "You weren't my first choice. But Amaziah backed out this morning, and besides, you need to get out more."

Jarrell laughed out loud. Roblin's easy confidence made it impossible to take offense. And doing him a good turn wouldn't hurt Jarrell's career any; even Phanom would recognize that. He looked at the report he had been analyzing, his uniform numbers written in painstakingly even columns covering several pages. The summary could wait until tomorrow, if he came in early.

Pushing his chair back from the desk, he rose and clapped Roblin on the shoulder. "You would inflict

Amaziah on a foreign woman? Good thing for you I'm available, or *both* ladies would hate your guts by the end of the afternoon."

They made their way from the Social Action offices through the marketplace toward the wide stone staircase leading to the temple's entrance. No time to change from his work clothes. Jarrell cast a covert look at Roblin's attire and breathed a sigh of relief. He, too, came directly from the office. If only Jarrell looked as good in his everyday attire as Roblin. His breeches encased muscular legs that Jarrell could never hope to have, and the blue jerkin with the bright yellow sun emblem of the Cabinet of Energy emblazoned on the right shoulder complemented the striking blue of Roblin's eyes.

"There they are." Roblin pointed at something behind Jarrell's head. "Holy Fires, look at her!"

Jarrell turned, his eyes drawn to a bright spot in the sea of white stone stairs where a pair of women stood on the first landing. The taller of the two fairly shone, with a thick head of sunlight-colored hair flowing unbound to brush at her well-shaped thighs. She was swathed in bright pink that looked more like a coat of fresh paint than clothing. She caught sight of Roblin's waving hand and waved back with enthusiasm, causing all heads in her vicinity to turn. Beside her stood an attractive but not nearly so flamboyant brunette wearing a flowing green jerkin over tight leggings.

"The blonde is mine," Roblin said in an aside, his eyes fixed on the pair as he took a step forward.

Jarrell suppressed a grin at the possessive tone. He had no doubt which of the two would attract the flashy Roblin's attention.

They arrived at the bottom of the stairs and greeted the priestesses. Roblin handled the introductions without taking his eyes off the blonde. "Jarrell de Asshur, meet Hanae de Helo and Bitra de..."

He fumbled for a moment before the brunette rescued him.

"de Adah," she supplied in a rich alto, "though that will mean nothing to you, since my father has never set foot outside the walls of Enoch his entire life."

Jarrell tore his gaze from Hanae to look at Bitra. An amused smile hovered about her lips as she watched Roblin practically drool while gawking at her friend. Her hazel eyes slid sideways to lock with Jarrell's, and the smile widened. To his amazement, Jarrell felt his pulse flutter. Hanae's flashy looks might draw attention, but Bitra was a lovely woman herself.

"I hope you haven't been waiting long," Roblin said. "Jarrell insisted on finishing some interminable report."

"Not at all," the blonde Hanae assured them, turning a blinding smile on Jarrell. "Do you work with Roblin?"

"No, I'm an analyst for Sub-Director Phanom."

"Ah, Social Action," Bitra said.

Jarrell turned a surprised look on her. "That's right. How did you know? I had no idea his name was known outside a small circle of politicians."

She shrugged. "We attend classes to learn about the political structure of Cainlan, in addition to our temple lessons."

"Bitra remembers all those political things. She's the smartest in our class." Hanae cocked her head to gaze coquettishly at Roblin. "But we both love Cainlan and are eager to see the city."

Roblin gave a cow-eyed sigh in return, and Jarrell suppressed a chuckle to see the normally self-possessed man acting like a moon-struck moron. He decided to come to his rescue.

"Roblin has the afternoon planned. We're in for a treat – we get to ride in his new landrider."

Hanae clapped her hands and turned an excited

grin on Roblin. "You have a landrider? I've wanted to ride in one since we arrived in Cainlan last season!"

"Then let's get started." Roblin gestured toward the walkway. "I store it in a shed near the Cabinet of Energy building, right over there."

Jarrell noticed that Roblin's hand lingered at the small of Hanae's back under the guise of directing her. He and Bitra fell in place behind them, and her sideways grin at Jarrell told him she had seen the gesture as well.

"You haven't ridden in a landrider before?"

Bitra shook her head. "We don't have them in Enoch yet."

"It's only a matter of time," Roblin said over his shoulder. "They're fantastic, you'll see. Something like this is certain to catch on everywhere."

"The problem is energy," Bitra said. "The energy cartridges to run a vehicle like that are still incredibly expensive."

"I've heard your government has applied considerable resources lately toward energy generation technology."

"That's true, but we're not making progress as quickly as Cainlan."

Roblin did not reply, and a heavy silence hung between them for a moment. Jarrell knew that Enoch's government had approached Cainlan with requests to share the technology they had developed to improve energy generation techniques. Cainlan's refusal made sense from a purely economic standpoint – energy had become the city's primary export. Sharing the technology would be stupid from a financial point of view. As an analyst in the Cabinet of Energy, Roblin would know that better than most.

"Plus," Hanae put in, "we're not surrounded by forests to harvest, as Cainlan is."

"Cainlan won't have them for long either, if they don't stop draining all the vegetation in the area for energy," Bitra said in a low voice.

Roblin's back stiffened, and Jarrell averted his gaze from Bitra, pretending a close examination of the fabrics displayed in the window of the shop they passed. The Enochian priestess seemed determined to touch upon the one topic certain to cause an argument. How long would the normally garrulous Roblin hold his tongue?

Turning back to Bitra, Jarrell plastered a determined smile on his face. "Why does Enoch send its priestesses here for training? Don't you have a temple there?"

She accepted his change of subject with a slight narrowing of her eyelids followed by the merest of nods. "Yes, but the first temple built to serve the god was this one. We want to learn from the descendant of the original high priestess."

"And are there just the two of you?"

Hanae turned her head to answer. "There are six of us in this class. We'll stay for the full five years of training until we become senior priestesses. When we return to Enoch we hope to take back some of the new practices and ideas we've learned here."

Roblin broke his silence. "Such as?"

"The SBP, for one," Bitra answered. "We don't have anything like that in Enoch."

"You don't?" Jarrell turned a surprised look on the priestess. "I didn't realize the Sacrificial Beneficiary Program was unique to Cainlan. What options do you offer to poor and indigent parents who have more children than they can afford to feed?"

Bitra waved a hand vaguely. "Oh, there are programs and food supplements. But Enoch can't afford energy credits in return for children given in service to the temple, as Cainlan can. Energy is too expensive there."

Her gaze slid to Roblin's back again, and Jarrell fought to hide a frustrated sigh. If the brunette priestess didn't leave off needling Roblin about energy technology, the afternoon wouldn't be any fun at all.

"Here we are." Jarrell detected a hint of relief in his friend's tone as he directed them through a gate in the decorative iron fence that separated the exclusive marketplace and temple gardens from the rest of the walled city of Cainlan.

"Ooh, look at all these landriders!"

Hanae clapped her hands at the sight of at least a dozen of the new vehicles stored in three neat rows in the covered and secured shed into which Roblin led them.

"This one is mine." Roblin guided them to one of the larger riders and opened the hinged door with pride.

Jarrell ran his hand over the polished surface. The thing was constructed of wood, like a regular wagon, though the finish was so smooth that he wouldn't have believed it. The canopy over the top was of the same thin sheets of polished wood, and would provide a good shade from the harsh rays of the sun during daytime journeys. The wheels looked like wagon wheels, but smaller, with iron spokes and thick rims.

"It's beautiful," Hanae said as Roblin assisted her up the step to slide to the far side of the front bench.

"Yes it is," Jarrell agreed, helping Bitra climb in after her friend. He clouted the proud Roblin on the shoulder. "This had to cost a bundle. The Cabinet of Energy must pay its analysts a lot more than Social Action."

Jarrell stepped into the vehicle, taking his seat on the second bench beside Bitra. The Enochian priestess seemed to have gotten over her determination to argue, for she flashed him an excited smile.

Roblin leapt into the front seat and reached forward to connect a metal lead to the largest energy cartridge Jarrell had ever seen. Then he turned to Hanae.

"Where would you like to go?"

"All around Cainlan," the blonde replied. "The only place we've been since we arrived is the temple. I want to go somewhere I can't see from my bedroom window."

"Then today you'll get a full tour." He grasped a lever between his knees and pushed it forward. "We're going to end with dinner in the finest pub found anywhere within the city walls."

As the rider rolled forward, Bitra turned a wide smile of excitement on Jarrell. She might be a bit prickly, but he had to admit feeling a grudging respect for the pretty brunette. How could he not admire someone who spoke her mind, and who was not afraid to contradict the supremely confident Roblin? She had shown herself to be in possession of a sharp intelligence, the point of which could cut like a sacrificial dagger at will. He returned her smile, determined to enjoy the afternoon in Bitra's company.

Nerves jangled in Eliana's stomach. From her vantage point behind the curtain she watched her mother stride with confidence to the center of the dais. She had waited for this day with conflicting feelings of dread and excitement. Excitement, because once her alliance was finalized she would be considered a full adult, no longer bound to her mother as a minor. Dread, because she would be legally bound instead to Caphtor, with whom she had never exchanged more than five words at a time. In the weeks since Liadan informed Eliana of his request, she had not laid eyes on the governor even once.

She looked better than she ever had, of that she was sure. She wore the customary dress for a first formal alliance, sky blue silk sweeping gracefully from shoulder to floor, the waist gathered close with a wide ruby belt. The traditional jewelry of rubies at her ears, throat and wrists were not copies, as they often were for the common folk of Cainlan. No, hers were real, a gift from the Council to celebrate the occasion. Her hair was twisted around her head in an intricate design of braids and loops, more sparkling red stones peeking out from its dark depths. Her mother stood on the same dais where the rituals of sacrifice to Cain were conducted. Through a gap in the curtain, Eliana glimpsed the marketplace gardens through the wide arched entryway. Fitting, she thought, for this alliance ceremony to be held in the same place as the bloody sacrifices she detested. She felt as though she were being stretched upon the altar herself.

Eliana expected a large gathering due to Caphtor's prominence in the city and the fact that the High Priestess herself would officiate. But the sheer number of people spread out before the dais left her breathless. She wondered if she would ever be able to stand before that many people with the ease that seemed to envelop her mother.

Her glance slid sideways toward Caphtor. He looked handsome in a sky blue toga, his ruby jerkin glittering expensively. His dark hair was combed straight back and gathered into a sober tail at the nape of his neck. He exuded conservatism and re-straint, but Eliana fancied she could see a calculating glint in his eyes, and it frightened her. When he smiled in her direction, she looked quickly away. She forced herself to focus on Liadan's voice.

"At this momentous time in history, we are fortu-nate to have such wise and far-seeing people as these two in our midst. Their union sets the standard for the upcoming generation; the rest of the world will gaze in wonder at the children of Cainlan. With such as these for our example we cannot help but lead the world in every aspect."

Eliana shifted her weight, uneasy. The High Priest-ess was turning a simple marital alliance announce-ment into a political rally. She caught her lower lip be-tween her teeth. On the other hand, how could it be simple, when it involved the High Priestess's heir and the Governor of Cainlan?

"I present to you the future High Priestess of Cain,

Eliana de Ashbel, and the Governor of the Council of
Cainlan, Caphtor de Chapra."

Two attendants pulled back the curtains before
them, revealing Caphtor and Eliana to the crowd.
Caphtor made a show of extending his hand to her,
and when she took it the crowd roared their approval.
His hand felt hot and damp. She kept her head lowered, not raising it even to look at Caphtor. But from
the corner of her eye she saw him grin widely at the
crowd. He raised their joined hands over their heads in
a gesture that spurred the mob to cheer louder. How
alarmingly tall he was! He towered a full head and a
half above her, and his hand dwarfed her petite one.
His grip was so firm it was almost painful.

Eliana felt the pulse of the mob, sensed their approval of this man with whom she was about to join.
The crowd was a creature in itself, and a powerful one.
To control an entity like this meant wielding control
unlike any other. This, then, is what Liadan spoke of.
What a weapon, to be able to dominate such a force.
Eliana raised her head, saw the smile of triumph on
his lips and the satisfaction in his eyes, and she shuddered.

Liadan approached the altar and stood with her
arms spread wide, her green robes blowing in a gentle
breeze.

"Come before the god, before almighty Cain." Her
voice assumed the musical cadence used for official
ceremonies, low enough so that the multitude became
silent, straining to catch her every word.

Eliana and Caphtor turned to face her.

"State your terms before the god, children of Cain."

Caphtor spoke, his deep voice rising to fill the sky.
"We seek to join in marital alliance. A commitment period of three years, retention of non-contractual rights
assured. One half of all proceeds to be retained upon
termination, and we acknowledge the right of legitimacy to all heirs."

Eliana drew a quick breath as a murmur rose from

the crowd. A request for legitimacy was uncommon for a first alliance.

"Are the petitioners in agreement to the terms?"

Liadan's gaze traveled to Eliana. An expectant hush rose over the crowd. Now was the time she could protest or change any of the terms. Though considered an insult and cause for weeks of scandalous gossip, occasionally a first-time female consort chose this time to voice her displeasure at any of the terms agreed upon by her legal guardian.

Eliana's heart pounded so heavily the silk at her neck pulsed. Though Liadan mentioned the required daughter, Eliana had not given serious consideration to children resulting from this alliance. The thought of having a child with the powerful man beside her terrified her beyond reason.

As her silence lengthened, the crowd began to murmur. Caphtor turned his head slightly to look at her. Eliana glanced up at him, and saw his eyelids narrow a fraction. She tore her gaze away and looked toward her mother. Their eyes locked, and the green ice in Liadan's dared Eliana to defy her.

Eliana swallowed. She was incapable of crossing her mother. She took a deep breath, proud of the clear, steady voice that projected to the back of the crowd.

"The petitioners are in agreement."

A collective sigh was expelled, of disappointment on the part of the crowd, and, to Eliana's surprise, of relief by Caphtor.

Liadan's forehead gave a slight dip. "The god approves the request. These petitioners will return to the presence of Cain six days hence to make the appropriate sacrifices. Observe the daily devotions as required by the god, and your alliance will be blessed at that time."

The crowd began to cheer, and the sound quickly increased to a roar until Eliana felt her eardrums numb in their attempt to reject the noise. She and

Caphtor linked arms and left the dais. As she walked down the stairs behind the curtains, Eliana caught a glimpse of Liadan motioning to one of her priestesses to take over performance of the sacrificial ritual about to begin.

As soon as they stepped off the lowest stair Eliana withdrew her arm. Caphtor studied her a moment and she struggled not to squirm beneath his direct stare.

"You gave me a tense moment. I thought you might deny the terms."

Eliana raised her chin. "The terms were unexpected, Governor."

Caphtor's eyebrows arched. "But you agreed... oh. I see."

"I am legally in my minority, so my mother is within her rights to make arrangements on my behalf."

"If you disagree with the legitimacy term, we can still change it."

Eliana studied him. His offer sounded genuine. Would he really be willing to undergo the indignity of changing the terms after they had been announced? It would appear as though she had discovered something repugnant during the period of devotion. If he was willing to suffer that humiliation for her, perhaps she had misjudged him.

She grinned up at him. "Can you imagine the scandal?"

He studied her for a moment, then relaxed into a conspiratorial smile. "The High Priestess would be furious."

An aide approached to hand Caphtor a note. He turned away, his brows drawing together as he read. When he turned back to her, his distracted air had returned. Their companionable moment passed.

"Whatever you decide. Now if you'll excuse me, there's a matter that requires my attention. If you want to talk about this further, make an appointment with my assistant."

He turned away from her without another word,

the aide following him down the temple corridor at something short of a jog to keep up with his long-legged stride.

Eliana watched his retreat, surprised at the speed with which he had dismissed her. If that encounter was any indication of their future relationship, perhaps she had nothing to fear. He might not deign to notice her at all.

By the time she reached her room, her anxiety returned. He might ignore her during the day, but what about at night? She had never stood next to Caphtor, had never looked up to see him towering above her. The reality of his size and his power with the crowd frightened her. What would the next three years be like, sharing a bed with a man like that?

That last thought set her chin quivering like a babe's. She jerked the door to her room open and slammed it behind her with a loud bang that shook the bottles on her vanity. Girta came through the doorway leading to her own room. She took one look at Eliana and crossed to her, arms outstretched. Eliana rested her head gratefully on Girta's soft shoulder, but her eyes remained dry.

"There now, lambling, you'll be fine, wait and see." Girta patted Eliana's back. "Tell me what happened."

When Eliana repeated the terms of the alliance, Girta was righteously indignant at the mention of legal issue.

"You're a babe yourself."

"I'm not." Eliana lifted her head to look into Girta's face. "Your own people are given in marriage much younger than I, and many of them have babes of their own soon after."

Girta sniffed. "That's different. They were raised to it. You were not. You can't begin to understand how different they are from you."

"Well, that's your fault." Eliana was in no mood to be reminded how easy her life was. "You're the one who taught me to be the way I am."

"I raised you to the life you were born to." Girta pitched her voice to soothe. "And it will be a fine life. You'll set that Governor right in no time. Have him falling all over himself to please you, if I know you."

"You've obviously not met our Governor, Girta. He's not the kind to fall all over himself for anyone."

A knock sounded on the door.

"Who could that be?" asked Eliana. "It can't be Liadan. She never knocks."

She cracked the door to peer into the corridor, and then swung it wide. In the hallway stood a temple guard, his red uniform crisp and clean. His impassive face wore the bored expression worn by most of the guards. Eliana had long ago given up trying to tell one from the other, convinced they tried to look as much alike as possible.

This guard accompanied a boy, slightly grubby with unkempt hair and rumpled clothing. His face bore signs of a recent scrubbing, as though he'd taken pains to improve his appearance before entering the temple. He carried a large oblong package by a wire handle in the top, the rest concealed by a black cloth. Eliana recognized the shape at once; it was a birdcage.

"Is that for me?"

Though she knew of the custom to send gifts on the occasion of a woman's first alliance, Eliana didn't know many people. She had assumed the Council's gift of rubies would be her only present. Who could have sent this one?

"Bring it in." She stepped back and gestured for the child to enter the room. He did, arms trembling under the weight of his burden. The guard remained in the hallway, watching the proceedings with detailed attention.

"Put it, oh, let's see." Eliana swung about in a circle, searching for the perfect place. "There, by the window."

She picked up a light table and dumped the display of decorative ivory boxes unceremoniously on her bed, then placed it directly before the window. The boy set the cage in place, then took a note from his jacket. "This is yers."

"Thank you." She turned to Girta. "Do you have any money?"

"Of course." Girta turned her back while she reached into her bosom. When she faced the boy again she handed him a coin, and winked broadly. The child grinned his thanks and bowed once more before hurrying out the door. Girta closed it behind him, while Eliana unfolded the note in her hands.

> *Eliana,*
>> *It is only fitting that the loveliest songs ever sung should accompany you on your new journey in life. But guard your heart, and don't forget this little beauty's reputation.*
> *Shem de Noah*

"Let's get a look at it." Girta sounded nearly as excited as Eliana felt.

She grasped the cloth near the top, and carefully lifted it over the handle. At the sight of the beautiful bird within, a thrill of delight sent her spirits soaring.

Girta peered inside. "How lovely!"

"He's a crested pisidia," Eliana told her, admiring the cage's occupant. "He's supposed to have the most beautiful song of any bird in the world."

"Who sent him to you?"

Eliana remained silent, watching the little bird hop about from perch to perch. He cocked his head daintily to look at her. She knew Girta wouldn't like the answer.

"That man I met in the mall the other day."

"The one who worships the True God?"

Eliana nodded. She fully expected a tirade on the

evils of strangers in the mall, and was surprised when
Girta, after a long calculating stare, shrugged and
turned her attention back to the bird.

"Well, he is lovely. Look, all the water has slopped
out during the trip. And I wonder what he eats?"

"Send someone down to the mall, to the animal
shop. The shopkeeper will have everything necessary."

Nodding, Girta left the room to find a page. The
room grew quiet. Eliana stood before the birdcage,
staring through the narrow bars with rapt attention.
The bird became still, returning her gaze with an unblinking ebony stare.

"You are a beauty, little friend," Eliana whispered
into the silence, and the bird turned his head at the
sound of her voice. "I will treasure you, and all the
more because of who sent you."

The bird extended his neck, the scarlet crest feathers quivering gently, and began to sing. Though quiet
at first, the song gained volume as it rose in pitch. The
sound was unlike any Eliana had ever heard, a high,
wild song in octaves far above those she had previous-
ly known existed. Caught up by the melody—for there
was a true melody, unlike any birdsong she had
heard—she wanted it to go on forever. Then the bird's
serenade became softer and softer until finally it
stopped.

Her whisper sounded harsh in her own ears after
the sweetness of the bird's. "I shall call you Melody,
and count myself lucky whenever you wish to share
your songs with me."

Unbidden, an image of Shem rose in her mind. Her
skin had warmed when he touched her in the mall. A
shudder rippled through her at the memory of
Caphtor's painful grip on the dais. A grip as firm as
the bars of Melody's cage.

A new journey in life. Tears slipped down her
cheeks as she watched the little bird groom his fluffy
feathers.

Chapter 6

Shem trudged up the mountain path, placing his feet in the prints his father left in the dew-covered grass. Behind him, Samson completed their parade, stopping every few feet to tear up a mouthful of fresh mountain grass. They left the wagon at the bottom of the path and piled bundles of supplies onto the horse's back for the short but steep climb to Grandfather Methuselah's cabin.

Shem looked up from the well-worn path, breathing deeply of the mountain air that seemed to grow sweeter with every upward step. Late afternoon sunlight filtered through the trees on his right, casting shadows at their feet. Though Father came to check on his grandfather and re-stock the larder every few weeks, too much time had passed since Shem's last visit to Grandfather Methuselah's cabin. The old man had been on his mind often in the weeks since his discussion with Jarrell.

Rounding a dense copse of trees, Shem caught sight of the cabin. The old man stood on the porch, leaning against a post and smiling in their direction. Shem grinned in return, as much to himself as to Grandfather. He'd been as quiet as he could, returning unconsciously to the games of his boyhood when he tried to sneak up the mountain pathway and surprise the old man. He had never been able to pull it off, and he still couldn't.

"How do you always know when we're coming," he called over Father's head.

"The knowledge isn't mine," Grandfather replied, as he always did. "It belongs to the mountain, and she shares it with me."

"Why do you call it a she?" Shem asked, continuing the ritual as they neared the porch.

"Because she nurtures me, like a mother nurtures her babe. She protects me as a cat protects her young. She sings me to sleep at night, like a bird crooning to her hatchlings. She is the earth, and God used her to give me life."

"And now God will destroy her." Shem broke the pattern of their ritual with a bitterness he wished he did not feel.

Father Noah turned to give him a piercing look, but Shem kept his gaze fixed on Grandfather. The three stood close enough to touch, though no one did. The old man looked first into Father's eyes, and then Shem's. Shem did not turn away, but let Grandfather see the confusion that lay in his soul.

"God will *cleanse* her," Methuselah said at last. "And He will make of her a new place, different than before and better for His purposes."

"But what are His purposes?"

"Ah, those are His alone to know," replied Grandfather. "But we must trust that He will always act in love for those who love Him."

Father turned a half-smile of agreement upon Shem.

Shem shook his head. "I envy you both your certainty. The One God is beyond my understanding."

Grandfather laughed, his head thrown back to let his mirth rise to the treetops while Father grinned.

"Grandfather has heard those same words from my lips," Father told Shem. "And I answer you the way he answered me – only a fool believes he understands God. So you've just called us both fools."

Grandfather stepped off the porch and embraced Father. Then he turned to Shem and caught him in the gentle hug of an old man whose arms have lost the strength of youth but have gained the strength of love.

"I'd give much to know how you always know when I'm coming," Shem said as he returned the hug.

"I tell you every time, but you don't listen. God made you from the earth, and you can learn from her if you know how to hear her. But when He remakes her, she will be different than now. You'll have to struggle to hear her then." The old man sighed and stepped back to peer into Father's face. "When the One God explained that to me, I was glad I would not be introduced to the new earth. I'm too old to learn a new way of life now."

Shem lifted a bundle from Samson's back. "The One God speaks to you of the flood?"

"Of course. I asked, and He answered. Are you surprised? Have you forgotten why we were made, Grandson? He desires closeness with us."

"Then surely you've asked what will happen to you?"

"I didn't ask, but He knows my unspoken questions and He answered anyway. I will not live to see the great waters, but he promised long ago that I would live to see Noah's work nearly complete. And I have." Father took another bundle from Samson's back and set it on the porch. "You disturb the boy, Grandfather, speaking of your death."

"Nonsense." The old man turned clear blue eyes toward Shem and smiled. "Shem knows I look forward to the next step. This will be the easiest one of all, for then all barriers between me and God will be removed." He turned toward the bundle on the porch with an eagerness found only in young boys and old men. "Now, what has Midian sent? I hope there's some of that sugared fruit glaze."

Father laughed and rummaged in the bundle. "Of course there is. Midian knows you well."

After they stored the supplies on various shelves in the cabin, Shem left Grandfather Methuselah and Father to prepare their meal while he took an ax into the surrounding forest to find deadwood. He worked to replenish Grandfather's dwindling woodpile, stopping long enough to eat the simple meal of his mother's stew and bread smeared with a thick layer of fruit glaze.

Only when the woodpile rose above shoulder level did Shem join the older men on the porch. The shadows cast by the tall trees surrounding the cabin deepened into a murky darkness. When Shem sat on a long bench beside Grandfather, Father stood.

"I'm going into the woods to pray." He smiled, though Shem saw only a flash of white teeth in the darkness. "Sometimes I think the One God makes His home in these woods. I feel closer to Him here than any other place."

Beside Shem, Grandfather nodded. "That is why I no longer leave my mountain home."

Father stepped off the porch and disappeared between the trees. The silence between Shem and Grandfather grew comfortable. A gentle wind rustled the leaves high in the trees, and blew a welcome cool breeze into Shem's sweat-heated face.

Grandfather broke the silence. "We could get those powered lights your father brought me."

"Only if you want," Shem replied. "I'm enjoying the night shadows."

Grandfather shrugged. "Don't tell Noah, but I never turn the things on. I prefer the One God's light to the manmade kind."

The darkness deepened, cooling the green earth with a gentle caress. From their vantage point high on the mountain, the forest spread out as a shadowy blanket over the earth, the remnants of the sun lighting a mountainous silhouette on the western horizon. Shem's gaze turned to the east as his thoughts drifted toward the city in that direction.

"Tell me why you are sad." Grandfather's voice was as soft as the night breeze and almost as low.

Shem didn't respond immediately. He sensed the old man waiting with infinite patience. When he did speak, his eyes remained fixed on the eastern horizon, on the spot where the darkness lightened and he could just make out the faint glow of city lights.

"Call me a fool, but I struggle to understand the ways of the One God. The people He created have turned from Him, but He could right that with one word. The power of all the heavens rests in His breath. I don't understand why He chooses instead to destroy."

Shem sensed Grandfather's smile in the darkness. "Our own will has chosen this path of destruction, not His. Though you may not understand Him, Shem, never doubt that the One God has a plan. His desire is to draw every person who has ever walked on this earth to Himself."

"Tell that to the people who will be destroyed." Shem was surprised at the bitterness in his own voice.

But Grandfather Methuselah laughed softly. "They wouldn't listen if I did. But do you mourn for all the people of the earth or for some more strongly than others?"

A shrewd question for an old man, and Shem was not surprised to hear it. Grandfather had ever been able to hear his thoughts.

"There are many people who still acknowledge His ways. Mara's people, and Timna's. And those are only the ones I know. There must be others who worship the One God and yet will be destroyed." Shem paused,

his eyes fixed on the horizon. "But, yes, there is one
who haunts my thoughts. She does not belong to Him,
but neither is she is His enemy. He could have her if
He chose."

Grandfather remained silent. Shem searched the
horizon as his mind struggled to answer the question
that burned in him. Finally he turned to the old man,
the one who spoke with God more often than he.

"But even then, she would be destroyed with the
rest. How do I convince her of the justness of the One
God when honesty compels me to tell her of His judgment as well?"

"If you feel compassion for this person, you will
speak to her not of this world, but of the next."

Shem felt the weight of Grandfather's stare and
shifted in his seat. Could his thoughts be seen? How
could they, when he couldn't see them clearly himself?
He turned away and retreated to the private battlefield
raging in his mind. There must be hundreds like her in
the city, thousands on the earth. Why did the fate of
this one girl weigh so heavily on him?

The next morning, after a nearly sleepless night,
Shem rose with the sun to find Grandfather and Father already stirring. After breaking their fast, Shem
whistled for Samson to begin their hike down the steep
trail. His farm called him to work, as the One God's
project called to Father.

Grandfather walked with them to the place where
the path began its downward slant. There they paused
to say goodbye.

"I'll be back in two weeks," Father promised as he
hugged the old man.

"I'll watch for you."

Grandfather turned to Shem, but instead of embracing him, he caught Shem's arms in his wrinkled
hands and held him away, elbows locked. Shem looked

down into watery blue eyes.

"I want to tell you something, Shem. The One God will reclaim the earth and the people on it. That is His plan, and the glimpses He has given me leave me shaking in awe. He will use the bloodline of your father, not because Noah is better than most men, but because he believed God and was obedient to Him. Remember that."

Shem looked away from the intensity in Grandfather's eyes. "How I wish God spoke to me as He does to you."

The old man smiled and pulled him forward into a hug. "He honors me, possibly because I spend every waking moment talking to Him. He enjoys fellowship with us, you know, and will often tell us of His plans if we ask."

He released Shem and turned again to Father. "That reminds me. Promise me that when I die you will change the coverings on my bed after you lay me in my cave."

Surprised, Shem laughed, and Father joined him. "What an odd request."

Grandfather's gaze moved from Father to Shem, his eyes twinkling. "Just promise me, and also that you'll take all the food out of the cabin so it won't spoil and cause a bad smell. Give it to the animals. Will you do that?"

Shaking his head, Father agreed. "Since you ask it, I will. Though I pray it will be a long time before that day."

As they began their descent, Methuselah's voice called after them.

"Remember Shem. It is amazing what God will tell you, if you only take the time to listen."

"Girta, do you ever make sacrifices?"

Eliana sat in a chair next to Melody's cage, watching the little bird crack seeds with a dainty beak. The lovely creature had grown accustomed to her new home in the two days since her arrival, and Eliana loved waking to the sound of birdsong as she preened in the morning sunlight.

The older woman gave her a surprised look. "You know I don't."

"I don't mean to Cain. I mean to the One God. Do you ever make sacrifices to Him?"

"Not for a long time. My father did, but they weren't sacrifices like people make to Cain."

"Tell me about them."

Girta seated herself on the bed facing Eliana's chair. "My father was a farmer, and at harvest time we all worked to bring in the produce. Then Father made an inventory and selected the finest of what we gathered to give to the One God."

"How? How did he do it, Girta?"

"We had an altar up on the top of a nearby hill, nothing more than a pile of rocks really, but flat. We piled our offerings on top. Then Father sang a song of thanks to the One God and we left."

"That's it?" Eliana arched her eyebrows. "Nothing else? No rituals, no chants? Just a 'thank you' and you left?"

Girta nodded.

"But how do you know the One God received your sacrifice? How do you know animals didn't come along and eat what you'd left for Him?"

"They may have." Girta smiled. "I asked the same question once. Father said if we are truly giving out of grateful hearts, then the gift is the receiver's to do with as He will. If He chooses to feed hungry animals, then He may do so. For all we know, the animals might not have anything else to eat and God used our offering to provide for them."

Eliana smiled. "That is beautiful. Did your father ever ask anything of the One God? Like the people here make sacrifices to Cain to ask him for things?"

"Oh yes. I remember once the crops were ready to fail, and Father made a special offering to ask for a blessing on the land."

"Did he say any special chants that time, any specific prayers?"

"No." Girta's voice lowered. "But I will never forget that offering. We all stood around the altar while Father prayed. I had my eyes closed and I heard my sister gasp. When I looked, the offering was in flames!"

"It burned?" Eliana asked in a hushed voice.

Girta nodded. "God set it on fire. I was young, but I do remember the smoke curling up into the sky."

"And did it work? Did He send you a good crop?"

"As I said, I was young and one year tends to run into another. But I think He did. That was the only one I ever saw burn, but they say God sometimes does that to signify an acceptable offering."

"Aren't all offerings acceptable to God?"

"They are, if they are from the heart. But every now and then a very special offering is made, as in the case of my father. He could scarce afford to feed us, yet he offered valuable food to God in hopes for His help. God chose to recognize his request in a special way."

Eliana turned back to the birdcage. This God who talked to Shem's father could send fire to burn an offering. She had seen signs during the sacrifices to Cain often enough, but she was almost positive they were contrived by the priestesses. Girta wandered through the door to her own room and Eliana's thoughts turned to her conversation with Shem. The man Cain and his brother Abel made offerings to the One God. Did Shem and his father do the same? She thought of the sacrifices made on the temple's altar, the animals and people whose blood was spilled to appease the god. Some day she, too, would be required to take part in those rituals. She shuddered. Would the One God hate her when she killed for a rival god?

Then she remembered the waters Shem said would cover the earth. Everyone would die except Shem's family. The One God would not spare a thought for the daughter of the High Priestess of Cain.

She lowered her head to rest on clenched fists, fighting an urge to weep. There were no detours in the road before her. She was headed straight toward misery in this world and the next, and there was nothing she could do about it.

The sun set and shadows darkened her room before Eliana moved from her chair. The thoughts whirling in her mind had circled around a recurring idea.

"Girta?"

Girta came hurrying at the agitation in her voice.

"What is it, lamb?"

"Can you drive a landrider?"

Girta's eyelids narrowed to slits. "No."

"Do you know someone who can? Someone who can be trusted?"

"Why do you need someone to drive a landrider?"

"Because I can't drive one myself, and I need to get into the forest."

Girta cocked her head, her gaze stabbing across the room. "And why do you need to go into the forest?"

"To make an offering to the One God."

Silence hung between them for a long time. Eliana held Girta's gaze and refused to flinch at the penetrating stare.

"Would you be so kind as to explain why the daughter of the High Priestess of Cain wants to make an offering to God?"

Eliana took a deep breath and forced her voice to remain calm. "I am about to enter into an alliance with a man who terrifies me. After the alliance, I will be expected to begin training for the priestly duties I will inherit. I'll be forced to kill people to honor a god in whom I no longer believe. I hope those reasons are sufficient, though I do have several others, which I prefer to keep private."

Her chin thrust upward, Eliana hoped she appeared regal but suspected that the quivering of her lower lip spoiled the effect. Girta stared at her for a long, silent moment, and Eliana saw that she was close to tears. That realization melted Eliana's resolve, and her own tears brimmed over her lashes.

"Oh, Girta, I didn't mean to make you sad." She rushed across the room to throw her arms around her nursemaid.

"I'm not sad, little lamb, except for you." Girta's tears mingled with Eliana's. "I want you to be happy, that's all I ever wanted."

They stood with their arms around one another until the tears subsided. Then Girta, pulling a hand-kerchief from her belt, dried first Eliana's wet cheeks and then her own.

"I know a driver," she said quietly. "I'll ask him to take us both."

"He can be trusted?"

Girta nodded. "With our lives if need be. He was raised to worship the One God, and I believe he would aid you if he knew you wished to do the same."

"Who is he?"

But Girta shook her head. "I'll talk to him first. I promised long ago never to betray his trust. If he will take us, then we go. If not, I know of no one else."

The following day, Girta told Eliana that her mysterious driver agreed to take them into the forest early the next morning. Now that she knew the deed was possible, her stomach remained in a constant state of tense excitement as she considered her offering. It must be sincere, the best of what she possessed. She spent a long agonizing time staring fearfully into Melody's cage. Finally, she decided that her offering to the One God should not involve killing a living creature, since that would too closely resemble a sacrifice to Cain. Once that decision was made, she approached her task with a lighter heart.

Girta woke Eliana early, when the darkness was still deep outside her window. They rose and dressed in silence, though the temple rooms were well insulated and their sounds of preparation could not have been overheard. Eliana dressed for the pre-dawn chill with warm leggings beneath a thick woolen tunic. Her brown hooded cape went over all. Grinning with excitement, she picked up her bundle and opened the door with exaggerated caution. Girta peered down the hallway before she motioned for Eliana to follow.

The halls of the west wing were deserted, not a page or servant in sight all the way to the temple's rear entrance. The absence of a temple guard at the door took Eliana by surprise. Where was the guardsman who should be stationed here? The door's heavy latch hung freely on the wall. Though they had made no sound, the windowless door cracked open as they arrived, and a large calloused hand beckoned. Girta squeezed outside and Eliana followed. The man on the other side of the door stood shrouded in shadows. He was taller than Eliana by a head, shoulders broad beneath a dark cloak, the hood of which concealed much of his face. Girta would have spoken, but he held up a single finger for silence. The finger crooked once, signaling them to follow.

He led them to the rear of the vehicle shed, moving without a sound. Night still clung to the earth and turned the barren field south of the temple to pitch. Eliana's eyes were drawn to a single bright spot beyond the field. As she watched, the blaze of the Eternal Fires of Cain leapt high above the surrounding protective wall, throwing fiery sparks into the night sky. That sacred place, visited only by Senior Priestesses during the secret rites they practiced, stood separated from the city as much by tradition as by distance. Approach by any but a Senior was forbidden by orders of none other than the god himself, and no one dared disobey. Though she didn't know why, the sight of the flames made her shudder.

Their guide led them to a landrider, its engine already humming with power. He clicked the door open, and then turned to assist her into the vehicle. The hand was strong and rough against her smooth skin, and as she leaned her weight on him to pull herself up she felt his arm tighten with solid strength. She slid across the padded bench inside and Girta climbed in beside her. The man stepped in easily, closing the door with a hushed click. He sidled past Girta's knees to sit in the single seat at the front of the vehicle, behind a panel of navigation instruments.

The silence continued while the landrider slipped forward. Beneath the vehicle's wheels, the ground crunched in the still night. To avoid the paved city streets, they turned at the southwestern corner of the temple onto a worn byway that was little more than a wide path of flattened grass. To the west of the city lay a wide plain, and beyond it, the dense forest she could see from her bedroom window.

When the temple and the city had faded into the distance behind them, Eliana finally gathered the nerve to speak.

"Driver, I don't know your name, but I'm grateful for the risk you are taking."

The driver shook his head, and Girta spoke.

"His name is Arphaxad de Mahalaleel." She turned to address him. "I thank you as well. You're doing us a great service."

Arphaxad. A familiar name, though she couldn't place where she had heard it. The hood of his cloak slipped off his head and she saw that his hair was dark, darker than the night though that could have been the poor lighting. When he turned his head to acknowledge Girta's thanks with a brief smile, the lights from the navigation panel outlined his face. It was craggy and creased, both with wrinkles and also by a deep scar running along one cheekbone. He had a long, straight nose over full lips through which white teeth flashed briefly with his smile. The face was familiar, too, though not one she saw frequently. Where did she know this man?

Then she remembered, and drew a swift breath. Arphaxad, the head of temple security. His was a face she saw infrequently, but one that had been around as long as she could remember. He was in charge of ensuring the safety of the temple, the priestesses, the servants and the residents. Nothing occurred anywhere in the temple without his knowledge and approval. If it were known that he worshiped the One God, the man's life would be forfeit.

Eliana drew a quick breath. She had placed them all in peril. "Sir, the risk you take is too great. If I had known who you were I would never have asked."

"No greater risk than yours, lady," he replied in a husky voice.

She shook her head. "I have the right to risk myself, but none to ask you to do the same."

He did not respond. Eliana glanced at Girta, whose gaze remained fixed on the view outside the rider. At least now Eliana knew the answer to Shem's question. Arphaxad arranged for another worshiper of the One God to become her nursemaid. She couldn't imagine why. The danger to both of them was unthinkable. She gazed through the window. How many worshipers of the One God were living in hiding around her? Certainly not many in Cainlan, but perhaps there were more outside the city. Did they all know one another? She drew a quick breath. Did Arphaxad know Shem's family?

"Have you ever heard of a man named Noah who worships the One God?"

"Noah de Lamech." Arphaxad nodded. "His lands lie beyond the forest, toward the great mountain. I've been there, though not in many years."

"Is he the one building that boat?" Girta asked.

"The same. He claims the design was given him by God Himself, along with a prophecy of the end of the world."

"Crazy old fool," muttered Girta.

Eliana turned to her. "You don't believe the prophecy?"

"Of course not. Why would God destroy the world?"

Arphaxad replied in a quiet voice. "You are too sheltered in the temple to see the corruption rampant in the world. Step outside for a few days, see what the people have become and you may not be so quick to question Noah's story."

Girta had no answer, and they fell silent. The darkness beyond the window seemed to have deepened. Eliana realized with a thrill that they were well inside the forest, farther from the temple than she had ever been. The energy hum of the landrider combined with the dim green glow from the navigation panel to create a cozy cocoon inside the vehicle.

Girta's voice broke the silence. "Where did you hear of Noah?"

"In the marketplace." Eliana avoided the suspicious look on Girta's face and directed a question at Arphaxad. "Will we be near his lands? Near enough to see his boat?"

"No. His lands are at least two hours on the other side of the forest."

Eliana smothered a wave of disappointment. Then she reminded herself that her purpose here was far more serious than trying to catch Shem de Noah's attention. She turned to gaze at the dark landscape gliding past outside the landrider. The other two kept quiet as well, as though they sensed her need for silence.

The landrider slowed, and Eliana's pulse quickened as it rolled to a stop. Arphaxad cut the power, and in a moment of complete silence and sudden darkness, all three of them peered into the thicket of trees around them. Then Arphaxad pressed a contact and a dull yellow light illuminated the interior of the vehicle.

He swiveled to face Eliana. For the first time he looked into her eyes, and she had never seen a gaze as

intense as his. The darkness rivaled that of the forest
around them, and yet they seemed to burn like black
fire.

"An offering to a god is not to be done lightly." His
gruff voice was almost a whisper. "Any god, but especially the only real God. I don't know your purpose,
lady, but I will give you a warning. Oaths made to Him
are sacred, and not to be broken. Know what you ask,
and speak only your true intentions."

He held her gaze a moment longer, and then gave a
quick nod before turning back to the front of the vehicle. Eliana gathered the pack into her arms and
stepped out. Girta leaned toward her, speaking in a
raspy whisper.

"Don't be too long. We must be back before daylight."

Eliana adjusted the bundle in her arms and
stepped off the path. Her feet crunched on the dried
leaves that covered the forest floor. Within minutes the
forest trees closed around her and she looked back to
make sure of the landrider's lights. There they were,
three bright beams visible through the trees. She
heard a sound that must have been the closing of the
vehicle's door, and turned back to the north.

The night air was cool and moist, with the heavy
nightly dew just beginning to settle. What she had at
first mistaken for silence soon became a roar of noise:
the chirruping of insects, the scurrying of night animals, and the rustling of leaves above her. The trees
grew close together for a distance, and then began to
spread out. The ground beneath her feet became soft,
springy, though each step still crunched with leaves
and sticks. She noticed that the air smelled different
than any she had ever breathed, spicier and somehow
cleaner. She came upon a small clearing, an empty
space in the trees just a little wider than she was tall,
but when she stepped into it she was bathed in a pure,
white light. The moon hung directly above, and a hundred stars scattered generously across the sky glit-

tered in the cold black night.

The perfect place. She set her bundle on the ground.

"Now for stones." Though she whispered, her voice sounded like a shout in the silence.

She had almost given up finding stones when she stumbled upon a creek. Icy water flowed over a stony bed. Eliana made a dozen trips to and from the creek, carrying as many large stones as she could manage to pry out of the water before she judged she had enough for a respectable altar.

Then she set about piling them, one upon the other in the exact center of the clearing. She had no experience at altar building, but when she finished she looked with satisfaction on the result of her efforts. Not a large altar, but sturdy enough. The stone on top was the largest, with with a surface made smooth and flat by years of the water's gentle caress. She was ready to begin. But how? How should she talk to this God who spoke to His people in plain words? She'd heard the chants and rituals of Cain many times, but she did not for a moment consider repeating any of them. She knelt before the altar and bowed until her forehead rested on the grass.

"I've been told You talk to Your people." She kept her voice low. "I'm a stranger to You, but I wish to be a stranger no longer. I believe that You made this world, and I believe that You have the power to unmake it.

"I've built this altar for You, One God. Though You deserve much better, it is the best I can do."

She unfolded her bundle and placed the contents in the grass. The linen she folded and lay across the altar so that it draped to touch the ground on either side.

"This is not a holy altar cloth, but it is the softest of my linens."

Then she placed her first offering upon the cloth, a doll in the shape of a lamb, the fluffy wool worn and darkened.

"This is the comfit Girta gave me when I was a babe. Many nights it kept me company, and You know that many nights even now it still does. I give it to You, because it is close to my heart. I hope from now on You will guard my nights."

The next item was a heavy glass bottle.

"They say this scent is costly and rare. Though You deserve much more, my hope is that You will find the odor as sweet as I do."

A jewel box was placed beside the bottle, and Eliana opened the lid to reveal a string of creamy pearls.

"Though I have more precious and expensive jewelry, this is my favorite. It is simple and pure and I think more beautiful than any stone."

The last object from the bundle was a covered basket containing an assortment of foods. Eliana arranged the fruit, vegetables and baked grains around the surface of the altar.

"I brought these from my dinner because Girta told me how You may want to feed the animals with them."

Eliana dropped her chin to her chest and closed her eyes.

"I'm sure You know who I am. One day soon I'll have to go into service for Cain. But I don't believe Cain is a god, so my service will have no meaning. And I vow to You now that no matter what I am called upon by duty to do, You will always be the only God I worship."

She paused, and the forest noises seemed to hush. "I've met one of Your people. We talked of You, and of other things. He isn't like anyone else I know."

Her head bowed, eyes still closed, Eliana slowly withdrew a note from her cloak. She silently read Shem's words one last time.

"I have no desire to offend You, but I would like to ask a favor."

Opening her eyes, she raised her head to look up at the stars. Her voice lowered to barely a whisper.

"Give me a man like this one. I'm afraid of what the future holds for me. With someone like him, I would not be afraid. Do not forget me, One God."

Silently her heart cried out for Shem. But what of his wife? She could not muster the courage to ask for her true desire. Instead she laid the note on the altar. As she did, tears rose painfully from her soul, and her vision blurred as they filled her eyes.

Through the blur she saw a shaft of light fall from the heavens. She blinked, wiping tears on the back of her hand. The shaft of light was no wider than a string of thread, but so bright she could barely look at it. It dropped from the sky directly down onto the altar, where it touched Shem's note. Slowly a trickle of smoke began to rise, and a brown ring appeared in the parchment where the shaft touched it. Then the parchment burst into flame.

Eliana's breath caught in her throat, her eyes wide as she watched the fire spread. The heat became un-bearable, and she backed out of the clearing on her knees, never taking her gaze from the small altar. The flame spread over the surface to consume everything upon it, even the bottle of scent. Leaves on the sur-rounding trees curled and withered with the heat, and she backed up further still.

When the surface of the altar was a red-hot mass of flame, the light disappeared abruptly. The heat di-minished, and Eliana crept forward, twigs pressing into her knees. In the short time it took her to ap-proach the altar, the heat dissipated, leaving a fine white ash to cover the stone. She reached out a tenta-tive finger and found to her surprise that the surface was cool to the touch.

Eliana threw herself to the ground, the wonder within her growing to fill her entire being. She lay prostrate until the moon moved beyond the opening above her clearing. Then she rose to her knees and crawled backward away from the altar.

She found the landrider with no trouble. Two anxious faces peered at her from inside. Arphaxad jumped from his seat to open the door. He looked into her eyes, and nodded once.

"You're ready to go, then."

Eliana accepted his hand to assist her into the vehicle. She expected Girta to be full of questions, but received only a reassuring squeeze of her hand.

"We saw the fire," she said, and then fell silent.

The sky began to lighten as they neared the edge of the forest. Eliana would have enjoyed the scenery had her mind not been buzzing with wonder. Peace filled her, a reassurance that things would turn out well after all. She wished with all her heart that she could talk with Shem, could tell him what happened and share the excitement that swelled inside her. And for once the thought of Shem did not throw her into a fit of sorrow.

They coasted smoothly into the vehicle shed behind the temple. Arphaxad cut the power and maneuvered his way out of his seat to open the door for them once again. He led them to the rear temple door through which they had exited.

"I leave you here," he said, his voice low. "No one will think it odd if you are seen in the temple halls at this time alone, but if I were seen with you that would be unusual enough to give the idle gossipers fuel."

His smile caused the scar on his cheek to deepen.

Eliana smiled in return. "I cannot thank you enough, Arphaxad. I sincerely hope this escapade does not cause you any trouble."

He shook his head. "Don't let that worry you. I am honored to have been able to help you in your endeavor. And..." He paused, his dark glance sliding hesitantly to Girta and quickly back to Eliana. "If you want to learn how to pilot a landrider, I can arrange to have you taught."

An elated thrill zipped through her. She looked toward Girta for permission, and met with the disapproving glare of her nursemaid.

"I see no reason to do any such thing." Girta's voice was flat, unbending.

"Oh please, Girta," Eliana begged. "I'll be able to go into the forest. That will be much better than wandering in the marketplace. Please!"

Girta remained unmoved, her arms crossed and her chin protruding in a classic pose of stubborn determination.

"Everyone should have a chance to get away from the city." Eliana wondered if Arphaxad ever spoke above a whisper. "She will be supervised at all times, and shortly she may have an opportunity to be grateful for a peaceful place to go."

Eliana watched as Girta's gaze rested on Arphaxad. She saw the nursemaid's eyes soften and suppressed the urge to bounce with excitement.

"Very well."

Arphaxad nodded, the shadow of a smile hovering about his lips as he produced a key and fitted it into the lock. He peeked inside before nodding for them to enter. Girta went first, and as Eliana stepped through the doorway she turned to squeeze Arphaxad's hand in gratitude.

"The One God be with you, lady," he whispered as the door closed behind her.

Chapter 7

The muffled blast from a horn echoed in the empty
stairwell. Jarrell stretched his legs and jogged up
the last few stairs two at a time. He hated being late.
And especially today, when rumors were flying that
this would be something more than a routine address.
Governor Caphtor himself was said to be making a
special announcement this morning.

He burst through the doorway on the third floor
and stopped. A crowd overflowed from the announcement chamber into the hallway. Drat! No chance at a
seat, and he probably wouldn't even be able to see the
governor.

Jarrell edged around the group and began the process of wedging his way through the press of bodies
that blocked the entrance to the announcement
chamber. He ignored the glares he collected on the
way, intent on getting inside the room so he could at
least see the platform.

There! He squeezed through the doorway and found himself at the front of those who had arrived too late to secure a seat in the crowded chamber. And no wonder the place was packed. Half the chairs seemed to be occupied by white-robed priestesses, proof that this would be more than a routine update to government employees. Priestesses rarely attended those.

Jarrell edged sideways and squeezed against the wall between two men wearing the emblem of the Cabinet of Economic Resources on their shoulders. Just in time, too. At that moment the five councilors filed through a side doorway and made their way to the chairs lining the rear of the platform. Jarrell picked out Councilor Tomsk, director of his own branch of Social Action. He doubted if Tomsk knew his name, though perhaps he might recognize his face as one of the sea of analysts who worked in his branch. Next to him, Councilor Asquith from the Cabinet of Energy dusted the seat of his chair before lowering himself into it, and turned to speak to the man standing behind him.

Jarrell's jaw went slack as he identified Asquith's aide. Standing behind the councilor, his arms clasped behind his back, stood none other than Roblin de Yibin.

Jealousy stabbed at Jarrell. How did he manage to land an appointment as Asquith's aide? Roblin enjoyed more than his fair share of luck, in Jarrell's envious opinion. They graduated from the same governmental training program, so Jarrell knew he was smarter than the dynamic Roblin. Jarrell finished every assignment faster, and always received higher marks. But upon graduation, Roblin somehow landed a job in the prestigious Energy Cabinet, while Jarrell became buried in Social Action. Roblin's assignments focused on the extremely visible topics of energy production and export economics. Jarrell spent his days analyzing an endless stream of welfare statistics.

And Roblin's good luck had landed him a place on

the platform during a major announcement as an aide to a member of Cainlan's Council. The fortunate fiend.

Jarrell tore his eyes from Roblin as Governor Caphtor strode across the platform to stand behind the podium. The man dominated the stage, towering above the others and dwarfing the petite High Priestess, who slid into single empty chair beside Councilor Limpopo. The hum of the crowd rose in volume at the unusual sight of High Priestess Liadan, magnificent in her formal green garment, in attendance at a government announcement. Caphtor waited, his expression polite, until the murmuring audience grew silent. His gaze swept the room.

"Thank you for coming. As you can see, we have the Council in full attendance today, which must mean we have something important to say."

The governor paused, and Jarrell chuckled along with the audience. The High Priestess's presence was not the only unusual occurrence. Rarely did a public address warrant all five councilors in personal attendance. Jarrell's own boss, Sub-Director Phanom, frequently attended in place of Councilor Tomsk.

Governor Caphtor continued. "As you know, the city of Cainlan was established long ago on the principles of self-defense. Our founders, peace-loving people who wanted nothing more than to live quiet lives, were forced to defend themselves against a vicious attack by an aggressive tribe intent on their slaughter. They were unprepared. Had the god Cain not intervened, they would have been annihilated."

Jarrell watched as Caphtor's gaze swept his audience, holding every person's rapt attention. At one point he seemed to look directly into Jarrell's eyes, and Jarrell stood straighter to think the governor noticed him personally. Caphtor spoke in everyday tones, but somehow pitched his voice to reach Jarrell in the back of the room, and even beyond, to the overflow crowd in the hallway.

"When mighty Cain established this city, he en-

dowed our ancestors with the ability to defend themselves against further aggression. He taught them to
construct the defensive wall that surrounds our city
even today. He blessed them and their descendants —
us – with strength and power and intelligence, so that
today, Cainlan is the mightiest city in the world."

Jarrell shifted his weight. He didn't believe Cain
had blessed anyone with anything, and what's more,
he didn't think the governor believed it either. No rational man could, and Caphtor was nobody's fool. Jarrell had not seen evidence that he was any more religious than the next man. High Priestess Liadan, on
the other hand, nodded in agreement, and he saw her
gesture echoed throughout the audience.

"We, the people of Cainlan, are leaders. The other
cities look to us to lay a path into the future. We lead
the world in technology. We lead the world in religious
devotion to our patron god. We lead the world in production of base metals. And soon we will lead the
world in military strength as well."

Military strength? Jarrell exchanged a glance with
the man standing next to him, his eyebrows arched.

"Today the Council unveils the formation of a new
elite branch of Cainlan's army. We will create a separate division within the Cabinet of Security, and have
selected General Brendolan de Ashern to command
this division."

Jarrell shifted his weight again. A whole division
dedicated to the army? They must intend for this army
to be much larger than the current one. Why? He let
his gaze wander throughout the audience. Every head
was turned toward the governor, listening as Caphtor
outlined the benefits of his new military branch. Unemployment. City Morale. Increased security.

A movement among a group of priestesses seated
along the wall to his right drew Jarrell's attention. A
dark head turned, and he caught sight of Bitra de
Adah. He hadn't seen her in the weeks since their tour
of the city with Roblin. He had enjoyed her lively wit,

but not the way she sniped at Cainlan's energy monopoly the entire evening. When Hanae and Roblin
disappeared together after dinner, Bitra had grown
quiet and Jarrell assumed she was bored with his
company. He left her at the temple entrance, certain
he would never see her again.

But now she looked directly at him and nodded a
greeting. He gave her a hesitant smile, pleased when
she returned it with a deep one of her own before turning around to give her attention to the governor.

Caphtor appeared to be wrapping up his speech.
"Cainlan's purpose is to honor the god whose name we
bear. We can do that only by establishing ourselves as
superior in all things. With this step, we will create a
tremendous military power, one unrivaled anywhere
men roam the earth. Once again, we will show the
world that Cainlan is the mightiest city in the world!"

The governor paused with an expectant air, and
the audience rewarded him with thunderous applause.
The councilors leaped to their feet, applauding, and
soon no one in the announcement chamber remained
in their seats. Jarrell lost sight of the podium behind a
multitude of heads.

Interesting announcement. As people moved into
the aisles, he edged his way through the crowd toward
the door. Would the other cities, like Enoch and
Manessah, follow suit and create larger armies of their
own? That could mean trouble. As he pushed through
the press of bodies, he decided that the governor was
correct about one thing. Cainlan did seem to lead the
world in every aspect of progressive civilization.

"Jarrell. Over here."

He turned to scan the mass behind him. A pair of
white hands waved above the crowd. Jarrell stopped to
allow the sea of bodies to surge past him, bringing
Bitra toward him.

"There you are." She grabbed at him before the
crowd pulled her past, and he steadied her with a firm
grip, stepping out of the press to stand near a wall in

relative quiet.

"What a surprise." He gave her a quick hug.

"A good one, I hope." Her hazel eyes sparkled with reflections from the energy lantern on the wall above his head. "I had a surprise today, too, when I saw your friend on the platform. I had no idea he had such a close association with a member of the Council."

Jarrell leaned toward her. "Honestly? Neither did I. I guess we should count ourselves fortunate that he stooped low enough to act as our tour guide."

"I suppose we should." A beguiling dimple appeared in her left cheek, and Jarrell suppressed an urge to reach out and place a finger upon it. Then suddenly the skin went smooth as her grin disappeared. "When I didn't hear from you, I assumed you preerred to avoid the troublemaking foreigner."

Delighted with her honesty, Jarrell gave a low laugh. "And I figured the beautiful foreign priestess must want to avoid the boring analyst from Social Action."

"Not at all. I told you how much I enjoyed the evening."

He shrugged. "I assumed you were being polite."

She grew serious, locking gazes with him. "I never lie. Not for courtesy, nor for any other reason."

The noisy hallway faded into the background as Jarrell gazed into Bitra's eyes. She really meant it. This beautiful woman had enjoyed spending time with him, Jarrell. His stomach fluttered as he drew a shallow breath. She stood so close he inhaled the subtle scent of orchids in her hair.

"Then perhaps you'd like to join me for dinner again. Alone, this time?"

The pleasure in her expression could not be feigned. "I'm free three days from now. Shall we meet on the temple steps when you get out of work?"

Jarrell found he could not squeak a sound through his suddenly dry mouth. She wanted to go out with him? Alone? Feeling like a thunderstruck fool, he nodded.

In answer, she leaned forward and brushed his cheek with her lips. "I'll see you then."

She turned and joined the crowd flowing toward the stairs, leaving him to stare after her like a moon-struck youth.

Eliana stood aside to wait for her mother, watching as the councilors and their aides swept through the doorway at the side of the platform. Councilor Tomsk, deep in conversation with his aide, caught her eye and nodded a greeting as he brushed by. Peeking through the doorway, Eliana saw Caphtor stop to speak to a man from the audience. The high priestess hesitated in front of her chair, obviously trying to decide whether to wait for the governor or to leave him behind. After a moment, Liadan raised her chin and crossed the plat-form.

"What did you think of the announcement?" She stepped through the doorway and continued through the narrow hallway without hesitating, inviting Eliana to walk beside her with a gesture.

Casting about for something intelligent to say about the speech, Eliana hurried to match her step with her mother's. "As the governor said, Cainlan will see a lot of benefit from this army. I'm sure the people will feel more secure with trained men patrolling the city streets."

Liadan nodded, and Eliana breathed a sigh. Thankfully she had paid attention to Caphtor's speech.

"Your alliance will be final in three more days. You're preparing the celebration feast?"

Eliana blinked in the sunlight as they exited the government building. With a start, she noticed that her mother and she were the same height. When did she grow those last few inches?

They were joined by an entourage of priestesses

accompanying them down the cobbled walkway beside the gardens toward the temple's main entrance. They kept a careful distance, allowing mother and daughter a semblance of privacy for their conversation.

"Caphtor's assistant, Melita de Lemlar, has arranged everything." Eliana kept her voice and her face devoid of expression.

Liadan's gaze slid sideways. "Watch that one. She's a favorite of the rumormongers."

Though not privileged to the temple rumor mill, Eliana was not surprised. From the moment she met Caphtor's assistant, she felt uneasy around the woman. Melita's eyes boasted secrets that Eliana suspected she didn't want to know. But Caphtor trusted the woman with everything, so avoiding her proved impossible.

"Actually, my alliance is the reason I wanted to speak with you. Was there any mention of living arrangements in the terms?"

Liadan's eyebrows arched. "No, but I prefer that my heir live within the walls of the temple. I assume you weren't planning on moving into Caphtor's bachelor quarters in government housing."

"*I* wasn't."

Liadan stopped on the path, forcing Eliana to stop with her. She leaned close, her voice low so the priestesses who passed them on the path would have to stop and strain in order to hear.

"Do not allow an aide to dictate to you. Remember who you are."

Eliana looked into her mother's eyes and drew strength from the arrogance she saw there. Liadan was right. She was the high priestess's heir. No assistant should be permitted to dictate where she lived.

"In fact..." Liadan's head swiveled to scan the faces of the crowd who filed past them. With a slender finger she pointed at a dark-haired priestess with a confident step and a smile hovering around her lips. "You. Priestess. What's your name?"

The brunette started, her eyes widening when she realized the identity of the one who had singled her out. She stopped on the path, her gaze darting to Eliana and then back to Liadan.

"Bitra de Adah, High Priestess." Her chin dropped to her chest.

Liadan rewarded her with a slight dip of her own forehead, and with a gesture gave permission for Bitra de Adah to raise her head.

"This is my daughter, Eliana de Ashbel." Liadan's hand swept toward Eliana, and the priestess flashed a nervous smile in her direction. "Her first marital alliance is upon her, and she has need of an assistant. Make arrangements for someone else to cover your duties. Tell your Senior you've been reassigned."

The priestess's hazel eyes widened before she bowed her head again. Eliana turned a surprised look on her mother and received a satisfied smirk as they resumed their walk toward the temple.

"Now you have an assistant too. Keep her as long as you like. And once you're settled, you must begin your training as a priestess."

Eliana stumbled, and her new assistant reached out a hand of support. Her daughter's problems solved and forgotten, Liadan swept ahead while Eliana slowed. Begin training as a priestess? *One God, please don't let that happen!*

"Are you alright, lady?"

Eliana watched her mother's retreating back, then looked up into the concerned face of her assistant and nodded.

The woman didn't look convinced. "You've gone pale."

"I... I'm fine." Eliana raised her chin. "And please call me Eliana."

"And I'm Bitra. So Eliana, what is my first assignment?"

They fell into step with one another, moving at an unhurried pace beside the neat garden hedge. The crowd of priestesses on the walkway trickled down to a few white-robed figures who hurried past them without notice.

"I honestly don't know. I need to find rooms in the temple suitable for the Governor to live, I suppose. And there's this party we're supposed to be hosting tomorrow night." She bit her lip. "But Caphtor's assistant probably has that already planned without me."

"I've heard of that one." For two steps Bitra studied her before giving a conspiratorial wink. "But don't worry. I can handle her."

Eliana felt sure that she could. She wished she felt as confident of her own abilities to 'handle' the governor. They reached the temple stairs and walked in silence up to the first landing.

"I'm sorry to have you reassigned so abruptly."

Bitra rewarded her with a huge smile. "I came all the way from Enoch to learn first-hand about Cainlan. What better chance than to assist the future high priestess and consort of the governor?" She lowered her voice, and a dimple appeared in her smooth cheek. "And this happened right after I arranged a date with a handsome government analyst. Today is my lucky day! I think I've just stumbled onto a path laid out by the god himself."

Eliana found herself returning Bitra's infectious grin. She liked this priestess from Enoch. A weight lifted somewhere in the vicinity of her chest, and she inhaled her first easy breath in weeks. She didn't believe for a minute that Cain had arranged their meeting, but maybe *the* God did.

Chapter 8

Shem straightened and stretched, his back muscles sore from hours bent over tender plants. He inhaled the musky scent of rich soil. With deep satisfaction he noted the straight lines of weed-free green straining upward to feed on sunlight. A dozen rows to go. He would be through this field by the end of the day.

A movement in the distance drew his gaze toward the farmhouse in time to see a man climb onto the back of a horse near the door. The pouches hanging at the horse's side bulged. A messenger. Shem watched the man urge the animal into a gallop down the path running the length of the far field, away from the house.

Unease stirred in his gut, but he ignored it. Messengers stopped by the farm every few weeks, bringing news from distant family or occasionally from Jarrell in the city. The trim figure of Abiri appeared in the doorway and, catching sight of him, waved frantically. His instincts were right. Something *was* wrong.

Shem deserted his tools and ran. He glanced sideways toward the ark. The men were working on the interior stalls, and no one was visible.

He burst into the house. One look at his mother's face stopped his words in his throat. Dread settled in his stomach.

"What is it, Mother?"

"Horrible, terrible news. A messenger came from the western hills."

"From Father's cousins?"

Mother nodded. "From a village nearby. Our kin have been slaughtered. All of them, Shem. They're all gone, killed. My father, and Mara's and Timna's too."

"Slaughtered." Shem's face went cold as the blood drained away. "How? Who?"

"Mountain bandits." A sob choked her. "A group of bandits cut down our people in their homes."

No. This could not happen. Not to his people, his own kin. How could the One God allow this to happen? He stood still as a statue, staring down at the agony in his mother's face. One of her tears splashed onto his foot.

Then he felt other eyes on him. Raising his head, he saw Mara standing in the doorway. Shock seemed to have frozen her into a statue. She stood with arms crossed, fingers biting into the tanned flesh of her arms. Her face lacked expression, but the pain in her eyes twisted his heart.

He opened his arms and she moved into them. Cradling her as he would a fragile child, he formed a silent prayer. *What can I do for her? Show me, One God.*

In the silence that followed, Mara's body began to tremble. Feeling like the most helpless man in the world, he tightened his embrace and held her as she sobbed.

"Slow down. I can't run in this dress."

Eliana walked as quickly as she dared without splitting the seams of her slender blue gown. She clutched at the heavy ruby necklace, a gift from Caphtor, not quite trusting the clasp to hold during a jog through the wide corridors of the Cabinet of Energy building. A lock of hair floated before her eyes, jarred loose from the intricate arrangement created by the hairdresser Bitra hired. Ahead of her, Bitra slowed and flashed a grin in her direction.

"Sorry. I don't want you to be late or your grand entrance will be spoiled. And in case you didn't know, you look beautiful."

"You do, too. Your analyst is going to fall all over himself when he sees you."

The foreign priestess did look lovely, her golden-hued skin and dark hair contrasting warmly with a gown the color of pale lemons. She slowed and fell into step beside Eliana.

"Thank you for letting me invite him."

Eliana dismissed her thanks with a wave. "You've worked so hard to plan tonight you should be able to invite whomever you want."

"The planning was already done. I mostly made a nuisance of myself with Melita to ensure everything was arranged to our satisfaction." Bitra winked. "And enjoyed the role immensely."

"Well, you've been busy finding and readying our new chambers, too."

Bitra succeeded in securing a suite of rooms in the temple's west residential wing. Eliana's cheeks flooded with heat at the thought of those rooms, and the night ahead. Bitra didn't appear to notice.

"And that was a mess, let me tell you. That woman apparently intended for you to join the governor in his pathetic little government housing room. I had to threaten to go to the High Priestess before she gave in.

But I think we now have the best rooms the temple has to offer. Here we are."

They came to a halt before a gigantic set of ornate doors, the entrance to the Council's assembly room. The uniformed guardsmen stationed on either side ceased their whispered conversation to stand straight when they caught sight of Eliana. She would have preferred holding the celebration in the temple's formal audience chamber instead of a cold government meeting room, but the plans had been made before Bitra inserted herself into the process.

Eliana stood still while her assistant gave her a quick inspection. Bitra fiddled with the errant lock of hair and tugged a wrinkle from the tight waistline of Eliana's gown before nodding her approval.

"Ready?"

Eliana faced the door with her shoulders held erect, steeling her queasy stomach. "Ready."

Bitra flashed a reassuring grin before she stepped back. One of the guardsmen opened the door wide. The noise of half a hundred chatting guests greeted Eliana's ears as her gaze swept the roomful of elegantly dressed people. They stood in small groups, sipping from wine goblets as they talked. The soft strains of music floated above the voices, though Eliana did not immediately see the location of the orchestra. She did, however, see the high priestess, resplendent in crimson, in the center of a cluster of adoring young men. The Council table had been removed, and instead elegant chairs lined two walls, and a long, cloth-draped table laden with silver platters waited to her right. A huge arrangement of multi-colored roses graced the center of the buffet.

"The music was my idea," Bitra whispered behind her.

Eliana would have turned to deliver a compliment, but at that moment Caphtor caught sight of her.

"And here is the lovely guest of honor, Eliana de Ashbel." He pitched his voice to claim the attention of

the assembly, who turned toward Eliana and applaud-
ed politely.

Eliana took his outstretched hand and stepped into the room, aware of a hundred eyes fixed on her.
Caphtor's gaze fell on the necklace, and his smile widened.

"My gift met with your approval, I hope?" Her hand
flew to the ruby pendant dangling at the base of her
throat. Though she would never have selected anything so large, she knew it had probably cost more
than a family in Cainlan spent on energy in a year. "It
is beautiful. Thank you."

As the guests resumed their conversations,
Caphtor lowered his voice. "I understand we're to es-
tablish residence in the temple."

Catching a hint of steel in his voice, her gaze flew
to his face. His lips hardened into a firm line. Did he
not want to relocate? But surely he didn't expect her to
move. And besides, her mother would not allow it. She
lifted her chin.

"The High Priestess preferred that her heir remain
nearby."

His eyelids narrowed. "There is one thing you
should know at the outset of our alliance. I will not
permit my life to be ruled by the dictates of Liadan."

He called across the room and went to join Councilor Asquith near the buffet, leaving her alone. As she
gaped at his retreating back, Eliana saw someone staring at her out of the corner of her eye. She turned her
head and looked into the face of Caphtor's assistant
standing a short distance away. Standing nearly as tall
as the governor, Melita had pulled her white-blonde
hair into an elegant twist and wore a low-cut gown
nearly as revealing as the high priestess's. An arrogant
smirk hovered around the woman's lips.

Bitra stepped to her side. "Look, there's Jarrell."

A slender man approached, a goblet in each hand.
He wore fashionable breeches and a brown leather
overtunic, green silk sleeves billowing to his wrists.

Shocks of silver at his temples stood out starkly amid straight brown hair that he had bound at the nape of his neck in a leather band the same hue as his over-tunic. As he approached, Eliana caught a whiff of new leather and hid a smile. Doubtless he was not the only one who bought new clothing for the governor's party.

"Wine for the two most beautiful ladies in the room." He held a goblet toward each of them, his eyes telling Eliana that his compliment was sincere.

"Not for me, thank you." Nerves made the idea of eating or drinking anything unimaginable.

Bitra claimed one of the ornate goblets. "Eliana de Ashbel, may I present my escort for the evening, Jarrell de Asshur?"

Eliana acknowledged his bow with a dip of her forehead. "I'm glad you could come, Jarrell. I'm sorry to have pre-empted your date."

"This is the most fun I've had since I moved to Cainlan." Jarrell's eyes danced as he looked around the brightly-lit chamber. "Just being in the same room with the governor and the entire of Cainlan's Council is enough to make my head swim."

"And I thought showing me around the city was the most fun you've had since coming to Cainlan." Bitra's lower lip protruded in a pretty pout.

Jarrell's eyes widened at his blunder. "I meant to say this is the *second* most fun I've had."

Eliana and Bitra both laughed, and after a moment he joined in. Eliana noticed a few people looking their way, and nodded in acknowledgement of a smiled greeting from Counselor Senset's consort, whose name she could not recall.

"So you're not from Cainlan originally?" she asked.

Jarrell shook his head. "I spent much of my boy-hood on a farm just beyond the western forest. But I moved to the city when I was accepted into Cainlan's analyst training program."

Eliana's heartbeat quickened. She willed her face to remain impassive. Surely there were lots of farms beyond the forest.

Bitra bestowed a look of surprise on Jarrell. "I had no idea you were raised on a farm. How extraordinary to end up as an analyst in Social Action. I thought farm people always stayed on their family lands for life."

"Oh, they do. But it wasn't my family's farm." Jarrell sipped from his goblet before explaining. "My parents died when I was a child, and I was taken in by some distant cousins. All three of the family's sons still live on the farm, and believe me, they will never leave."

Eliana's heartbeat fluttered to new speeds. Three sons? And all living on their father's land? She schooled her expression into one of polite inquiry.

"I met a farmer from that vicinity not long ago. His name was...:" She paused, tapping a finger on her lips. "Shem. That was it. I don't remember his father's name."

"Shem de Noah!" Jarrell's face lit with delight. "That's the very family. Shem is like a brother to me. How odd that you've met him."

"Eliana, my dear, allow me to congratulate you," boomed a female voice.

Eliana found her arm captured in the clutch of a round woman who's piled and powdered hair resembled one of the pillars at the main entrance to the temple.

Smothering the urge to jerk away, she smiled. "Thank you, Lady Kenara. And thank you also for the lovely alliance gift you and Counselor Limpopo sent."

She searched frantically in her mind for some clue as to which of the gifts that filled her room had come from Kenara and Limpopo, so she could expand appropriately on her expression of gratitude. But she was rescued from further comment when Kenara tugged her toward the center of the room.

"You must let me introduce you to my sister. I had no idea you two had not met."

Eliana cast a regretful glance toward Jarrell and

Bitra. Bitra lifted her glass in a silent salute before turning her attention on Jarrell.

Eliana plastered on a polite smile as she faced the group toward whom Kenara led her. She would find a way later to ask more about Shem de Noah.

Despite her determination to corner Jarrell and ply him with questions, Eliana found her attention monopolized the entire evening by first one guest and then another. Her desire to enjoy the party proved impossible, since every time she turned around she found Caphtor at her elbow, or Melita staring from across the room in that haughty way of hers. As the evening wore on, Eliana's dread swelled. Fear of the night ahead sent her heart into her throat whenever she looked into Caphtor's face.

The wine flowed like floodwaters, and the noise level of the guests rose on the tide. The sun had long since disappeared when High Priestess Liadan plucked at Eliana's arm, pulling her away from a cluster of gossiping women.

"Have you forgotten your manners? The guests won't leave until you do."

A shaft of terror shot through her. The time had come. She turned round eyes on her mother.

Liadan's eyebrows rose. "Are you afraid of the night ahead?"

Swallowing convulsively, Eliana could only nod.

Liadan stared at her, a perplexed line creasing her forehead. Then it cleared, replaced by a slow smile.

"Don't worry. You're my daughter, after all. No doubt you'll find the experience quite...enjoyable."

She gave a low laugh before clapping her hands to gain the attention of the room. Eliana ducked her head, wishing she could hide behind her mother's skirts as she hid behind Girta's when she was a child.

"The governor's consort has decided to retire for

the evening," she announced. "Tonight my daughter becomes a woman."

She placed an arm across Eliana's shoulder, her smirk suggestive. Those in the vicinity of Caphtor clapped him on the back as a few ladies giggled. Someone in the back of the room shouted a bawdy comment in the governor's direction, causing Eliana's face to flame.

Bitra came to her rescue. The priestess appeared from nowhere and took Eliana's arm. As the comments became vulgar, Bitra led Eliana from the room like a child.

When the door closed behind them, Bitra put an arm around Eliana's shoulders, where her mother's had been a moment before.

"That was fun!" She grinned sideways at Eliana as the two made their way down the corridor, toward the exit and the temple. "Jarrell and I had a great time lording it over that insufferable Roblin de Yibin. He nearly dropped his goblet when he caught sight of us. And when he heard we'd been invited by the guest of honor herself..."

Eliana tried to smile at the chattering priestess, but the effort must have looked more like a grimace. Bitra's grin became a frown of concern.

"You don't look well. Did you eat something that disagreed with you?"

Eliana shook her head. "I didn't eat at all."

"Well, no wonder you look ill. You spent the entire party talking and not eating. I'll have a page rush something up from the temple kitchen before the governor arrives." She gave a broad wink. "You need your strength tonight."

Blood roared in Eliana's ears, drowning out the priestess's voice as she rattled on about her plans to meet Jarrell to continue their date. What would Bitra say if she confessed how the approaching night chilled the very blood in her veins? She quickly dismissed the thought of revealing her feelings. Their friendship was too new, and after all, Eliana was the high priestess's heir, and Bitra a priestess.

As they entered the temple's west residential wing through a side door, Eliana remembered her mother's words. Maybe Liadan was right, and the night wouldn't be as bad as she feared.

When they arrived at Eliana's new suite, Bitra rushed ahead to throw the door open. She stepped aside for Eliana to enter, her eyes flashing with excitement.

"I've given you an alliance gift to celebrate your first night as Governor Caphtor's consort. In here."

Eliana followed her across the sitting room and stood in the doorway of the bedchamber. At least two dozen candles flooded the room with a golden glow, while the delicate scent of jasmine tinged the air. Golden candlelight reflected on the silky fabric of a filmy nightgown displayed on the bed. Eliana's palms went clammy at the sight of the nearly transparent garment.

"It's...beautiful. Thank you." She tried to make a show of enthusiasm, but fear kept her jaws clenched together, and her lips refused to smile.

Bitra's forehead creased. "I'm going to find a page and send up that food." She wrapped her arms around Eliana in a hesitant embrace. "I'll see you in the morning."

No sooner had the door closed behind Bitra than it opened again. Eliana whirled, her heart pounding in her throat. Had Caphtor arrived already?

At the familiar sight of Girta, she flew across the room and threw herself into her nursemaid's arms, pent-up sobs finally erupting from her tight throat.

"Hush, now," Girta soothed, "you mustn't take on so. Your eyes will swell. Everything will be fine."

Would they? What if Girta was wrong? Maybe nothing would ever be fine again. But she had no choice, and allowed Girta to help her into the revealing gown. What could she do? She was the governor's consort. Whatever the night held, she could not avoid it now. She sat unmoving at her dressing table as Girta unwound her elaborate hair arrangement and brushed the silky dark tresses until they shone. She even choked down a few bites of the cheese and bread delivered by the page Bitra promised.

When they heard the door open, her heart thudded to a halt. She stood, crossing to stand in the center of the room, her breath coming in shallow gasps nearly indistinguishable from sobs. Girta gave her a reassuring hug and whispered into her ear.

"You look beautiful, my little lamb."

Then Girta disappeared. Caphtor's figure filled the entry. Eliana swallowed her breath. He must not hear her sob, must not know how terrified she was. He swayed slightly, and reached out a powerful hand to steady himself against the wall.

"So, this is the place you expect me to live." His glance circled the room, and he turned to examine the sitting room behind him.

"There is a space beyond the bathing chamber that I thought you might use for business." To her relief, her voice did not quake, as her knees were doing within the white silk.

Caphtor snorted. "There is only one business I will conduct within these rooms." His words slurred.

Eliana gulped. He was drunk.

"One thing you should know, little high priestess-to-be." He stepped toward her, looking down into her eyes through narrowed eyelids. "I will not be dictated to. Not by your mother and not by you."

Her stomach knotted as fear surged. She lowered her gaze, hoping to hide her rising panic. A powerful hand reached out and cupped her chin, jerking her head upward. Before she could react, the hand moved to the back of her head and yanked her forward, his mouth bruising her lips with force.

When he released her, his dark eyes stared into hers with an intensity that set her head throbbing.

"I...I have wine." She stammered, no longer able to keep the fear from her voice. "I thought you might–"

"I've had enough wine."

He grabbed her arm, causing her to wince with pain, and pulled her toward the bed. Instinctively she tried to jerk away, but his fingers bit into her flesh in an unbreakable grip.

"Caphtor, you're hurting me."

He shoved her toward the bed with such force that she flew onto its surface. Her head hit the backboard with a loud crack that echoed in her ears. For a moment her vision dimmed and sharp pain sliced through her skull. Dazed, she blinked. When she looked at Caphtor again, he towered over her, a smoldering black fire in his eyes.

Breath froze in her lungs as she realized that the pain of the night had just begun.

Chapter 9

Jarrell hurried through the crowd, applying his elbows liberally to create a path for his slim frame. He spied the pub ahead and glanced toward the sun hovering directly overhead. Late, though not horribly so. Maybe Shem arrived early and grabbed a table. If not, they had no chance at a seat and he'd have to skip the meal.

He stepped inside the doorway and blinked in the dim light. As his eyes adjusted, he spied a pair of waving arms. Shem sat against the back wall at a small table in the corner near the serving counter. Jarrell hurried across the room and grasped his friend's right forearm.

"Sorry I'm late. I lost track of the time trying to dig my desk out from beneath a mountain of reports waiting to be done. The creation of this army has wreaked chaos on my office in the past four weeks."

Shem cocked his head as Jarrell sat. "How so? I

thought the expansion of the army would mean more jobs, and therefore fewer applicants for public aid."

"You would think so, wouldn't you?" Jarrell snorted. "Instead the instance of fraud has tripled. Lots of people are eager to collect the wages of a soldier, but few are willing to give up the government aid they've grown accustomed to. Enough about the army." He dismissed the topic with a wave. "I'm too busy to think about that." His lips twitched sideways as he looked at his friend.

"What?" Shem demanded. "Something big has happened. Were you promoted?"

"Nothing like that." Jarrell looked away under the pretense of locating the tavern keeper in the crowded room while he tried to regain control of his mouth.

Shem's lips parted in a wide smile. "Only one thing could put that goat grin on your face. You've found a lady."

Jarrell let the grin explode across his face. "I have."

"Tell me of her," Shem demanded. "What is her bloodline? What is she like? When will you marry?"

Jarrell shifted in his seat. Shem was his best friend, his almost-brother since boyhood. But like his father, Shem was old-fashioned. He probably wouldn't understand. But the news had to be shared sometime.

"Uh, well...

I'm not exactly considering marriage yet. It's not foreseeable right now, for either of us."

Shem's smile wilted a fraction. "She does worship the True God?"

Jarrell shook his head.

A guarded expression came over Shem's face. "Is she of Seth's blood?"

Jarrell shook his head again.

"I see. At least assure me that she doesn't actively worship Cain."

"I'm afraid she does." Might as well deliver all the bad news at once. "It's worse than that, actually. She's a priestess in the temple, and she's a foreigner from

Enoch."

His friend's eyes squeezed shut. Jarrell waited, letting Shem work through the news his own way.

Finally, Shem sucked in a resigned breath. "I had a feeling it would be something like that from the stupid, mountain goat look on your face. Well, it was bound to happen, with you running about among the pagans. Tell me more. What does she look like?"

Jarrell's shoulders relaxed. "You're not going to preach to me about my bloodline and keeping myself pure and all that?"

Shem shrugged his shoulders. "I'm not your conscience, even if you sometimes treat me as such. How you spend yourself is between you and God. I'm here if you need me." He paused, his gaze fixed on the scarred surface between them. "And besides, lately I've come to understand that the One God loves all people, whether they love Him or not."

Relieved, Jarrell reached out to clasp Shem's shoulder. Then he grinned. "She's beautiful. Dark hair and eyes, and the most exotic lips you've ever seen. They pout just a little when she's thinking about something. And she's smart, too, so smart she intimidates my friend Roblin."

Jarrell described Bitra, and didn't bother to keep the pride out of his voice. He still found himself stunned that someone so beautiful and smart actually enjoyed his company. But she did, as she had proven by spending every free moment with him in the past four weeks.

A harried server interrupted his verbal tribute to the dark-haired priestess by finally arriving to take their order. When the man left, Jarrell drew breath to continue, but Shem interrupted.

"You mentioned her duties in the Governor's household. I thought you said she was a priestess."

"She is." Jarrell's shoulders squared with pride. "She's also assistant to the Governor's consort. The High Priestess tapped her for the position several weeks ago. Bitra had to step in and–"

"Do you mean Eliana de Ashbel?"

Jarrell sat back, surprised. "Yes, of course I mean Eliana. But she's officially the governor's consort now."

Shem's lower lip disappeared between his teeth, and his gaze slid toward the far side of the room. "Of course she is. Have you seen her?"

"Occasionally. I attended the alliance party as Bitra's guest, and met her there. Oh!" Jarrell slapped a hand to his forehead. "I completely forgot. You've met. She told me at the alliance party. But we never had an opportunity to speak again, so I didn't hear the story of how it came about."

Shem expelled a breath.

Jarrell narrowed his eyes. Why wouldn't Shem meet his gaze?

"Do you remember our last meeting, when I was late? I told you I rescued a girl."

Jarrell nodded. "By the pet store?"

"That was Eliana."

"Really?"

Shem nodded. "This morning I arrived in time to see the ritual at the temple—"

"You?" Jarrell sat back, shocked. "Shem de Noah actually attended a pagan sacrifice?"

Color lit Shem's cheeks. Jarrell had never seen him look so discomfited. "She has been on my mind lately, and I wanted to see if she was there. I left before the ritual began." He leaned forward. "But not before I saw her on the dais, looking pale and thin. In fact, she looked ill. Do you know if she's well?"

Jarrell shrugged. "I didn't think you'd be interested in government gossip, but I'll tell you what I know. She has seemed sick lately, and rarely leaves the temple. The talk is that she may be carrying a child."

"Already?" Shem's face drained of color. "But their alliance is only a few weeks old. And she's so young."

Jarrell folded his hands in front of him. How interesting. Why did the possibility of Eliana's pregnancy disturb his old friend?

"She's old enough to form an alliance, and older than Mara when you married." At the mention of his wife, Shem sobered and looked away. "Actually, Bitra told me that she doesn't think Eliana is expecting a child. She says her relationship with the Governor is strained, and that Eliana seems frightened of him."

"Frightened." Shem stared at a point behind Jarrell's head.

"Bitra is worried about her. Says the only thing that makes her happy are her landrider lessons, and they're only twice a week. The rest of the time she's withdrawn and sullen. Bitra can't get her to confide. She remains tight-lipped, not the same girl as before her alliance." Jarrell reached across the table and grasped Shem's arm, forcing him to look down. "If she considers you a friend, it might help if she heard from you. I could ask Bitra to deliver a message if you like."

Shem's eyes widened, and Jarrell thought they lightened, but only for a moment. Then his gaze dropped to the table, and he shook his head.

"No. I don't think that's a good idea."

"But if –" Jarrell stopped to draw a sharp breath as realization slapped at him. "Do you mean to tell me, Shem de Noah, that you have feelings for this girl, this … pagan, daughter of the highest pagan of all?"

"Of course not," Shem hurried to say.

But Jarrell saw the truth reflected in his eyes. He held the gray gaze until Shem's head dipped forward. "Maybe a little. I know you'll find this odd, but the One God has put a tenderness for this girl in my heart. My feelings don't dishonor her, or Mara." He lifted a single shoulder. "I just want her to be happy."

Jarrell studied his friend through narrowed eyelids. There was more to Shem's feelings than he admitted. Maybe he didn't admit them even to himself. But he was right in one thing. A follower of the One God had no business making overtures of friendship to the future High Priestess of Cain. Any relationship between the two of them could only lead to disaster.

"You're right, of course," he said. "Best to let things lay."

When Shem smiled, the gesture looked strained. "Tell your priestess to watch out for her. She needs a friend. I don't think she has many."

Eliana winced as the brush raked over a tender spot on her scalp.

Girta dropped the brush like it burned red-hot. "I'm sorry. I didn't mean to hurt you."

A glance into the mirror showed tears shining in the nursemaid's eyes. Eliana hurried to look away from the pity she saw there. Instead, she bent to retrieve the brush and finished arranging her hair so that it covered a fresh bruise high on the side of her forehead.

She forced a smile at Girta's image. "I'm fine. Don't worry about it."

"You are not fine." The nursemaid's lips tightened. "What kind of monster is he?"

Eliana did not answer. Many sleepless nights after Caphtor left her bed had been devoted to that question, but no answer presented itself. Finally, she gave up trying to understand why Caphtor took pleasure in hurting her. Instead, she focused on presenting the meek countenance he desired in his consort. If she took exactly the right attitude with him, and did not look him in the face nor speak overmuch, his attentions were almost tolerable. But the slightest show of defiance, even a glance that held a hint of boldness, brought on a violent episode that ended leaving her bruised and sometimes bloodied.

As last night's had.

"If you won't speak to the High Priestess," Girta said, "perhaps I should."

Eliana whirled on the stool to clutch Girta's apron

with trembling fingers. "No! Please, don't do that. It will make him furious, Girta. He hates any mention of Liadan. I don't even want to think about what he would do."

Girta grasped her hands, and her warmth calmed Eliana's shaking. Tears threatened, but she blinked them back. She would not ruin the day by starting off with eyes red from crying.

She rose from the dressing table and crossed the room to retrieve a short jacket from the foot of the bed. Though the days had turned warmer, the jacket's sleeves would hide an ugly bruise on her forearm. She slipped it on, and then turned to smile at Girta.

"You should get out and enjoy the sunshine while I take my rider lesson. Maybe walk in the gardens."

Girta stared at her for a long moment through narrowed eyelids, and then gave a brief nod. "Melody could use some seed, and I wouldn't mind a visit to the fabric merchant. You need a new blue dress."

Because Caphtor destroyed mine last week. She buried the reminder and brushed a quick kiss on Girta's cheek. "Buy enough fabric for us both to have a new dress."

As she walked through the temple corridors away from the chambers she shared with Caphtor, the darkness that seemed to hover over her in those rooms receded. She avoided the hallway leading to her old chambers, where happier days were spent. No sense looking backward. Life was as it was.

This new life wasn't without its benefits. Money, for one thing. As the future High Priestess, Eliana's daily needs had been provided by the temple from the moment of her birth. But as the Governor's consort she was awarded an actual salary from Cainlan's treasury. Her chambers must be furnished in a way befitting the Governor of Cainlan's Council, and she and Bitra were taking full advantage of the opportunity to pour through the marketplace shops to find exactly the right accouterments. The place was starting to take shape.

Not that Caphtor ever entertained there. He spent more time in his government apartment than with her. Eliana shuddered. That arrangement was fine with her. Preferred, in fact.

Two guards at the temple's rear exit lifted the heavy latch and pushed open the door when she approached. Awarding each of them a brief smile of thanks, Eliana stepped outside.

She stopped and raised her face toward the sunlight, breathing deeply of the grass-scented air blowing across the wide empty field behind the temple. A hint of smoke tainted the breeze. A glance toward the Eternal Fires showed a thick, dark line rising above the circular stone walls that stood like a lone tower, bereft of a castle to guard.

"There you are," said a familiar voice.

She whirled to see a man approaching from the direction of the rider shed. He wore breeches laced at the calf over boots that crunched on the stone-strewn path. A smile deepened the scar on his right cheekbone.

"Arphaxad!" Delight bubbled inside her, erupting in a happy laugh as Eliana closed the distance between them with three quick steps. "Are you my rider instructor today?"

"More than that." The skin around his dark eyes crinkled with his smile. "I intend to test you. If you've learned well, you'll be done with lessons."

Disappointment tugged at the corners of her lips. These rider lessons took her away from confines of the temple. What would she do when she no longer had that excuse?

Then she realized the meaning of his words. "Do you mean I'll be able to take a rider out alone?"

His smile widened. "That's right."

Her heart thudded in her chest. She would be able to leave, to go anywhere she wanted. Like into the forest … and beyond.

"But first you have to prove that you can handle the rider." Arphaxad leveled a stern gaze on her.

"I'm ready," she assured him with more confidence than she felt. She followed him through the wide doorway into the vehicle shed where the temple's three landriders were kept. The one Eliana piloted in her lessons was smaller than the others, and much nicer, with room for only two people. She pressed a release switch and stepped backward as the entry panel opened outward and upward.

"I'm surprised the temple has one this size," Eliana told him as she slid across the bench. "Who uses it, besides me?"

"This one is mine." He gave her a sideways grin. "All my needs are supplied by the temple, so I splurged on a luxury rider. I enjoy the opportunity to escape every so often."

Eliana understood the need for escape better than most.

"Where shall we go?"

He waved a hand vaguely. "Wherever you like. I'm merely along for the ride."

Grinning, she connected the leads to the energy cartridge, grasped the lever, and eased it forward as she had been taught. The vehicle rolled ahead, through the open doorway and into the sunshine.

Though a beautiful day surrounded them, Eliana focused all her attention on delivering the smoothest ride she could manage. She followed the road around the western corner of the temple, and then ran alongside the high city wall for its entire length. At the northwestern corner of the city she veered the rider onto a wider roadway. Arphaxad's eyebrows arched when he realized she intended to pilot them through the busy outer-city streets. She awarded him a confident smile and kept her attention fixed ahead.

Within moments they slowed to a crawl behind a herd of curly-furred naugabeasts on their way to the shearing center. The shepherd directing the herd stoutly ignored their rider. He kept his head turned away and refused to speed his pace one jot.

"Why doesn't he move the herd onto the grass and let us pass?" Irritation made her voice sharp.

Arphaxad laughed. "Disregard for the wealthy. Often, the best defense against the poison of envy is to become haughty yourself." Eliana considered that as they crept along behind the herd. "Is it a defense against envy, or a side effect of it?"

"A good observation, and you may be right. Envy is a disease that goes back almost to the beginning of man, and there are not many who haven't felt a few of its symptoms."

"All the way back to Adam's first two sons?" She chanced a sideways glance to see his reaction.

She was not disappointed. Arphaxad turned his head slowly to give her a high-browed stare.

"There are certain historical events which should not be discussed within the temple walls. Girta has told you more history than she should."

An unspoken question hovered in his voice. Eliana answered it. "I didn't hear that from Girta. Someone else told me, a man I met in the marketplace."

"You should take care who you speak with." Though he spoke in a calm tone, Eliana sensed his concern.

"I do," she assured him.

She found her eyes drawn to the buildings lining the streets. Some were commercial, like the shearing center where the naugabeast herd veered off. These were made of wood, or sometimes stone, and bore carefully-lettered signs declaring the trade practiced within. As they gained distance from the city wall, the buildings became smaller, most formed from mud and straw, with cloth-covered doorways and windows, or without covers at all. These were dwellings, and the people swarmed around them.

The road they traveled marked the western border of the outer city. On Eliana's right stretched an endless sea of roofs. She caught a glimpse of crisscrossing paths too narrow for a rider, each lined with various sorts of buildings and people. There was no grass, only the dark earth where feet and hooves had crushed the life out of any vegetation that may have been brave enough to poke its head up into the sunlight. After what seemed ages they left the northernmost border of outer Cainlan. Just ahead the crisscrossing paths combined to form one wide road heading into the forest. She steered the rider onto the grass beside the road and turned to look Arphaxad full in the face.

"Well?"

He returned her gaze with a noncommittal one of his own. "First, a few questions. Tell me what the gauges mean."

Eliana placed a finger on the first gauge on the instrument panel. "This one shows the temperature of the internals. If that needle rises above the half-mark, I'm to disconnect the energy leads until it cools."

"Why?"

"Because using energy causes heat, and when the heat gets to a certain point it will jam the internals. And then," she straightened and assumed the tone of her first instructor, "the rider becomes nothing more than an expensive pile of junk."

He chuckled. "Go on."

"This one is the energy gauge. It tells how much energy we have left."

"How much have we used so far today?"

She glanced down. "Not quite one tickmark."

"And what will you do if you run out of energy?"

"There are two spares stored behind the seat, so I'll just change out the cartridge."

He nodded. "And what if the cartridges are empty? What if the last person who used the rider forgot to replace them?"

"Well, that wouldn't happen because—" She stopped. She forgot to check the spares before they left the rider shed. Heat flooded her face. "Because I would

have checked to be sure they were fully charged before
I left, except I was sure that the head of temple security checked them before accompanying the Governor's
consort for a morning ride."

Arphaxad put his head back and laughed. "You're
right about that. But you should have checked anyway. Do you know what happens if you don't have a
spare cartridge?"

"I walk?"

"You walk," he agreed. Then he grinned. "You've
learned well."

Eliana's pulse fluttered. "So I can take a rider out
alone?"

Creases deepened the lines in his forehead. "I'd
prefer that you take Girta or your assistant with you,
for safety reasons. But you no longer need an instructor along, and you're free to use my rider anytime you
wish."

Eliana bit the inside of her lip. Having Girta or
Bitra along would completely spoil her plans to pay a
visit to the farm of Shem de Noah. Hiding her disappointment, she nodded and grasped the lever.

They rode along the main road beside the city's
western wall in silence for a while. She stole a glance
at his profile. How had this man, a worshiper of the
One God, come to hold the top security position in the
temple? And why was he so far from his people?

"Arphaxad, where is your family?"

"Dead," he replied, staring ahead.

"How did you end up in Cainlan?"

"I was a violent youth, always picking fights with
the other boys. When my father died, I think it was a
relief to the entire village when I announced that I
would leave."

"Surely not," protested Eliana.

"I was horrible," he said in a low voice. "Had my father lived, I would have broken his heart. I renounced
his lifestyle and his God."

"The One God?" Eliana shook her head. "But now

you are a worshiper again."

"Not truly, my lady. I have forsaken everything He gave me in life, and have sold myself away from Him."

The pain in his voice wrenched at Eliana's heart. "But you led me to Him."

"No, He drew you to Himself. Though He may have used me in some small way." Arphaxad heaved a sigh. "I do not fully understand how, but the One God has a grip on my heart. I don't think He has led me into the places I have gone, but He has been with me even so. No matter how many times I've tried to loosen His grip, He does not let go."

Eliana fell silent. Did the One God have a grip on her heart, too? If so, she couldn't see any sign of it. Her life had done nothing but grow darker since the night of her offering to Him. "Why did you never marry?"

He didn't respond at first. She waited for his answer as the rider slipped along the road.

"I gave up the lifestyle that sanctions marriage, remember? But there was a lady I once loved. She wouldn't have me."

"Did her rejection hurt you very deeply?"

"She didn't reject me. I never told her of my feelings, so there was never a chance to reject me. But she must have known I had some feelings for her, or perhaps she even had some for me. One time, when she was truly in need, she came to me for help. It was the most wonderful, and also the most difficult thing I've ever done, helping that lady."

The last was said so quietly, almost in a whisper, that Eliana dared not ask anything further.

She navigated the turn around the northwestern corner of the city, and the temple rider shed loomed before them. She pulled the lever toward her to slow the vehicle and steered through the doorway. When they came to a smooth stop, she locked the lever and disconnected the energy leads, then turned a triumphant grin on Arphaxad.

"Well done," he said, and she preened at his praise.

She followed him out of the vehicle and into the sunshine. The temple doors loomed before her, like the entrance to a dark tunnel of her fears. She cast a long-ing glance toward the forest. "How I envy you the abil-ity to escape." She felt him watching her, but did not turn her head. "I know my duty. But every so often, it would be nice to leave duty behind, if only for a little while."

They approached the temple door and Arphaxad paused before opening it for her. He looked down at her, his dark eyes soft.

"The city streets are too dangerous for a beautiful young woman to travel alone. But perhaps you could take the rider into the forest. That southern path we took the night you made your offering is rarely used, and the drive through the trees in daylight is ... peace-ful."

Her heart swelled, and she reached out and grasped his forearm. "Oh, thank you, *adame.*"

Arphaxad started at her use of the title of honor. Eliana had never spoken it, since she had no male rel-ative who had given her support and encouragement in life. Though Arphaxad was not her relative, she felt right using it now.

He pierced her with a dark gaze, and gave a slow nod. Then he opened the door. Eliana entered the temple with a lighter step than when she exited. She had been handed the gift of freedom, and she intended to use it.

Chapter 10

Caphtor ignored the sideways glances of the temple guards and threw open the door to the suite he shared with Eliana. The heavy wood swung inward and crashed into the wall. He didn't care. He hated this place, and the ever-watchful eyes of the guards who scraped and bowed before Liadan. Loathsome creatures.

"Eliana," he shouted, infusing his tone with a hint of command. He liked watching her scurry to answer his calls.

The woman who stepped through the bedchamber doorway into the common room did not scurry. Instead, she moved at such a slow pace as to be insulting, and stared at him through wary brown eyes. The nursemaid. What was her name?

"You. Get Eliana immediately."

The woman drew an even breath before answering. "She's not here."

Irritation flooded him, and caused his hand to clench into a fist. "Where is she?"

"She has her rider lesson this morning. I expect her back before the noon meal."

Rider lesson. The irritation receded a bit. Caphtor approved of Eliana's landrider lessons. Landriders were a thing of the future, a symbol of Cainlan's domination of the world's energy production. It was fitting that his consort have the skill to pilot a rider. One day he, too, intended to learn.

"When she returns, bring her to my office."

Caphtor turned to go, but the woman took a step forward, her hand raised. He stopped, and turned an arrogant expression her way, one that had melted many junior government workers who dared to interrupt him.

She did not melt. Her chin rose in a posture of defiance. "I want you to stop hurting her."

Caphtor examined her through narrowed eyelids. This woman, this *servant* dared to use a commanding tone with him?

"Your wants matter little to me. Your attitude, however, is most upsetting. I advise you to change it. Quickly."

The only sign that his threat hit its mark was a slight trembling in her chin. Her expression hardened into a determined mask.

"My wants may not matter, but those of the High Priestess will carry some weight, I daresay."

Caphtor snorted. "The High Priestess cares nothing for Eliana. She wouldn't bestir herself to act on her daughter's behalf."

"Perhaps not on her daughter's behalf, but certainly she cares about the reputation of the temple. If word got out that her heir is being abused, she wouldn't stand idle."

"Are you threatening to go to the High Priestess?"

Caphtor took a step forward. The woman clasped her hands to still the sudden trembling, but she did not retreat.

"I'll do whatever I have to in order to protect Eliana from being hurt by you, or anyone else."

Caphtor allowed his lips to curve. He knew the effect the gesture projected, had practiced it, in fact. It was not designed to make the recipient comfortable.

"Before you speak with the High Priestess, perhaps you should consider your own safety." A slight widening of her eyelids betrayed her surprise. "She might be interested to know that the nursemaid who has raised her heir from infancy does not worship her god. In fact, follows an old fashioned sect that she has determined to wipe out of existence."

She drew a quick breath and hid her quaking hands behind her back, removing them from his view.

"That's right," he went on. "Liadan may not bother to check the background of those in her employ, but I don't make that mistake."

Fear rose in her eyes. This time, his smile was genuine. He enjoyed seeing fear in the eyes of underlings.

"Understand this. I care little what god you worship. Stay out of my way, and you may do whatever you like." Another step forward brought him within reach of her, though his hands remained at his side. "If you threaten me again, you won't live to regret it. But Eliana will."

As her broad peasant face drained of color, he whirled and strode from the room.

Her spirits high from her rider lesson with Arphaxad, Eliana found her suite empty. Girta was still shopping. A note lay on the bed, telling her that Caphtor wanted her to come to his office.

A cloud of dread darkened the pleasure of her ride. She glanced at the new energy-powered timepiece on her dressing table. Nearly lunch time. Bitra would be finished with her priestess duties shortly, and could go with her to the Cabinet of Energy building. Bitra could put Caphtor's assistant, Melita, in her place every time. Whereas the woman assumed an arrogant attitude whenever Eliana encountered her alone, leaving Eliana with the desire to creep away like a coward.

She changed out of her jacket and leggings, donning a sweeping brown gown of which Caphtor approved. She hated the thing, the way it washed out her pale skin and made her look like a wraith. But maybe if he liked the way she looked, the interview would be easier and she could get out of there quickly.

Bitra arrived in time to help fasten the pearly buttons at her wrists.

"You've got so many lovely gowns," the dark haired priestess said, her nose wrinkled as she surveyed the dress, "I can't imagine why you'd want to wear that."

Eliana forced a smile. "I don't know. I kind of like it."

Bitra looked unconvinced, but shrugged. "Whatever you think. Do we have time to grab something to eat before we go? I'm starving."

Eliana hesitated. If Caphtor found out she hadn't hurried to his office as soon as she received the message ... She bit her lip and gave Bitra an apologetic glance.

"If you don't mind, I'd like to talk with the Governor first. Hopefully it won't take long, and then we can get something to eat in one of the taverns in the marketplace."

Bitra shrugged. "Fine with me. Though I don't know if I can handle that pinch-faced Melita on an empty stomach."

They left the suite and walked through the temple corridors to the main entrance. Normally talkative Bitra remained quiet, staring ahead with a blank expression. Eliana, her stomach growing tighter at every step, missed her lively chatter. Bitra could always be counted on to distract her with the latest temple gossip.

"How are things with Jarrell these days?" she asked.

The pretty brunette beamed. "Wonderful. He took me to a concert a few days ago, and afterward we spread a blanket under the stairs and talked almost until the sun came up."

Eliana smiled. "That must have been the day you nearly fell asleep while answering my correspondence."

"It was." She giggled. "He's so smart, and he has such tenderness for the poor people of Cainlan. They're not just numbers in the reports he analyzes, they're hurting people and he genuinely wants to help them."

Eliana swallowed a sigh. Of course Jarrell cared about people. He grew up with Shem. Someday Eliana would arrange to speak with Jarrell alone, so she could press him for details of his boyhood and Shem's. But she had no desire to betray her fascination for a worshipper of the One God in front of the intelligent priestess. That wouldn't be safe, for either her or for Shem.

They arrived at the entrance to the Cabinet of Energy. The floors inside the impressive building gleamed as those in the temple did not, regardless of the dozens of government workers who rushed across them all day long, intent on whatever business they had to conduct. Eliana's pulse picked up speed as she and Bitra climbed the stairs leading to Caphtor's office. She schooled her expression. She would not show fear. She was the future High Priestess of Cain.

Bitra's smile took on a hint of challenge as they approached the blonde seated behind an elegant desk. Melita looked up, her gaze insolent as she caught sight of Eliana, but growing wary as it slid to Bitra.

"Tell the Governor his consort is here." Bitra's voice held the merest hint of command, as if she spoke to a servant instead of the assistant to the most powerful man in Cainlan.

Melita bristled. "He is occupied. You can sit there until he's free."

She gestured toward a divan in the corner. Rising to the challenge, Bitra's smile widened.

"He left word that he wanted to see his consort as soon as she became available." She took a step toward the closed inner door. "Perhaps I'll just let him know she's here."

Melita rose and stepped out from behind the desk, blocking Bitra's path. Two spots of color appeared high on her pale cheeks. She towered a full head over the priestess, and the glare with which she speared Bitra would have set Eliana's knees quaking.

Admiration rose in Eliana as she watched Bitra return the glare with a calm and determined smile. The two women locked gazes for a moment, and then, amazingly, Melita took a half-step backward. Her gaze slid to Eliana.

"I'll see if he's free."

As she turned to open the door, Bitra winked at Eliana, her smile growing broad. She was actually having fun. Eliana shook her head. If only she possessed a fraction of the brunette priestess's confidence.

"Ah, Eliana," Caphtor's voice preceded him to the doorway. "Come in."

Eliana straightened her shoulders in an effort to hide the internal quaking the sound of his voice produced. He would not hurt her here.

He closed the door behind her, leaving Bitra in the outer office with a fuming Melita.

"Sit, please." He gestured toward a chair in a corner of the room.

The tension in her shoulders lessened as she sat and he took a chair next to hers. His voice was professional, even friendly, the one he used for business.

"How was your rider lesson?"

"Fine." She managed a smile. "In fact, it was my last. I've been cleared to pilot a rider alone."

"Excellent!" His obvious pleasure in her accomplishment took Eliana by surprise. "You should buy a rider of your own. Perhaps you could instruct me to pilot it."

"Of course."

She looked toward the window behind his desk to hide her wariness. Caphtor was never friendly without a purpose.

"In fact," he continued, "that fits into my plan nicely. I've been thinking about our living arrangements."

Her gaze flew to his face. "What do you mean?"

"My dear, I told you at the beginning I wasn't happy living under Liadan's roof. Surely you've noticed that I spend no more time in our temple suite than necessary."

Eliana certainly had noticed. And was grateful. She dipped her head in acknowledgement.

"It isn't right that an alliance couple live separately, and yet I know my meager quarters in this building are unsuited to someone of your position. So I've decided we must purchase a home elsewhere in the city."

"Elsewhere?" Eliana shook her head. "But where?"

Caphtor waved a hand. "I don't care. I'll leave that up to you. You can keep an office in the temple, and with your new rider skills, you can easily get there every day. You can even pilot me here every morning, until I learn how to do it myself."

Leave the temple? Eliana's throat threatened to close around a sudden lump of panic. The temple was the only home she had ever known. She couldn't live elsewhere, not with Caphtor. Not with anyone. Liadan would be furious.

Caphtor gave her no opportunity to react. He rose, and held out his hand to assist her to her feet.

"Melita will help. She knows my tastes. Find us a place suitable to both our positions, and don't worry about the cost. The treasury can afford whatever you spend."

Eliana didn't trust herself to speak. She nodded. With a satisfied smile, Caphtor opened the door and ushered her into the outer office. Melita's painted eye-lids narrowed as she saw Caphtor's hand on the small of Eliana's back. Eliana ignored her.

"I'll see you tonight, my dear," he said.

Eliana tried not to think of that as a threat.

Chapter 11

Eliana eased the lever backward and felt it slip into a slower notch. She had passed through the forest without mishap, and the path coming up on her right seemed to head toward the great mountain looming in the distance. Was this the right one? She decided in a flash that it was and pushed the lever to the right, guiding the rider gently onto the path. She smiled at the pleasure of a smooth turn, and could almost hear Arphaxad's deep voice full of praise.

She giggled. Freedom made her giddy. What a light, wonderful feeling to speed through the forest, trees growing on either side of the path to join leafy hands above her and form a canopy of green under which the rider flew. Perhaps she should do as Caphtor suggested and buy one of her own. Then she wouldn't be forced to evade Arphaxad's eyes when she asked permission to take his rider into the forest. If he suspected her true destination today, he would never have let her out of the shed.

Eliana lowered her gaze to the heat gauge, noting that the needle was still well within the safety area. Energy was also doing well, though she planned to switch cartridges before the return trip just to be safe. It couldn't be too far now. Shem said his father's farm lay just a few hours from the city, and she'd been piloting through the forest nearly that amount of time already.

Her stomach tightened at the thought of him. What would he think of her showing up at his home? Would he think she was throwing herself at him? *Was* she throwing herself at him? She pushed the disturbing questions to the back of her mind. She just wanted to see this phenomenal boat, that's all. He couldn't describe the thing and then expect her to forget all about it. Especially after he'd explained the reason for its construction. No rational person would be able to put it out of her mind.

Anyway, she was just out for a day's enjoyment, nothing more. She'd brought a basket packed with cold stewed roots and chopped vegetables, soft bread and sweetened spreads. Enough for two, if he had a mind to share it with her. Shem had treated her to pastries and and ice at their last meeting, and she simply wanted to return the treat. Surely his wife wouldn't mind that.

The justification settled in her mind, she set herself to enjoy the day. A mild eastern breeze rustled the leaves of the trees to her right. The path, not defined enough to be called a road, ran beside the forest and weaved in and out of the trees in some places. The quiet hum of the rider's internals provided a comforting background. On a day like this she could almost forget she was the Governor's consort, or the future High Priestess of Cain. She could almost forget the nights filled with fear and pain.

Like last night. Her smile faded. Caphtor was unhappy that she had failed to find a suitable home in

the six days since his request. It wasn't for lack of trying. She and Bitra had toured every available structure, but found an unacceptable flaw in each one. She
didn't dare select one that Caphtor would find fault
with.

She thrust those thoughts from her mind. Today
was a free day, her very first as an allied adult with
freedom of movement. She intended to enjoy herself.

The path veered westward away from the forest,
though scattered trees continued to dot the landscape
and grew quite thick in some areas. The mountain
loomed larger and larger above her, dwarfing the valley
through which she traveled. It was a small forerunner
of a giant mountain range, one the people of Cainlan
referred to as "the Grandfathers" since it was from
there that their founders had come. The lush green
grass and trees blurred to a rich blue toward the
mountain's peak.

She came upon an even smaller path veering off to
the left, one obviously not often used, just the kind
that might lead to a farm. She turned, and the rider
bumped along the seldom-traveled path. Trees grew
quite thick on both sides, as though she'd driven into
an outcropping of the main forest. Then suddenly the
trees on her right dropped away to nothing as she entered the clearing of a large farm. The southern, western and eastern boundaries were marked by the thick-
est of forest. She could not see a northern boundary,
but a bluish line at the base of the mountain in the far
distance looked like it might serve that purpose.
Shem's farm was much larger than she had guessed.

And it was without a doubt Shem's farm. The path
on which she traveled ran along the tree line around
the southern and western borders of a well-plowed and
planted field, though another path branched off to the
north toward a sprawling single-level home. Several
more neat fields lay north of the house, but these
Eliana noticed only in passing. Her eyes were drawn
toward a large wooden structure rising from the

ground at the northwestern edge of this field. A giant boat.

Ark, Eliana corrected herself as she pulled the lever back to its stopping position. The rider rolled to a halt as she gazed in fascination at the edifice. It rose impossibly high, higher than even the tallest trees nearby. The frame was longer than the temple of Cain itself, or appeared so to her untrained eyes. Even at this distance she was awed by the size of the thing, and by the idea of its undertaking. This was not a quick, easy project. This was a task of many, many years, requiring devoted and undivided attention. The man who agreed to undertake this goal, even at the request of the One God, must be completely convinced of its necessity.

She swallowed against a suddenly dry mouth. The reason for this project meant the death of the entire world. Her death. But not the death of Shem, nor of his family.

Eliana glanced toward the house. There was no one in sight. Had anyone been outside the house she would have felt compelled to stop there first. Instead she eased the lever into the first notch, and the rider rolled forward across the uneven path. She rode the entire length of the field, and then curved around to the north, the forest thick on her left. The ark loomed tall before her, and she tore her eyes away from the awesome sight to watch the path lest she roll over some of Shem's neatly planted rows of vegetables.

As she approached the ark she caught her first glimpse of a person, and her heart began to beat a faster rhythm when she recognized the familiar shape. He carried a load of wood upon his shoulders from a pile nearby. At the sound of the rider's hum he turned, and Eliana saw with a surge of disappointment that it was not Shem but someone very much like him. A brother. He did mention two younger brothers, though she couldn't remember their names. The man stopped in his tracks, balancing the long strips of wood on his shoulder while he watched her approach. As she got closer she recognized a family resemblance in the squared jaw and strong nose, but his features were covered with a look of distrust she could not imagine Shem ever displaying.

She pulled the rider to a stop a few lengths from him and drew in a breath to gather her nerve before flipping the release lever. The door rose with a *whoosh* and an inward rush of soil-scented air. Eliana steeled herself, assuming a mask of nonchalance as she stepped from the rider.

He wore a short informal robe over durable leather leggings, the common dress of a laborer. His hair was dark, like Shem's, though he looked at her through brown eyes wider-set than Shem's gray ones. His mouth was firmer, and in Eliana's opinion less sensitive. He nodded, excused from a more formal bow by virtue of the heavy burden he bore.

"I am Ham de Noah." His voice was lower and gruffer than Shem's gentle tenor.

"And I am Eliana de Ashbel," she replied, also without the formal bow. She bit at her lower lip. She hadn't intended to use her pre-alliance name, but now that it was out, she wouldn't correct herself. Maybe her father's name would be less recognizable than Caphtor's.

Ham's eyelids narrowed. "You're the High Priestess's daughter." His voice dripped accusation.

So much for anonymity. "That's right." She tilted her chin upward.

He watched her carefully. "Odd that someone from the temple should come here today."

"Oh?" She added a touch of arrogance to the syllable, an imitation of her mother. "Are people from the temple not welcome on these lands?"

"Of course they are," said a friendly voice behind her.

She whirled to see an ancient man approach from within the trees, a load of long wooden strips balanced

on his shoulders. Ancient though he appeared, his
back was straight, not bent with age, and he seemed
to have no trouble with what looked to be a very heavy
bundle. White hair hung long and thick over his
shoulders to mix with a bushy beard across his chest.
His eyes, which Eliana could see were blue even at a
distance, twinkled with merriment while a soft chuckle
dimpled his cheeks. As he drew close he stooped to
deposit his load on the grass, then turned to bow formally before her.

"I am Noah de Lamech, and you are most welcome
to my home, daughter of Ashbel."

His hands reached to clasp hers. Eliana liked the
old man instantly, and found herself grinning back at
him. An eager search of his features revealed much
resemblance to Shem. Here was the source of that
warm smile and sparkling eyes, though these were
lighter and of a different hue than Shem's. This man
was tall, too. She had to tilt her head to look up at
him. The hands that grasped hers were strong and calloused, not one whit less in strength than those of a
man in full prime. He too wore the dress of a laborer,
though both his clothes and those of his son were well-
sewn and clean.

"You must forgive my son's suspicious manner,"
Noah said. "We've had a rash of vandalism lately, and
just this morning we discovered considerable damage.
All my sons have become suspicious of strangers."

"Vandalism?"

"I'm afraid so." Noah sighed. "Always there are men
who prefer to attack rather than accept beliefs contra-
ry to their own. This was the worst so far. A main
spine support was damaged and will have to be replaced. Thankfully it was on the far side and we haven't completely finished closing in the stalls there."

Eliana had no idea what a spine support was, but
she gathered from the seriousness of his tone that it
was critical to the architecture of the ark. That explained Ham's suspicion. This sort of attack was just

the type of action the High Priestess would sanction to sabotage a project of which she did not approve.

"I promise you, sir, I had no knowledge of –"

Noah cut her off with a snort. "Of course not. The temple is not to blame. I am convinced that this and the other attacks are the work of isolated men acting alone upon their fears. I've not made our purpose secret, after all, and the news has not been well received."

"I don't mean to contradict you, sir," Eliana said, "but your son is right to question my presence. Though to my knowledge no one at the temple is aware of your project, if they were, this is the sort of attack you could expect to receive. At least at first, while they still considered you little more than a nuisance."

"Just what I said." Ham's distrustful expression softened. "And if the temple is not aware of us now, they soon will be if you consider the number of spectators we've attracted lately. Father, we should hire a guard."

"Nonsense." Noah dismissed the notion with a wave of his hand. "We labor under the direction of the One God. Do you think He will not guard His project? Until He tells us to hire a guard, we will not."

Ham voiced Eliana's thought. "Then why didn't He protect it last night?"

Noah's chin took on a stubborn set.

"Listen, Father," Ham said, "how many times have you told us that our God gifted us with the wisdom and knowledge that allows us to survive in this hostile world? Is it a tribute to Him to ignore that wisdom? Do we pretend ignorance in the ways of the harvest, expecting Him to drop food upon our doorsteps? No, He taught us how to feed ourselves, expecting that we would."

Eliana knew Ham was taking advantage of her presence, guessing that his father would listen with more consideration before a stranger. He appeared to be correct. Noah looked at his son as if he had never considered the idea just presented.

"But He *can* drop food upon our doorsteps," Noah argued. "He has done so many times."

Ham nodded. "He has. But not always, and not until we experience great need. Even then He used other people to fill our need. This is the same. I believe you, Father, that He will not let the project come to disaster. But that does not mean He wants us to stand by while nightly we see our work destroyed a bit at a time."

Noah's thoughtful expression showed that he was close to being convinced, but then his features gave way to stubbornness again.

"To hire guards would be to invite trouble. Once we hire a guard the word will spread, and it will be viewed as a challenge. Instead of minor vandalism we will have groups of angry men attacking the ark, and we do not have the coin to hire an army."

Eliana felt like an intruder eavesdropping on a private conversation. The men seemed to have forgotten her presence for the moment, and she cleared her throat softly to remind them that she stood listening to their argument.

"Have you considered leaving one of you to sleep here?" She turned to look toward the home at the far end of the pasture. "It is too far to shout, but perhaps you could install an alarm bell or something of the sort to call for help should the need arise."

Ham smiled in triumph, glancing at his father with an almost-concealed smirk, and Eliana knew she had voiced a solution that had been discussed before. Noah shook his head slowly.

"I suppose you're right, though I dislike having to take precautions of this type. It presents a display of mistrust to other men. If we do not treat them with respect and trust, how will they ever learn to treat each other so?"

When Ham answered, it was with a gentler voice. "Father, there lies the reason the One God has instructed you to build this ark. They do not trust each other, and they do not trust Him."

Noah sighed. "Let it be so, then, though I want it known that no violence will be done to any man. I will not be responsible for taking the life of even one man, condemned or no. That I leave to the One who knows all men's hearts."

Noah turned to Eliana with a smile. "Enough on that ugly subject. My dear, would you like a tour of our little project?"

At Eliana's nod, Noah tucked her hand into the crook of his arm, patting her fingers with a fatherly gesture. He guided her away from the rider toward the eastern side of the ark, the side closest to the house. Ham, with a nod toward Eliana, carried his burden to the opposite end.

"I've been working on it for many years, since before your birth, if you'll forgive me a guess at your age." Noah's blue eyes teased. "I am lucky to have three strong sons to help me, and lately a fourth helper as well. What a shame you shall not meet them all today...but you've already met Shem, have you not?"

Eliana nodded. "In the marketplace. That's how I knew of this place."

"He's gone to the city today with his wife and our young helper."

Eliana's heart sank. Not here? When she'd come so far?

Noah looked straight ahead, his expression thoughtful. They walked a few steps in silence.

"I am sorry to have missed him." She took pride in the fact that her voice remained even. "But I have been curious about this project of yours ever since Shem explained it to me. I only hope I'm not keeping you from your work."

Noah shook his head, his dimpled smile once again in place. "I look forward to the occasional break," he told her in a confiding tone. "Here we are."

The structure towered over her head, the unfinished end closest to her stretching bare fingers of criss-crossed wood heavenward. Noah led her to a giant doorway, bigger even than the doorway in the rider shed. Large enough to allow entry of the biggest animal on earth.

They stepped through the frame and onto a steep ramp, following it upward to a flat deck.

"This is the lower deck," Noah told her, gesturing to the floor. "As you can see, we've finished this floor and nearly finished the second as well."

The floor did indeed stretch as far as Eliana could see to the right. To her left the ark's finished sides darkened the interior, but they had left several gaps that were not yet filled in. Through one of them she saw Ham, a tiny figure at the far western end, deposit his load of wood on the grass just outside the ark. A second deck formed a roof for the level upon which she now walked, but she saw that it did not yet reach the outside frame at the far end, and gaps had been left in it as well. Probably for ease in hefting wood and other supplies up where they were needed. From this vantage point she could now see where Noah's other son worked—he was atop the second deck, on his hands and knees with his back to them, busily hammering slats of wood on the cross beams to expand the surface upon which he worked.

"How many decks will there be?" She craned her neck to see the top row of wooden beams that stretched above her from the sides like fingers curved around a butterfly.

"Three in all," Noah replied. "Seems high, I know, but we'll need enough room for the tallest animals to live comfortably for what may end up being a long time. Plus, we've got storage space beneath this lower deck for food, and we'll suspend whatever we can from the ceilings."

"I hope you're building plenty of ventilation shafts," Eliana told him, remembering the gamey smell that sometimes came from the animal shop in the mall.

"None." Noah smiled down at her. "The sides will be finished to within eighteen inches of the top all the way around, and any ventilation we have will come from there. We'll have one window, at the top of this side," he gestured toward the eastern side of the ark. "Remember that the ark will need to be as waterproof as we can make it."

Eliana nodded, an odd tickle in the center of her stomach. This man was talking about her death, and the deaths of not only everyone she knew, but of everyone and everything in the entire world. To him a worldwide flood had become a commonplace thought. He had lived with the knowledge of the earth's doom for longer than Eliana had been alive. Was he moved any longer by the awesomeness of it all? Could he be, after such a long time?

Noah seemed to read her mind, for his next words answered her thoughts.

"I pray daily that I will not become insensitive to the needs of those who will suffer the wrath of the righteous God. But sometimes I get caught up in the planning, and forget the reason for the event. It is my greatest sin." He bowed his head.

Respect washed through Eliana. No wonder the One God had chosen Noah to survive. No wonder Shem was such a wonderful person, with a model like this.

Laying a gentle hand upon his arm, she smiled at the older man.

"Not so, *adame*," she told him, bestowing the title for the second time in her life. "'Tis no sin to devote one's life to the ambitions and goals of one's God. I see in you more love for people, including those who would harm you and your purpose, than in all the priestesses who serve the false god Cain. The task has not fallen to you to redeem the world, only to save a remnant of it."

Noah nodded, his head bowed. Still, a troubled expression blurred his features.

"It is my constant hope that some who see our work will turn to the only true God of heaven. If enough do that, He may change His mind."

Eliana shook her head. "I'm afraid your hope is a desperate one, without much chance of success."

"Father! Who have you got down there?" A voice from above interrupted their conversation.

"A visitor from the temple, and a friend of Shem's."

"I'll be right down."

Eliana turned in time to see a man leap from the high deck toward the one upon which she stood. She gasped, sure that he would fall crashing to his death. Instead, he swerved wildly in an arc, swinging from the end of a rope. He swayed back and forth a few times, before he let go with an exhilarated laugh, to land lightly on his feet.

Noah shook his head. "If we ever finish this thing," he told her with a grin, "it will be because of Ham's perseverance, not because of the foolhardiness of that one. I've even come upon him and Devon, the boy who is helping us, wrestling in the mud like a pair of hogs."

Eliana laughed at Noah's expression. "I'll wager that was a sight not to be missed."

The reprobate approached, grinning, and executed a graceful bow. Noah introduced him.

"Eliana de Ashbel, this is Japheth, youngest of my sons."

"A pleasure to make your acquaintance." He straightened, humor still dancing on his face. "De Ashbel? The High Priestess's heir? My brother spoke of meeting you. I am honored, lady."

He bowed again, and when he raised himself upright his eyes searched her face. "What brings you so far from the city? We don't often have guests of such position as yours, you know."

Eliana smiled. She could like this younger brother of Shem's. "I've heard of this great undertaking, and had an urge to see it. Besides," she confessed with a grin, "I've recently learned to pilot a rider, and I needed an excuse for a trip."

Eliana gestured through the entrance toward Arphaxad's rider.

Japheth drew a noisy breath. "You've got one of those little two-passenger vehicles! Could I look at it?"

He rose to the balls of his feet, bouncing up and down, and looked so much like a child excited at the prospect of a long-awaited treat that Eliana couldn't help laughing.

"It's not mine," she told him, "but I'm sure my friend won't mind if you pilot it a short distance. Help yourself."

Japheth's gray eyes, so much like Shem's, lit with pleasure. He bowed once more, a hurried gesture, and then took off toward Arphaxad's rider at a trot.

"He has wanted one, you know." Noah's face lit with paternal pride as he watched his son race down the ramp. "All my sons have urged me to get a landrider. But I have a hard time justifying the expense. In a few short seasons it will be worthless."

Eliana once again felt an odd surge of emotion, unnamed and unidentifiable, flood through her at the veiled reference of things to come.

Noah looked down at her, his eyes suddenly gentle. "I'm sorry, dear lady. I forget sometimes that I speak to those who are not of my faith. Let us continue our tour. This main level will hold our quarters, up toward the front there." He gestured to the end of the ark that faced the house. "We'll also quarter some of the gentler and more fragile beasts here. We expect that the motion of the waves will not be as fierce below the surface, and this level will be under water. As you can see we've already framed all the stalls."

Eliana looked toward the place he indicated, but to her it looked like nothing more than a sea of leafless trees, all straight and evenly placed. At the other end, though, she saw how walls had been built between the posts, forming uniform square alcoves.

Noah pointed toward the rear. "The back wall of

the outer stalls will be curved, for that will be the outside hull of the ark. Our quarters will be a bit bigger.
On this and the second deck we'll have four rows of
stalls, with two aisles. The top deck will have two rows
of stalls only, and larger than these, for the larger animals."

"What about the fierce ones?" Eliana asked, shuddering at the thought of spending any amount of time
closeted with some of the flesh-eaters she'd heard of.

Noah smiled. "My wife has spent a few restless
nights thinking of that. All the stalls will have doors,
some of them will even be a complete enclosure, but I
sincerely hope we don't have to shut any animal in
completely. We trust the One God with our lives, so
would He allow us or any of our charges to be devoured by one of His creatures? I don't think so."

"But how will you feed them all?" For the first time,
Eliana realized just how large an undertaking this
was. There had to be hundreds of different types of
animals, and some of them had never been seen near
Cainlan. "And how will you find them all in the first
place?"

Noah laughed. "Now you sound like Shem. Again, I
trust in the One God. He will feed all of us, and He will
bring them to us. But as my son Ham likes to put it,
we do not expect Him to drop food on our doorstep, or
on our deck as the case may be. We're stockpiling food
in preparation for the time when we'll enter the ark."

"When will that be?"

Eliana held a breath, fearful of the answer, but Noah shook his head.

"Only the One God knows the day. We have a lot to
do on the ark still, but we make more progress each
day. The seasons rush past me like a bird soaring on a
breeze. All too soon we'll be finished."

His voice held an infinite sadness, and his eyes
peered into the distance toward the forest and beyond
that, Cainlan.

Eliana's voice matched his for sadness when she

echoed, "All too soon."

Noah started, looking down at her with a gentleness that caused tears to spring to her eyes. When he spoke he said the last thing she expected.

"I see that you are not a stranger to the One God."

She smiled, using a finger to brush a stray tear from her eyelashes. "I've just met Him, *adame*, though I fear He's more stranger to me than I to Him."

Noah nodded. "That is true even of those who have known Him all our lives. We find His ways odd at times, hard to explain and often harder to bear, but always He is just, and He acts from the great love He has for us."

"For all of us?" She asked the question that had been burning inside her since her offering in the forest. "Even those of us who are of the line of Cain?"

Noah turned to face her. "Cain was His son as well as Seth. And though Cain performed an evil deed, the One God treated him with more mercy than he deserved. Do you know that even though Cain had taken the life of his own brother, the One God protected him, because of His love?"

"And yet that same God will take the lives of all His children." Eliana hesitated to say the words, but they burned inside her.

"Ah, but Cain, even in his lowest moment, continued to acknowledge God. His greatest punishment and torment was not that the ground would be cursed for him, but that he would be sent from the One God's presence. Are these people today His children, when they refuse to acknowledge even His existence? That's what Cain lost for his children—God's presence with them."

"Some of us do acknowledge Him," Eliana answered in a small voice, thinking of Arphaxad and of Girta.

Noah bowed his head, placing a gentle hand upon her shoulder. "I know, child. If I knew the answer to all things I would have no need of a God, for I would be

one. All I can say to you is this—perhaps He has prepared for you the easier way. If you live as His child in
this life, He will catch you up to Him in the next one,
for all eternity."

Looking into the blue eyes, Eliana saw his great
desire to comfort her. His words offered little comfort,
though, for she did not want to die. But neither did
she want to tax him further, so she smiled and
changed the subject.

"What of the animals that run, like the mountain
deer? Won't it be hard on them being shut in a stall?"

"Oh we don't plan to shut them all in at once," Noah told her as he steered her toward an unfinished
side. "The second deck will include an open area where
they, and we, can move a little more freely. And there's
always the aisles, though Midian would not be happy
with animals running up and down the aisles."

They joined together in a chuckle at the idea of a
parade of wild animals trotting around the corridors of
the ark in a controlled sprint. They were still laughing
when the rider pulled up alongside the structure. The
door rose and Japheth gave a whoop of delighted joy.

"This little vehicle flies like the wind!" he shouted
as he leapt from the pilot's seat. "I won't tell you how
fast I had her moving for fear you'll never let me pilot
her again, but I promise you she'll outrun a mountain
cat! Oh, look who I found on the way."

He turned back to the rider to help a figure from
the opening. A brightly printed skirt and dainty san-
daled feet exited first. Japheth pulled the woman from
the vehicle, a pretty girl with dark hair twisted in a
rope hanging over her shoulder and down the front of
her blouse. Japheth draped an arm about her waist.

"This is Abiri, my wife," Japheth called as Noah led
Eliana toward them. "She was bringing our lunch, so I
picked her up along the way. I hope you don't mind."

Eliana shook her head, and Abiri gave Japheth a
playful shove.

"She may not mind, but I most certainly do. Father

Noah, do not *ever* buy one of these things, or you may find yourself with one less son, and I without a husband. He pilots like a wild man of the mountains, veering here and there around the place, dashing between trees and then out again." Abiri grinned at her husband, shoving him again toward the rider. "Get the baskets, you reckless youngling."

Eliana and Noah approached a gap in the exterior wall, and Noah leapt down to the ground with an easy grace. Eliana stood poised on the edge, gripped by a sudden vertigo as she looked toward the ground. It was a long way! Abiri had turned to face the rider, and Noah approached Japheth, who had his back to them rummaging in the storage area behind the seat. Eliana stood still. Did they expect her to jump as Noah had? Surely she could do it, for she was young and he quite an old man, but the thought of leaping toward the ground filled her with dread. Then Ham approached from the west and stood below her.

"Sit down and swing your feet over the edge," he told her. "Good. Now put your arms out and lean down towards me."

"But I can't reach." Eliana tried to keep the panic out of her voice.

"No, but I'll catch you, I promise. If you prefer, you can walk back to the ramp."

He looked up at her, his brown eyes very much like his older brother's at that moment, even given the different color. Shem's gentle smile turned a stranger's face into a familiar one. She stretched her arms toward his and leaned. In the moment before his hands caught her around the waist she tumbled in the air. Then she grabbed his firm shoulders. He lowered her to the ground with a fluid motion so that she was not even jarred, and released her the moment her feet were firm upon the soil. With a sigh of relief, she smiled her thanks up at him, and together they turned toward the others.

Time for the midday meal had come so quickly

Eliana hadn't realized how hungry she was. She pooled her food with that of Noah's family, and together they had an enjoyable meal. Abiri was shyly interested in life at the temple, and asked questions with an engaging smile. Japheth kept up a running dialog on any subject that happened to come up, and so kept the conversation flowing.

When the meal ended, Eliana stood and brushed crumbs from her leggings. "I must get back."

"Must you go so soon?" asked Abiri. "Mother Midian and Timna will be disappointed if they don't get to meet you."

"I'm disappointed too," Eliana told them all, "but my friend who owns the rider will be worried."

"Will you give Abiri a ride back to the house on your way?" asked Japheth. "You can show her how a rider like this is supposed to be driven, and save her the walk at the same time."

"Of course."

The baskets loaded, Eliana stood beside the rider facing Shem's family. She smiled her farewell to his brothers, but when she looked at Noah her smile faded and she fought the tears that threatened to spring to her eyes. He seemed to sense her melancholy and took a step toward her. Placing a hand on each shoulder, he forced her to look up into his face.

"Remember, He is always just, and always loving."

Eliana looked into his blue eyes, then nodded once before she got into the rider. Abiri followed her in, and Eliana flipped the lever that lowered the door. The men stood by while she turned the rider on the worn grass, and Noah raised his hand as she pulled away.

"I've enjoyed meeting you," Abiri told her as the rider glided away from the ark. "I wish Shem was here, so he could convince you to stay for the evening meal."

"When will Shem be back?" Eliana asked, keeping her voice even.

"Not until later. I know he'll be disappointed when he finds he's missed you. He told us all about meeting you that day in the marketplace."

That day in the marketplace. Did he not tell them about their second meeting? And his alliance gift?

"I want to hear what life in the temple is really like," Abiri went on. "I used to live in a city, you know. I came from Enoch. My father crafts and sells pottery there. Japheth's only taken me into Cainlan a few times, and we always have to leave so quickly."

Eliana judged that Abiri was not much older than she, maybe three or four years. A fitting spouse for the fun-loving, childlike Japheth.

"You're from Enoch, and yet you married Japheth."

Abiri was quiet for a moment. "And I'd do it again, even though Father was not happy about it. Mother was, though. Her people were from the same mountains as Father Noah."

They approached the house. Eliana flipped open the door and waited until Abiri stood on the ground, her baskets slung on her arms.

"I'm glad you came, lady," Abiri told her.

"Please call me Eliana, and I'm glad I came, too. I hope to see you again."

"I hope so too. Take care and be safe." Abiri waved as the door descended to snap in place.

Eliana cast one last glance toward the ark. A melancholy feeling settled over her as she filled her eyes with the sight of the structure that would house Shem and his family in safety when the One God's wrath destroyed the only world she knew. With a sigh, she pointed the rider toward Cainlan, and home.

The rider rolled to a stop inside the shed. Eliana opened the door and stepped out, half-expecting Arphaxad to appear and chastise her for staying gone so long. But the shed was empty, save for two temple guards stationed at the entrance.

With a sigh of relief, she waved toward the men

and headed inside the temple. She would not be so lucky when she got to her suite. The time was mid-afternoon, and Girta expected her hours ago. Her nursemaid was certain to be furious.

At the door, she paused to draw a fortifying breath. Then she pushed into the room.

"Girta, I'm back," she shouted toward the bed-chamber.

The woman who stepped into the doorway was not Girta.

"Bitra?" Eliana cocked her head. "What are you do-ing here on your free day?"

The priestess crossed the room with outstretched hands, her normally tanned face pale. A wave of alarm washed through Eliana as she caught sight of Bitra's wide eyes.

"What is it?" she asked, reaching to grasp her hands. "What's wrong?"

Bitra swallowed, then drew a breath. "It's Girta."

Eliana's mouth went dry. "Is she ill?"

"Not ill." Her voice cracked "Girta … she's dead."

A black hole opened up at Eliana's feet. She felt herself tipping toward it, further and further until she was covered up by blessed darkness.

Chapter 12

Jarrell sat at his desk, a mountain of reports before him. On days like this one, he actually missed the life he'd left behind, the life of a farmer. The work had been hard, but rewarding in a different way. And if plowing and weeding and planting had eventually become monotonous, at least he could see the sunshine. He glanced around the crowded office, his desk one of a dozen with identical mountains of paperwork, and stifled a sigh.

The sound of hurried footsteps in the corridor outside the room drew everyone's attention. Jarrell looked up in time to see the red, excited face of Sub-Director Phanom. He'd been attending a general Council meeting this morning. He usually returned from these meetings bored and struggling to stay awake. But today when the fat old man waddled into the room, excitement lit his broad face. He scanned the occupants, and his gaze lit on Jarrell.

"Jarrell, just the man I want to see." His voice boomed through the silence in the room. "I got a new project today, and you're going to be my top analyst."

"Me?" Jarrell stumbled to his feet. His fellow analysts didn't bother to conceal their envious stares.

"Yes you. You're perfect for this job."

Phanom thrust his case into Jarrell's arms. Jarrell took it and followed his immense leader into his private office, all eyes fixed on them as they approached the door of polished wood.

The weight of the case didn't bode well for the assignment. It must be stuffed with parchments. Had Phanom once again agreed to perform work that didn't fall under his jurisdiction? Jarrell swallowed a sigh. Since he'd proven his sharp skills as a statistical analyst, the Human Services studies almost always found their way to his desk. To be published under Phanom's name, of course. Phanom's assistant, an ornamental young woman who had no skills that Jarrell had yet been able to detect, smiled blankly at them as they passed her post. Phanom didn't acknowledge her at all. She was the niece of Councilor Tomsk, the Councilor over Social Action and Phanom's leader.

The large window behind Phanom's cluttered desk faced east, affording him a spectacular view of the mall gardens and a glimpse of the main temple gates. In the distance the mountains stood majestically against the blue sky. Many times Jarrell had stood here while Phanom bent over a document, and dreamed of holding a position that afforded him an office like this.

"Great news!" Phanom exclaimed as he lowered his large body into a chair. "The Council just approved a lottery."

"A lottery." Jarrell repeated the word, surprised. "I thought they voted against a lottery last season."

"They did, but Councilor Limpopo has been doing some research into the project, and he brought it before the Council for a second vote. It was an excellent presentation, excellent." The fat little man rubbed his hands together with glee. "He was proposing, of course, that Economic Resources run the whole thing. I waited until the proper moment, after he had won the Council over, then I explained why it should be handled by Social Action. After all, our very charter states that we will administer all government-mandated programs. Councilor Tomsk was quick to defend me, though Limpopo turned nearly purple with rage. In the end the Council approved the lottery, and us as its administrators!"

Jarrell stood silent. Another governmental program. More paperwork for his already overloaded desk. Why was Phanom so enthusiastic about the project?

"It's all arranged," he said. "The lottery will start in the fall, and we will begin advertising in early summer. Ticklers to grab their interest, then more substantial details that will snare them, and finally we will announce the prizes. They'll be falling all over themselves to purchase chances. The merchants will love it, and the entire economy will benefit."

Jarrell began to get the drift of the program. "The population will focus on the lottery, and the wonderful prizes, of course, and they will pay less attention to other disturbing news, like the reasons behind the formation of this new army."

He voiced the comment as a veiled attempt to gauge Phanom's opinion of the army. Rumors had begun to rumble among the government employees that Caphtor's new army had its roots buried in frightening soil.

"Exactly." Phanom waved a hand. "And there's that threatened ore laborer's dispute. This will become the new focus, and in the meantime the city will prosper with the proceeds." A wide grin split his pudgy face. "I knew you would grasp the situation, Jarrell, that's why I immediately thought of you to design the program. I want you to take charge of everything. The design. The advertising. The selection of the winners. Can you handle it?"

Jarrell was stunned, knocked almost breathless by this evidence of Phanom's trust. This assignment wasn't merely another paperwork project. He was being asked to design something entirely new. Excitement stirred his insides. This could be a huge boost for his career.

He raised his chin and returned Phanom's grin. "I can handle it."

"You must start work immediately." Phanom waved at the heavy case. "Councilor Tomsk will be watching my every move, and yours too."

Phanom stood after being seated almost no time, and ushered Jarrell toward the door with a congratulatory clap on the back. The sudden thought of the work waiting on his desk nearly suffocated him.

He dug in his heels. "I'll need a couple of assistants to help me with the details."

"Of course. Conscript anyone you need. Just see to it that you have a presentation ready for me to give to the Council by the next open session." Phanom clapped him on the back once more before opening his door and giving him a firm shove. The door closed behind him.

Jarrell stood, clutching the case to his chest. This was it, his chance to propel himself into the public eye. No doubt Sub-Director Phanom saw the lottery project as an opportunity to launch his career toward a Council chair, and that wasn't unlikely. If Jarrell could make his boss look good enough to be awarded the next available Councilor's seat, he was certain to be appointed Sub-Director as Phanom's replacement. Forget Roblin and his promises, Jarrell could win a big promotion on his own.

All work had stopped, and a dozen curious gazes were fixed on him. Jarrell grinned and nodded at the surprised assistant, who was accustomed to being ignored. He hurried to his own desk, eager to get started on the biggest project of his career.

Mara stood between Devon and Shem at the top of a rise, staring down a sloped path at the outer city marketplace. Behind them, the last section of forest through which they'd traveled stretched out like a wasteland. Thousands of trees stood barren, stripped of their leaves, the bark falling off their trunks. The aftermath of energy harvesting. They had passed by a harvesting crew on their way to the city, had paused to watch the workers attach probes to the sides of strong, living trunks for the draining process that would turn them into so many brittle twigs. True, the convenience of those household energy cartridges couldn't be denied, but how many trees had been destroyed so she could grind wheat more easily?

Her unease reached deeper than a devastated forest. One day, maybe soon, would the entire earth look like this, lifeless and wasted? And what of the people?

With a shudder, she turned her back on the dead trees and faced forward. At the bottom of the hill the path grew wide and split into two with an island of activity between. Booths and tables, tents and pavilions lined each side of the twin pathways, the variety of colors and patterns a happy assault on her eyes. And so many people. The first time Shem brought her to Cainlan after their marriage, she had been stunned at the sheer numbers, more people than a poor girl from a sleepy mountain village had ever dreamed existed in the entire world. She studied the boy beside her. Judging by his slack jaw, Devon was as dazed by his first glimpse of the city as she had been.

"It's a bit overwhelming, isn't it?"

He gulped, and nodded.

Shem's head turned as his gaze swept the valley. "Before we take off, let's pick a place to meet if we get separated."

Mara cast him a grateful look. He was so logical.

"Where's the weaver's stall?" she asked. "The one

with the fabric imported from Enoch?"

Shem cupped a hand over his eyes to scan the marketplace, and then pointed. "Do you see that pavilion, the one with the green and white stripes?"

Beside her, Devon nodded. She saw it, too, about halfway through the market booths on the right. "That's the first place I wanted to go anyway. Abiri's yearning for a new dress lately, so I promised to look for fabric." She turned to Devon. "You can see that striped canopy from practically anywhere in the market. If we get separated, make your way there and we'll be waiting."

Devon nodded. He really did look frightened. Mara knew how he felt. Even though she had been to the city many times, her heart pounded at the thought of entering that mass of people. The idea of having to wander around down there alone made her stomach queasy.

"Shem's hands are full with the baskets, but I'll just grab his belt, like this." She slipped the fingers of her left hand through the leather around Shem's waist, and then held her free hand toward the boy. "Now it will take a riot to separate us."

Devon grasped her hand and ventured a tentative smile.

Shem started down the path, and they followed along behind. Though it looked like a great distance from above, they came to the weaver's stall quickly and without losing one another in the crowd. The green and white pavilion spread out above several rows of tables piled high with many lengths of fabric. Beneath, the crowd thinned to a few individuals walking slowly through the tables. They fingered the fabrics and chatted with each other and with the merchant, a short man with a red sweaty face and a toothy smile.

Once they stepped out of the crowd Mara dropped both Shem's belt and Devon's hand and plunged in amidst the piles of cloth. Here, she was at home. She smiled a greeting at the merchant and began testing the make of his wares. Shem followed her for a minute, shuffling his feet in the dust and looking bored.

She turned on him. "Don't you have some errands to run?"

He looked startled. "I did want to check on the price of grain from last season."

Waving a hand, she shooed him away. "Go. I'll not have you hovering about, making me feel like I have to hurry."

Relief flooded Shem's face, and she hid a smile.

"Devon, do you want to come with me?"

They both looked at the boy, whose indecision showed plainly on his face as his eyes moved from one to the other. Clearly the idea of watching her shop held no interest for a child his age, but he didn't enjoy an easy companionship with Shem. Since Shem spent most of his time in the field and Devon at the ark, they hadn't grown close. Not like he had grown close to Japheth. Or to her.

In the weeks since Devon's arrival, that wrenching desire for a child of her own had eased as she lavished her affections on this love-starved boy. That he obviously loved her in return filled her heart with joy.

"Mara will need someone to carry her purchases," Shem suggested.

Devon's forehead cleared. "I can do that."

"Good man." Shem clapped him on the shoulder. "I won't be long."

Mara called after him. "If we're not here we'll be in one of the booths that way." She pointed, and he sauntered off, whistling a quiet tune.

She turned back to the piles of fabric, and finally found a soft linen she knew Abiri would love. The price was outrageously high, and she set about haggling with the merchant. Here, her youth in the mountain village served her well. Her bargaining skills had been honed on wayfaring merchants, notorious tight-fists who traveled with their wares into the mountains to make a profit on those they considered ignorant villag-

ers. There she'd learned to squeeze a bargain out of a
rock.

She piled her purchase in Devon's arms and strode
with purpose into the next booth, this one under a
white tent with the sides open to catch the infrequent
breeze. The tables here were not as wide but more
numerous, and lined with every kind of metal
cookware imaginable. For a while Devon followed Mara
from table to table, but cookware couldn't hold a boy's
attention for long. She hid a smile when he wandered
toward the front of the tent to stare at the passing
crowd.

She picked up a large pot and turned it over in her
hands. Mother Midian's soup pot was wearing thin.
After the waters came – her stomach fluttered at the
thought – utensils like this would be impossible to
find. The sturdy metal of this one would be just the
thing to take—

"Balek!"

Devon's shout pierced the low hum of the marketplace. Mara turned, and her heart leaped into her
throat when she saw the boy rush into the crowd outside the booth. His sudden movement sent two metal
pans clanking nosily to the ground. He continued to
shout, so loudly that everyone in the vicinity turned to
look.

As did the man at whom he shouted. Mara's breath
stopped as she looked at the one who turned toward
the boy. Dark, unruly hair framed a face with a short
nose that was a mirror's reflection of Devon's. The
young man's eyes widened, and then he shoved his
way through the crowd. He threw his arms around
Devon and lifted the boy from the ground.

"Little brother, you're alive! I thought I'd seen the
last of you."

Pulse pounding, Mara rushed toward the two as
the stranger deposited Devon back on his feet.

Devon turned a glowing smile on Mara. "This is my
brother."

Joy lit the boy's face, and Mara's heart twisted. Was this the brother for whom he had gone searching? That search had brought Devon into her life. What would the end of the search bring?

Shem stepped from the crowd into the shade of the pavilion. He crossed to Mara, a question on his face.

"It appears that Devon has found his brother." Her voice sounded flat, even to her.

Shem reached for her hand, his gray eyes looking down into hers. As always, her husband knew when she battled fear.

The stranger turned a wide smile their way. "I am Balek de Diarmid."

Shem returned the greeting, "Shem de Noah. My wife, Mara."

Mara nodded, and Balek, after giving them a curious look at Shem's choice of word, bowed in her direction. Then he turned to Devon.

"Amazing that we should see each other here, of all places. What are you doing here? Where have you been all this time?"

His voice betrayed the same mountain burr as his younger brother, only more pronounced.

"I'm working with them." Devon nodding to indicate Shem. "But I thought you were going to the mines."

Balek spread his hands wide. "That's a tale best told elsewhere."

"You two should take some time to catch up on family news," Shem said. "We're here for the day. We can meet somewhere later, maybe for the evening meal?"

Mara turned a sharp look on her husband. She certainly did not want to send Devon off with this stranger, brother or no. But he squeezed her hand.

Balek nodded, enthusiastic. "I have the day free. How 'bout it, Dev? Let me show you the city, and we can talk."

Devon turned shining eyes her way, and her heart

leapt into her throat. He looked so happy, happier than he had looked in the many weeks since he arrived at their farm. Fear squeezed her throat, but she forced a smile and nodded her approval of the plan.

As Shem and Balek arranged a time and place to meet later, she reached into a deep pocket on the inside of her wrap and extracted a small leather pouch. This she pressed into Devon's hand. He turned a startled gaze on her.

"In case you see anything you want to buy," she whispered.

"Come on, Dev." Balek's voice boomed above the noise of the marketplace crowd. "Is this your first trip to Cainlan? Then I've got a lot to show you."

Balek nodded farewell. Devon slipped a finger through his brother's belt, as Mara had done with Shem's. They disappeared into the crowd.

She buried her face in Shem's shirt, fighting an urge to cry.

Mara spent the day fighting panic. What if Devon didn't come back? What if he decided he would rather live with his brother? Of course he wanted to be with his own family. But she had come to think of Devon as *her* child, and losing him would be devastating.

Shem was unusually attentive all day. Normally, she would have been thrilled, but she spent the day distracted. Would Devon leave her waiting at their meeting place and disappear forever?

The day crept slowly until finally Mara entered the Twilight Tavern, her hands clutched around Shem's guiding arm. The moment Mara's gaze fell on Devon the dark foreboding that had plagued her all day lifted. The boy waved at them from across the room, his smile bright enough to light the dark interior of the tavern as well as her heart.

Shem led her across the floor and Balek rose, ges-

turing for her to take his seat. Now that he had indeed
kept his appointment to return his brother to her, Mara was able to smile at him.

"I hope we're not late." Shem slid into the chair
next to her and signaled for the server.

"No, we were early," Balek assured him. "We spent
the whole day sightseeing, so we didn't have much of a
chance to catch up on news."

"Then I hope we're not too early!" Shem laughed.

"We were finished, and starving."

Upon cue, the server brought goblets of fresh juice
and a tray of fruit and cheeses, with a crispy loaf and
several different spreads. He set the feast before them
and left.

Mara eyed the young man across the table. "Balek,
have you been in the city long?"

"Just two weeks. I came to join the army."

"Ah." Shem nodded. "I've heard a lot of young men
are eager for the life of a soldier."

Balek laughed. "I don't know about the life of a
soldier, but the money sure was tempting."

"Good pay, I've heard. And how do you like it?"

He shrugged. "I'd tell you if I knew. I didn't make
it."

"Then you don't have a job?" Mara asked.

"I'm going back to the silver mine tomorrow. I hope
they'll take me back."

She tried not to look toward Devon. Would he follow his brother to the mines, as he'd initially planned?

"Was the army full by the time you got here?"
Shem asked.

"Nah. I made it past the first cut, actually went into the initial training period. But I knew pretty early I
wouldn't make it. You can't believe how hard they
worked us. I'm a blacksmith's son, but I've never
worked that hard in all my life. By the second day I
was so exhausted I was slipping and falling with every
step. I wasn't surprised when the captain handed me
my trainee's pay and told me to leave."

"At least they paid you," Mara said.

"That's right. Army pay's better then miner pay, but miner pay is a lot better than the village black-smith's son can make. Any job is better than none."

Mara decided she liked this young man. His face was thin, like Devon's. He had the same short, up-turned nose, the same thin brown lips. He wore his hair longer, pulled back in the fashion of today, but she could see it was as thick and wavy as the younger boy's.

"Hey, Dev." Balek nudged his younger brother with an elbow. "You plan on giving your gift today?"

Devon fixed a shy smile on Mara. From inside his tunic he brought forth a woolen packet the size of his hand. He held it across the table to Mara, who stared at it in surprise.

"For me?"

Touched, she took the packet. It was light, and she carefully unfolded the thick wool. Three pairs of eyes fixed on her, Balek's knowing, Shem's curious, and Devon's eager. As the last fold opened, she caught her breath in surprise. It was a piece of silver formed into the likeness of a ship, with double sails and a curved prow. From the bottom to the top of the mast was no longer than her smallest finger. At the very top of the mast was a loop of silver, where a thin strip of leather might hold the charm around her neck.

She gasped. "Devon, it's beautiful! I've never had anything this fine in my life. But it's far too expensive for me."

"No it wasn't." Devon's earnest eyes grew round. "Balek took me to see a friend who forms silver from the mine he works in. He let me have it for a good price. As soon as I saw it I thought of you. And be-sides, I want you to have it."

Sincerity gleamed in the child's eyes, and his obvi-ous desire to please her went straight to her heart.

Tears brushed at her lashes as she refolded the wool around the little ship and placed it inside her tunic. "Thank you, Devon. It's the most beautiful gift I've ever received."

Devon grinned, and silence fell around the table for a moment.

Balek wondered aloud, "What's happened to that server? My cup's empty."

"Mine, too." Mara looked at Devon. "Would you please run over to the counter and tell him we'd like more juice?

Devon nodded and left the table, making his way toward the back of the tavern to find the server. As soon as he was out of earshot Mara turned to Balek.

"Will you tell us about Devon? He's so quiet we've discovered almost nothing. I knew he had a brother, and we've known he was from the mountains by his speech, but little else."

Shem rested an arm across the back of her chair. "He showed up on our farm, bedraggled and alone with a tale of looking for you. Since then he's not said a word about his past."

"I'm not surprised. Devon's had a hard time. When he left home he was running for his life."

"For his life?" Mara shook her head, uncomprehending. "Who would want to hurt a boy that young?"

"Our parents."

Shock froze Mara's tongue.

"The temple's Sacrificial Beneficiary Program?" Shem asked, and Balek nodded. "I wondered if it might be something like that."

"What kind of a family would..." Mara began, then stopped as she realized she spoke of Balek's parents.

"It's all right." His fingers trailed the rim of his mug. "I'll tell you what kind. Poor ones, who have no regard for their children except as laborers or moneymakers. Father had me to help in the shop, and they have my sister to work in the house. Devon was a mouth to feed, that's all. I overheard them discussing it one night, deciding how to spend the credits they would receive when they gave him to the SBP. So I told him." He turned his head to find Devon across the room. "I should have gone with him, but I couldn't leave my sister alone. I scavenged as much food as I could and pointed him in the direction of the mines, told him I'd join him when I could. I figured he'd have a better chance there than with us."

"I had no idea people could be like that." Mara's voice shook. Imagine, having the gift of a child and selling him for money.

"A lot are," Shem told her. "Jarrell worked with the families for a while, helping them receive their credits and the like. He used to tell me how much it bothered him whenever he had to see the children before they went."

Mara followed Balek's gaze and saw Devon, still standing at the counter, finally attract the attention of the server.

She spoke quickly. "Before he comes back, I want you to know that he has a home with us. We'll see that he has clothes and food and shelter for as long as he wants to stay."

Beside her, Shem nodded.

Balek clasped his hands on the table and speared her with a direct gaze. "Devon's happy now, I can see that. He talks about you, ma'am, all the time. You should have seen him searching the shops for the perfect gift."

He looked down at his hands, and when he raised his head pity shone in his eyes. Mara's heart screeched to a halt. "But he told me he wants to come live with me and work the mines."

A lump formed in her throat around which no words could pass. Beneath the table, she groped for Shem's hand.

"Do you think the mines are a good place for a boy his age?" How Shem managed to speak in such a calm tone she didn't know.

Balek lifted a shoulder. "There are younger ones. They don't actually go down in the tunnels, but they're

paid a good wage for work top-side." He leaned forward. "Look, I've tried to talk him out of it all day. I
know he's better off with a family like you. But he's
determined. Even if you convince him to go home with
you today, he'll leave soon on his own."

A dark pit of grief lay yawning before her. As Balek
spoke, Mara felt herself slip over the edge. A child had
finally come, and had stolen her heart. And now he
would leave, and break it.

Chapter 13

Eliana lay on her bed, her face to the wall. Girta's death pressed against her like a shroud. Why had she not seen the signs of her increasingly weak heart? How easily she tired, how her breath often came hard and heavy after even mild exertion?

The sound of the door in the outer room closing alerted her that someone had arrived. She didn't bother to turn. Maybe they would go away.

"Lady, you need to get up." Bitra bustled into the room and hurried around the bed to stand in Eliana's line of sight. "The high priestess is on her way here."

Once, that news would have sent Eliana scurrying to tidy the room while her heart pounded, but no more. What could her mother do to her? A little more misery in her life wouldn't even be noticed.

"Eliana!" Bitra leaned down and shouted into her face. "Get up. You look terrible, like you haven't bathed in days."

"I haven't." Without Girta here to help her, what was the point?

She allowed herself to be lifted to a sitting position on the edge of the bed and returned Bitra's worried stare.

"No time to get properly dressed." The priestess disappeared into the dressing room and returned with a silky robe. "Here. Put this on. We'll just tell her you're not feeling well."

Eliana did as instructed, and then sat quietly at the dressing table as Bitra yanked a comb through her tangled locks. Her reflection in the mirror stared back at her, dull-eyed and pale. She did look awful. No wonder Caphtor hadn't visited in over a week.

Well, at least that was one bright spot in the gloom surrounding her.

"There." Bitra pulled the mass of her hair back and clasped it with a comb. "That looks a little better. I don't think we have time to apply color and kohl, though. But if you've been ill, you wouldn't be wearing that anyway."

She whirled and raced to the bed to jerk the coverings into a semblance of order. Eliana watched. She ought to get up and help, but what did it matter if Liadan saw her bedclothes in a shambles? Girta was dead. Nothing mattered anymore.

A loud rap sounded on the outer door, followed immediately by the squeak of hinges.

"Daughter!" Liadan made the word sound like a summons. "Where are you?"

Bitra's eyes went round as goose eggs.

With a sigh, Eliana rose from the bench. "I'm here."

She headed toward the doorway, but in the next moment her mother stepped into the bedroom. Liadan's presence flooded the room like a tidal wave. Her gaze circled, slid over Bitra, and then came to rest on Eliana. Dainty nostrils flared.

"You look like a wraith."

"Thank you" Eliana tinged her voice with sarcasm.

Liadan's eyebrows arched, and no wonder. Eliana had never spoken to her mother in any tone other than hushed respect. But now she didn't care what Liadan thought. What if she became angry? What would she do – hit her? Eliana had grown used to that.

Liadan looked at Bitra, and jerked her head toward the door. In an unusual display of meekness, Bitra left the room without a word.

Liadan strode to the window, then turned to face her. "I'm told you haven't left these rooms in more than a week. Are you ill?" Without waiting for an answer, she swept ahead. "Don't tell me you're grieving over the loss of your servant."

A band squeezed Eliana's throat. Girta had not been a servant. She was the only mother Eliana ever knew, far more than this cold woman standing before her.

She wrapped her arms around her middle and hugged. "She was my nursemaid, and I loved her."

"You're no longer a child to need a nursemaid. You're an adult, consort to the governor. And in less than a year you'll enter the priesthood and begin training. You don't have time to wallow in grief over a nursemaid."

Anger sparked deep inside. How like Liadan to disregard her feelings so quickly. "I'm not even sure I want to be a priestess."

Liadan's brows inched upward toward her hairline. Mouth dry, Eliana swallowed. She hadn't planned to say that, but once the words were out, she wasn't sorry. She fought the urge to fidget beneath the high priestess's penetrating gaze. And yet she felt none of the fear she'd suffered in the past. Caphtor had shown her there were worse things in life than the wrath of her mother.

Finally Liadan responded. "The law states that succession must remain in the direct bloodline of the current High Priestess. There is no escape for that."

Her matter-of-fact tone stunned Eliana. No angry

raving? No verbal barbs about ignorant daughters? The calm, almost calculating tone gave Eliana the shred of courage to voice a question.

"But what if there is no direct heir?"

Liadan shrugged. "The writings of Jaline address that. The title would be thrown into contention, and a lottery would take place among the senior priestesses to select another. But that has never happened. It is the duty of each and every Primogenitor to produce an heir within five years of assuming the title of priestess at age twenty-one."

Eliana couldn't believe they were having this conversation, and that her mother wasn't shouting. "There's never been a time when an heir was not produced?"

Liadan shook her head. "Never. The writings state clearly that at the twenty-fifth celebration of the birth of the Primogenitor, if an heir has not been produced, then she is put to death and her blood used as sacrifice to seek a blessing on the ceremony to select the next candidate. So far no one has volunteered to be the first."

Death. She hadn't considered that, though knowing the temple's preoccupation with the subject she wondered why it hadn't occurred to her. Was her desire to avoid the priesthood stronger than her fear of death?

One God, is that what You want of me?

A thought occurred to her. "You yourself were close to the deadline when I was born, weren't you?"

Liadan nodded. "You were born the season before my time was over. And thank the god you were female. Had you been male we both would have been put to death, and my mother would have had another successor. As it was, not only was I designated as future High Priestess, but I was awarded the title a full twelve years early when Theresina was killed."

Eliana nodded. She had no memory of her grandmother Theresina, but knew that she had been killed in an unfortunate accident with a sacrifice — she'd slipped on the blood and fell on the sacrificial knife before the entire city.

Liadan's eyes narrowed. "Surely this decision isn't a result of your nursemaid's death."

No, her struggles had begun long before Girta's death. Even before she pledged her allegiance to the One God. And they went beyond her distaste for blood, though that was a compelling factor. "I've watched you when you're performing your priestly duties. I've seen the way you control the crowd, the way they worship you with their eyes while you're in front of them. You have a...presence. You collect the respect of a crowd, and use it like some kind of power. Caphtor can do the same thing." Eliana allowed a sad smile to show on her lips. "I cannot."

That explanation wasn't the entire truth, but perhaps it would provide just the right amount of flattery that Liadan would not question the reason further. Judging by the slow, pleased smile that spread across her mother's face, she had judged accurately.

"You are correct about the presence." She purred with pleasure. "It is an art, a gift if you will, that is granted to only a few. There have been High Priestesses in the past who have not had this gift, and during their terms the temple has suffered a decline in popularity and a loss of power. Had I been Jaline I would have had an entirely different way of choosing the head of our religion." She sighed, apparently not at all disturbed to have committed near sacreledge by questioning her ancestress. "You're correct in your self appraisal as well. I've never seen you exhibit this gift." She raised her chin. "But you are not without hope. There is a way for you to comply with the laws of Jaline and yet not become High Priestess."

Eliana drew in a breath. A flicker of hope ignited the darkness inside her. "How is that?"

"Produce an heir before your twenty-fifth birthday. Of course it must be a female heir. You may then release your claim on the title in favor of the child. The writings indicate that as the current holder of the title, I would remain High Priestess until the child reaches the legal age to assume the role. This would extend my term by another forty years, more than triple the original time." Her gaze became distant, and her smile deepened. "I would be quite satisfied for this to happen. You may not aspire to this position, but I am loathe to release it."

"And if I fail to produce an heir in time?"

Liadan shrugged. "Your choice is to serve Cain by becoming his living priestess or his dead sacrifice."

A shudder shook Eliana's body. Though her thoughts had centered on death since Girta's heart failed her, she had not seriously considered her own. Death was a way out of the misery of her current situation, but to die as a sacrifice to Cain? "I don't wish that."

Liadan's lips twisted her smile tight. "In that, at least, we are agreed. I suggest you re-think your decision. You could still become a priestess, but produce the necessary heir within the required time and release the title to her. Then you have the livelihood of a priestess, but you aren't required to perform any but the simplest ceremonies. And I shall retain the title until your child is forty."

She gave a decisive bob of her head, apparently well pleased with the solution. Eliana was less certain. Could she consign a child to her fate?

Of course, if Shem's father was correct, there was an entirely different fate awaiting her and any child she had.

Liadan crossed the room to Eliana's dressing table to finger each of the jars and pots on its surface as she spoke. "Is there any truth to the rumors that you already carry a child within you? Have you bled?"

Eliana gave a bitter laugh. Caphtor had asked the same thing the last time he visited these rooms. "I have. The rumors are unfounded, and spread by people who have nothing better to do with their time."

Liadan's brow creased in question. "And yet, there is some truth to what's being said. Your manner has changed since your alliance, even before the death of your nursemaid."

She said nothing, only shrugged and shifted her gaze to the wall.

"Has your union been…satisfying?"

Eliana was hesitant to discuss the subject with her, but her confidante had died, and she didn't feel free to discuss Caphtor with Bitra, who, after all, was a foreign priestess.

"No, it hasn't." She faced Liadan, untied the sash of her robe, and let the garment fall. She caught a glimpse of herself in the mirror as she revealed her shame to her mother. Fading bruises marred the smooth skin of her arms. She slipped a shoulder out of her nightdress to show another ugly bruise on her collarbone.

"I have more," she said, "but you probably don't want to see them."

Liadan's face paled as she scanned the bruises, and then flushed with rage. "How dare he injure a favorite of the god? Governor or not, I'll have him whipped."

"No." Eliana spoke quickly. Caphtor would be furious if he knew she had spoken with her mother about him. She picked up her robe and hid the evidence of Caphtor's rage. "You yourself told me how important it is for the temple and the government to work together in these uncertain times. Besides." She lowered her gaze to the ground. "He'll be angry if he discovers you know."

Liadan's nostrils flared. "I care not one whit for his anger. And neither should you." Her spine straightened, and her voice assumed a tone of authority. "You are the Primogenitor, the daughter of the High Priestess. If he treats you roughly, it is because you allow it. You're far too meek, daughter, which is another reason you are not suited for my role."

Eliana opened her mouth to argue, but closed it again. Liadan was right. She *was* too meek, and no doubt that's why Caphtor felt free to abuse her.

The high priestess paced across the room. "This explains so much. He would never dare to raise a hand against me openly, so he searched for a subtle way to strike at me, and at the temple I serve." Rage flared in her eyes as she turned on Eliana. "Hurting you is his cowardly way of striking at me. By abusing you, he expresses his contempt for me and for the god. I will not have it." Her dainty chin thrust forward. "I will put a stop to this immediately."

When she turned toward the exit, a wave of panic rose to choke Eliana. She raced forward to stand between Liadan and the door. "No. Please, I beg of you. He will kill me if you say anything."

The glittering eyes narrowed to slits. "He would not dare."

Why, oh why had she let down her guard enough to show her bruises? "Let me talk to him." She swallowed the fear that threatened to shut her throat. "I'll threaten to tell you if he doesn't stop. Please."

A speculative expression crept over Liadan's face as she held Eliana's gaze. When she gave an almost imperceptible nod, Eliana nearly wilted with relief.

"I've encountered men like Caphtor. They like the power their physical strength gives them. But that is not true power. You must stand up to him, Eliana. Show him that you have *true* power. You have the regard of the god and of the people."

"But so does Caphtor. The people love him."

"Exactly." Liadan's head jerked in a nod. "And he loves the power that gives him. So that is a tool you can use. What do you think would happen if you made it known that the people's darling governor treated the Primogenitor, the god's chosen, roughly?"

Eliana stared at her, a glimmer of hope flickering to life. The people would rise up against Caphtor if they knew. Liadan was right. This was a tool she could use. If, that is, she could muster the courage to wield it.

She would. Somehow, she would find a way.

Her back straightened and she awarded her mother the first real smile she'd given anyone since Girta's death more than a week before. "That's the perfect solution. Thank you. I wish I'd spoken to you weeks ago."

Liadan preened at the compliment. "Remember, daughter, that you know nothing about power. And I know everything."

She swept out of the room, her robes billowing behind her. Eliana stared after her. Her mother's parting words were certainly true. She knew nothing about power. But she'd just had her first lesson. And no one could deny her instructor was, indeed, a master.

Now, if she could only manage to face Caphtor without trembling.

The sun had dipped below the horizon when Eliana made her way down the corridor atop the wide wall that surrounded the inner city of Cainlan. Behind her lay the temple, and ahead of her loomed the main government building, where Caphtor kept his office. A pair of temple guardsmen trailed behind. To her right stretched the barren field that gave Cainlan's guards visibility to anyone who approached the city. In the distance lay the wall that surrounded the Eternal Fire. A flame leaped into the sky, a bright place in the darkness.

She entered the government building, and her nerves tightened into a knot in her stomach. What would Caphtor do when he saw her? The presence of the guards provided only a measure of safety, though they'd been ordered by the High Priestess to protect her from harm from *any* source. Would they act against the Governor if they saw him hurting her? She hoped she wouldn't have to find out.

The hallways were mostly deserted, the workers long since gone home to their suppers and beds. Even Melita's desk outside Caphtor's office sat vacant. A dim yellow light shone around the edges of the door. Not the white light of an energy powered lamp. Caphtor was working by candlelight?

Eliana stopped before the door, the guards a few steps behind her, and raised her hand to give a timid rap. She paused. Tension battled fear in her stomach. He hated to be disturbed when he was working. He might become angry.

A shudder of fear made her hand tremble. She pushed the feeling aside. That's why she was here, to stop being a slave to fear. The speech she'd prepared resonated in her mind. She'd tell him his bullying days were over, that she refused to be the object of his aggression one more night. She was the Primogenitor, the daughter of the High Priestess. Her spine stiffened as she assumed a pose she'd seen her mother take often. In this case, Liadan was the perfect model to imitate.

She tightened her fist and rapped on the polished wood, then immediately opened the door and entered the office.

The room was aglow in candlelight, and it took a moment to refocus her eyes. When she did, her gaze was drawn to Caphtor's surprised face. He lay on a padded bench along the far wall. His bare chest glowed warmly in the flickering light.

He was not alone.

Warm light reflected off of white-blonde hair. Pale limbs were wrapped around his body. Silky skin, with no sign of bruises.

Melida.

When Caphtor's assistant caught sight of Eliana, her initial expression was one of shock. But that was quickly replaced by a look of gloating, a superior smirk that made Eliana want to slap her face.

Caphtor jerked away from his assistant and off the bench. His face held a touch of shamefaced alarm that gave Eliana a boost of confidence. As he scrambled to don his tunic, she turned to the guards.

"Wait here, please. I won't be long." She stepped inside the office and swung the door shut behind her.

Melita rose from the bench in a slow, lazy manner, completely unembarrassed by her nakedness. She awarded Eliana another smirk as she sauntered around the room, picking up scattered articles of clothing. Eliana ignored her.

Shouldn't she feel something other than the wild desire to laugh? After all, she'd just found her consort in the arms of another woman, and a particularly annoying one at that. Her lack of jealousy proved what she'd known all along – she had no feelings for Caphtor at all except fear, and that was about to end.

With his tunic in place, Caphtor regained his poise. Anger darkened the eyes that fixed on her. "What is the meaning of this? You have no business here."

Eliana's body almost reacted with an instinctive shiver, but she stopped it. Her head high, she steeled her tone to match her mother's.

"What? No business in the office of my consort?" She allowed a cold smile and dropped the sarcasm. "Actually, I do have business to discuss with you. But I will not do it here." She slid her gaze to Melita. "Not in front of the servants."

The woman's mouth dropped open, and poison filled her eyes. "If you think—"

Caphtor stopped her mid-sentence with a raised hand. He eyed Eliana with a speculative glance. Was that a touch of grudging respect on his face?

"You'll excuse us long enough to, ah, cover ourselves?"

Eliana made of show of letting her gaze sweep him from bare feet to his head. He looked ridiculous standing there with his white legs sticking out beneath his tunic, which barely brushed his thighs. Though she much preferred to have this discussion with Caphtor at a disadvantage, she'd like even better to do it in her own rooms, where she felt comfortable. And without Melita.

"I'll do more than that. I'll give you time to finish your *business* meeting." She gave a generous nod. "I'll expect you at my rooms within the hour."

Caphtor's jaw dropped. She'd never dared to give him an ultimatum, and it felt good. Was this what power felt like?

She whirled and opened the door, then marched away, not bothering to close it. The guardsmen fell in step behind her as she headed toward the temple.

Chapter 14

The bell had not chimed the passing of an hour before Caphtor arrived. Eliana sat in a chair in the main room of their apartment, her demeanor calm, when the door opened.

"You can leave now." His growl was directed at the temple guardsmen stationed outside her door.

"Please don't." Her request caused Caphtor's head to whip toward her. She caught the eye of the guard behind him. "I prefer that you stay nearby." She almost added, *within shouting distance,* but didn't have the nerve to defy the governor that openly.

Caphtor's jaw tightened, but he closed the door without further comment. The sight of the barely suppressed fury on his face would have made her quiver with fear yesterday. But her conversation with Liadan had given her a touch of bravado. With a guard stationed right outside the door, he wouldn't risk creating a scene. At least, she hoped not.

He chose a chair opposite hers, one that faced her directly as an inquisitor would face a common thief. Eliana maintained a stone-faced expression, neither pleasant nor offended. Anything she said would only make her appear shrewish, so she waited for him to begin the conversation. He did, though not before a long and uncomfortable silence.

"I expect you want to discuss the incident tonight." His voice was remarkably void of emotion.

"Not particularly."

Surprise flashed onto his face. Displaying an uncharacteristic nervous gesture he smoothed his black hair back from his forehead. Good. Let him suffer from nerves, wondering what she would do. Though relationships outside of a formal alliance were not forbidden, keeping them secret was frowned upon. In a progressive society such as Cainlan's, open relationships were common, though always disclosed. But an alliance that had been formed with legitimacy of heirs was different. The partners were expected to focus only on one another until an heir had been produced. The scandal of an undisclosed sexual relationship between the governor and his assistant this early in his alliance with the Primogenitor would certainly become a source of gossip, and Caphtor would hate being the center of a scandal.

"I suppose you're wondering why I didn't tell you about Melita before now."

Eliana chose her words deliberately. "I do wonder why you didn't *disclose* your relationship."

The barb did not go unnoticed. Menace flashed in his eyes, and she willed her pulse to slow. His seat was far enough away that she could scream if he tried to …

Enough of this. She was done with cowering.

"Before we discuss your undisclosed relationship, allow me to inform you of a change in our relationship. From this moment forward, you will not hurt me, ever again. I'm tired of bearing the brunt of your abuse."

One eyebrow cocked upward. "Oh?"

Though the contempt on his handsome face made her insides quake, she fought to keep her expression calm. "If you hurt me again, I will create the biggest scandal Cainlan has ever seen. I'll file for a dissolution of our alliance on the grounds of brutality, and let the entire city know how you enjoy taking your pleasure."

His lip curled. "Do you really think anyone would take your word over mine?"

"Oh, I think I'll be believed. The High Priestess has pledged to support me." She lifted her sleeve to display the latest angry bruise. "And I'll take my clothes off and parade across the temple dais during the morning ceremony if I have to."

Her threat hit its mark. Blood drained from his face as, apparently, he realized she had already spoken with Liadan. Or perhaps he realized the repercussions of such an act. He actually squirmed in the chair. She did not look away until he jerked a nod of acknowledgement.

A thrill of victory zipped through her, but she forced herself to remain outwardly calm. One minor success, but she had a bigger agenda tonight. And the best way to approach this, she'd decided, was to blurt it out at once. There might be some advantage in the shock value.

"This morning I informed the High Priestess that I don't wish to enter the priesthood, or to inherit her position."

"What?" Caphtor exploded out of his chair and stood looming over her, his face purple with rage.

She couldn't help it. She shrank into the cushions.

"You can't do that." He ground out the words through gritted teeth. "You'll spoil everything."

Her instinctive fear dissolved, replaced with curiousity as his words registered. "What do you mean, spoil everything?"

Hands tightening and releasing repeatedly, he paced the length of the room. "Tradition demands I father your heir. I could have chosen an alliance with Liadan but..." He shuddered. "I chose you."

Because I'm easier to bully. Eliana maintained her placid expression and nodded for him to continue.

"But the heir is always a female. Firstborn male infants of the Primogenitor are disposed of." Caphtor's voice lowered, but at the same time his eyes blazed with intensity. "I want to change that. You agreed to legitimacy of heirs in our alliance. I plan to enforce that agreement. If we have a son first, I will not allow him to be put to death."

Battling emotions assaulted her. What Caphtor said was true. Tradition dictated that the Primogenitor's first *living* child must be a female. She had steadfastly refused to consider the possibility of her firstborn being male. She would not, *could* not put a son to death. Had Caphtor devised a way to have a son without that worry? A sudden longing filled her. Might she one day truly hold her own babe in her arms?

She spoke sternly, lest Caphtor detect her thoughts and twist them to use against her. "But this is law, ancient and holy. I must produce the next High Priestess, and she must be my first living issue. You know that."

"That's the way it is now," Caphtor agreed. "But other laws, laws of government, mandate that I have rights to any children, because I have no other heirs. You agreed to the terms of our alliance."

Eliana saw the direction of Caphtor's logic. "You intend to contest the religious laws, claiming that the governmental laws will dominate."

"Exactly. If you give birth to a male, the matter will be brought before the Council." Caphtor smiled. "The Council is full of men who have devoted their lives to the furthering of the government. And to me. Not one of them is a genuine worshiper of the god."

"But if you are successful in defying one religious tradition, others will fall into question. The temple could lose influence in the city."

It was becoming more and more difficult to school the hope from her voice. What did she care if the people lost their regard for a religion she found increasingly repugnant?

"Not all influence, and not right away." Conviction blazed on his face. "But the temple holds too much power. If Cainlan is to prosper it must shed its cloak of old-fashioned values and rules. It has only been in the past generation that we've advanced ahead of rival cities in some aspects of progress. We must push past the boundaries set by the temple, and secure our place as the uncontested ruler of the world."

Eliana's mind reeled. This was a complete overthrow of the balance of power her mother held so dear. "But why destroy the temple's power? The temple and the government have always ruled equally." She leaned forward, arms planted on her knees. "What purpose will it serve to take away Liadan's power?"

Caphtor's eyelids narrowed, and he watched Eliana for a full four breaths. She waited, sensing that his answer would reveal something of utmost importance.

His lips tightened. "Liadan wields more power than you know as yet." He avoided her eyes as he avoided a complete answer to her question. "Power that will someday be yours, if we are unable to produce a male heir before a female one." His eyes glittered. "I have watched you. You're not close to your mother, nor do you hold the same convictions."

Frustration knotted Eliana's hands into fists. What was he talking about? What could he possibly gain by the temple's loss of prestige?

And what if their first child were a girl? Would he destroy the position to which his daughter would one day lay claim?

The answer dawned, and his plan became clear. "If we produce a son, you will contest the child's death on the grounds of governmental law, and overthrow the temple. If we produce a girl, she will become Primogenitor when I am confirmed as High Priestess, but she will also be your legal heir. If you can control her, you'll effectively control the temple's influence over the city." The depth of his plan became clear, and she had to admit a grudging admiration. "Either way you will be in a position of control over both the government and the temple fairly soon."

Caphtor smiled. "You have a good mind."

"But how did you expect to persuade me?" The question fascinated more than offended her. "I am, after all, heir to one of the two most powerful positions in all Cainlan. I might not be willing to relinquish any of that power. My mother certainly would not be, and you have no reason to believe I'll be any different."

"But I do." His manner was open, almost eager, the first time ever that he'd conversed with her on anything approaching a peer level. "You don't possess the fiendish drive of your mother. I think in time you'll come to see that religion must take its proper place in our city. It's an important one, but not a law-setting one. Cainlan will benefit from my vision for her future." The look on his face became sly. "Add the fact that you were raised by a nursemaid who does not worship the god at all, and some of that attitude would naturally have been passed along to you."

Eliana gasped at his last sentence. Caphtor chuckled, cocking his head to one side. "Things like that cannot go unnoticed to someone diligent in investigation. Have no fear. I'm not a worshiper myself, though it does benefit me to play the part of a loyal devotee."

Eliana tightened her lips. Girta was beyond Caphtor's reach, but she was not. Nor was Arphaxad. Though the governor may not be aware of her own conversion to the service of the One God, it would not take long to discover her accomplice within the temple. Arphaxad might be in danger. She stilled her racing thoughts. It was time to regain control of this conversation.

"I assume that your plan, at least where I am concerned, has not gone as you expected." She adopted a dry voice, and was pleased to see discomfiture flash across his features. He lowered himself once again into his seat.

They stared at one another in silence, her thoughts whirling. Caphtor was right about one thing — she was not averse to changing the role of the temple since she cared very little for the worship of a murderer. And she thought him wise not to strip all authority from the religious leader. The people of Cainlan would revolt and plunge the city into civil war, a dangerous thing at any time. A city with that sort of strife would be ripe for invasion. And if his plan went well...

A child! A tiny baby of my own to love and cherish.

Caphtor had been honest with her. The realization left her slightly amazed. If even a whisper of his plans were made known he would be unable to leave these rooms in safety. If one of the city's religious zealots didn't get him, Liadan's agents most assuredly would.

He broke the silence. "So you see why you can't relinquish your position as Primogenitor."

Eliana permitted herself a tiny smile. "You're quite right. My mother informed me that I am not within my rights to *surrender* the title. But I can *release* my title in favor of a female heir, provided she is born before the twenty-fifth anniversary of my birth. So as you can see, it also benefits me to produce a child as quickly as possible."

"I don't believe you'd do that."

Her gaze dropped away. Guilt had plagued her since the conversation. Could she honestly give birth to a child and place her in the same heartrending position that she faced?

She raised her chin. "I'd have forty years to influence my daughter. Who knows? By the time she reaches her majority, she will have no more taste for the position than I do."

"Forty years?" Caphtor's brows bunched to form a furry black line. "Not an ideal solution. Why don't you want the title?"

Honesty required honesty. Eliana sighed. "I will not sacrifice people to a dead and unresponsive idol. Human lives, even when willingly given, are more valuable than that."

For a moment she considered telling him about the One God. If she were to be completely honest she *would* tell him. But something stopped her. Her confession was weapon enough jeopardize her life, as was his. That was enough ammunition to entrust to each other's hands for one night.

Besides, at the thought of the One God, a flicker of anger stirred. She'd pledged her life to Him, and what had it gotten her? Far more misery than she'd had before.

Caphtor was watching her with an odd expression. "I agree, but my definition of value is probably not the same as yours."

Again, his secretive smile held something back. What wasn't he telling her?

She let it go. She'd gotten more from him tonight than she'd expected. Best not push for more. "If we have a son first, that would solve your dilemma."

Caphtor nodded. "In the short term. You would still have to become a priestess, though certainly changes in the temple would come about faster once the government becomes the primary law-setter. And my understanding is that you are not required to perform human sacrifices until you're a senior priestess, so we would have time to bring about those changes." His expression transformed into a leer. "In order to have a child of either gender, we have to ... cooperate."

The idea left her cold. But did she have an option to offer? Either way, she would have a child. A boy would live, and change the government of the city in the short term. A girl would live, and she would have years to shower her with love and instill the values Girta had passed on to her. That girl would one day wield the power to change the city in the long term.

And if Shem's father is right, none of this matters

anyway.

An image of Noah's ark loomed large in her mind's eye. Would the One God really destroy even innocents? Even a child? Surely not. Perhaps a child of hers, raised in the love Girta had lavished on her, might change more than just the destiny of Cainlan.

A vivid memory from this evening flashed into Eliana's mind. She hardened her gaze. "There is one condition I insist upon."

"And that is?" Caphtor asked.

"Melita must go." Caphtor's head jerked upward, defiant, but she pressed on. "And not only from my presence, either. How will we overcome our—" She searched for a word. "—*difficulties* if you're invested elsewhere? I insist on complete fidelity, at least until we've gotten an heir."

A struggle played across his fluid features. Eliana tightened her lips. She would not budge on this.

After a moment's pause, Caphtor dipped his head. "Truly, I've grown tired of her. But Melita won't go quietly. Her silence may have to be bought."

Little did she care how he arranged the woman's departure, so long as she was gone. She replied as sweetly as she could, "Surely no price is too great, if it means the fulfillment of your goals."

He gave her a sharp look, his dark eyes intense. "Agreed. My sacrifice will be the forfeiture of my relationship. And yours? Do you agree not to relinquish your title in the short term, and to become a priestess at the appointed time?"

Eliana hesitated. She felt uncomfortable compromising her beliefs, even though she was in the throes of a minor feud with her chosen deity.

"I won't sacrifice a person," she insisted, her expression firm.

"But you will fulfill your duties up until the moment that is required, if ever? And you will work with me to accomplish what we've outlined here tonight?"

Caphtor watched her, his expression expectant.

Eliana lowered her gaze, her thoughts warring. Did she have another option? Yes, she did. She could send him away now, and reveal the entire plot to Liadan. Throw herself fully under the protection of the High Priestess and the temple. But at what cost? Liadan would relish the opportunity for an open confrontation. Cainlan would revolt. Caphtor might still hold enough sway over the Council and the people to wrest a measure of power from the temple. In the end, she'd either lose her life or be forced to search for another to father her heir.

Gray eyes hovered in her mind, and heat crept into her face. She pushed the thought away before it could form. Shem's duty was to his wife, and she would not interfere with that.

Meeting Caphtor's eye, she nodded.

"Fine." He picked up his satchel and stood, ready to return to his office. "I'll see to my end of the bargain immediately, this very night. And since we'll be—" He speared her with a heated gaze. "—cooperating, we need to be under one roof. I'll make another sacrifice and move in here." He gestured toward the second bedroom, which had not been occupied since they moved in. "I'll need a personal attendant. Will you see to it?"

Eliana also stood, and was at once sorry. He towered over her so that she felt like an impotent dwarf beside him. Still, she forced herself to remain outwardly calm, even though she felt like a child craning her neck to look up at an adult.

"I'll take care of it."

He left the room. In the moments after the door closed behind him, discomfort twisted her stomach.

Why am I uncomfortable with this arrangement? I have no ties of loyalty to the false god or to his temple. I don't even think he is a god, just a dead man who was horrible during his life.

Had she just betrayed her mother? Her discomfort increased when she thought of Liadan. It would not be easy for the High Priestess to accept any decrease in status or prestige.

Striding to the doorway that led to her bedroom, Eliana brushed the thought from her mind. Liadan would survive. It was time for Eliana to be concerned for herself. No one else would.

Then she smiled at a new thought. Caphtor wanted her to find an attendant for him. She'd enjoy that. She intended to hire the sturdiest, plainest, most competent middle-aged woman she could find. Just let him try to complain about it.

Chapter 15

Jarrell sat at a table in an almost deserted tavern, parchments spread out in disarray before him. There were only two other patrons, and the bored barkeep dozed noisily in a corner beside the serving counter. Jarrell had chosen this pub for its lamentable yet useful lack of regular customers.

The parchments piled on the table represented his work on Cainlan's lottery. He tried to organize all the lists into a logical order, first marketing, then selection, then awards. The mess represented a full week's work, and he was dismally aware that he'd barely begun. And that the beginning hadn't been a good one. The knowledge that his future rested on his performance of this project weighed heavily on his mind.

He'd struggled with these lists for several days before finally admitting to himself that he needed help. His peers in Social Action would be more hindrance than help. Since the day he'd received this assignment, they'd taken every opportunity to let him know that they resented his luck. Roblin wasn't much better. Each time Jarrell approached him he'd been enthusiastic about helping, but when it came time to commit an hour to the project, he couldn't scratch one out of his day.

In frustration Jarrell had finally fallen upon an idea. The temple had experience conducting a lottery. And he just happened to know a priestess.

The tavern's door opened. Bitra entered and approached his table, eying his parchments with skepticism. He rose and executed the half-bow greeting of friends. Her lips were painted and wet, as if stained by a freshly bitten redberry. The golden chain draped around her neck and waist ended in metallic stars that jingled as she moved. Jarrell let his gaze sweep over her in appreciation, and she returned his grin.

"Thank you for agreeing to meet with me." He gestured for her to take the seat opposite his. "I could use your help." He indicated the pile of parchment between them.

"Your note didn't say much." Bitra squinted to read the words scrawled upside down before her. "Only that you had some questions about a lottery."

"First, would you like something?"

"Enochian wine, if they have it."

Jarrell left the table and approached the counter. He returned in a short while with two large goblets.

Bitra sipped from hers. "So what is all this?" She nodded to indicate his lists.

"This," Jarrell said in a disgusted voice, "is the project that will ensure my professional future, be it bright or dismal. And it's looking pretty gloomy."

"What kind of project?"

"A lottery."

"Ah." Bitra nodded. "I've heard rumors that Cainlan was planning to begin a lottery. And you've been given the task of designing it?"

Jarrell nodded miserably. "I haven't a clue where to

start. My 'assistants' would all as soon see me fail. Roblin agreed to help with the marketing of the thing-"

Bitra snorted, her opinion of Roblin's help obvious.

Jarrell awarded her a mock-scowl. "—but he's been so busy he barely has time to nod if we pass in the corridor."

"What makes you think I can help?" By her grin Jarrell knew she was pleased he'd sent for her.

"I wanted to ask you about Enoch's lottery, and the lotteries at the temple you've seen."

Bitra nodded. "All right. I don't know how much help I'm going to be, but I'll tell you what I know. First things first. What's the purpose of this lottery?"

"Purpose?" repeated Jarrell.

"Yes, purpose. What's it for? Who is going to gain the most, and how much do they expect to gain?"

"I, uh," Jarrell stuttered, "I think the Council means for..." His voice trailed off into silence. He hadn't anticipated having to confide.

"What's the matter?" she asked.

"You can't tell anyone this."

"Alright."

He leaned across the table and lowered his voice. "The people of Cainlan are unsatisfied. Prices here are high, taxes are higher, energy is unaffordable yet necessary. The only thing low are wages, and there is unrest lately because of perceived unfairness in wage distribution. And the reasons behind the formation of this army have everyone whispering."

"So the primary purpose for the lottery is to distract the people from their complaints?"

Jarrell nodded.

Her expression cleared. "That makes sense. From what I understand, Enoch's reasons were much the same."

"Oh?" Jarrell was surprised. "And did it work?"

"For a while." She sipped from her goblet. "But measures like these can only quiet the grumbles temporarily. It's like a crying baby—you can show him his thumb and that will keep him quiet for a moment, but before long he will realize he's still hungry. In Enoch the grumbling has begun again."

"There's more. I think the Council has an idea that the city will profit from the program."

She lifted her shoulders. "It probably will. I don't know the numbers, of course, but in Enoch part of the renewed grumbling comes from the fact that a few smart have-nothings figured out that the value of the prizes wasn't even close to the amount collected by voucher sales. Someone is making a lot of profit on Enoch's lottery, and it's not the lottery winners."

"Can you tell me how it works?" Jarrell removed a writing implement from his tunic and flipped one of his lists over in search of a clean patch of parchment.

"Pretty simple, really. The cost of the voucher is kept small, so people feel as though they can afford it. Of course, no one buys only one voucher, because they want more chances at the prizes."

Jarrell jotted a note. "How do the prizes work?"

"A big prize is given away each season. That's always a large currency prize. The amount changes season by season, and I think it's determined by how many vouchers were sold or the previous drawing."

"That would make sense." Jarrell scribbled furiously.

They drained their goblets while they talked. A plan began to take shape, and Jarrell's pen flew across the parchment, trying to keep up with the ideas. Excitement stirred in the base of his skull. This thing might really work after all.

"I have a confession," she said after another silence.

"What's that?" Jarrell asked, his eyes on his work.

"I agreed to help you so I could spend time with you. Alone."

He looked up. A blush colored her cheeks, and released an answering flutter in his stomach.

"I'm honored." He dipped his head in a bow without releasing her gaze. "I requested your help because I wanted to enjoy you alone, too."

Her smile heralded the return of the charming dimple. "Really?"

"Really." He leaned again over the table, and glanced over his shoulder to ensure the waiter could not overhear. "The food here is lousy, but I know someplace better. Why don't we go get something to eat?"

"I'd love that." A playful smile hovered around her lips.

Jarrell began gathering his parchments into a neat stack. This lottery had finally brought him good luck

Shem lay on his makeshift cot on the ground. His stomach and legs lay sheltered by the ramp leading into the ark, leaving his chest and head exposed to the night air. It was his turn for nighttime guard duty. He shifted on the hard ground and spared an envious thought for Ham and Japheth warm in their beds.

Above him, a million pinpricks of light glittered in the black sky. He should have allowed Mara to spend the night here with him. She wanted to, but an uneasy feeling had niggled at the thought. Abiri and Timna stayed home in their beds alone when Japheth and Ham took their turn. Mara should do the same. The whole reason to post a guard was in anticipation of danger. It wasn't right to take the women into a potentially dangerous situation.

He clasped his hands behind his head. Of course, Abiri and Timna hadn't just lost a child. In the days since they left Devon in Cainlan with his brother, Mara walked with a slower step. Her shoulders slumped in a way Shem had never seen from his steady, reliable wife. Would it have hurt to let her come with him just this once?

A clod of dirt beneath his shoulder pushed uncomfortably through his pallet. He scooted sideways to find more even ground.

The real reason he insisted on Mara staying at home this night was a selfish one. He needed time alone, time to think. Time to talk to the One God.

"Remove these thoughts, Almighty One."

His whisper, directed toward the heavens, hushed an enthusiastic chorus of crickets that had taken up residence beneath one of the support structures.

Since the day he returned from the city to discover that Eliana had been here, he couldn't rid his mind of thoughts of her. He'd missed her by just a few hours. Why had she come? Was it merely to see the ark, as she told Father? Or was there another reason?

"I love Mara. You know I do."

Love had not been the basis for their union. When Shem came of age to take a wife, love was not considered in the decision. Raised here on this farm, he was seldom exposed to Father's distant relatives. When he attained the age to take a wife, it was to a village of strangers he traveled. How could he fall in love during a two-week journey made for the sole purpose of choosing a spouse? By virtue of her age and kinship, Mara had been the perfect choice.

The right choice, too. She complemented him, a suitable helpmeet, with her steady devotion and her dedication to excellence in accomplishing any task she undertook. Her quiet ways and easy manner enabled her to slip into his family as though she had always been a part of them. The love that grew between Shem and Mara was not a sudden flash of emotion, destined to fade with familiarity. No, their love grew stronger with every day that passed, every task they accomplished together.

"I don't understand why thoughts of *her* plague me," he whispered.

Why did the One God remain silent? Did He not care? Shem writhed on his pallet. Of course He cared. All Shem's life had been spent in the shadow of a visible reminder of God's care for Father and his family. If only He would speak to Shem, as He spoke to Father and Grandfather. If only He would explain the ache Shem felt when thoughts of Eliana haunted him. If only He would take that ache away.

Father's words, delivered long ago after a minor boyhood infraction and the resulting punishment, resounded in his head. "The One God does not expect us to be perfect. He knows we aren't capable. He only wants us to give our imperfections over to Him. Then He can use them for His glory."

Shem closed his eyes. "I don't know if these thoughts are imperfections or not, but I gladly hand them to you. And I promise I will never dishonor Mara, or the vow I made to You when I took her as my wife."

An unnatural sound interrupted his prayer. He looked up to see a line of riders approaching the ark, coming straight across the fields and carving a destructive path through his carefully tended crops. None were heading toward the house. They were all heading for the ark. At this time of night that could only mean one thing, and it wasn't good. He jumped to his feet and ran to the large bell mounted on a high post. With a metal rod, he struck the bell as hard as he could, over and over. The convoy of riders drew up behind him, but he kept on, ignoring the shouts of the approaching men.

Then he was grabbed from behind, his arms pinned to his sides while someone jerked the rod out of his hand and threw it aside. But Shem saw what he hoped for – a light from Japheth's window on the western end of the house. His alarm had been heard.

Shem was spun around and found that he was the center of attention in a group of a dozen men. Some held torches, others energy-operated lanterns, so there was enough light to see their faces. He recognized a few daytime visitors to the ark, and those he did not recognize wore the same hard expressions. The smell of intoxicants on the breath of the one who held him was sour and overpowering. Shem turned his head in an attempt to get a breath of untainted air.

"Wha' was 'at fer?" asked a slurred voice in his ears. "Ya callin' for help?"

Shem didn't reply, but struggled to escape the man's grip. He was strong. The onlookers laughed at Shem's efforts, and he saw several tilting jugs and bottles to their mouths.

"Ain't nobody kin help you, but they kin come anyway. They cain't stop what we're gonna do," said someone on his right.

"And that is?" Shem turned his head toward the voice.

"We're gonna teach your crazy old papa what a real disaster is all about." The sneer came from the man who held him.

Shem twisted to the left and jerked forward. He broke free and whirled to face his would-be attacker. But the man tilted his head back and laughed, a deep guffaw from a belly as full of spite and poison as his voice.

"Keep him away from that bell," warned someone in the crowd.

"He ain't got nobody to call worth nuthin'." The man in the front spat on the ground, his glare glinting in the torchlight.

"Well, here comes somebody."

The men all turned toward the house. Samson galloped toward them, carrying double. A third figure, Shem couldn't tell who, followed at a run. His brothers and father had gotten ready in a hurry. Relief washed over Shem, but the feeling was quickly crushed. The four of them would not be much use against a dozen men bent on destruction.

The crowd's mumble grew loud as Samson approached. A ripple of expectation and excitement emanated from them. Father and Ham slid off the horse's bare back before he came to a stop.

Father stepped toward Shem, the torchlight reflecting yellow in the white hair flying wildly around his head. But there was nothing wild about his manner, his voice. When he spoke Shem was amazed that anyone could be so calm.

"Friends, we welcome you to our farm." His gentle voice carried to the back of the crowd. "You've come to see the handiwork of the One God, the true Creator of the earth, and I welcome you on His behalf."

The crowd stood silent a moment, then someone in the back laughed. The insulting sound was quickly joined by the others. Ham's hands clenched into fists, though his face remained impassive.

Father raised his hands, and the laughter quieted. "Let me tell you the tale of this magnificent construction, how I was given its design—"

"We've heard that, old man," cut in the unofficial leader, the drunken one who had pinned Shem's arms to his sides.

He turned his attention on Father, and for the moment Shem was ignored. He took the opportunity to step to his father's side, just as a panting Japheth ran into the circle of light.

"Then you've come back to ask questions," Father responded.

"You're crazy, old man. So crazy you're dangerous, and we've come to make sure you don't hurt anybody with your craziness."

Japheth, his breath coming in heaves, took a menacing step forward. Father did not turn but gestured behind his back for his sons not to interfere.

"Often the ways of our God are hard to comprehend. To some they might seem crazy, but I have lived a lifetime of service to Him and I can tell you—"

"We don't wanna hear what you can tell us," shouted someone from the crowd, and many roared agreement.

"Then what do you want?" Ham's shout carried over their voices. "Wasn't cracking the spine support enough?"

"We wanna teach you a lesson," said the leader. "There ain't no god tellin' you what to do, and you're gonna admit that."

Noah shook his head. "My friends, there is nothing you can do, nothing, to convince me of that. I've heard His voice too many times, seen His hand in my life and the lives of others. The harder you try to convince me that He does not exist, the more convinced I will become."

"Yeah, well let's see how convinced you are in a minute."

He gestured toward Shem and his brothers, and the crowd surged forward, dividing and coming around them from all sides. Once again Shem found his arms pinned to his side. Then someone grabbed his hand and twisted it up toward the middle of his back, jerking as he did, and pain shot through Shem's shoulder. He struggled once, but his captor twisted again, and he subsided to avoid his arm being broken. Looking around he saw that Ham and Japheth were in similar situations, though Japheth's captor was having a hard time dodging some vicious backward kicks. Someone punched Japheth in the stomach. Shem winced, and Japheth stopped his struggle, gasping.

No one touched Noah. He watched, his forehead a map of concern, and turned again to the mob's leader.

"I must warn you that we are children of the One God. What you do to us, He sees. The pain we feel, He also feels."

"Well, I hope he's watching now, 'cause he's really gonna like what we do next."

The man grabbed a torch from one of his band and moved toward the ark. Many of the mob moved with him, laughing, and then roaring, their voices filling the night with derision. Shem watched with blooming horror as several approached from the parked riders carrying liquid containers. The contents splashed onto the sides of the ark. The scent of flammable oil stung his nostrils.

"Friends," Father called out again, and this time his voice held an edge. "Please listen to my warnings. You are not hurting me or my family by your actions. But you are attacking the handiwork of the One God. He has already expressed His displeasure with this generation. Take care that you do not anger Him further."

The men laughed and continued to douse the sides of the ark as far up as they could with oil. The empty containers were thrown to the side. As one, the group turned to their leader, waiting for a signal. He twisted his neck to look behind him, his eyes haughty and cruel as they pierced Father's. Shem could not see his father's face, but he knew by the stiffness in his back that the old man returned the glare. The leader laughed once, throwing back his head and letting his voice explode into the night. Then he took a step toward the ark, the torch held high.

The ark was instantly engulfed with the brightest glow Shem had ever seen. His stomach clenched in horror as his eyes slammed shut against the glare. Father's lifetime of work, in flames. When he opened them he had to squint through narrowed eyelids, so bright was the fire upon the ark.

But wait. This brightness wasn't the glow of fire. It was a white light, whiter than the brightest sunlight, harsher and more pure than any bonfire. Figures moved in the whiteness, shining figures with silver armor. As his eyes grew accustomed to the light Shem made out people, mighty warriors dressed for battle, their shields shining in the light. Or maybe their shields shed the light, or maybe it came from their faces, for Shem had a hard time looking directly at any of them.

His captor released him, but Shem hardly noticed. Everywhere he looked the most incredible beings he had ever seen stood between the mob and the ark. A few brandished long spears, more of them swords. Shem couldn't begin to count their number, for it was almost impossible to look at them, but a multitude formed a protective line from one end of the ark to the other.

Everyone froze. Laughter died in men's throats. Shem's senses were so full of the shining warriors that he seemed to hear a mighty chorus of voices raised in battle song. The sound flooded his mind until he was aware of nothing else. The group of once-hostile men, now a terrified rabble, turned toward their riders and fled. If they shouted their fear, Shem could not hear their cries. He heard only the song of the host of heaven as they proclaimed their victory over the worldly forces they had come to defeat.

As suddenly as it began, the light went out, and the host disappeared. Dazed, Shem turned to find the riders gone, and he and his family alone before the ark.

Father turned to face his sons, his eyes wide with the wonder of what they had just seen. A glance at Ham and Japheth showed the same. But more than that, an intensity lit Father's gaze that Shem had never seen. A smile, victorious and mighty, spread over the old man's face while his eyes blazed.

"Our Father God will not be defied." His voice rang in the night, full of suppressed joy and righteous justice.

Shem sank to his knees. "Praise to the True God of Heaven." His whisper came from a heart overflowing with awe.

And yet, in a deep, hidden recess of his soul, an unanswered question cried out to be heard.

But what of Jarrell...and Eliana?

Part Two

Judgment of the One God

Chapter 16

Five Years Later

Jarrell paused outside his apartment door to compose himself. He must shed this foul mood. Bitra would be inside, cooking one of her favorite Enochian dishes in his tiny kitchen. He didn't want to spoil her free day and special dinner with grumbling. He shifted his package and pushed open the door.

Bitra rushed into the common room. "I thought you'd never get here."

The tender kiss she placed on his cheek sent a thrill coursing down his spine. She pulled back and looked into his eyes. "What's wrong?"

The woman was too astute for her own good. He thrust the flowers into her hands.

"Nothing's wrong. I brought these to thank you for

cooking my evening meal."

"They're lovely." She buried her nose in the bundle of sweet-smelling blossoms and inhaled. "Thank you. Now sit down and tell me why you've got such a long face."

Jarrell didn't bother to hide a grimace as he sat.

"Here." He pulled a document out of his jerkin and thrust it toward her. "Read for yourself."

Bitra dropped onto the divan beside him and tucked her bare feet up under her legs. She scanned the document with eyes that grew wider as she got toward the end.

"Roblin has been named sub-director of Energy Generation?" She looked up, disbelief etched on her face. "Isn't that a huge jump for someone in his position?"

"Four levels." Jarrell failed to keep the bitterness out of his voice. "I don't know that it's ever been done before."

"Who is this Chapra? The one taking his place."

"No idea. No one has ever heard of him." Jarrell's hands clenched into fists. "That's my position, you know. Roblin always said he'd stand up for me when the time came. I knew something was wrong the past few weeks. He's grown distant. The other day we passed in a corridor, and he barely acknowledged me. Like I was no more than a spot on the rug."

"Roblin is an idiot," Bitra said.

The pronouncement brought a delighted laugh from Jarrell. He grabbed her by the waist and pulled her into his lap. Oh, how he would miss her when she returned home to Enoch. The day of her departure loomed in the near future, a far greater disaster than Roblin's promotion.

Jarrell had first mentioned the possibility of her leaving the priesthood last year, and had been gently but firmly rebuffed. In Enoch, being a Priestess was a rare privilege, even more so than here in Cainlan where worship of the god was more common. Families of priestesses were given special allowances, including energy credits which were far more expensive in Enoch than in Cainlan. Jarrell understood why Bitra couldn't give up such an esteemed profession, but he still felt hurt by her choice.

She snuggled against his shoulder. "I can't tell you how good it feels to be free of the temple, even if only for a few hours."

"Oh? Is something wrong?"

She didn't answer at first. When she did, her lips moved against the soft skin of his neck. "I think I need to take a sabbatical. The longer I serve, the more disillusioned I become. If I had known all the things I'd learn here, I would never have come to Cainlan."

Jarrell tightened his arms around her. She'd said that more than once lately, and he responded with his usual comment. "Then you wouldn't have met me."

"That's the only reason I'm glad I came."

"Besides, would you have learned the same things in Enoch? Surely the worship of Cain is not so different from here, for all this is the source. The tricks are the same."

Bitra nodded. "That's what bothers me, the tricks. I used to really think they were signs from the god."

"As does everyone not associated with the temple," Jarrell told her.

"Not everyone." She plucked at a loose thread on his breeches.

Jarrell studied her profile. "What do you mean?"

"If a god named Cain exists, why do we have to use tricks to bless an alliance, or select a sacrifice? Why doesn't he do these things himself? And why does he allow his temple be filled with people who are totally self-centered, concerned for nothing but their own self-gratification and tricking the public as much as they can?"

"You sound like you don't believe in him either," he said quietly.

Bitra went very still. After a moment she pulled

away and sat cross-legged on the cushion beside him, her dark eyes wide.

"You know what, Jarrell? I don't. I haven't for several seasons now."

"Then why don't you quit?" he asked.

"And do what?"

He didn't hesitate. "Stay with me. I'll take care of you here. Or we can move to Enoch and open a shop of some sort. Or buy a farm. I've experience being a farmer."

Her eyes filled with sadness. Tears welled up and spilled over the lids, sliding slowly down her face and disappearing into the dark hair.

"I've worshiped Cain since I was a child," she said softly. "I went with my father to the sacrifices, and was terrified and exhilarated that one day I, too, might be given in sacrifice to the great god. And I was, in a way. I have sacrificed my life to his service, I promised to give myself to him forever. And now I realize I made a promise to nothing, to a statue with no spirit within it." Her voice lowered until he could barely hear her. "I miss my god."

That single sentence sparked a longing within Jarrell's own breast, unlooked for and unwanted. He, too, had worshiped a God since childhood. He was also estranged from that God, though not due to His nonexistence. While Bitra had been betrayed by her faith, Jarrell had betrayed his God.

He pushed the thought from his mind. Now was not the time to think about that.

"You don't seem surprised," Bitra said. "Denying the existence of the god these days is practically confessing to a death sentence. I expected a bigger reaction."

He shrugged. "I'll act shocked if you want, but the truth is I have always wondered how an intelligent woman like you could believe in the existence of Cain to begin with. I suppose childhood faiths are hard to put behind you."

She turned on him, giving him a shocked look. "You don't believe in him either."

"Never have."

"But you go to all the services, participate in the worship ceremonies. Why?"

"You said it a moment ago. If I don't I might as well stand up on the temple stairs and announce that I wish to be executed. Not to mention the fact that I would have lost my job a long time ago."

Bitra nodded, and the silence descended again. She slid beneath his arm, her head resting on his shoulder in a quietly intimate way that made him deeply glad he'd contacted her that day to help him with the lottery.

Thoughts of the lottery darkened his mood yet again. He'd put so much hope into that project, and to what end? Cainlan's lottery was a huge success. Money poured into the city treasury, far more than the Council originally expected. And who received credit? Phanom, that's who. Oh, he'd fattened Jarrell's pay as a result, but had the promised promotion materialized? No. Jarrell still sat behind the same analyst desk. Only a very few knew that the design and implementation had been his.

He pushed dark thoughts away. The lottery had brought him Bitra, and that was reward far beyond anything he'd expected.

"So what brought all this on today? Did something happen, or did you just get tired after so many days of service?"

Bitra sighed. "It's Hanae. Since becoming Senior Priestess last season she's been increasingly withdrawn. Lately she's begun to snap at me for no reason, and then flounce off without a word. Even when she does apologize she doesn't offer any explanation for her behavior."

"You had another argument today?"

She nodded. "I mentioned to Hanae that we should consider logging where we send all the SBP candidates who aren't selected for sacrifice, so we can at least tell the parents who come asking. She rounded on me, shouting that I had no idea what I was talking about, and I'd better keep my mouth shut." Bitra shook her head. "She stomped out of the room and was gone before I could even answer her."

"What do you suppose she was so upset about?"

Bitra frowned. "I don't know, but I can tell you one thing. She seemed more frightened than angry, and Hanae isn't normally afraid of anything."

"That doesn't make sense. Why would she be afraid to help keep parents more informed?" Jarrell could think of several reasons why that was not a good idea, but none of them should cause fear.

"I don't know," Bitra answered, "but I intend to find out. And soon. I'll become a Senior in another few weeks, and I don't want the same thing to happen to me."

Jarrell pulled her even closer, giving her a cuddle. "I don't want to talk about that."

Bitra was quiet. After she'd been a Senior Priestess for a single season she would be sent back to Enoch, to begin her service there in her own temple. That meant in just a double handful of weeks she would be leaving Cainlan. Unless Jarrell could convince her to stay.

"Something else disturbing happened today." Her voice acknowledged that she had followed his thoughts and wanted to change the subject. "Eliana's blood arrived."

Jarrell stirred, still uncomfortable discussing that private female function, though Bitra exhibited no embarrassment and spoke of it freely. Especially in the past year, and especially in regards to the Primogenitor.

"Not good news," he said.

"Not at all. It's been years since her alliance, and she's still slim as a virgin."

Jarrell tightened his hold. When she told him the

fate of a Primogenitor who failed to produce a female heir by the twenty-fifth anniversary of her birth, he'd been horrified. To think of the lovely young woman put to death for lack of a daughter was further proof of this religion's barbarism.

"Hanae told me, before she got angry with me that is, that some of the Senior Priestesses are hoping she'll fail. They say they don't want to serve under someone who is so obviously a tool of the governor's."

Jarrell sensed Bitra's discomfort with the vicious gossip, for she truly liked Eliana. Jarrell didn't have occasion to see her often, but could never hear news of Eliana without thinking of Shem. His friend had stopped asking about her, but Jarrell made a point to mention her name occasionally just to watch the reaction. It was always the same, even after so many years. Hunger would shadow his friend's face, and he would drink in news of her like a dying man gasps for air. Jarrell wondered if anyone else knew about his friend's deep fascination with the Primogenitor, especially Shem himself.

"Let us hope, for Eliana's sake, that she and Caphtor can produce an heir soon. It must be terrible living with something like that looming over your head."

Bitra agreed with a nod. Jarrell tightened his arm about her again. He ached to offer her comfort, and he was prepared to give her that in abundance, for as long as he had her here.

Shem scooted the container of grain toward the back wall, lining it up neatly with several dozen others just like it. He turned to survey the stacks that surrounded him, mentally tallying the numbers of crates and barrels. Not enough, but a start. Another good harvest later this season and they would finally make some real progress toward the provisioning. But this grain wouldn't keep forever, even wax-sealed as it was. If only the waters would come soon, before it all spoiled.

He jerked his shoulders with a start, realizing what he wished for. Images flashed into his mind, bringing the accustomed feelings of guilt with them; Jarrell, and Amibelak the vegetable merchant, Tomolin the animal shop owner. One other came to mind, but that one he quickly pushed away. Too much guilt was associated with that mental image, so much that he'd become expert at denying himself that particular pain.

Still, personal feelings aside, the ark was very close to being completed. The outside was sealed now and probably watertight, though they planned to coat it once more with the sticky but effective sealant found in the haybark tree during harvest times. The remaining work was all inside—building the walls that subdivided the interior into stalls and quarters, the fences that marked off runs and pens. Father was convinced that the flood would hold off until they were completely finished, but that would not be long. Then the waters would come with frightening swiftness.

Shem stood in the storage section below the main deck, completely sealed but for a single trap door above him. He'd been stockpiling for a full season now, and had finally convinced Father that they should send for provisions unavailable in the region around Cainlan. Some of the vine vegetables, for instance, that prospered in the eastern mountains, and also some of the more exotic fruits that animals from other areas of the world were accustomed to. The shipments had started arriving.

He glanced toward a crate in the far corner, one he himself had painstakingly filled and stored, experiencing a surge of satisfaction at the sight. It was full of pouches, all individually sealed and safely watertight, containing as many different kinds of seeds as he had been able to find during many seasons of searching. When the waters had done their work and left the

earth, and when his family had found a land to settle
in, he would begin his task. Father may be acting under a directive to save a remnant of animals and men
for the new earth; he would concentrate on what he
knew better than anyone—plants.

His insides twisted as he spied the lettering on the
surface of a barrel. Devon's markings. The boy had
surprised all but Mara by returning to the farm as often as he could, helping with the ark and sharing news
with what had developed into a canny wit none of
them had seen that first night when he'd showed up,
dirty and starving.

That was the same day he'd first met Eliana. Guilt
seeped into his gut and rested there, a hot, heavy
weight

There. He'd said her name in his mind. Shem sat
down upon the barrel he had just placed, looking
gloomily up at the light that swung from its peg on the
ceiling. He tasted the guilt, welcomed it in a perverse,
self-punishing sort of way. Long ago he'd stopped trying to analyze that guilt. He'd never done anything to
deserve it, had never once acted upon any of the wild
thoughts that used to occur to him, had refused even
to dwell upon them. Yet the guilt persisted, especially
when he thought of Mara at the same time, as was inevitable.

He let the guilt wash over him, and then stubbornly thought of her again. Eliana. How was she? Whenever he was in the city he could not keep himself away
from the temple, hoping for a glimpse of her. Glimpses
came far too infrequently, and when he did see her it
was with a mixture of joy and anguish. She was still
lovely. Her features had matured from childish pretti-
ness into true beauty. Had she changed inside? Had
she become infected by the pagan life that surrounded
her?

Jarrell was irritatingly uninformative. He could tell
only of her social actions, her public image. He knew
nothing of the real Eliana, the person behind the Pri-

mogenitor. Jarrell spoke of the Governor's consort.

Shem's teeth set as he thought of Caphtor. Guilt scooted to the side to make way for another uncomfortable emotion. Caphtor was a stunningly handsome man, large and powerful, muscular beyond belief. They made a striking pair on the occasions he'd seen them together. Shem refused to think of their relationship, for those thoughts invariably led to mental pictures he preferred not to see. And behind all the gnawing, agonizing feelings was the thought that Eliana must be happy. Hadn't she renewed their alliance two years ago?

"Shem." A deep voice called from above, echoing in the belly of the ark like the voice of God might echo in the mountains when He spoke with Grandfather Methuselah.

But it was only Ham from the first deck. Shem looked up and saw his head silhouetted in the square hole in the ceiling. He brushed aside his thoughts, though the feelings lingered, and stood.

"Timna is here with the noonday meal," his brother said.

"I'll be right there." Shem grabbed the last barrel, hefting it upward to rest upon the one he'd just placed. He took the light and headed toward the ladder, steeling himself against any further betrayals of mind. She wasn't his concern. She was a grown woman who could take care of herself.

Eliana swiveled the stool with her feet. She held the silk gown away from the dirty shed floor, and didn't care for a moment if anyone saw her looking less regal than a Primogenitor should, with her skirts gathered in a bunch in her lap. Arphaxad wallowed on the filthy floor, the leather of his work breeches black with dirt. His legs protruded from beneath the two-seat rider, and his voice, when he spoke, was muted.

"You can always leave," he said.

"And go where?"

"Enoch is far enough that you wouldn't be known, yet the culture is similar to ours. You wouldn't stand out as a foreigner there."

"I'd stand out as a lone woman trying to escape from something. Women don't move to a new city by themselves."

Arphaxad was quiet for a moment, and when he spoke it was in a lower voice. "I'd go with you, you know."

Eliana felt a rush of feeling for the older man. He would go with her, if she asked him to. He'd leave his life behind without a second glance and become a fugitive just to keep her safe. Their relationship had deepened with time, and she felt closer to him than she ever had to another human being, even Girta. She wondered again why this should be, for they were from vastly different backgrounds and the difference in their ages was great. Their only link was the True God of Heaven, and neither of them were devout. They couldn't be, and keep their lives.

"I know you would, my friend," she told him, "and then we'd both be put to death when we were caught. No, running is not the answer. I don't know anything else but being Primogenitor. And Caphtor would search the world over for us."

"He might look, but I think we could escape him. We could go to the mountains. We could join with the hill folk and become a part of a mountain village."

Eliana laughed. "I'd be useless in a mountain village, *adame*. I can't draw water from a well. I wouldn't know the front end of a goat from the rear."

"You could learn."

"Besides, how do you know there are any mountain villages left that would have us? That band who killed your folk last year might have gotten them all by now. I don't think we could find a village that doesn't bow knee to Cain these days, and if they do they'll know me instantly."

Arphaxad was quiet for another moment. "You're right about that, lady. I've begun to think we may be the only believers in the One God left."

"No," Eliana told him quietly, "there are others."

"Ah yes. Noah's clan. Well, there's another possibility. You could go there. Old Noah would certainly keep you safe."

Longing to see Noah's farm—and his family—again struck her with force. "No." The word flew from her mouth.

Arphaxad came out from under the rider, eyebrows arched high. "I thought you liked the old man."

She averted her eyes. "I do, but it would put him in terrible jeopardy."

His eyes narrowed, and she forced herself not to squirm beneath his suspicious gaze.

Finally he shrugged. "If we believe Noah it won't matter in any case. We won't be around when your twenty-fifth birth anniversary occurs."

"Have you spoken with him?" Eliana asked in an eager voice, her mind not on Noah's disaster, but on Noah's son.

"No, not him. I spoke with a soldier in the marketplace not long ago. Seems old Noah has made quite a name for himself these days, proclaiming to anyone and everyone that the floods are on their way."

"A soldier?" Eliana's mouth went dry, remembering that day so long ago and the damaged spine support.

"Yes. He and some of his buddies had been to see the ship they've built on that farm. They say it's a spectacular sight. They also say the old man is crazy."

"Do you think he is, Arphaxad?"

Arphaxad pursed his lips, a thoughtful look in his eyes. "No. I believed him from the first, and I still do."

Eliana sighed. "So do I."

"Then what are you worried about?" Arphaxad said cheerfully. "We won't be around much longer, so it won't matter."

"That doesn't let me off the hook, unless this flood happens soon. I can't become a Senior Priestess, Arphaxad. And I can't have a baby either, it seems."

Arphaxad leaned against the rider, his face very serious. "Eliana, have you considered the possibility that the fault is not with you?"

She nodded, and then shrugged. "But what difference would that make? Even if Caphtor is unable to father children, and I'd make a wager on that, I'm still without an heir. Fault is not the issue."

Arphaxad looked at the floor, uncomfortable. The scar on his cheek turned pink. His lips moved, then slammed shut, as though they held on to words he would not release. Finally, words struggled past his lips. "You could find another to father your child."

"I—" She snapped her mouth shut. To say the thought had not occurred to her would be a lie. But to cuckold Caphtor? Despite their agreement, she was aware that the governor shared his bed with many besides her. Still, the idea of doing the same left a cold, sick feeling in her stomach. There was only one man who...

She shook the thought from her head with a violent jerk that sent hair whipping into her face. Down that trail lay heartache.

"I understand." Arphaxad watched her with liquid eyes. Just what he thought he understood, she didn't know and dared not ask.

He cleared his throat. "Rest assured, lady. I won't let anyone harm you."

Warmth washed over her. That he meant his vow, she had no doubt. But what could one man do in the face of a centuries-old religion and a powerful government that wanted to undermine it? Between the two she was nothing but a pawn, and her inability to conceive left her powerless to do anything about it.

"Thank you, *adame.*" She slipped off the stool and pressed a tender kiss to the scar. "I know you won't."

Chapter 17

Eliana pulled the door to her chambers shut behind her.

"Bitra? Davina? Is anyone here?" She crossed the front room, divesting herself of her dusty jacket as she walked.

Caphtor's attendant, who also served as her personal maid when Bitra's duties called her elsewhere, came scurrying into the room at a pace which was at odds with her immense body. Davina's grey hair was awry as usual, locks standing at attention in odd patterns around her head.

"Needn't shout." Her thick eyebrows pulled down into a scowl. "I heard the door, and was on my way."

Eliana smiled an apology and entered her bedroom, Davina behind her. "I'm almost late. Would you help me dress? I can never get those back laces by myself."

Grim faced, Davina marched into the dressing

room and returned with a plain but creamy yellow
robe and a silk under gown. Though she'd been a
priestess for several years, her special role as Primogenitor allowed her to avoid the typical white robes required of the others. She'd intercepted some envious
glances from the younger priestesses, though the older
ones never exhibited anything but stern faces and the
occasional scowl. Except, of course, when Liadan was
in the room.

The outer door opened and closed, and a moment
later Bitra entered. "I can do that, Davina."

The older woman rolled her eyes and huffed as she
shoved the clothing into Bitra's hands. When she
stomped out of the room, Eliana and Bitra exchanged
a grin. Davina was sour-faced, but she used exactly
the same attitude in her service to Caphtor. Eliana
took perverse pleasure in watching.

Bitra helped her slip the silk over her head. "Where
are you working today?"

"There's a sub-director progress meeting this
morning." Eliana imitated Davina's sour-faced scowl.
"The High Priestess used to attend, but she has decided the Primogenitor can act in her place for that meeting. It's her way of getting me involved in the inner
workings of government without giving over any real
authority. It's also a very boring meeting, and she has
never liked attending it. I'll be tied up there most of the
day." She wrinkled her nose to show her displeasure.

"Interesting stuff, huh?" Bitra tightened the laces
at the small of her back.

"You've no idea," Eliana returned drily. "From the
behavior of the Sub-Directors you would think the
meeting attended by ill-mannered children. They try to
outdo one another, and their reports are so long and
boring it takes all my willpower not to fall asleep. And
of course Rabat will threaten to evict someone, as he
always does, and Amur and Chapra will argue, and
well, you get the point."

Bitra laughed, a clear, ringing sound that echoed

pleasantly off the walls. "I certainly do. I'm going to spend my day in the temple stables, shoveling manure and trying not to breathe the stench. I'd say I have the easier day."

"I'd say we're doing much the same thing," Eliana shot back with a laugh.

The priestess helped her settle the yellow robe over the gown, and tugged at the loose waist. "This is almost too big. Have you lost weight?"

A bitter sigh blew from Eliana's lips. "Well, I'm certainly not growing with a babe, am I?"

Bitra looked uncomfortable. "I'm sorry."

She picked up a brush and pointed toward the stool. Eliana sat, and the priestess began pulling her hair into a neat braid. Her reflection in the mirror showed a brow creased with lines.

"What is it, Bitra? I've grown to recognize that worried frown over the years."

"There has been talk." The priestess shrugged, her fingers busy in dark tresses. "Gossip really, among some of the Senior Priestesses. They're wagering you'll be the first Primogenitor to not produce an heir since Jaline established the religion."

Eliana pushed away a stab of fear. "I don't know why so many of the Seniors dislike me. I don't think I've done anything to offend the priesthood or any of them personally."

Bitra bit her lower lip. "I think many are envious."

"Envious? Of what?"

"Your youth, your beauty, your innocence. And they're afraid, some of them, that you're not ready to assume the role of High Priestess."

Eliana laughed, though the sound contained very little humor. "They're right on that account. I'm not. But that's why the writings of Jaline call for a training period that lasts from my twenty-fifth birth anniversary to my fortieth. And the last five of those are intensive training with the current High Priestess. Liadan herself didn't have the full tr-...Oh, I see." Eliana took

a breath as understanding dawned. Bitra's expression
confirmed her suspicion. "The Priestesses aren't happy
with the way Liadan has handled things, and they fear
that I'll be much the same as she."

Bitra nodded. "That, and also that you're too pliable, and far too influenced by the High Priestess to be
independent. And, I must tell you, by the Governor as
well."

Eliana nodded, her face impassive. Caphtor would
be furious if he knew that the temple gossips had
pegged her as being too easily swayed, especially by
him. That barb was a little too close to his scheme.
And there was some truth there too. Though she didn't
feel personally influenced by either Liadan or Caphtor,
she didn't care enough about the position of Primogenitor or High Priestess to exert her own will in any matter dealing with temple or governmental leadership.
And if she had, her efforts would certainly have been
immediately quashed by her strong and influential
mother.

Eliana knew she owed Bitra an answer, and
wished she could confide in her. But there were so
many things happening behind the public image of the
leadership of temple and government. Arphaxad knew
part, but he was in charge of temple security. It was
his job to know things. She wouldn't endanger her
friend by revealing them.

"If only the Priestesses understood that Liadan
doesn't even care that I exist, much less take the time
to try to influence me. And Caphtor...well, the Governor is so busy with his work that he barely has time
for anything else." Both were true enough. Eliana ex-
erted enough effort to keep her voice clear of self-pity,
though when she explained her plight in those words it
was difficult not to feel a little sorry for herself.

She toyed with a bottle of scent on the dressing table. "Actually, if I were they, I'd be more concerned
that I will fail to produce an heir. If the role of Primogenitor is thrown into contention, the god might select

someone even worse than me."

Bitra's lips pressed together for a moment. She finished the braid and tucked it over Eliana's shoulder. Their gazes met in the mirror. "They're talking about that too."

Of course they were. Inside, Eliana shrank from the second reminder of the day that death loomed in her future. She forced a smile much braver than she felt. "I'm not defeated yet. You may not know it, but I was born a very short time before Liadan's twenty-fifth birth-anniversary. Maybe putting things off to the last moment is common with my bloodline."

Bitra's eyes shone with concern. Then she turned away to retrieve Eliana's discarded clothes from the floor. "I thought you'd be interested in knowing that Jarrell is having lunch with an old friend today. Shem de Noah."

Eliana froze, wide eyes staring back at her from the glass. Shem, coming to Cainlan today? Longing swelled from her chest to her throat. Oh, to see Shem again, just once more.

The priestess disappeared into the dressing room with the clothes, then returned. "They're meeting at the tavern in the temple marketplace for the noon meal." She kept her eyes averted, a guilty flush riding high on her cheeks. "If you plan to be in the area around then, you might run into him."

Realization clashed over Eliana like a thunderclap. Was Bitra suggesting... She gulped. And a short time ago, when Arphaxad had pinked and suggested the fault lay with Caphtor and not her. Was he hinting the same thing?

Thunder crashed in her mind, and echoed inside her ribcage.

"Just where is this tavern located?" she asked.

Chapter 18

Shem and Jarrell lingered outside the tavern. They'd paid their tab and exited the crowded establishment, giving up their seats to two of the patrons standing in a long line of hungry people waiting to be served.

Shem was hesitant to leave. All through the midday meal Jarrell had been distracted, and though Shem had tried several times to turn the conversation in a way that encouraged confidences, his friend stubbornly refused to talk about anything but the most superficial subjects. The bright sunlight highlighted the lines that had appeared in Jarrell's face since their last meeting.

Shem lowered his voice. "You're avoiding something, my friend. Can't you tell me what it is?"

At first Jarrell did not reply. When he did speak, his eyes fixed on some painful place buried deep within his soul. "I have lately begun to question things I

thought were true, and to wonder if those I had reject-
ed as untrue, are not truer than I always believed." He
looked up at Shem then, and gave a twisted grin. "I
know that makes no sense. You were always sure of
your direction and your reasons."

Now it was Shem's turn for twisted lips. "That is
perhaps the most untrue thing you've ever said. I
question my direction at every turn and my reasons
every day." He paused. "Is something wrong between
you and your Priestess?"

Jarrell shook his head. "My only problem is the
lack of time I have with her. No, this is a personal
question, strangely enough brought on by Bitra's own
doubts. I have begun to..." he raised his eyes, looking
intently into Shem's before he finished the sentence,
"...to think a lot about when we were boys, you and I."

Shem didn't understand. "Our friendship, you
mean?"

But Jarrell shook his head. "No, not that. I mean
the things we believed, the way we were raised. Those
stories Grandfather Methuselah told, and how Father
Noah would recite the prayers before the offerings,
and..." He gestured helplessly, unable or unwilling to
pinpoint what he meant.

But Shem understood. Jarrell was questioning his
faith. Or rather, his actions in becoming absorbed in
the values and faithlessness of the culture in which he
lived. He had convinced himself all these years that he
had grown past the need for faith, that religion was a
thing for old men and children, and now he was wondering if he had been wrong.

Shem placed a hand on his friend's shoulder. He
knew very well there was nothing he could say to resolve Jarrell's conflict, that the battle could only be
fought by him. But there was one thing Shem could
offer.

"I've told you many times, though not so much recently, that you are always welcome at home. Maybe
now is the time for you to visit. The old stories are still

there, my friend, and Grandfather is always willing to
repeat them. Come with me the next time I go to the
mountain."

Jarrell looked at him a long moment, then smiled.
He placed his hand on top of Shem's, squeezing, and
nodded his head. "Perhaps I will." The bell began to
toll the hour. "Holy fires, I'm late! Phanom will have
my hairtwist for a sash decoration if I'm late for another meeting." He whirled and dashed away.

"I'll send word when I'm going next," Shem called
after his retreating figure, and Jarrell waved a hand
wildly in acknowledgment.

Shem shook his head and turned in the opposite
direction. Jarrell was a barrel of contradictions, and in
that he hadn't changed from childhood. If God was
tugging at Jarrell to get him back on the path of truth,
Grandfather was the best person to give him a shove
in the right direction.

He made his way down the mall pathway toward
the common market and his meeting to pick up a
shipment of exotic foodstuffs for storage in the ark.
He'd not gone more than a dozen steps when a heavily
robed figure stepped out in front of him, blocking his
path. He started to mumble an apology and side-step,
but a pair of dainty hands reached up and threw back
a heavy hood, and suddenly he was staring into a pair
of dark, dark eyes set in the loveliest face he had ever
seen. Eyes that had haunted his dreams, waking and
sleeping, for five long years. Her lips were a touch
fuller than when he had seen her last, or maybe her
face was thinner. Faint lines creased the smooth
creamy skin of her brow, and her hair, blacker even
than her eyes, was pulled back in a twist that disappeared down the back of her robe.

Her eyes roamed over him. What did she see?
When they once again locked gazes, they exchanged a
brief smile, acknowledging the changes that had taken
place since they had last seen each other.

"It has been a long time, lady, but you are even

lovelier than when I last saw you."

"And you are remarkably unchanged." Until he heard her speak he hadn't realized how much he had longed to hear her voice.

"I hope to see you every time I come to the city, but it seems you don't spend as much time in the mall as you did before your alliance."

There. Acknowledge the alliance right up front to put the conversation on a safe path.

"My time is more in demand now." She lowered her gaze, fingers fiddling with a fold in her robe. "I'd like to talk to you away from all these people, if you have a moment to spare."

"Of course." His meeting with the food vendor could wait.

He followed her through the twisting paths of the mall gardens to the center alcove. The stone bench there was empty. Eliana breathed a sigh of relief and sank onto it after removing her robes. She patted the stone beside her, and he slid onto the edge, leaving a comfortable distance between them. She stared at the stone a moment, then spoke. "How is your family? Your father Noah, and your brothers Japheth and Ham?"

"They are fine, and will be pleased to hear that I saw you. For several weeks after your visit to the farm they spoke of nothing else."

Eliana didn't meet his gaze. "I came to see you, you know, but you weren't there." He struggled to find a safe way to respond to that, but she corrected herself. "Actually, that's not the whole truth. I did want to see the ark too. How is that progressing?"

Here was a safe subject. "Almost finished. It's an awesome sight."

Eliana smiled. "I'm sure it is. It was awesome at the time I saw it, and that was without most of the walls. And that boy, what was his name, the one who was helping with the boat? Is he still with you?"

"Devon. No, he's a miner, working in the silver

mines northwest of here. But he comes home most free days and helps."

Her nod jerked, and she shifted uncomfortably on the bench. "I have a confession. Our meeting today wasn't by chance. I discovered you were meeting your friend, and waited for him to leave."

Shem didn't know how to respond. After a brief silence he decided on levity. "It seems the last time we met you'd done much the same."

Eliana blushed, but she did raise her eyes to his with a grin. "You're right. And you saved me from harm that day." Her tongue appeared and ran across her lips. "I'm hoping you'll do the same this time."

Not from bandits this time, since none lurked in the shrubbery around them. "You have only to ask."

"You'd better hear me out before you say that. What I'm about to ask could have serious repercussions."

"You can trust me with your life, Eliana," Shem told her, and he meant it.

"I am doing exactly that." Shem felt the first stab of fear, not for himself but for her. She drew in a breath. "If I don't give birth to an heir by next year, I'll be sacrificed on Cain's altar." Her eyes fixed on his face. "Sacrificed to a false god. I believe that there is only one True God, thanks in great part to you, Shem de Noah."

Her great dark eyes watched as he digested this piece of information. Eliana, the Primogenitor, acknowledging the True God of Heaven? Shem was so stunned he was unable to think of an appropriate response.

"This heir you speak of. Will she be raised in the temple?"

Eliana gave a tilt of her head, acknowledging that the question was a fair one. "She will have twenty-five years before she is faced with the same decision. Besides." She gave him a piercing look. "Do you believe that the temple, or these people, or this world for that matter, will exist as we know it in twenty-five years?"

Shem was silent a moment. He knew what she was asking. If the flood occurred, *when* it occurred, both Eliana and her child would be killed along with everyone else.

She was watching him, waiting for an answer. What could he do but shake his head?

"Neither do I. But I am not dead yet, and until I am..." She lowered her gaze, a becoming blush rising high on her cheeks. "I long for a child of my own. Someone to love, as I was loved. By Girta."

He'd seen the same longing on Mara's face. Something in his chest twisted. "I understand."

Eliana shook her head. "I don't think you do. So far I have not conceived, and I have reason to believe I will never bear Caphtor's child."

The way she spoke Caphtor's name told Shem a great deal. Contempt curved her lips as though she tasted something rotten. They were treading dangerous waters with this subject. He thought of several questions to ask, but could not think of a delicate way to state any of them.

Her fingers plucked at her silky robe. "So you see my dilemma. By law I am required to produce an heir. By custom that heir is to be fathered by the Governor. Yet the Governor is unable to father my heir."

Shem remained silent. A suspicion was born within him, and quickly grew to maturity. His heart began a heavy thud, and threatened to push the breath out of his lungs. What was she asking? *Dear God in Heaven, don't let her ask that.*

But before the prayer had even finished forming in his mind, Eliana spoke again. "And now we come to my request."

Shem stood abruptly, unable to hear her speak the question. He paced quickly toward the statue of Cain, his thoughts whirling. How could she ask this of him? It was wrong, a sin. She knew the vows he had taken, to God and to Mara. Did she expect him to lay those promises casually aside?

And yet, how could he be angry with her? She was a child of her culture. In her world, the request was a perfectly reasonable one.

One God, help me explain.

Behind him he heard Eliana rise. Taking a deep breath, he turned.

But his words, whatever they were, died before he could speak them. An angry red stained her face, and her eyes sparked with black fire.

"I see your answer." She turned and snatched her robe off the bench.

"Eliana, wait. Please believe me, anything else you ask of me, anything."

"Anything except save my life." Tears filled her eyes, and she swept them away. Her voice grew angry. "I understand. The children of Seth are special, chosen. You dare not mix your blood with the lowly descendants of Cain."

"That's not true." Shem kept his voice calm in the face of her rising anger.

"Isn't it? It's not enough that we will die at the hand of the One God. We're all doomed anyway, so why dirty yourself by associating with me?"

She fled the alcove before Shem could recover from her blistering attack. He stood stunned, staring at the empty bench.

Eliana ran, ignoring the stares of the people in the mall, not caring if they recognized her or what they thought. She was totally humiliated, without a shred of dignity left to bolster her mutilated self-esteem. How could she have been so stupid? Of course he would say no. He was so *righteous.* Fury warred with humiliation, and the anger surprised her.

But just now she was too upset, too furious, too mortified to consider why. She fled to the temple, to the only home she'd ever known. A home that held no safety anymore, no security. She would die in this home.

What was I thinking? One God, why did I ask of him the one thing I know he can't give?

The guards stared as she ran through the halls. She ignored them. She burst into her apartment and ran to her room to fling herself across the bed.

The anger faded and the pain in her soul became an agonizing throb, bringing tears to her eyes and forcing them down her cheeks. How stupid she had been. Of course Shem would never agree to anything so underhanded, so dishonest. And how many times had Girta told her that the One God joined His people to one another in marriage? It was unthinkable that he would ever open his arms to another woman. He was far too noble.

And now she could think with surprise on her angry words. Did she really believe Noah's clan thought themselves better than others? Did the children of Seth look with contempt on the children of Cain? Of course not. But that feeling, that deep gut impression that she was dirty because of her parentage, had crept into her consciousness so quickly she had to admit that it had bothered her for a long while. From the first time Shem told her about Cain's true identity, the feeling had lurked like a worm under the surface. As though she was caked with filth that she could never wash away.

She tossed to the other side of the bed. Yes, she was tainted because of her parentage. But did Shem think so? In all honesty, he had never treated her as such. She'd done him an injustice in that, throwing her own feelings of inadequacy at him, hoping to smear him with her dirt. She owed him an apology. But the thought of facing him again brought another wave of humiliation over her, and she thrust the idea away.

One God, help me. I was wrong to ask of Shem

what he couldn't give without stepping away from you. But I don't know what else to do.

Silence reigned in the room. The One God didn't answer. He never had. Maybe if she were of Seth's blood instead of Cain's, He would.

From her cage in the corner, Melody warbled a tentative song. As the sweet notes washed over her, Eliana's breath ceased its shuddering heaves. Though her pain did not lessen, a gentle calm descended. Perhaps God did speak, only without words.

One God, help me to trust you.

She could think of nothing else to say.

Chapter 19

Jarrell was in his sleeping room, having exchanged his work toga for a more comfortable and less constricting one, when he heard the front door slam. He jerked around to find Bitra standing in the entryway. A flush stained her face, and a good portion of hair had escaped its bindings to fly wildly around her head. She met him halfway across the floor and threw her arms around him, burying her face in his shoulder. Jarrell held her, felt the trembling of her body and tears close to the surface.

"What's happened?"

She took several deep breaths before answering. "It's Hanae. She's gone, missing, and I'm sure something has happened to her."

He turned her gently and guided her to the sofa. When they were comfortably seated amid the soft cushions, her body snuggled close to his right side.

"Tell me."

"I returned to our room after my temple service and Senior Priestess Remotra waited inside. She told me Hanae had been sent on a special mission for the temple, and would be away indefinitely. She asked me to pack up her things, because her bed was being reassigned." A sob forced its way out, and her eyes flooded. "It's not true, Jarrell. Her clothes had not been touched. Her beauty paint was all still in place. Hanae would never go anywhere without her clothes and her paint."

That was certainly true.

Bitra sniffed, and scrubbed at her eyes with her hands. "And I'm certain our things have been disturbed, hers and mine. I know something has happened to her, something terrible."

The idea of someone searching Bitra's room disturbed him nearly as much as Hanae's disappearance. "Was anything missing?"

She shook her head. "Not that I can tell. But what could they have been looking for in my belongings?"

Discomfort settled deep in his gut. "Is it possible Hanae really is on a secret assignment?"

Bitra shook her head. "She would have said something to me before she left. I know it."

"She may not have been able to. You've told me Senior Priestesses are not permitted to talk to anyone about the things they learn or do."

"Seniors have secret assignments, but I've never heard of any like this, none that take them away from the city for an extended period of time. And besides, she would have taken something, clothes, beauty paints, slippers."

"Maybe it was sudden. Maybe that's part of this assignment, that the priestesses had to leave suddenly, without even packing. Maybe all that stuff will be provided for her wherever she goes."

She looked thoughtful, though not convinced. "Priestesses, you said. Remotra didn't mention anyone else being sent. Was Hanae the only one, or are others gone with her?"

He shrugged. "That's one thing to check on. Do some asking around, or just listen and watch to see if anyone else is gone too."

"I will. But I can't help thinking this is somehow related to her strange behavior lately. She always talked to me before. Even if she was a Senior, if something bothered her that much she could have confided in me. Hanae was never one to stick by the rules, so why would she now?" Creases lined her brow, and then her eyes widened. "Unless she'd discovered something so terrible she was in danger, and she didn't want to expose me."

They looked at one another with solemn expressions as the impact of that statement became clear. The idea of Bitra in peril tied his stomach into knots. He didn't trust those who ran the temple any more than he trusted those who ran Cainlan's government, but would they really harm one of their own?

He shook his head. They had to think logically. That was the only way to figure out what had happened to Hanae and ensure Bitra remained safe.

"What was it Hanae said a few days ago when she was so upset?"

Her hand crept up to her mouth, and she chewed a fingernail with a pensive expression. "I had mentioned that we ought to log where we send the SBP candidates who aren't selected for sacrifice, and she told me to mind my own business."

"Candidates for sacrifice? I can't imagine she would have found anything that has to do with the candidates that could cause her to be afraid for her life."

Bitra was silent for a long time, and Jarrell could tell she was thinking hard about something. "Something has bothered me for a while about that SBP. We take in so many children, more than I would have dreamed possible. Human sacrifices are done twice each week, and we house only enough for four weeks at a time in the temple. That's eight candidates at one time. But today I worked the SBP desk, and I took in seven children. And today was a normal day."

The number surprised Jarrell. "Seven a day? I had no idea there were that many."

Bitra nodded. "I know. And the ones who don't stay in the SBP hall are sent to work programs around Cainlan, like harvesting energy, or the fields, or even the ore mines. But we don't record where we send them. Why not? And the daily registers for the SBP desk are taken up at the end of the day and sent away. I've never seen them again."

Jarrell stood and paced to the other end of the room. Seven SPBs a day? Where did they all go? Turning, he faced Bitra. "I can help here. I have access to information concerning the Sacrificial Beneficiary Program. I can find out how many families have received the subsidy in the past couple of weeks, or even years if I dig."

"Can you find out where those children are?"

Jarrell shook his head. "We wouldn't track that. Only the subsidies."

"But do you agree that it is odd? Why wouldn't the temple want to keep track of where they go?"

"I can't think of any reason, except that they don't want anyone to know where they're sending them. And Hanae got upset when you mentioned this?"

Bitra nodded. "But that wasn't the first time we've talked about it. We've wondered the same thing since we came here. The SBP is something we don't have in Enoch, so we were both curious about it. We wanted to find out as much as possible so we could consider setting it up at home. But something about it just isn't right. And every time either of us tried to ask anyone we could never get a straight answer. So when she jumped all over me the other day, that was definitely not normal."

Bitra paused, swallowing hard. When she went on her voice was calm, but Jarrell could hear the edge of panic creeping in.

"I think something strange is happening with the SBPs, and it has something to do with the Seniors. Hanae found out about it, and now they've done something to her. And they probably think I know about it, too, or else they're worried that I might."

They stared at one another and Jarrell tried to keep the fear out of his face lest he upset her further, but knew he failed. He came back to the sofa and sat beside her, pulling her close to him.

"I want you to be careful." He loaded his voice with concern. "Take a few days off. Stay here with me."

But Bitra shook her head. "That would be stupid. If we're right I'll be watched. I have to act as if nothing unusual is happening." His doubt must have shown, for she smiled and placed a hand on his cheek. "I'll be careful. Besides, I do have a few other friends in the temple who won't be afraid to tell me sacred secrets, if they know them."

He covered her fingers, trying to warm them between the skin of his face and palm. "I'll worry about you every minute we're apart."

"I'll come here as often as I can. And if they give me a new living partner as grouchy as Senior Priestess Remotra, that will be often."

Jarrell grinned. "Then I hope she's a pucker-faced old crab."

Chapter 20

The hike up the mountain seemed longer each time Noah came. While work on the ark had helped him stay strong, his stamina during the long uphill trek was not what it used to be. He almost considered Shem's longstanding desire for a rider, one that could negotiate this path. But in the next moment he dismissed the thought. The closer they grew to the ark's completion, the more convinced he became they would not have enough time to get good use from a rider. Samson served their purposes well enough. He gave the animal an affectionate slap on the neck and continued.

Grandfather Methuselah was not waiting on the porch as he normally did, and Noah felt a tug of anxiety. Was the old man all right? He quickened his pace, startling a pair of doves into flight as he passed the bush where they rested. He mounted the wooden stairs, unslung the bag from his shoulder and dropped it onto one of the porch chairs. The door was open, and Noah peered inside.

Methuselah lay on the bed in the one-room cabin facing the side wall, his back to the door. Was he...

"Grandfather?" Noah said in a soft voice.

Methuselah's head jerked, and he rolled over. Rubbing his eyes, he sat up on the bed with a smile. "You're early. Caught me sleeping in the middle of the day."

Noah entered the cabin and crossed to embrace the older man who rose to greet him. "On your birth anniversary you're permitted to rest in the day if you want to."

Methuselah felt frail in his arms, shrunken and fragile, as if the pressure of Noah's embrace might snap his bones. Noah hugged gently, then made as if to help the old man back onto the bed.

"No, no, it's time to be up." Methuselah brushed feebly against Noah's hand. "Let's go out where we can sit and talk."

When the old man was seated in his customary chair, Noah sat next to him, glad for the opportunity to rest after his hike. Though the sun had barely begun its descent, giant trees surrounding the cabin cast cooling shadows across the weathered porch.

"I made it another year." Methuselah gave a satisfied nod. "I didn't expect to, but the True God of Heaven is gracious."

"He is indeed. And next year will be ninety-seven decades. No one will ever catch up with you, Grandfather."

A knowing smile hovered about the old man's lips. "This is the last birth anniversary I will see. But you're right that no one will ever catch up with me. The One God told me that. In fact, in this new world of yours a man's years will become shorter and shorter. And after that..." He waved a hand. "That's a long way off and nothing you need to worry about. Tell me of the work.

It is progressing?"

"It is almost finished." Noah leaned back and balanced on two of the chair's spindly legs. "In fact, we could use the ark now if the need arose, but the True God has not yet sent the animals. And the harvest is almost upon us."

"An important harvest," Methuselah observed.

"It is. The crops will be loaded onto the ark to preserve us and those animals God sends to us, until He delivers us to our new land. We will cease all work on the ark and assist Shem with the gathering."

"Ah, Shem." Methuselah crossed his hands across his stomach. "I hoped he would join you this time. He has been much on my mind these past few days."

His thoughts, too, had hovered on his oldest son rather a lot lately. "He's distracted. Something happened on his last trip into the city, and he's been closed into himself since."

Methuselah nodded, as if he already knew that. "He searches deeply inside for meanings to the things that plague him, yet they evade his grasp. Shem has yet to learn that the only way to truly understand the world is to look outside, to listen to the Maker."

Noah sighed. "I, too, struggle to understand, Grandfather."

"What's to understand?" Methuselah reached over with a gnarled hand to pat Noah's arm. "The One God chose you because you have loved Him all your life. He will continue to guide you."

Some of the knots in his neck loosened. Grandfather was right. He didn't need to understand the why of everything. All that was required of him was to place each foot where the True God of Heaven directed. If he kept his eyes on the Creator, things would come out right.

Birds serenaded them from high in the treetops, and Noah allowed his eyes to droop closed. He could almost be persuaded to take a nap too. Something about this mountaintop relaxed him as no other place on earth did. Peace reigned here, and God was as close as breath.

Methuselah's voice slid without a ripple into the pool of solitude surrounding them. "The One God has honored me lately with His plans for the age that will come after this one. He will take the earth back to Himself, Noah. He will reclaim her and all who call her home, and He will use your bloodline to bring His plan to fruition. The line of Noah, and of Seth. He will do great things in the earth, mighty things that leave me shaking with awe."

Noah felt the truth of Grandfather's words, felt it affirmed inside him. A sense of awe crept over him, and the fine hair along his arms rose. That the One God, the Creator of All, would choose him to help with this wonderful future was almost more than he could grasp.

He cracked open an eye and found the old man watching him. "How I wish that God would speak with me as often as He speaks with you."

"He honors me often, possibly because I speak to Him all my waking life. He enjoys fellowship with us." He settled back in his chair with a smile. "Or it could be that I am old and close to death, and I have fewer ties to this earth than you.

"And that reminds me." Methuselah's tone relaxed. "Do you remember your promise? That when I die, you'll change the coverings on my bed and empty the house of food that might spoil."

Noah laughed. "Yes, I remember and I will. But I still think that's an odd request."

A twinkle appeared in the watery blue eyes. "It may seem so to you, but I happen to know that this old cabin will have one more important use before it's washed away in God's wrath."

Chuckling, Noah shook his head. "The True God of Heaven tells you more than He has ever told me."

The sun had inched lower in the sky as they talked. Shadows from the towering trees danced across the furrows in Methuselah's cheeks as he relaxed against the back of his chair. "The One God talks all the time. You only have to open your ears and listen."

They talked into the night, only breaking long enough for Noah to assemble a light meal. Methuselah must have been well rested from his nap, for he was in good humor and much more alert than Noah when they went to bed.

Noah lay on an arrangement of cushions on the floor as he had done since he was a boy coming to visit after Methuselah retreated to this secluded spot. Methuselah bade him a good night and lay on his bed, and the last Noah heard as he drifted off to sleep was Methuselah's rough voice humming a snatch of a tune. Noah smiled, recognizing it as a lullaby his mother sang to him as a child.

The next morning Noah woke to find Methuselah's body cold and empty, his spirit gone on to be with his God. Try though he might, Noah was unable to feel as saddened as he should. Methuselah had been a man of God, and he had been ready to quit this earth. From their conversation, he had known his time was short, had probably even known when his life would end, and had been happy with that knowledge. When Noah searched inside himself, he realized he had known it too.

He prepared Methuselah's body with the wrappings and herbs he found ready in the cabin. He had long since known the location of the cave Methuselah had chosen as his crypt, and there he laid the old man's body, sealing the entrance with the many large rocks he found in the area. Then Noah stood outside the sealed cave, looking not down but upward, and he gave loud thanks to the God of Creation for the life of Methuselah de Enoch de Adam, the father of all.

In the cabin he put clean, fresh coverings on Methuselah's bed. He emptied the shelves of all the food that would spoil, setting it in the grass outside for the animals that had been the old man's only physical companions for many years. When he had closed the door and latched it so the wind would not blow it open, he stood looking at the little house. What plan did the One God have for this humble place?

Shaking his head, Noah secured his pack to Samson's back. They began the long hike down the mountain. If they hurried, they should make it home before his family sat down to the evening meal.

Chapter 21

Mara removed a bowl from the washtub and hand-ed it to Abiri to be stacked on the shelf with the other clean ones. The men had finished breakfast and headed for their day's labor at the ark and in the fields.

An unusual noise from outside drew her attention. What was that? It sounded like a landrider.

Midian, busy mixing dough for the evening bread, looked up with some alarm. "Someone's here."

Visitors to the house were rare. Most people veered toward the ark when they approached the family's lands. Mara dried her hands on her apron and stepped toward the door, while Abiri and Timna hung back.

Standing in the open doorway, her gaze went im-mediately to Shem in the far field. He had already seen the vehicle approach, and was running in their direc-tion. She relaxed. The stranger, who had just stepped outside his rider, had also seen Shem.

"It's all right." She spoke over her shoulder in a voice loud enough to be heard inside the house but not outside. "Shem is on his way. Timna, set what's left of the morning's brew back on the fire."

She stepped outside the house and approached their guest. The stranger was tall, taller even than Shem, but uncomfortably thin. His beard had gone unshaven for several days, and his face showed no signs of washing in the same amount of time. Snarled locks of hair were caught back in a simple leather strip to fall halfway down his back.

At Mara's approach, he bowed low. "Name's Blasien de Jarett, lady. This be the house of Noah?"

He glanced toward the ark. Mara detected a note of fatigue in his voice

"Yes, it is. I'm Mara, wife to Shem de Noah."

"I carry a message from the mines t'the east."

Mara's pulse quickened. "From Devon? Is everything alright?"

"He's alright himself, though his brother was taken in the blast and he's fair upset wi' that."

The world reeled around her, and she leaned against the doorjamb to steady herself. "You mean Balek was killed?"

Sadness tinged the man's bulging eyes as he pulled a small scroll from within his leather vest. He handed it to her just as Shem arrived.

She removed the strip that closed the scroll and unrolled it with shaking hands, and scanned the note.

Family of Noah de Lamech,

In case you have heard of the tragedy that has be-fallen us, rest assured that I am unharmed. But I grieve the loss of my brother Balek, who was killed along with thirty others when the mine exploded three days ago.

The air here is thick with grief. The most pitiful of course are the children who lost parents—

A sob escaped Mara's lips. Children without parents. She blinked away tears so she could continue reading. Shem placed a comforting hand on her shoulder and read with her.

—when it blew. Blasien, who brings this message to you, lost his brother as well. He is delivering messages to the families of the dead on his way to the city to buy supplies—food, medicines and emergency equipment have become unavailable through the government store. We suspect that is purposeful, because we have refused to work the mine until measures are taken to make it safer.

It may be a while before I visit. There's so much to do here.

Devon

Shem spoke to Blasien in a voice filled with compassion. "Devon says you lost your brother in the explosion. I'm truly sorry."

Blasien bowed his head. "He were my younger 'un."

"Won't you come inside?" Midian spoke from the doorway behind Shem and Mara. "We have a good morning brew, and it will only take a moment to put together a meal."

But Blasien shook his head. "I thank ye, but I'm goin' to t'city and want to be back afore nightfall. The store's stock is dwindlin', and ole Wildon's thinkin' they won't send no more 'till we go back to work." His eyes, protruding and reddened, took on a determined gleam. "We ain't gonna let 'em run over us."

Midian disappeared and returned in a moment with a steaming mug of brew and the half loaf of bread left from their morning meal. "Take this. You need nourishment."

Blasien took it with a bob of his head by way of thanks. Mara stood beside Shem and Midian, watching him pull away, heading toward the forest that bordered the family's farm on the southeast corner. They watched until the rider was out of sight, lost in the trees of the surrounding forest.

Shem turned then to Mara. "Devon's all right, thank the True God of Heaven. It must have happened during the day shift."

"I've got to go to them." Mara knew her tone had been rough when they all looked at her with startled expressions. "There are grieving children, and Devon grieving the loss of his brother." She turned to Shem. "Balek was the only family he had."

Shem replied in a soft voice. "He has us."

"Exactly." Mara lifted her face to his. "That's why I've got to go."

Shem looked skeptical. Mara thought for a moment he would forbid her outright. Her hands tightened into fists, and she shoved them into the deep pockets of her apron. She was rarely at odds with her husband, but the compulsion to go was strong. "Would the One God turn His back on children?"

"Of course not, but that man, Blasien, sounded as if they expect some sort of trouble. Do you want to get mixed up in a problem with the government?"

"If Devon is, yes."

A gasp sounded from behind her, where Timna and Abiri stood watching. From the corner of her eye she saw a frown on Midian's face at her argumentative tone. But how could she stay here when someone she loved was in need and in pain?

"The harvest is almost upon us." Shem gestured toward the field from which he'd just run. "I can't be gone more than a day, two at the most."

Shem, go? Why would he suggest such a thing? "You don't have time to go. Father Noah needs you here."

He gave her an odd look. "You can't possibly think I'll let you go alone."

"You won't?"

"Of course not." His voice became gentle. "You're my wife, and Devon is as close to a son as we have yet.

I love you both. My place is at your side."

Tears flooded her eyes. She stepped forward, into his open arms.

Emergency Council sessions had become almost commonplace in the past few years, so the faces around the Council table were calm, some of them even a little bored. Caphtor took his seat at the head of the table and awarded the room a chilly smile.

"Here we are again, gentlemen and High Priestess. Thank you for gathering on such short notice."

Feren rolled his eyes. "Let's get on with it. I see you more than I see my consort lately."

"For which she is eternally grateful, no doubt," put in Seneset.

Feren glared but did not respond, and Caphtor sighed. If they would only act like adults instead of bickering children, these meetings would go far more quickly.

Caphtor raised his voice to command their full attention. "Councilor Limpopo has made me aware of a volatile situation in the silver mine southeast of the city. Limpopo, would you enlighten the Council?"

Limpopo's square jaw tightened. "You may have heard of the mine explosion three days past."

"I haven't heard what caused it." Virdin spoke from the opposite end of the oblong table.

"A new cross-cut was being carved for ventilation between two shafts, and uncovered a natural gas pocket. The odorless gas ignited when the worker continued to chisel the rock with a metal hammer. Of course the shaft had been timbered with energy-harvested wood, which is highly flammable."

Someone whistled, and several Councilors winced. Caphtor nodded for Limpopo to continue.

"The workers were unable to extinguish the fire, though they did have the wits to wet the second shaft to prevent it spreading there. But they've refused to work the second shaft."

"Refused?" Virdin cast an outraged glare around the table.

"Refused," Limpopo confirmed. "They claim the second shaft is unsafe, that the smoke from the timbers in the burned shaft infects the air. They also say the rock is probably full of gas pockets, and they won't continue to work it without detection devices."

"Workers refusing a government command." Liadan's eyes snapped. "What have you done about this outrage?"

"We stopped sending supplies."

"And is that working?" asked Tomsk.

Limpopo shook his head. "They've sent representatives to the city for food."

"Then why don't we let them sit? If they're buying their own supplies, their money will run out soon."

"Not a good idea. If word gets out that they are manipulating us in that way we could have the same thing happen in other mines. We'll have labor strikes at every turn."

"Then are their demands reasonable?" Chapra asked.

Several indignant shouts met the question. Caphtor held up a hand to gain their attention. "We considered that. We could have supplied them with the necessary equipment, ventilators and gas detectors, charged to the mine."

"Are you mad?" His face purple, Seneset rose from his chair. "If word gets out that we met the demands of a few rag-tag troublemakers, we'll appear as indulgent idiots, ready to be walked over by any group of low-life workers who take it into their minds to want something they don't have."

Heads nodded agreement around the table.

"I say answer their demands with a show of force." Seneset's hand formed a fist, which he raised in the air. "Let them know Cainlan's Council will not be manipulated."

That was exactly the answer Caphtor hoped they'd reach today. "What do you propose, Seneset?"

"General Brendolan has been cooling his heels on the Manessah border for several years now, only an occasional skirmish to occupy his time. Let's recall a squad and garrison the mine for a while. That should convince the miners to return to work."

The suggestion produced a few shocked expressions, and more than a few thoughtful ones.

"It might work." Caphtor stroked his chin. "They needn't use force. Their presence alone would probably do the trick. But if force is required..." He shrugged. Every councilor wore an openly supportive expression.

Liadan caught his eye and nodded. "I say yes."

Satisfied, Caphtor spoke to Seneset. "Ask the General to send a squad. Their order is to show the miners we will not be manipulated."

Seneset nodded, a smile on his face.

Caphtor stood, his hands opened flat on the table in front of him. "Gentlemen, High Priestess, enjoy what's left of your day."

As he swept out of the Council chamber, he glanced toward the hallway that led to the temple's residential wing. Eliana would be there. He considered going to her, but dismissed the idea as distasteful. These days she looked at him with resentful eyes, as though her inability to conceive were somehow his fault.

A twinge of discomfort plagued him. Not one of his many partners had given him a child.

Ridiculous. He inflated his chest and squared his massive shoulders. No one was more powerful than he, more virile. The fault lay with Eliana.

Rage smoldered in him at her unspoken accusations. He was wasting his time with her. Five years he'd committed to this fruitless relationship, and he was no closer now to realizing his plan than the day he'd begun. Perhaps it was time to make alternate arrangements. If Eliana were to die early, another would be selected to take her place. Someone younger, and potentially more pliable.

He turned his back to the temple and walked with a purposeful stride toward his office.

Chapter 22

"I've examined the registers for the SBP program, and something is definitely odd here," Jarrell told Bitra on her next free day. "The temple issued two hundred thirty-seven SBP credits last season."

"More than two hundred." Bitra gave a low whistle. "I had no idea. Are you sure? I haven't seen that many people come through the temple."

"How often do you work that desk?"

Bitra cocked her head. "Not often. Once every couple of weeks. It's considered a task for Seniors, but since I'm close to that rank I've filled in a couple of times."

Exactly the answer he'd expected. "They want to limit the number of people who know the details, so no one gets suspicious."

"Suspicious of what?" Frustration raised the level of her voice. "I'm suspicious, but I don't know what of."

Jarrell felt the same, but had no suggestion. They

sat in silence a moment, then Bitra's eyes opened wide.

"I found out something yesterday that may be important. I finally got another of the Enochian priestesses to talk with me, though she was extremely cautious. Almost fearful. Word of Hanae's *special assignment* has spread, and though no one voices her questions, the explanation isn't sitting well. Sollenia told me there's a special training that the Cainlan Seniors go through to which we from Enoch are not privy. She's heard whispers of something called—" She lowered her voice. "—the Chamber. But as soon as she mentioned the word, she became so fearful she refused to say anything else."

Interesting. The religion of Cain made liberal use of mysterious rites, but he'd never heard of a secret chamber. "So you think this Chamber has something to do with the SBP?" Jarrell narrowed his eyes, thinking.

"I don't know, but I feel in here," she pushed on her stomach with a fist, "that they're connected. And Hanae, too."

Jarrell stood and paced to the other end of the room, trying to organize his thoughts. He faced Bitra. "If there is something that Cainlan Seniors learn, something that outsiders aren't permitted to know, what would happen if Hanae discovered the secret?"

"You mean like a mistake? Someone confided something they shouldn't have?"

Jarrell shrugged. "Or maybe she heard rumors and investigated. Whatever the reason, she saw something she wasn't supposed to, and it was terrible. She was frightened."

Bitra's fingers tapped on her folded arms. "And maybe she carried that secret around for several weeks, waiting for someone else to realize that she knew."

"That's right. She would have been terrified and afraid to say anything."

"That would explain her behavior these past weeks." She shook her head. "What could she have found out that is terrible enough to put a priestess's life in danger?"

Jarrell couldn't imagine. "Not only that, but why did they search your room? What did she have that they wanted back?"

Fear flickered to life inside him. If Bitra was suspected of having the same knowledge as Hanae...

The thought was not thinkable.

Jarrell paced across the room, thoughts raging with emotion. "It's something involving the SBP, so it involves children. What are they doing with all those children?"

"Slavery?" Bitra proposed. "They're selling them to other cities?"

A possibility. "How's the slave situation in Enoch?"

Bitra shook her head. "I don't believe we've an overabundance of child slaves, but I haven't been there in over five years."

"Hmmm. Manessah, maybe?"

"All those children being shipped to Manessah?" A scowl scrunched her lovely face. "How are they transporting them without being seen?"

She had a point. Plus, Cainlan's trade relationship with Manessah had been shaky for several years.

A thought occurred to Jarrell. He spoke slowly. "What is Cainlan's primary export?"

"Energy." Bitra supplied the answer with a shrug.

"Right. And why are we the main suppliers of energy to the other cities, when they are surrounded with just as many forests and natural sources as we are?"

"The other cities suppose it is because Cainlan has discovered some secret in the harvesting process, a way to expand the amount of energy taken from a limited source, and they— oh." Bitra's mouth hung open as she caught his meaning. "Are you suggesting that the temple is somehow using the SBPs, using *people*?"

"To harvest energy." The more he considered the

idea, the more it rang horribly true. "You said Enoch doesn't have an SBP program, so why do we? When did we start it?"

"It's been eight or nine years." She held his gaze. "Right around the time Cainlan's energy monopoly started becoming obvious to the other cities."

A long, heavy silence fell over the room as they both weighed the gruesome idea in their minds.

"We have to find out what this Chamber is," Jarrell told her.

Caution overtook her features. "If we're right, then my life is in danger if anyone suspects I've discovered the existence of this Chamber. And since I've made no secret of our relationship you'll be suspect as well."

He cared nothing for his own welfare, but hers? The thought of Bitra coming to harm chilled his blood. She had to get away, to escape. And he knew where.

He dropped to the cushion beside her. "Let's go away together. I know a place we can go. The people there will shelter us, I know they will."

Noah would welcome them, of that he had no doubt. He would praise the One God for sending Jarrell back to the family who cared for him. Or maybe he should take her to the old man, to Grandfather Methuselah. She could hear the stories of his childhood, get to know the God he had turned his back on. They both could.

For a moment he thought she might agree. She clamped her lower lip between her teeth, her eyes clouded with indecision. Then she shook her head.

Before she could speak he rushed on. "Then you go alone. Tonight. Return to Enoch. You can leave word that someone has died, and your family has urgent need of you."

A tender smile curved her lips. She raised a hand and brushed gently against his cheek. "I can't do that. We have to know the truth behind this Chamber."

Fear crept along his spine. "No we don't. The only thing we have to do is keep you safe."

"I'll be safe as long as I don't raise suspicion. And there's someone who might be willing to tell us what she knows."

Eliana sat before the window, her gaze fixed on the distant forest. She forcibly kept her mind as empty of thought as her heart was of comfort. If she let herself consider the farm that lay west of that forest, her world would shatter like a clay pot dashed against a stone.

A noise from the other room alerted her to Bitra's entrance. When the priestess entered, the distress apparent in her face intruded on Eliana's melancholy mood.

"What's happened?"

Bitra held up a finger, closed the door behind her, and spoke in a whisper. "Where's Davina?"

Curiosity stirred within her. "At the market. Why?"

Bitra dragged another chair across the room and placed it beside hers. "I need some information, but I want to be honest with you. If what I suspect is true, I may be risking my life by asking the question."

The priestess's manner was so cautious Eliana couldn't help but be intrigued. "I am your friend. Ask your question."

Bitra's chest expanded as she drew a breath. "What is the *Chamber*?"

The emphasis she gave the word was at once fascinating and frightening. Obviously she wasn't asking about a regular chamber, such as bedchamber or the Council chamber.

Eliana shook her head, perplexed. "What chamber are you referring to?"

Bitra studied her face silently a moment, then her shoulders deflated. "I hoped you'd heard of it. It has something to do with the temple, and the Seniors, and a lot more, if what I suspect is true."

"What is so important about this Chamber? What is it you suspect?"

Bitra looked away, her struggle apparent. "My friend is missing, and I think something terrible has happened to her."

During the priestess's tale, told in an urgent whisper, Eliana's curiosity changed to concern, and then to alarm. She straightened in her chair, her spine rigid.

When Bitra paused, she asked, "How could they get energy from people? Is it even possible?"

"I don't know, but then I don't understand how they get it out of vegetation either. Do you?"

Eliana shook her head. "It takes a scientist to understand the process, and I'm not that. But there's one flaw in your theory. There would have to be a lot of people who knew about this."

"I know. But there are a lot of Seniors, and their vows of secrecy are broken at the cost of their lives."

The import of her words sifted in Eliana's mind. "The High Priestess." Would Liadan approve something as horrifying as killing a child to harvest energy? With a sinking feeling, she knew the answer. Not only would Liadan approve, she could very likely have come up with the idea of the SBP for the sole purpose of providing a constant supply of children. Acid soured her stomach and sent the bitter taste of bile into her throat.

"It wouldn't be only the temple," Bitra went on. "Some of the Council would have to be involved."

She had no problem believing Caphtor's involvement, or any of the councilors for that matter. "But surely word would leak out somewhere."

"Apparently it did. I think Hanae discovered something, and now she's disappeared." A tear slipped beneath one of Bitra's eyelids and trailed down her cheek. "I have to find her. If she's still alive, maybe we can save her."

A terrible thought came to Eliana as she watched Bitra dash that tear away. "It may be too late to help your friend. Have you seen what happens to a tree when they take the energy out?" The sight of the wasted forests to the northwest of Cainlan loomed before her, trees withered and dried to matchwood while still rooted in the ground.

Miserable, Bitra nodded. "I don't care. I have to try." She raised her eyes to Eliana's face. "And I need help. You're *from* here, and you have contacts. You can ask the questions I can't. "

The decision was already made. Eliana leaned forward and grasped the priestess's hands in hers. "Of course I will."

Bitra launched out of the chair, and Eliana found herself gathered into a hug. She returned the embrace, her mind already planning the questions she would ask.

Chapter 23

Eliana did not seek Arphaxad out at once, deciding instead to wait a full day after Bitra's visit. If there were any truth to this crazy story, and she was convinced there was, the priestess may have been followed. To run to Arphaxad immediately would only cast suspicion on him, and possibly endanger him as well.

She made her way to the temple security office on the main floor of the residential wing mid-morning. Arphaxad's eyebrows arched when he caught sight of her. He gestured for her to enter his office and be seated. "You arouse my curiosity, lady. If you want to use my rider, you have only to send a page with your request."

She didn't return his smile. "Have you heard of something called the Chamber?"

Though normally passive even under the most stressful situations, he reacted to the question with surprising emotion. He jerked backward in his chair as if slapped, the scar on his face growing white.

So. He knew.

He rose, came around from behind his desk, and shut the door, closing them in to his office together. Then he swung on her. "Where did you hear that word?"

Now Eliana was frightened. His eyes bored into hers, blazing in a way she had never seen. She tried to answer, compelled by that intense gaze, but could not choke any words through her dry mouth.

"It's true," she finally managed. "About the children."

He watched her for a long moment. "I don't know what you've heard, lady, but these are questions that should not be asked."

Her fear seeped away when he addressed her as "lady." For a moment he had looked so fierce that she had been afraid, but now she saw that this was still the Arphaxad who was devoted to her, as she was to him.

She leaned forward and clasped his hands. "I've heard that it's somewhere here in the temple, and that children and others are taken there and never seen again. I've heard that it has something to do with the city's energy generation, and that the Senior Priestesses are involved."

Arphaxad's hands remained limp in hers. "Your informant is good."

Eliana drew in a breath. "Then it's true?"

He didn't answer at first, nor did he release her hands. He leaned against the edge of his desk, as close to her as he could be. "Much of what I suspect is just that – suspicion. But over the years I have uncovered some facts."

"Such as the number of SBPs taken not matching the number sent out for placement in work programs? Or that the records are taken away somewhere, not available for research or viewing?"

Arphaxad nodded. "Also that there are rooms within the temple, or more specifically *beneath* the temple, that are not accessible to anyone but the High Priestess, the Senior Priestesses, and certain government officials. I have been given the names of people who may access those rooms, and they include the Governor of the Council, the Director of Energy and his Sub-Director in charge of Generation. It doesn't take long to fit the pieces together."

"Who is responsible, Arphaxad?"

Eliana braced herself for his answer, and was not surprised when it came.

"The same person who gave me the names. The High Priestess, from whom I take my orders."

Eliana's gaze dropped to the clean surface of the desk. Disappointment whipped at her. Why? Had she thought Liadan was hiding noble qualities beneath the layers of greed and ambition? Hadn't she always known her mother would sacrifice anyone, including her own daughter, to feed her enormous sense of self?

When she raised her eyes, Arphaxad watched her with a curious expression that she could not read. "Don't judge her too harshly, lady. She lives the life she was raised to live. We can't despise her for living it well."

Eliana jerked her chin upward. "If that is true then why am I horrified? My heritage is the same as hers."

Arphaxad's smile held a note of secrecy. "But you had another influence, an outside factor that your mother never had."

He meant Girta, no doubt. She couldn't allow herself to be distracted by thoughts of her lost friend, or loneliness would overtake her. She had no time for that. "Where is this Chamber?"

For a moment she thought he wouldn't answer. Then he did. "There is a stairway in the northeast section of the temple, beneath the temple dais. At the base of that stairway is a locked door, and beyond that, corridors beneath the temple. It is my belief that the Chamber lays at the bottom of that stairway, though I've never ventured beyond that locked door."

Eliana nodded. "I think I know that stairway. There are usually guards posted there."

"Yes. They don't know what they're guarding, except that it is a holy place. During one shift in the early morning there are no guards stationed in that corridor. I was given instructions to have the corridor cleared for a period of two hours each night."

"That's when they take the sacrifices down to the Chamber?" Arphaxad nodded. Eliana narrowed her eyes. "How do you know, if no one is permitted in the corridor?"

Arphaxad ducked his head. "I'm very good at issuing commands, but have never been much for obeying them. I've spied." He raised his head and looked at her, eye-to-eye. "I know what you're thinking. You wonder how I could stand by and let this happen? I offer no excuse. Though I am of Seth's bloodline, I am no good servant of the One God. I've performed many acts for which I deserve condemnation. Only two that I can recall that the One God may consider praiseworthy." His smile grew tender. "The second was piloting you into the forest for your offering. And I was forced into that."

An odd choice of words. "Forced?"

"I could never deny my sister. When we were younger, because she would sit on my head until I complied. But in later years, because of my love for her." A smile tugged at the corners of his lips. "And for another."

Realization dawned on her, and she sucked in a breath. "Girta! She was your sister." Girta obtained the position of nursemaid to the infant Primogenitor because of her relationship to the head of temple security.

He inclined his head. "And if she were here, she would no doubt have my hide for a handbag. Forget the Chamber, my lady." He leaned toward her and squeezed her hands. "You not only endanger yourself, but your priestess friend."

A chilling reminder. And yet, Eliana had promised Bitra she would find out about the Chamber.

A knock on the door relieved her of the burden of an immediate answer.

Arphaxad released her hands and straightened. "Come."

A page entered the room. His gaze flew to Eliana, and a flush suffused his face. "I have a message from the priestess in charge of the stables, sir."

A sigh blew between his lips "Forgive me, Primogenitor. This will only take a moment."

He stepped out of the chamber, pulling the page along with him.

Eliana settled back in her chair, prepared to wait for his return. Her gaze rested on an object on the side of his desk. A large ring of keys. An idea formed in her mind, both frightening and exciting.

With an anxious glance toward the empty doorway, she reached for the key ring.

Within two hours of their arrival at the mine site Shem was ready to leave. These people made him uncomfortable. Their grief and pent-up rage beat upon him like heat from a potter's oven.

Devon's demeanor had changed from the quiet boy Shem knew. The weight of grief sat heavy on his features. Mara gathered him in an embrace, while Shem thumped his back with an awkward gesture.

Mara released him and held him at arm's length. "Take me to the children."

There were twelve orphans in all, varying in ages and sizes. The miners, male and female alike, seemed only too pleased to release them into Mara's care. Their relief bore evidence that Mara had been correct in her concern—the children had no one here to care for them.

"I need your help," she told her wide-eyed charges. "We've a wagon full of supplies that need to be unloaded."

When Shem tried to begin the unloading, she shooed him away. "They need a task to keep their hands busy." So he folded his arms while grief-stricken babes, some no older than six years, unloaded the supplies they'd brought. Some of the foodstuffs had come from the ark's stores, but Father had given unstintingly.

Devon stood beside Shem, watching Mara organize the effort. "I knew she'd take care of them."

Shem observed him from a sideways glance. Sorrow carved lines in his young cheeks, and his mouth formed a hard line. Not long ago, that mouth had gulped the food set before him as though he couldn't consume enough to overcome the hunger of weeks alone on the road. The memory tightened Shem's gut.

"I'm..." He gulped, and shifted his gaze to Mara and the children. "I'm sorry about Balek. He was a good man."

Devon nodded, staring in the same direction. "He was."

What words of comfort could he offer to soothe a grief so stark? "I don't begin to understand the purposes of the One God, but I believe in His goodness. Someday we will see Balek again."

The boy's eyes shifted to Shem, and a smile played about his lips. "I know. Thanks to you and your family, I know."

Shem placed an arm around Devon's shoulders and embraced him in a sideways hug.

After a supper of vegetables and bread, Shem watched Mara march the children off to a natural spring where Devon said the workers and their fami-

lies bathed. She loaded the older ones' arms with dry-
ing cloths, and the younger ones' with bricks of soap
she'd made at home. Shem sat on a bench outside
Devon's tent, looking westward. The sun was below the
tree line, but its light had not yet faded completely.
Devon had gone with Mara to show her the way, but
she had not suggested that Shem join them as well.

He sighed. Was he feeling sorry for himself? Probably. The fields at home waited for him, but here he
served no purpose. Mara had found a mission in the
needs of these orphaned children, and she didn't need
him to fulfill it.

He thought back on Mara's expression this morning when he told her he loved her. Obviously he had
not said it often enough, else the words would not
have moved her so. The memory left him ashamed.

*I will do better, One God. In the new world, I will tell
her so more often.*

In the world the One God would re-create, they
would have children of their own to care for. The idea
sent a shiver down his spine.

He wandered around the mining camp, amid the
framed tents and clusters of miners' families. Grief invaded the very atmosphere, even as twilight's finger
began to paint the sky with darkened colors.

The sky still held a remnant of light when Shem
heard the sounds of shouting men and women. They
drifted toward him from the direction of the government store, in the center of the mining camp. Angry
tones carried on the evening breeze.

He headed in that direction, behind a row of tents,
and eventually stepped between two temporary dwellings onto the camp's main path. A crowd of grumbling
men and women blocked his way. The air snapped
with swelling anger, fed by their murmurings. A shouting voice in the center rose above the others, and firelight from torches flamed above the heads in front of
him. He shouldered his way through the press of people, aiming for a place where he could see what was

happening.

Shem hadn't realized there were so many people in this little mining town. An elbow pushed him on one side, a shoulder on the other. Finally he was shoved in the right direction and found himself out in the open, at the front of the crowd, facing the last thing he expected to see.

A group of uniformed men with odd-looking weapons stood in the center pathway. Several carried torches, their weapons strapped to their backs. Behind and beside Shem were most of the people in the town. The soldiers' gazes occasionally strayed toward the crowd, but their main point of concentration was elsewhere.

On the other side of the clearing, gathered around the place where a path through the surrounding forest split apart from the main trail and headed uphill to the springs, stood a group of eight or ten men. All were red-faced and angry, But none more than the one in front, who glared poison at the leader of the soldiers. Devon.

As if that weren't alarming enough, Shem's gaze was drawn to the small cluster of people standing directly behind Devon. Fear flipped his heart like a flapjack. A dozen damp-haired children gathered around Mara carrying towels from their bath. His wife was frozen with fright, eyes wide and terrified. Shem tried to get her attention, to tell her to retreat to the springs, but her gaze was riveted on the soldier arguing with Devon.

"My orders are from General Brendolan himself." The man's voice filled the clearing with contempt. "You are to go back to work immediately."

Devon's reply held even more contempt. "Did the general tell you when we can expect the equipment we've requested?"

The commander spat in the dirt at his feet. "It ain't your place to *request* nothin'."

Devon raised his chin. "We won't return to work until we get our supplies." The men around him nod-

292   Virginia Smith

ded.

The commander's face flushed a deeper shade of red. "For the last time, I'm tellin' ya to get your stuff together and get down in that mine."

"And what if we don't?"

The commander's glare took on a new level of menace. "I've been authorized to do whatever is necessary to get your lazy carcasses down that hole."

Tension cracked between the two groups. Shem's gaze slipped up toward Mara. If she would only look at him he would tell her what to do. Take the children and return to the spring. Hide in the cover of the forest.

A movement behind her drew his attention. A sense of coming disaster gnawed in his stomach. A man slipped down the trail behind her, his movement almost covered by the underbrush. Was this a miner, coming to take Mara and the children out of harm's way?

Then Shem saw the weapon. The man raised it and pointed it over Mara's head, toward the soldiers.

Though he had no idea what the weapon might be, Shem gauged the man's intent. The miner was going to fire on the soldiers.

He leaped out into the clearing, toward Mara, and shouted, "No!"

Too late. There was a noise unlike anything Shem had ever heard, a sort of whistling explosion. The commander fell backward. Horrified, Shem watched the crimson of his short vest became sticky and dark with blood.

Chaos erupted. A young soldier looked in shock from his commander toward the man who had fired the weapon. He shouted something. Shem was too horrified to hear the words. And all the soldiers pointed their weapons toward the man, and toward Devon, and toward...

"Mara!" Shem screamed a warning, but he was too late. His ears filled with explosions as the soldiers' weapons discharged. Paralyzed, he watched Mara crumble backward, and land in a heap with the children. In front of them, Devon, too, was thrown backward into the jumble of bodies. In a matter of seconds no one was left standing.

Shem, and all the miners around him, stood riveted in place, their minds unwilling to comprehend what their eyes saw. A long, deadly silence descended.

It was broken when the young soldier who had opened fire on Mara and the children, shouted in a voice filled with hysteria. "See what happens when you don't obey Cainlan's army, scum? Get back to work or we'll do the same to you."

As the soldiers broke ranks and ran, Shem sank to his knees in the dirt. His numb mind refused to accept the horror he had just seen. Somewhere in the crowd behind Shem someone began to cry.

Shem was the first to regain the use of his arms and legs. He struggled to stand on trembling knees and ran toward the bodies. When he reached Devon, he stopped to peer down at the face of the boy he'd grown to love. His throat thawed enough to constrict, and he opened his mouth to get a breath, but a sob escaped instead.

He stepped around Devon, across three other bloody bodies, and then arrived at Mara's side. She lay on the ground, her lower half buried beneath the corpses of dead children, her eyes open and staring into the trees above her. Across her chest was smeared the wet, sticky blood that had pumped from her body when the weapon's projectile tore a hole in her chest the size of Shem's fist. He stepped around her, his eyes never leaving her face, and sat on the ground behind her head. He put his hands under her shoulders and scooted his body so that her head rested in his lap. When he closed her eyes, his fingers lingered on her immobile face.

One God, she doesn't deserve this. She's going with me into the new world. We'll have children, repopulate the earth with our offspring. She'll make a terrific moth-er.

He was aware of others watching him. No one moved. No one tried to pick up any of the bodies. No one cried. They all watched Shem, and he watched Mara's face.

Chapter 24

Jarrell stifled a sigh and shook his right leg. It had gone numb from standing immobile so long. He leaned forward and peered down the corridor, then jerked back when he saw the flash of red uniform from one of the temple guards stationed at the top of the stairway. The alcove in which he stood was dark and crowded, obviously used as storage, though he'd not been able to open any of the crates and see what was inside for fear of being overheard. He had no doubt that this was the same alcove used by the Primogenitor's friend, for the arrangement of the crates allowed for a man to crouch down in a tight place against the rear wall and remain hidden from anything but an outright search.

But it was impossible to maintain that crouch for any length of time, so staying hidden for the entire night was out of the question. At least the position of the alcove allowed him to move around in several directions without fear of being seen, unless the guards decided to walk this way. The alcove was situated at the intersection of three corridors, which made it easy to see in any of three different directions.

Having spent more hours here than he had antici-pated, he could say with certainty that traffic in this section of the temple was extremely sparse. There probably wasn't much need for guards. The doorways and alcoves here were used exclusively for storage, and the only people who came this way appeared to be us-ing it as a by-way to an entirely different section of the temple.

The perfect place for a secret chamber.

When he told Bitra he wanted her to keep a safe distance from this part of the temple, she'd launched a heated argument, insisting that she be allowed to come with him tonight. Wisdom had prevailed, but on-ly because she refused to hand over the key she'd got-ten from the Primogenitor. Jarrell ground his teeth. If he had that, he could enter that locked door without endangering her. But her stubbornness had won out.

A sound from the guards sent Jarrell scurrying for cover behind the crates. The guards' footsteps receded down the stone hallway toward the temple. A grim sat-isfaction overtook him. Eliana had been right. The guards were leaving their post.

Time passed in silence. Finally, Jarrell stood and stretched his cramped body. Another sound reached him. Someone was approaching from far down the western corridor. There were many feet slapping the cold stone floor. In addition he heard voices, small, high-pitched, their tones whining and questioning. Jarrell shifted his position in the shade of the crate to see their approach.

A small parade appeared. Five children in varying ages followed a white-robed priestess, with two more priestesses trailing behind. The face of the woman in front was straight-lipped, immovable and dispassion-ate as though carved from stone. She placed one foot before the other in a rhythm akin to a march, her mind on her mission and not on the little ones behind her.

Jarrell's gaze dropped to see the younger members of this grim procession, and his heart twisted. Three little girls, two of them clutching each other while the third followed behind, whimpering. The solitary one held tightly to a scrap of fabric, a dirty and tattered blanket. As Jarrell watched she brought it up to her cheek to scrub away the wetness there. Dark, stringy hair fell into her eyes. Jarrell guessed her age at around five years.

The group passed out of Jarrell's line of vision as they reached the intersection of corridors directly in front of the alcove in which he hid. He followed their progress by the sounds of feet and sniffles, together with an occasional quiet sob, as they turned north along the corridor leading to the stairway the guards had vacated. After they passed out of visual range, Jarrell crept as quietly as possible along the wall. He peered around the corner with one eye and saw the white backs of the trailing Priestesses as they descended the stairway. In the silence of the corridor he could easily hear the jingle of keys and the soft scratch of metal on metal as a lock turned. The click of a door closing echoed toward him across the distance, followed by silence.

Jarrell remained where he was for a long while, afraid to move. How long would the Senior Priestesses be behind that door? He paced the small area behind the crates, and had decided that they would not return when the door opened a second time. He dove for his hiding place and huddled there. When he risked a peek after they had passed, relief flooded him. All three priestesses had left, heading in the direction of the temple's SBP unit. The children were nowhere in sight.

When they had gone, Jarrell forced his muscles to relax. If Eliana's information was correct the guards would resume their post in little more than an hour.

He was supposed to watch for anything that happened during this period — that's what he and Bitra had agreed upon.

But Jarrell had to know what was behind that door. Maybe he could hear something if he pressed his ear to the wood. After a good look around, he stepped out of hiding. His shoes made a loud noise on the floor, and the sound echoed in the empty corridor. On his way to the stairway, he stopped often to listen for noises. Nothing.

The short stairway led downward, maybe ten or twelve poorly lit steps. At the bottom was a door, closed but not in any way ominous or threatening. He crept down the stairs quietly and at the bottom approached the door to place his ear against it.

Nothing. He plugged his other ear with a finger.

The sound of a throat clearing behind him sent him leaping into the air. A hot, sick flood of alarm turned his stomach to liquid fire. He jerked around to face his attacker.

Bitra stood at the top of the stairs, her arms crossed, watching him from between narrowed eyelids.

"What are you doing here?" Her harsh whisper echoed in the silence.

After a moment his breath returned, though his heart continued to pound like a ceremonial dance drum. He mounted the stairs two at a time and stood beside her, glaring. "What are *you* doing here? You're supposed to be up in your room, sleeping."

Bitra returned the glare without flinching. "Let's talk about what you're supposed to be doing." Sarcasm weighed her words down. "And about promises, and what it means to keep them."

Guilt stabbed at him. "Alright, so I decided to see if the guards really do leave their posts every night. But that doesn't explain your presence."

A falsely sweet smile spread over her features. "I thought we might need this." Her hand opened to reveal a key in her palm.

He shook his head. "I'll not allow you to—"

His voice fell silent when fire appeared in her eyes. He gulped. Wrong word choice. He sighed in defeat. One quality he loved about Bitra was her adventurous nature, though at times like this it could prove disastrous. If he didn't go with her now, she'd only return alone later. And then who would protect her?

"Alright. But promise me we'll retreat if there's danger." He grasped her arms in both hands and forced her to see his soul in his eyes. "I couldn't go on if something happened to you."

In answer, she stepped forward and brought her lips to his.

Who could argue with that?

They descended the stairs. Once again Jarrell placed an ear to the door. Still no sound from the other side. Those children hadn't been quiet. Surely if they were just inside this door, noise of their presence would betray them.

He nodded to Bitra, and she slipped the key into the lock. It clicked open with a soft *snick*. Opening the door a crack, he peered in. He saw only blackness.

Jarrell swallowed against the dryness in his throat. He opened the door wide enough to allow his body to slip through. Bitra followed.

After a moment, his eyes adjusted to the dim light from the stairwell. They stood in another corridor, though the ceiling hovered just above their heads. The floor beneath his feet was of stone, as were the floors of the temple corridors, but not polished smooth. The surface was rough and almost gritty.

"Look." Bitra's whisper sounded loud in the empty space surrounding them.

Jarrell stared into the distance and saw a pinprick of light far ahead of them. Perhaps that's where the children had been taken.

"Let's come back tomorrow night with a light," he whispered.

"We can't use a light. We'll be seen." Her expression shifted into a stubborn mask. "Let's go now."

She grabbed his hand and plunged forward, out of the scant light from the open door and into the darkness of a long, cold corridor. Jarrell sighed. Stubborn woman. He clutched her hand, and stretched his other out in front of him, his gaze fixed on the dim light in the distance.

After an eternity of wandering in the darkness, the light ahead disappeared.

Jarrell halted. The blackness around them was so deep for a moment he was disoriented. "We should go back." That is, if they could figure out which direction was *back*.

"No." Bitra's hand clutched his, her nails biting into his skin. "I know where we're going."

He'd never heard her voice so full of fear. His stomach knotted in response. "Where?"

"To the Eternal Fires, outside the city gates."

The direction was right. The protective stone wall, high and round, lay to the southeast of the temple, across a vast, barren field.

"I should have realized it before," Bitra said. "Only Seniors are allowed to see the Holy Blaze, the base of the Eternal Fires."

Dread built in his gut. They'd gone far enough. Any further would be foolish. "We've discovered what we wanted to know. It's time to go back."

"No!" She jerked her hand out of his, and he knew a moment of panic in the darkness.

"We haven't proven anything," she said, "only fixed the location. We can't leave now. We can't leave those children to who-knows-what fate."

His mind conjured a picture, the stringy-haired child scrubbing her face dry with a filthy and tattered blanket. If he did nothing to help, he would see that miserable face in his dreams for the rest of his life, looking up at him with fearful eyes, begging to be rescued.

We can't leave them.

Fear for Bitra warred with his desire to rescue those children. But even if he insisted, Bitra would continue without him. He couldn't let her go on alone.

"Alright."

A relieved sigh sounded beside him, and a soft, groping hand traveled down his arm to grasp his hand. He took a great deal of comfort from the warmth of her skin.

Gradually, a dim light appeared ahead of them. Jarrell squinted and blinked, not convinced his eyes weren't conjuring a mirage. When he decided the light was real, he began to hear a noise. Though unfamiliar, it resembled the hum of a rider engine. But beneath the hum was a noise he had no trouble identifying. The sound of children crying. Sweat broke out on his forehead, and the cold air in the tunnel chilled it against his skin.

Bitra surged ahead, tugging him along. The outline of a door became visible as she inched it open. What in the world was she doing? The silhouette of her head appeared in the light as she pressed an eye to the crack. He heard her gasp, and then she shoved him forward to look. Jarrell's eyes were dazzled by the brightness on the other side of the door. The room was large, larger than his entire house, and the hum was loud. The source could be any of a number of large metallic devices scattered about. He had an impression of levers and pipes and coils, and several odd-looking chairs. All this he registered in a flash, and in the very next second he realized that there were people in the room, moving about. Several priestesses, clothed in their traditional white robes, and also two uniformed men. He was just about to back away when one of the priestesses moved aside and gave him a clear view of something that had been hidden a moment before.

One of the chairs had an occupant. Strapped by her arms, legs, torso and head was the child he had seen being led down the corridor. Her tattered blanket lay on the floor beneath limp fingers. The chair was reclined, more like an adjustable single-width bed, and it was attached by something beneath her head to one of the machines that hummed behind her. A wide black strip covered her mouth. Blank eyes stared at the ceiling.

Jarrell stood rooted to the floor. What were they doing to that child? Horror spread over him as he realized that he and Bitra had been correct. The machine with the coils and wires was somehow draining energy from the child. And finally he saw something he did recognize—an energy canister on the floor connected by a shiny tube to the humming machine.

In the next instant, the door shoved open and slammed into his face. Stunned, Jarrell fell backward. Stars danced in his vision, and then rough hands jerked him upward.

"Here, who are you?" a deep voice growled in his ear.

Bitra! Even before his vision cleared, his shout echoed against the stone walls of the corridor. "Run!"

But she didn't. Her face, stricken and terrified, turned his way as a guard grabbed her and jerked her through the doorway. Jarrell tried to twist out of his captor's grip, but failed.

"Bring them in here," came a female voice from inside.

Jarrell was half-carried, half-pushed forward. He blinked, his eyes dazzled by his sudden plunge into light. When he could finally see, a familiar face blurred into focus. Shock zipped through his body.

"Roblin! What are you doing here?"

Roblin snorted, shaking his head. "More to the point, what are you doing here, my friend?"

Jarrell ignored the question. "What do you know about this..." His gaze slid to the child's body, and back. "This torture chamber?"

"What have you done with Hanae?" Bitra wrenched against the grip of her captor, a guard wearing the uniform of Cainlan's army.

"Ah, Hanae." Roblin's smile displayed a cruelty that sent chills marching over Jarrell's skin. "So lovely, and so dim-witted. The perfect companion, if only she'd had a less inflated opinion of herself. But some things are meant to be, and it seems she was meant to die tragically young."

"Die?" Bitra's voice wavered.

"Oh yes." Roblin waved a backward hand, toward the chair. "The procedure is fatal, which is why this location is so fortunate. The priestesses dispose of the bodies up above, on the Eternal Fires. So you see, Hanae really did sacrifice her life to her god. And her energy will benefit the city that bears his name."

A choked sob rose from Bitra's throat. Jarrell longed to go to her, to hold her in her grief. But the soldier's grip could not be broken.

He glared at Roblin. "You are horrible."

Roblin rewarded him with a pained look. "Am I? I'm only doing my job. If you'd been appointed to the Department of Energy Generation you would have been in the same position. I doubt if you'd have acted differently."

"You're wrong about that," Jarrell assured him, but before he could elaborate they were joined by a group of senior priestesses, ones Jarrell had not seen before.

The oldest, a stern-faced woman with grey hair and thin lips, stepped forward to stand before Bitra and glare down at her.

"I knew something like this would happen." She shook her head. "You foreigners won't stay in your given place. I told the High Priestess it was a mistake to ever allow you into the temple. Now look what's happened." She whirled to face Roblin, whose expression had become lazy and indolent the moment she entered. "How did they get in? I found the other foreigner's key when I searched their room."

Another soldier stepped forward and searched Jarrell with rough hands. Jarrell tried to jerk away from him, but he found the key in the deep pocket of his jerkin. Remotra snatched it from his hand.

"A pass key. Where did you get this?" She whirled around to glare at Bitra.

Bitra clamped her lips shut and raised her chin, her manner belligerent.

"It doesn't matter. There aren't many of them around. I'll have temple security account for all of them, and I'll find out sooner or later." She turned back to face Roblin. "What do you intend to do with them?"

Roblin shrugged. "Same as the others. Have you a better suggestion?"

Remotra's eyes narrowed. "The High Priestess won't like this. The second foreign Priestess in one season, and a government aide besides."

Jarrell stiffened. High Priestess Liadan knew of this, this atrocity? He shook his head. Of course she did. Why was he surprised?

Roblin snorted. "You mean you don't want to re-mind the High Priestess of your mistake with the first one, letting her into a training session she should nev-er have been privy to? I'm surprised we didn't have you strapped in an energy chair, Priestess."

A snide curl appeared on Remotra's lips. "Watch your mouth, government man, or you'll find the god Cain breathing down your neck, and you won't like the smell of his breath." With one final glare at Bitra, and an even colder one for Jarrell, Senior Priestess Remotra turned and left the room, the pass key clutched in her hand.

With her gone, Roblin seemed to lose his taste for the game of playing with Jarrell and Bitra. He covered a gaping yawn with his hand. "I do wish you'd chosen a more convenient time to suicide, Jarrell. I have an important meeting in the morning, and now I have to report to Virdin. He hates news of this sort first thing in the day."

"Listen, Roblin." Jarrell schooled his voice of the

contempt and distaste he felt. "Bitra didn't have anything to do with this. She's trustworthy and she won't
say a word to anyone. Why don't you let her go? She'll
go back to Enoch and you'll never hear from her again.
You'll still have me, and you can do whatever you want
with me."

Bitra began a loud protest, but stopped when
Roblin's laughter told her what he thought of Jarrell's
suggestion.

"You must think me an idiot." Roblin shook his
head at his one-time friend. "She's got more brains in
her right big toe than you've ever had, and far less
cowardice. I'd let you go before her. You're far more
controllable than she is." His gaze shifted to the soldiers. "Bring them."

Jarrell and Bitra were shoved forward, toward one
of five empty chairs.

Roblin's voice took on the tones of an instructor,
slightly bored. "I want you to get a good understanding
of what happens here, Jarrell, so we'll let your lovely
friend go first."

The guard who held Bitra pulled her forward, and
she struggled. Jarrell writhed and twisted, desperate
to come to her aid, but his guard delivered a vicious
punch to his gut, and fresh stars of pain exploded before his eyes. He struggled to retain consciousness.
When he could see clearly again the guard and one of
the priestesses were holding Bitra down in the chair
while the other strapped her in place. The guard
wrapped a black leather strip around her mouth, mut-
ing her screams of fear and rage.

"You see," Roblin said, "we're able to get as much
energy from one child as half a forest of trees. And it
takes only a fraction of the time. Oh I understand your
protests, Jarrell, really I do. When I was first told
about this I felt much the same way. But I quickly realized how much sense it makes. Why should we destroy all the forests surrounding Cainlan when we can
be so much more efficient using the one resource

which the City possesses in over-abundance? Even
you must admit that the population cannot continue
to grow at the rate it has been. The children we take
are not wanted, and would only grow to be a drain on
the city."

Roblin's voice droned on, but Jarrell barely heard
him. His eyes were fixed on Bitra, who had been
strapped so securely into the chair that she was unable to move. They attached bands to her ankles, her
knees, thighs, hips, torso, arms, shoulders, neck and
forehead. Her screams stopped when the neck strap
was tightened. Bile mingled with desperation, and rose
in his throat as he heard her struggle to breathe.

"Oh don't worry, she won't suffer long. When the
procedure starts the breathing rate slows to almost
nothing, and all struggling stops," Roblin said.

Though he wanted to hurl insults at the man,
words failed him. He could not look away from Bitra.

She stared at him, her gaze locked on to his.

"I love you." Jarrell shouted over the suddenly loud
noise of the machine.

Her gaze softened and tears sprang to her eyes.
Her head dipped a fraction, the only movement she
could manage, and Jarrell knew she was telling him
she loved him too.

"Touching, really." Roblin, pretended to wipe a tear
from the corner of his eye. "But it's time now. Say
goodbye, Jarrell."

Jarrell ignored him, his eyes fastened on Bitra's
while he tried to pour as much love as he could into
his gaze. And then one of the priestesses flipped a lever and the chair reclined, tilting Bitra's upper body
backward while her feet came forward until she was in
a prone, horizontal position. Jarrell could no longer
see her eyes, and he sobbed aloud. He wanted to shout
to her, to tell her he loved her, but the words would
not form in a mouth already full of grief.

"Here's the really interesting part," Roblin said in
the tone of a lecturer. "In order to drain the energy we

have to have access to the brain. And of course the only way to do that is to go through the skull. It gets messy sometimes."

The priestesses spread a plastic cloth beneath Bitra's head, and then one of them swung a metal arm from the machine behind the chair. Two metal rods, each sharpened to a fine point, protruded from the end. The arm swung around, the points aimed at the back of Bitra's head.

Jarrell's breath stopped as he watched, unable to tear his eyes from the horror taking place before them. When the priestess had positioned the points, she flipped a lever. The arm was now securely in place beneath Bitra's skull.

Roblin walked over to stand above her. "Don't worry, priestess, after the first few seconds you won't feel a thing."

Jarrell froze, gripped with a horrified numbness as he watched the torture being done to his love. Roblin nodded toward the Senior Priestess standing beside the giant machine, and she pressed a contact button. The humming noise increased in pitch, and the arm moved slowly toward Bitra's skull. In a matter of seconds it had reached her, and Jarrell watched in shock as blood splattered the white cloth beneath her head. Bitra's body arched, and over the sound of the machine he heard her muffled voice give one, long scream.

And then Jarrell lost consciousness.

He awoke to find himself in the same chair that had so recently confined Bitra. Pain shot through his body as the straps were tightened around his arms and legs. He was already bound from the chest down, but they had not covered his mouth.

"Welcome back." Roblin stepped into view. "You missed all the fun."

"Where is she?" Jarrell's shout wavered.

"Gone. You'll be happy to know that we harvested more energy from her than we did from Hanae."

Shock numbed Jarrell's brain. "I don't believe you."

Roblin shrugged. "See for yourself." He stepped aside and pointed.

Jarrell turned his head, and immediately closed his eyes. In the corner stood a handcart, the sort driven by farmers during harvest or planting. Bodies were piled across the bed. He recognized the clothing of the children he had seen earlier. Bitra lay across the top, her arms and legs dangling at an unnatural angle.

A howl of grief started in the pit of his stomach, and he threw his head back to let it out. Bitra, dead. His love, his life, killed by a monster who used to be a friend.

Roblin wrinkled his nose. "Gag him. I can't stand that noise."

A priestess approached from the right, and Jarrell's mouth was tightly bound. The scream continued, as had Bitra's, but the sound was now muffled even in his own ears. And then a strap was tightened around his forehead, and another around his neck, and he needed all his strength to breathe. The chair reclined until his body was prone. The panic inside swelled, and he moved his eyeballs wildly around, trying to see what was happening. He caught a glimpse of fluttering white cloth on one side, and then the priestess on his left dropped from view as she swung the arm into place beneath his skull.

His panic dissolved. A calm crept over Jarrell, and his thoughts became clearer than he would have thought possible, even when the hum of the machine sounded so loud in his ears.

True God of Heaven, I'm sorry I've been such a disappointment. But if You ever loved me can I ask a favor? Let Bitra get to know You in eternity. You'd really like her, and I know she'll love You. If only I'd told her about You before.

His prayer was interrupted by the onset of the most brilliant, horrible pain he'd ever felt as the metal pinpoints pierced his skull. With a gruesome clarity he felt pressure leave him as blood erupted from his skull. And then the pain was gone.

Jarrell sank into oblivion.

Chapter 25

Shem brought the bodies home for burial. The shock and grief that met him upon his return did nothing but drive his own anguish deeper within. In silence he observed the five-day rite of mourning appropriate for a lost spouse, stoically going through the motions of the prescribed rituals for each day. The emotional cleansing the exercise was supposed to impart was as distant as Mara's and Devon's souls, lost to him forever. That his family were concerned was obvious, but he could not force himself to care. At the end of the fifth day he folded the mourning cloth and placed it in his clothing bag, packed and ready for a hasty departure upon the command of the One God.

He was up before the women the next morning, and left the house without breaking his fast. The fields called to him. The harvest was upon them, and he needed to lose himself in its gathering. And there, alone with his carefully tended plants, he finally began to find solace for his troubled spirit. There he was able to give vent to the feelings he could not express, the deep and tearing guilt that he had not loved either of them enough. The horrifying fear that he had somehow caused their deaths by his lack of attention. And finally the sickening shame that he had betrayed them both with his long-denied feelings for another. Was this God's way of punishing him? Was he to go into the new world alone? In the repetitive working of the harvest he acknowledged his sin, and humbly accepted the role given to him by the True God of Heaven. The role of a man destined to live his days alone.

By the second day after his mourning period had ended, a sense of urgency gripped them all. That this would be the last harvest, no one doubted. Progress on the ark was suspended while they worked from sunrise until the sun had sunk so low they could not see the produce on the vines. And then they worked long into the night preserving the fruit of their labor.

Messengers arrived to deliver the exotic foods and plants Shem had ordered during the past several seasons. Hardly a day went by without a delivery of one sort or another, and the response was always similar. They parked their riders near the house, and by the time Shem had arrived from whatever section of the field was being worked that day the cargo was usually unloaded. They stared at the ark, an awesome sight of towering height and immense length.

"By the Eternal Fires of Cain, what is that?"

"It's an ark," Shem always replied. "A boat."

"How you gonna get it to the water?"

"I'm not. The True God of Heaven is going to send the water to the ark."

In the past he'd been embarrassed to talk about the ark, and ashamed of himself for feeling so. But as the reason for its construction grew closer he found himself almost eager to discuss it with anyone who cared to listen. Meeting the skeptical gaze of his audience, he would describe Noah's vision and the pro-

nouncement of disaster by the One God. Usually he
didn't get much farther than that.

"What are you, crazy?" A hasty departure was usually imminent.

But if everything within Shem's body weren't already crying for him to *hurry, hurry, hurry*, the arrival
of the first animals certainly produced an urgency unlike any he had ever felt.

They had almost finished the harvest, and it had
been done in record time. While they worked the far
western field, the women labored to cure and pack the
immense amount of fruit and vegetables they had
gathered. The bounty of this season's produce surpassed any Shem had ever seen or heard of. Preparing
all the food for storage in the ark would consume their
time in the coming weeks.

Shem raked what Ham cut, and worried. An immense bounty, but would it be enough?

"God of Father Adam, would you look at that."

Japheth's exclamation drew his attention from his
work. Shem raised his head, unaccustomed to hearing
an oath of any kind spoken by his brother. Japheth
and Father both stood frozen, ignoring the grain at
their feet. Shem followed their gazes, and his muscles
locked at the sight that greeted his eyes.

"What is that?" asked Ham, awed.

Shem wondered himself. There appeared to be a
herd of them, but they moved slowly so he was easily
able to count seven. In body their shape was similar to
a horse, but their fur was far shaggier and longer.
Their long necks stuck straight up, topped with round
heads. As Shem watched, one lowered its neck and
tore at the grass, easily able to reach it without bend-
ing its knees.

"At least they're grazers," commented Noah,
"though I can't imagine what they're called."

But Shem had heard of something like them before.

"They're llamas, from the grassy plains beyond the

barren lands. Remember the story of Mahalelel's journeys into the southern deserts and the strange animals they found there?"

"I remember." Japheth's voice held the enthusiasm
of a child. "And they look just like Grandfather described. Do you think we're going to see the ones with
humps too?"

"Of course we are." Father nodded, his voice confident. "The One God will send all animals to us for
safekeeping in the ark."

Father's gaze shifted to Shem, a smirk hovering
about his lips. It was as close to, "I told you so," as Father Noah ever came.

"He'll send the ones we don't already have," Shem
shot back, and father and son exchanged a grin. It was
the first easy conversation they'd had since the deaths,
and a burden lifted inside him.

"What do we do with these in the meantime?"
asked Ham. They had all begun to graze, and were
cropping the grass around the rear of the ark.

"Nothing." Noah waved a hand. "There is plenty of
grass, and we have already finished the harvest of this
field nearest them. They can graze upon the stubble of
the field, and there is water just a few short steps into
the forest."

"But shouldn't we try to get them inside?"

Noah shook his head. "The One God will tell us
when to move them inside."

Ham shrugged. "Alright, but it's going to get awful-
ly crowded around here pretty soon."

"More so every moment. Take a look there." Japheth said, and he pointed toward the sky.

Gliding toward the ark from the north was a flock
of large birds, their extended wings reaching almost as
long as a man-length as they coasted on the air. From
beneath Shem saw white underfeathers fringed at the
tips with gold. The sunlight shone off them like a
crown.

"Eagles," he breathed, taken with awe at the sight

of the mighty flapping of one pair of immense wings.

"We must hurry. It has begun." Father Noah's voice, though quiet, held a note of finality that stirred Shem's blood.

Stirred his blood, and yet he felt something else. Fear? That too, but fear of the unknown was to be expected. Excitement? Urgency? Dread? Yes, all those as well. But that wasn't the feeling that disturbed him. The four men returned to their tasks, working with a renewed intensity. And Shem worked harder than anyone, trying to smother the anguish that threatened to overpower his outward calm.

As the days passed with no news from Bitra, Eliana grew fretful, then anxious. Finally a cold fear settled in her stomach as the days dragged into a week with still no word from the Enochian Priestess. When she finally mustered the courage to ask a Senior about the location of her assistant, she was told that a new assistant would be assigned within the day. Fearful, she didn't question the woman further.

In the end she decided to go to Arphaxad. Guilt churned in her stomach as she made her way to his office. When he looked up from his desk and caught sight of her, the creases in his face deepened with a layer of sadness. With a wordless gesture, he indicated the chair where she had sat before.

She closed the door behind her, but then paced the length of the small room. With a fortifying intake of breath, she faced him.

"I've done something I shouldn't have, and I'm afraid I've put a friend in terrible danger."

Arphaxad's expression did not change. "I know."

"You know?"

Arphaxad shrugged. "I know you stole a pass key from my ring. I know you gave it to that Enochian priestess who was asking about the Chamber. I know you told her and her government-worker friend about the guards' posting schedule."

"And do you also know that both she and her friend are missing, nowhere to be found?" Hot tears sprang to her eyes, and she wiped them away with the back of her hand.

Arphaxad watched her a moment, an odd expression on his face. When he spoke his voice was softer. "It seems I know more than you do at this point."

"What do you mean?" Sudden fear rose within her. "What's happened to them?"

Arphaxad took a breath. "Their bodies were discovered five days ago in an alley just east of the house the government-worker was leasing. They'd apparently been robbed and murdered, then dumped in a poorly-lit alley. There was no identification on them, but she was wearing her priestess robes so they were brought here to be identified."

Eliana's breath halted in her chest, then returned with painful gasps. She closed her eyes and let the tears flow unhindered, Bitra's image clear in her mind.

One God, what have I done?

Waves of guilt warred with grief to batter her mind. Arphaxad's arms circled her and she rested her head against his chest and wept deep, painful sobs. He held her, quiet, until the sobs lessened and she was able to accept the offered handkerchief to dry her cheeks.

"It's my fault." New tears sprang forth with her admission.

"No it isn't."

"Yes it is. I stole the key. If I hadn't given it to them, they'd still be alive."

Arphaxad cut her off with a shake of his head. "Not true. There are keys to that door all over the temple. Every senior priestess has one and Bitra would have found that out eventually. Even if they didn't have a key, locks are not hard to pick if you're determined to get through them."

"They wouldn't have known where the place was if

not for me, or that the guards would leave it unguard-
ed."

"Did they appear to be stupid people? Slow mentally?"

"No." She sniffed, and wiped her nose "No, they
were both very bright, I'd say."

Arphaxad nodded. "How long do you think it would
have taken them to figure out that there is only one
deserted corridor leading away from the SBP wing?
And since the Priestess knew the SBPs were housed
there, she would eventually decide to wait in one of
those empty rooms to see where they were taken. She
would have observed the guards herself."

He spoke the truth, but she was not yet ready to
absolve herself of all blame. "Maybe so, but the information I provided certainly hurried them along. And
without that key they'd have had a longer delay and
might have changed their minds."

Arphaxad gave her a skeptical look, then shrugged.
"You may wallow in a pool of guilt if you want. But I
believe those two would have acted on their own eventually." He went on in a different tone. "No one knows
who took the pass key, or even where it came from."

Relief washed over her, immediately followed by
another stab of guilt that she could be concerned with
her own safety so soon after learning of her friend's
death.

"Was it found on them?"

Arphaxad shook his head. "I've heard no mention
of it, but several days ago Senior Priestess Remotra
asked me to conduct an audit of all pass keys in the
temple. I reported all the keys safe and accounted for."

Arphaxad gave her a tender smile, which she found
she could return, if somewhat tremulously. He had put
himself in danger once again for her.

"Thank you, *adame.*"

"You can thank me with a promise." He released
her and returned to his chair. "Do nothing else about
the Chamber. I fear for your safety."

Eliana strode to the window and stared with un-
seeing eyes down on the top of the rider shed. Investi-
gate? Was she going to hide in a deserted corridor all
night, or steal another key and see what horrors lay
behind that locked door?

She turned to bestow a brief smile on Arphaxad. "I
don't plan to do anything."

But of course that didn't stop her from asking a
few questions.

Eliana planned to confront Caphtor with her
knowledge that very night. She dismissed Davina early
and set herself to wait for him. The hours passed,
more and more of them, and still Caphtor did not come
home. She grew impatient, then angry, and finally resigned to spending the entire night curled into a knot
on a big chair in the common room. It was well past
the middle mark of the night when she fell asleep.

She was awakened by the opening of the door. She
sat up quickly, ignoring the cramps in her legs and
neck at the awkward position she'd assumed during
her nap.

"I'm glad you're up." Caphtor told her. "Something's happened." A note of excitement tinged his
voice.

"What is it?" Not that she particularly cared, but
unless she allowed him to tell his news she'd never be
able to talk to him on the subject that was foremost in
her mind—the Chamber.

At his next words, all thoughts of the Chamber
vanished.

"Manessah attacked our army post today, an un-
provoked assault. We held our own, our losses were
minimal, but the two forces were well-matched. We've
received word that Manessah is sending reinforce-
ments to the site." The excitement in his voice glittered
in his eyes at well. "We're at war."

Dumbstruck, Eliana could only stammer. "War? With Manessah?"

"Yes with Manessah. Who else?" He planted his hands on his hips and glared down at her. "Are you completely ignorant to what's going on outside these walls? The days when we can hide our eyes and sit isolated in our city are gone. Cainlan is going to become a force to be reckoned with in this world."

"Is Liadan aware of this?" The high priestess would be furious.

"Exactly what I mean," Caphtor responded. "If it doesn't happen within Cainlan's walls Liadan doesn't care to hear about it. She was shocked, so taken by surprise that she had nothing at all useful to say. Her focus is so narrow, she's become a stone around our necks." Caphtor gave a start, as if he suddenly realized to whom he spoke. "Anyway, I'm leaving immediately for the front."

"The front?"

"The Manessite border," Caphtor explained with exaggerated patience, as though to a child. "We're sending the rest of our army to join the fight, as Manessah is doing. And our army needs a strong leader in the early parts of this war. Brendolan is a fine general, a brilliant strategist, but he's not a dynamic presence. The men need someone to encourage them."

Though Caphtor had faults aplenty, he could certainly provide a motivating presence. The people loved him. But to leave the city without leadership during a time of war?

"It doesn't make sense to have Cainlan's Governor absent. The people are sure to panic."

He waved a hand, impatient with her comment. "The Council's discussed that at length. That's where I've been. We're all agreed this is the best course, the only course to be taken."

With a look that told her he'd not hear any further arguments, he left the room. The sounds of his preparation for departure drifted through the open doorway.

Why had she bothered to argue at all? It mattered little to her that he was leaving. All she cared about was the fact that people, mostly children, were dying to provide energy for Cainlan.

Energy. That's what this war is all about.

Caphtor might think her ignorant of anything outside the walls of the temple, but she was at least aware of the fact that other cities coveted Cainlan's energy supply. And the reason for that jealousy concerned her a great deal.

"Davina!" Caphtor's voice bellowed through the open doorway.

Eliana rose from her chair and followed Caphtor into his sleeping room. "She's gone into the city for the night, visiting her family."

"Well I need help. I can't find my clothing bag."

Swallowing a sigh, she retrieved the bag from his dressing room. He did not thank her, but began tossing articles of clothing into it. Eliana perched on the bed, watching.

Perhaps she should feel some concern for his safety. But as she watched him, so big and vital and full of confidence, she could not force herself to feel anxious for him. He seemed not the slightest bit uneasy himself. In fact he exuded an air of barely suppressed excitement, noticeably eager to rush toward this threat and defeat it.

He's in his element, like a barbarian warrior eager for a new foe to fight and defeat. An action like this is what he's been waiting for to prove himself, to show everyone in Cainlan and the rest of the world what he can do. The thought sent a shiver down her spine. What would he do once he met and defeated this foe? A victory against Manessah would surely make him lust for more. And since Enoch did not appear to be a threat now, and surely would not if Cainlan's army defeated Manessah, would he begin to search within his own city for his next victory? Which foe would he attack next?

An urgent need to escape the presence of this pow-er-hungry man flooded her. She rose and headed for the door, where she turned to look once more at him. His task was almost finished, and his gaze darted around the room in search of something he may have missed.

"I wish you luck." Did she really mean it? She wasn't sure, but neither could she think of anything else to say.

Caphtor nodded once, the only sign of acknowl-edgement she would receive, and bent over the cloth-ing bag to fasten the straps around its bulging sides.

Eliana left. Frustrated, she went to her own room and closed the door. She'd not been able to ask him about the Chamber.

News of the war was received with more enthusi-asm than Eliana expected. The temple hallways buzzed with the murmuring voices of priestesses and guards as she made her way toward the high priest-ess's rooms.

Two priestesses attended Liadan in her chambers. Eliana entered and watched as they stripped her mother of night clothes and dressed her in a day robe.

When they finished, she asked, "May I speak with you privately?"

Seated at her dressing table, Liadan tossed Eliana a measuring glance, then nodded a dismissal at the priestesses. Alone, she arched an eyebrow. "Well?"

Eliana drew a breath to steel herself. "Is it true that the temple uses children instead of trees to gen-erate energy?"

Liadan grew very still, her eyes locked onto Eliana's face. A series of emotions played across the High Priestess's features, beginning with surprise and ending with a dawning realization.

"It was you who told those two about the program."

Eliana schooled her features to nonchalance, but her heartbeat picked up in tempo. "Actually, no. They told me, after having figured it out for themselves."

"Impossible." Liadan's head shot up. "No one has figured it out in all the years since we started."

Eliana shrugged. "They did. Apparently your people are not as careful or as cunning as you thought. If they were, they wouldn't have let the first foreign Senior find them out."

She was probing, and the tactic paid off.

The High Priestess's eyes rolled, and she gave an undignified snort. "That idiot Remotra let one slip through. Foreigners are supposed to be excluded from that training session. That was the first mistake since the induction of the program."

"That mistake," Eliana told her, "cost three people their lives."

Liadan narrowed her eyes. "The lives of three people mean nothing when the overall benefit of Cainlan's superiority is at stake."

"I suppose if the number of lives given to this cause were measured, three are insignificant." Eliana tried to keep the sarcasm from her voice, but anger threatened. How could her mother be so cavalier toward Bitra's death?

Liadan's lips curved into a chilly smile. "You disapprove of the program."

Eliana struggled to maintain control. Never had she felt such fury toward her mother. Fear, yes, but there was no trace of fear now. She paced across the room to hide her expression until she mastered her emotions. "I don't understand how you can end the lives of children who have been dedicated to the god."

"Their lives belong to the temple, given freely by their parents and rightfully purchased."

She whirled around. "In service or sacrifice to Cain?"

Liadan's eyes narrowed. "But they *are* serving Cain. Cainlan is the god's city. Cainlan's superiority in the world is in the god's best interest. His worship will spread everywhere our energy goes, as it already has. There are temples in both Enoch and Manessah, and their popularity is growing. Within a few years, even within your time as High Priestess, both those cities will come to depend more and more on direction from Cainlan's temple. We are proving ourselves to be the dominant force in the world."

"Obviously Manessah is resisting our dominance," Eliana said in a dry voice.

The High Priestess dismissed that with a flick of elegant fingers. "A natural reaction. We can't expect them to lay their cities at our feet freely. Of course there will be resistance, but nothing we can't overcome. And the reason we can overcome it is because of our energy generation program."

"Our energy generation program is the reason for the resistance to begin with." Eliana's fingernails dug into her palms.

Liadan looked at her as if she were speaking insanity. "Didn't you hear what I just said? One day you will be one of the rulers of the entire world because of this program. If we hadn't discovered it, one of them would have eventually. And then you, daughter, would find yourself without power of any kind, or even without a temple to serve."

"I don't plan to serve the temple in any case," Eliana told her.

Liadan's lips curved into a twisted smile. "Are you still talking that foolishness?"

Eliana tossed her head upward and looked down her straight nose at her mother. "I have too much integrity to devote my life to the service of a lie, and especially one that causes so much destruction and death."

Liadan's laugh mocked her. "What you have is a superior case of ignorance, inherited from your father no doubt. I'd hoped it could be overcome, but I see that I was wrong. Blood always tells, they say, though

I thought mine would carry some weight."

Eliana was taken aback. Her mother had never referred to Ashbel in such disparaging tones. She was still struggling to think of a response when Liadan went on.

"Does the Governor know of your refusal to become High Priestess?"

"We've discussed it."

Liadan laughed again, this time shaking her head in disbelief. Eliana's cheeks grew warm. The High Priestess rose and approached, a cold glint in her eyes even as her laughter died. Eliana stiffened, trying not to flinch at her approach, but Liadan was not coming to her. Instead she went to the door and opened it, then turned to address her daughter.

"Get out now. I grow tired of your questions and of your ignorance. If you want to throw your life away, that's your decision. Perhaps you should go ahead and present yourself for sacrifice, and save me the trouble of denouncing you. It will have to be done shortly anyway. Your belly's still slim as a virgin's."

For a moment, she could not move. Though she'd never fooled herself into thinking her mother loved her, tears burned her eyes at the harsh dismissal.

But she had inherited a sense of pride from the woman standing before her, and it had sharpened during the years of her association with Caphtor. She might be dismissed, but she would not go groveling or sniveling. She raised her chin, cutting her eyes sideways once to deliver her best contemptuous glance, and left the High Priestess's dressing room without a backward look.

It wasn't until she reached her own sleeping chamber that she allowed her hands to tremble, and the tears to roll down her face, though she didn't quite understand why they should be there at all.

Chapter 26

The area surrounding the ark had become an animal sanctuary in barely a week. More types of animals than Shem had dreamed existed grazed in the spent fields, and more arrived each day. Now the reason for the immense size of the ark was made real to him.

His eyes were drawn to a pair of elephants tearing at the trees. What would it be like, confined within the ark's curved walls with these wild and wonderful creations of the One God? At least He had sent young ones — these wouldn't see their full growth for a few years.

Shem guided Samson past four landriders, and halted the animal near the ark. Father stood on the entrance ramp, halfway up so he could be seen by his audience, a group of a dozen men.

"Who's that?" shouted a man in the back, indicating Shem.

"My oldest son." The old man's voice projected to

the back of the group.

"Are you as crazy as your old man here?"

Shem answered while he made his way to the back of the cart and hefted off the first heavy crate. "If you mean, do I have faith in the prophecy delivered by the True God of Heaven, the answer is yes."

Both Japheth and Ham appeared to help, and Shem knew they'd been hovering just inside the ark, watching over Father.

"More of 'em, and all of them crazy."

Japheth's jaw tightened, and he caught Shem's eye. Given the slightest provocation, Japheth would flare into righteous rage. With a slight shake of his head, Shem carried his load up the ramp.

Even though his audience displayed no indication that they were receptive, Father would not pass up an opportunity to try to turn the men's hearts back to their Creator.

"We're not crazy, friends, though I understand how we must appear. I ask you, if the True God of Heaven spoke to you, giving you warnings of the end of the world and the death of civilization, would you not heed His voice and strive to do what He asked?"

A pleading note saturated his father's voice. Shem shook his head. How could he continue to feel compassion for these men, considering some of the insults he'd had hurled at him lately? But that was why Father had been selected by the True God. Someday perhaps Shem would understand.

"If that happened to me I'd run right to the saloon and buy ten more bottles of whatever I'd been drinking." Loud guffaws of laughter met the insult.

Inside the ark, Shem nodded for Ham to stay by the door and watch over Father until he and Japheth returned. In the almost-full storage section in the belly of the ark they stacked crates of baked clay jars, filled with salted produce and sealed with waxed cloth. Once those were secured, they hurried to rejoin the group at the ark's entrance.

"...and it grieves Him to do this terrible thing. But He will not be ignored, and He will turn His people back to Him. I believe you can stop this tragedy before it happens. Turn from your unholy actions, turn to the One God and beg His forgiveness. I know He will welcome you."

"What, and miss all the excitement?" a man's voice answered. "Water pouring from the sky, from nothing up above us? That's something I've got to see."

"How did you get all these animals here?" someone else asked, and this man sounded more curious than degrading.

"The True God of Heaven sent them to us, for safekeeping inside His ark when the floodwaters come. As you can see, He has drawn them from all over the world, and brought them here. Does that not convince you?"

Shem looked over the faces in the group, and one or two did seem convinced as they watched a herd of giraffes grazing nearby. But several burst into loud and insulting laughter.

"If you want to start a zoo out here in the middle of nowhere, that's your business." The man who spoke turned his head and spat. "But don't blame it on a weird prophecy from a non-existent god with no face and no name. Come on, let's get outta here."

They turned away, most of them laughing loudly and shaking their heads. Several men glanced toward some of the animals, and one even threw a cautious look toward Father.

"You, stay with us and we'll talk more," Noah said at once, walking down the ramp. "You're welcome here, and in my home as well."

But the man turned away and hurried after his friends. Noah stopped, his hand outstretched toward the retreating men. He shook his head sadly as he watched them climb into their riders, still shouting and hooting at the animals and at one another.

"I've failed again. Will no one turn to Him?"

Japheth approached and put his arm around the old man's shoulders. "I think we're the only ones who will hear Him. The only ones left."

Father dropped his head, and nodded once. "Then how can I wonder that He will destroy them all and begin again? If the only one He can find is someone such as me, what heartbreak He must feel."

"They seem to be getting more hostile." Shem watched the riders disappear in the distance.

Ham nodded. "I think so too. It's like the animals have changed something."

"They're frightened," Father said. "This is not natural, and they know it no matter how loudly they protest otherwise. God is trying to speak to their hearts, but they refuse to listen."

When they'd unloaded the cart, Shem led Samson back toward the house for another load. He glanced in the direction the riders had taken. They had once again faced the hostility of the world, and had come away unscathed. Physically, at any rate.

Caphtor loved war. He loved seeing the camp spread out before him, sprawled across the hilly plain in an array of men and equipment and war vehicles. He loved the smell of the fires at night, the sight of a thousand spots of flickering light scattered evenly across the plain. He loved the way the men looked at him, the way they listened to his commands and obeyed without hesitation. He loved the cramped, close meetings with General Brendolan and his field commanders, loved listening to the strategies being formulated and hashed out into detailed tactics. Most of all he loved the battles, the piercing whistles of the hand-held weapons with which his men were armed, the explosions of the projectile bombs tossed back and forth between the two armies, the smell of sweat and fear that rose above the battle ground on all sides of him, and even from himself. He had found his niche, his element, his place in the world.

The only problem was the small, nagging itch in the back of his mind that reminded him he knew absolutely nothing about leading an army. The commanders obviously recognized that fact, General Brendolan especially, but at least the troops did not. They saw him as a leader to be obeyed.

The war progressed well. Manessah was a formidable opponent, their army well-trained and deadly, but Brendolan had chosen Cainlan's site well. They backed up to a high palisade on the western side. Easily defensible, the position also served to shelter them from the worst of the wind that blew with fury across the plains from the west. At the northeastern edge of their encampment stretched a wide river, an excellent source of fresh water for the troops and also a natural barrier that must be crossed in order to attack them.

Caphtor sat at the head of a makeshift table in the tent that served as Brendolan's field headquarters. The position was honorary only, and everyone knew it. Still, he held his head high and listened closely to the conversation.

Brendolan rested his clasped hands on the table in front of him. "Let's be honest among ourselves, my friends. The Manessite force trained a full year longer than ours, and they outnumber us. Their leader has an uncanny way of deploying his troops precisely where they will do the most harm, at our weakest points."

Squad Commander Markian leaned forward, his gaze sweeping the table. "I've heard General Andon has uncanny abilities, like mindreading. And that he consults demons before every battle."

The commander beside him nodded. "They say his mother was raped by a god, and that he's stronger than five men."

"I've heard of those cross-breeds, the spawn of demons and woman," affirmed another, his eyes wide.

"They're supposed to be giants."

The mood in the tent had shifted toward the fearful. Caphtor cleared his throat, determined to restore the men's confidence. "Those are rumors. I've never seen a giant on the battlefield."

Markian awarded him a somber look. "General Andon does not ride into battle. He commands from behind, using an intricate network of pages and avian message-carriers to direct the fighting from a safe distance."

A general who cowered behind in safety while he sent his men into danger? Caphtor scoffed at the idea. Who would follow such a man?

Brendolan's expression remained solemn. "Andon is a brilliant commander. If we could remove him, the Mannesite army would fall."

Silence filled the tent as everyone considered those words. Finally, Markian ventured a thought. "A full-blown attack would never work, but a small patrol might be able to infiltrate their camp."

Commander Updonolit's eyes ignited. "It might work. No more than five or six troops. And they'd have to go at night, under the cover of darkness."

Excitement itched at the base of Caphtor's skull. If they were successful in assassinating General Andon, the Mannesite army would collapse. The war would end.

And if I play a part in the assault, I'll be welcomed as a hero when I return home.

He resolved at that moment to lead the attack squad, even if he had to pull rank on Brendolan.

"Can we locate the General's tent within their camp?" asked Updonolit.

A grimace that might pass for a smile crossed Brendolan's face. "I don't think that will be a problem."

Squad Leader Raynor did not accept Caphtor's involvement in his covert mission with good grace. He glared, growled, and threatened, but Caphtor stood his ground. Finally, Raynor tossed his hands in the air.

"If you wish to commit suicide on the battlefield, I won't stop you. Just see that you don't bring harm to any of my men in the process." He held up a finger. "But I'm assigning two guards to watch you."

Though he chafed at the restriction, Caphtor held his tongue.

In the blackest part of the night, the squad set out. Raynor led, his black-clad figure dissolving into the darkness of the trees. Caphtor stayed in the rear, flanked by his guard. Though he moved as silently as he could, the sound of his footfalls seemed magnified in the still night. The men around him slipped from tree to tree with no sound at all, their bodies feather-light and their feet silent.

They reached the river, and Raynor led them south to a ford. On the other side they marched east for a full hour into Manessite territory.

Winded by the unaccustomed exertion, Caphtor's breath came in loud gasps. None of his guard seemed affected in the least by their long march. The knowledge did not sit well with him. Still, he trudged on, trying to control the length and volume of each inhale and exhale.

After an eternity they reached a place where the tree growth was even more meager than the sparse wood through which they'd marched. Raynor called a halt and the squad drew near, forming a tight knot of men ready to hear their commander's orders. Caphtor pressed himself into the center.

"Here's where we split." Raynor glared at Caphtor, daring him to disagree.

"Here? In the middle of the forest?"

Raynor nodded toward the north, behind Caphtor's back. The Governor turned and noticed for the first time the unmistakable site of an army camp in the distance — flickering splotches of firelight and dark

shadows of what could only be tents. He hadn't realized they'd arrived so near the southern edge of
Manessah's camp.

He'd agreed to the role of observer on this mission,
which was the only reason Raynor had let him come. A
shame to come this close and sit out the action, but at
the sight of all those campfires, a ribbon of fear twined
through his mind. Rather than risk being overheard,
he nodded. Raynor gestured for his two guards to stay
with the Governor until the squad returned. If the men
were disappointed in not being able to complete the
mission for which they had trained, they hid it well,
and took up their positions on either side of Caphtor
as the rest of their squad disappeared into the darkness toward the north.

Caphtor watched the men become one with the
black of night until no one remained but the three of
them. A sigh escaped his lips, a sound louder in the
silent wood than he intended. He selected a large tree
and lowered himself to the ground in front of it. His
guard paced in irregular circles around him, peering
into the darkness.

How long would Raynor be?

Diligence might be praiseworthy, but it wasn't very
interesting. Caphtor watched his guards pace, but
soon grew bored with it. The warm air and sounds of
the night relaxed him. A soft breeze high above stirred
the leaves of the tallest trees, and their gentle whisper
was better than a lullaby. Caphtor slipped into a light
sleep.

He was awakened by a sharp and painful kick to
his left thigh, and a bright light shining in his face. He
jerked upright and glared upward at the idiot who
dared to treat him so. The curse died unspoken on his
lips at the glimpse of a yellow beard. A quick glance
told him he was surrounded by Manessite soldiers.

He scrambled to his feet, expecting at any moment
to be knocked down again. Another glance told him his
own guards were not in evidence.

"They won't be much help to you." A deep voice spoke from the darkness just beyond his range of vision.

Caphtor lifted his chin high. "What won't be much help?"

"Your guards. They put up something of a struggle, and we were forced to kill them. Show him, Dicksel."

The light swung away from Caphtor's face, and he blinked to see past bright spots in his vision. When he could focus, he saw two bodies in Cainlan uniforms dumped in an unlikely tangle on the ground. A streak of fear shot through him. How long had he been asleep? And where was Raynor? If he kept these Mannesite soldiers occupied, perhaps the squadron leader would return and take them by surprise.

The light swung back to his face, and the authoritative voice spoke. "Your friends can't help you. We caught them before they entered the camp."

Caphtor said nothing. Raynor was too good to be caught so quickly.

"He wasn't as good as you think he was. If he was the best you've got, Manessah will have an easy time conquering Cainlan."

"You haven't had an easy time so far," Caphtor snapped. But as the words left his lips, he realized the voice had responded aloud to his thoughts.

Fear punched him in the gut. What had the men said? That the general could read minds. If that were true—

"You're right, Governor. Dicksel, put away that beam-light and give us a broad one so we can be properly introduced."

The light snapped off, and a dimmer, broad range light was flipped on. Caphtor could see the owner of the voice, and he almost wished he couldn't.

Andon was huge, a real giant. He towered at least half again as tall as the tallest of his soldiers, and none of them were small men. Muscles bulged in his arms and thighs as big around as Caphtor's waist. His face was almost beautiful, with a strong nose, perfectly formed chin and full, sensuous lips. Caphtor had no trouble believing the tale about his father being an angel or maybe a demon.

The giant threw back his head, and laughter rang like music through the night air. "Rumors of my parentage have spread to Cainlan, have they? Well, I don't know if he was an angel or a devil, but I've benefited from the gifts he bestowed. Such as the one you've just become aware of, the trick of hearing thoughts. Which is how I knew where to find you. Your man Raynor was extremely concerned that you remain hidden, and imagine my surprise when I discovered that the Governor of Cainlan's Council lurked nearby in our forest. Of course I had to find you, to meet you. You and I have a lot to talk about."

Caphtor kept his face impassive, but chaos reigned in his thoughts. If this man, this giant, could read his thoughts, Cainlan was in jeopardy. City secrets, conversations with other Councilors, army strategies – they all flashed quickly into his mind before he clamped down.

Concentrate on something inconsequential. Think about Raynor. He already knows about Raynor.

Andon smiled. "It's no use, Governor. All I have to do is mention a subject and you'll think about it. For instance, I'd like to know when Brendolan plans to attack our forces...ah, I see. He won't, until he gets me out of the way." Andon's smile widened. "That won't happen anytime soon, but it's a wise decision. Brendolan is a good strategist, though there is one thing I don't understand. How could he be so stupid as to send the Governor of Cainlan along?"

Beads of sweat broke out on Caphtor's forehead. *I will not think!*

Andon's laugh rang out again. "You should have listened to your general, Governor."

"What do you intend to do with me?" Caphtor ground out the question, horrified when fear leaked into his voice.

"Nothing." A pause, and then he continued in a tone that sent chills marching across Caphtor's arm. "At least, not right now. First, I have some questions that need answers. For instance, is there a way for my men to get into the city of Cainlan without being seen? Think of a way, Governor."

Caphtor struggled not to think. His mind grasped for anything else. Eliana. Liadan. His latest lover lying back on the pillows of his couch. But no matter how he struggled to avoid the thought, the tunnel leading from the Chamber to the temple popped into his head.

"The Chamber?" A low chuckle filled the clearing. "Interesting. We'll get to that in a moment. First, tell me where that tunnel leads."

Though his teeth ground with the effort, Caphtor couldn't stop his thoughts. His mind was laid bare for the general to read.

Andon's voice held a satisfied smile. "A plan begins to manifest. You're doing well, Governor. On to the next question. Tell me about the production of energy."

I'm going to die. The realization hit Caphtor with the weight of a boulder.

The giant drew close and stooped until his face hovered inches from Caphtor's. "Of course you are. But not before you've told me everything I need to know."

A dark pit yawned in Caphtor's mind. Helpless to stop himself, he stepped into it.

Chapter 27

The day after news of Caphtor's death reached the city, Eliana awoke itching with irritation. Her skin felt sticky, as though she'd rubbed oil into it the night before and then slept between dirty sheets. She refused to eat before she had a bath, but scrubbing her body in the clean, scented water did little to alleviate the stickiness or lighten her mood. She broke her fast in silence, ignoring the nervous page who brought it.

Davina moped about the apartment, readying Eliana's clothes for the day with a face pulled long in grief. Eliana supposed her own attitude could be attributed to grief as well, though if that were so, it felt nothing like she'd expected. She'd received the news of Caphtor's death in silence, her face stoic as the messenger relayed the words sent by the High Priestess. It hadn't occurred to her until late at night to question why the message from the battlefront had been delivered to Liadan instead of to her.

"I'm not wearing that." She lifted her glare from the soil-colored gown laid out on her bed to Davina.

Caphtor's attendant scowled. "You don't have anything else that suits."

"What does it matter?" Eliana huffed a vexed breath. "I'm stuck in here for five days, unable to see anyone but you and an occasional page until his body is returned and entombed."

Davina turned an exasperated expression toward her. "If the Primogentor doesn't follow tradition, who will? You must wear this color for five days, and this is the only thing you have." She paused, then added an accusation. "You didn't wear it yesterday."

"The day was almost over by the time I got the news, and I wasn't going to change that late. And anyway, no one will know if I wear the proper color or not as long as I show up decently attired at the interment ceremony."

Davina's eyes narrowed. "I'll know."

Eliana ignored her. "Besides, if I wear that today I won't have anything to wear tomorrow. Or the next day, or the next."

"I've taken care of that. I've ordered four more gowns like this one. They'll arrive by evening."

Davina's mouth snapped shut, and Eliana fought to maintain her composure. Liadan would never allow herself to argue with a servant. None would dare to cross her.

She drew herself up. "I will choose my own wardrobe today. You are dismissed."

Davina's glared continued for a moment. Then she turned on her heel, a swifter movement than Eliana had ever seen the large woman make, and marched out of the sleeping room.

A few moments alone restored her calm somewhat and she regretted her actions. Why was she so out-of-sorts today? The cause might be grief, but more likely could be attributed to the odd, heavy feel of the air. She was a little ashamed of herself, after having spent so many years with the man, but she'd felt nothing more than a sense of shock upon hearing the news. The shock had been as much at the loss of the Governor of Cainlan's Council as at the loss of her consort — probably more.

She circled the room, then settled in a chair beside Melody's cage. Sunlight shafted through the window, and the little bird preened in a bright ray, using her tiny beak to separate the fine new scarlet feathers sprouting in her wings.

There would be a new Governor soon, selected by lottery from among the Council members. Virdin, Seneset, perhaps Limpopo?

Regardless, it made no difference to her. In the days since her meeting with Liadan, she'd come to a decision. She would no longer bend a knee to a false god, nor to his high priestess, who took the lives of children to feed the city's hunger for power. Her heart felt no sorrow, not any longer. She'd given her life to the One God five years before, and she would honor that vow until she drew her last breath. His ways were beyond her understanding, and she had stopped trying.

Did You do this to me? Did You bring Girta here so I grew up knowing there was something else besides service to Cain?

And what of Shem? His name, even unspoken, sent a dart of pain through her heart. Why would the One God lead her to him, and then deny her? The question had remained unanswered for years. No doubt it would for the rest of her short life.

Melody hopped onto a smooth branch in her cage and cocked her head to fix a bright eye on Eliana. Her beak opened, and her sweet whistling voice rose high and light. It seemed almost to mix with the rays of light that filtered into her cage from the brilliant sky outside. Eliana raised her head, watching the delicate bird trill a song so intricate that the notes seemed to blend with one another in a complex harmony. The melody was new, a composition of love and passion and pain all together, born in the tiny brain of this amazing creature. Eliana's heart responded to the song, and tears rose to her eyes.

When the song faded, the bird continued to fix her with an unblinking stare. This little gift from Shem had given her years of pleasure, and Eliana loved her.

What would happen to Melody when she died? What would they do with her?

An idea occurred to Eliana. She rose and hurried to her dressing table. If she took time to consider her action, she might change her mind. Extracting a slip of parchment and a writing implement, she penned a quick note.

While the ink dried she called for a page. Eliana handed the note to the boy, then lifted Melody's cage from its stand and placed it in the child's arms.

"Take this to Arphaxad in Security," she said. "Tell him I want it delivered to Shem de Noah. He'll know where that is."

The boy left, struggling to carry the cage that was almost as tall as he himself. Eliana returned to her seat and stared out the window, across the open field, into the trees that spread across the horizon. She spent a long time there, trying not to picture Shem as he read her note.

Chapter 28

Shem unloaded the cart, storing the last of Mother's crates in the belly of the ark. He straightened and looked at the result of his family's labor in the flickering lamplight. Hundreds of crates of food, plants, supplies, clothing and other necessities lined this storage compartment. Not a handspan's space remained. Still, Shem experienced a nagging worry that this wouldn't be enough.

"The One God will take care of us," Father had assured him when he'd expressed that concern a few days before. "If necessary He can multiply our supplies. He would not go to all the trouble of saving us from disaster simply to let us die of starvation afterward."

That did make sense, but Shem worried nonetheless.

Stepping outside into the sunshine was always a shock. No matter how many times Shem saw all the

animals that had gathered here, awe overtook him
when he looked at them again. If ever anyone needed
proof that Noah's prophecy was true, here it was. They
were everywhere — in the grass, which they'd cropped
almost bare, in the fields, which they'd picked cleaner
than any gleaner could, and in the forest, which had
been stripped of every visible sign of greenery and
most of the bark.

Shem glanced at the sun to gauge the time. The
men had decided to stop using all energy-powered
gadgets in preparation for the time in the not-too-
distant future when such things would be unavailable.
The women had steadfastly refused, insisting that they
had the rest of their lives to learn how to do without,
they saw no reason to start before they had to. Mother
had even become something of a lavish spender, a big
change from her spendthrift habits of the past. She'd
ordered and received more fabric than Shem thought
could be used by five generations. They also had more
metal pots and utensils than Shem considered necessary, but she said she had no idea how long the tech-
nique of metal work would take to develop. Shem
agreed with her on that — he and his brothers had no
idea how to extract and work raw metal.

The sun rode high in the sky. Shem walked down
the ramp toward Samson. He left the ark open, since
some of the animals had already taken up residence
inside. They'd laid their claims on stalls, and even carried in their own bedding material.

As he and Samson neared the house, a rider
turned from the forest and headed down the path. He
urged Samson into a trot. The rider slowed when a
pair of adolescent bears strayed across the path in
front of it, stopping for a playful swat at the nosepiece.
Shem had arrived and stood near Samson's shed, a
pair of raccoons frolicking at his feet, when the rider
glided to a halt.

A young man, little more than a boy really, stepped
out of the vehicle with wide, round eyes. Shem smoth-

ered a grin at his awed expression as his gaze fixed on the ark. He didn't wait for the inevitable question, but offered his often-repeated explanation.

"It's an ark, a type of boat, and we don't plan to move it to the ocean. We believe the True God of Heaven, the Creator of all mankind, will shortly send flood waters to cover the earth, and He has directed my father to prepare a place where a remnant of His creation can be kept safe."

The boy eyes became uninterested. "Oh."

He turned away to unload his delivery from the rear cargo panel of his rider. He set the birdcage in the grass at Shem's feet.

What could this be? I've already received all the special orders I placed. Shem's pulse quickened when he recognized the bird's breed. A crested pisidia.

"Here's a note. My boss says sorry it's late; we got busy and couldn't get out here 'till today."

Numb, Shem took the sealed note without a word. The young man didn't wait for thanks, but slipped into the pilot seat of his rider and closed the panel without a backward glance. Before Shem had broken the seal on the note the rider was on its way back to Cainlan.

Hunger rose inside him as he lifted the flap of parchment and devoured the words written in an even, flowing script.

Shem de Noah,

Do you remember what you told me about this little bird? The tale must be true, for she carries my heart with her. I send her to you, for safekeeping against what comes. Maybe the One God will allow that much of me to go with you in His ark.

I wish you well,
Eliana

Shem read the note again, and then a third time. A

fourth reading proved impossible, for tears blurred his vision.

Invisible bands around his heart, placed there years before, released, and the anguish hidden there seeped outward. He sank to his knees in the grass beside the birdcage, the note clutched in a trembling fist

Why do I love someone who is so completely out of reach? Is it too much to ask to love someone of my faith, of my bloodline? His gaze swept heavenward. *Am I to go into your new world alone? Because if that's your plan, I want no part of it. Leave me here, and give my place to another.*

He sank to his knees and buried his face in his hands. Tears burned as they left his eyes.

A bright light surrounded him. For an instant, he thought the end had come. His eyes were blinded, as though the sun had exchanged its yellow hue for one white and pure, and had drawn close above to cover him with the warmth of its brilliant rays. He'd seen this white light before, the night the ark had been attacked.

"Peace to you, Shem son of Noah." The voice spoke in a tone deep and rich. Anger and pain fled, replaced by a peace so complete his heart soared. "I bring tidings to soothe your soul. The Lord your God has heard your plea, indeed has known your innermost feelings from before you walked this earth. He is a God of compassion. Know this, that the woman you desire will be the mother of your children. From your loins and her womb will spring forth a generation after God's own heart, the fulfillment of His desire. Make haste and take her unto yourself. And blessed will be your path."

Then the bright light disappeared, and Shem blinked. The sunlight seemed dingy and dull after the brilliance of heaven's messenger. His thoughts reeled, yet his heart felt light and free. Eliana was his!

The angel's command burned inside him. *Make haste.*

He leapt up and snatched at Samson's lead. A

sense of urgency speeding his movements, he freed the horse from the cart.

Wait. He couldn't leave without letting someone know. With a pace quick as a cheetah, he dashed to the house and burst through the door. His family, all six of them, turned astonished gazes his way.

"I'm going to get her." The words flew out of him, fueled by the joy that overflowed his heart. "The One God said I could!"

Chapter 29

The room was getting smaller. Eliana awoke on the fourth day of enforced confinement to discover that the walls of her bedroom seemed to have shrunk. While she knew that wasn't true, she opened her eyes and fixed a hateful glare on the sameness that was beginning to drive her to distraction.

Her skin again felt sticky between clammy bed sheets and the air seemed charged with an energy that caused an almost uncontrollable evil temper to have taken up permanent residence throughout the apartment. Davina strode about with a perpetual scowl of disapproval, and Eliana found herself doing things purposefully designed to irritate her. To make matters worse, a dull ache pressed against her skull.

The page deposited her breakfast tray on a table next to the window.

Davina lingered a moment longer, fixing Eliana with a determined stare. "When you've broken your fast, I'll help you dress for the day." She cast a meaningful glance toward the dressing table, where another dull brown gown lay ready.

Eliana heaved an audible sigh as the woman left the room. Silence pressed against her ears, the same silence she'd endured for days. Her head pounded. Perhaps food would help.

She sauntered over to the table and sat gazing out the window as she made her breakfast from the tray of fruit and sweet cakes. She'd just finished her first sweet cake when she heard someone come into the room behind her.

"I'm nearly finished, Davina."

No answer. When Eliana turned, shock slammed into her like a fist. There, standing beside her dressing table, was Caphtor's long-ago personal attendant and lover, Melita. She held a dagger, the blade long and bloody. It swung casually from her right hand, as though it were nothing more than a timepiece on a chain. Blood splattered the front of her sky-blue robe.

She smiled, and the expression sent a shaft of terror through Eliana.

"Davina is gone." Her soft voice held the cold of the grave. "I'm afraid she won't be back."

Fear tightened her throat and threatened her breath. "What have you done with her?" She meant it to be a demand, but to her horror what came out was nothing more than a whisper.

"I've done her a favor, really."

Eliana couldn't force a word through her throat.

"Don't you want to know what kind of favor I've done her?"

She didn't respond, but Melita answered anyway.

"I saved her from a terrible death by savages."

She's deranged. Maybe, if she kept talking someone would come and—

Her fists tightened. No one would come. She was in mourning.

Keep her talking.

"What kind of savages?"

"We've been attacked." A drop of blood slid from the dagger's blade to the floor. "They got into the temple through a secret tunnel and they've spread throughout the government buildings, killing everyone they see."

For the first time, distant sounds registered on Eliana's ears. A muted scream, shouts, the pounding of feet in the corridor outside her door. Acid churned in her stomach.

"I've just saved your attendant from a terrible death. I'm sure she'd much rather die at the hand of one of her own kind than a foreigner." Melita brandished the knife. "Wouldn't you?"

Eliana shook her head. "I'd rather not die at all." Her glance flickered around the room. There was nothing that could be used as a weapon, nothing she could get to.

Melita's eyes narrowed. "You don't have a choice, little High Priestess-to-be. I've waited for this, planned it a thousand times. If it hadn't been for you I would have been here with him, all this time."

Eliana's knees began to quake. Her grip on the chair tightened. If she let go, she'd collapse to the floor.

"Now he's gone, and so are his plans." Melita's voice maintained a deadly calm. "And shortly, you will be too."

Melita lunged forward and raised the dagger. Acting by instinct rather than design, Eliana jerked the chair from behind her with her right hand, intending to use it as a shield. Panic gave her strength, and the chair swung around her body and flew out of her grasp. It hit Melita in the chest, and the dagger clattered for the floor.

Eliana leapt toward the door at a run. Melita lunged after her. For an instant she thought she might make it, and then a hand closed on her arm. She was flung sideways, and her feet became tangled in a toss rug. A moment later she crashed to the floor. Melita landed across her body. With a profane perversion of a smile, she reached for the dagger.

Eliana squeezed her eyes shut, anticipating the feel of the blade.

An odd noise filled the room, a whistle and whir, followed by an explosion that left her ears ringing. Melita was thrown backward, off her body.

She opened her eyes, and shut them again. The woman had been flung against the foot of the bed, her chest a gruesome mass of torn flesh. Blood pumped from the wound.

Eliana jerked her head toward the door, and a relieved sob rose from her lungs.

Stunned, Arphaxad looked from Melita's body to the odd-looking weapon in his hands. "I had no idea it would be so devastating. How evil have we become, to create such a thing?"

Eliana scooted to the wall and leaned against it for support. A knot of tears almost choked her. Arphaxad dashed forward and jerked her to her feet with a strong grip on her arm.

"We've got to hurry. We don't have much time." He pulled her toward the door.

"Where are we going?"

"Away. The Manessite army has invaded Cainlan, and they're massacring everyone they see. They've already killed the High Priestess, and no doubt they're on their way here."

The impact of Arphaxad's words struck her. She jerked to a halt, numb. "The High Priestess? Liadan is dead?"

Arphaxad nodded, his expression sad amidst his obvious desire for speed. "I'm sorry, my lady. I just came from there." He hefted the weapon. "I took this from a fallen Manessite soldier. My guards are trying to hold them off, but our weapons are no match for theirs. We've got to hurry."

Eliana looked down at her body. She still wore her

night shift, though now it was smeared with blood. Moving quickly, she snatched the brown grief gown, then followed Arphaxad through the doorway. In the main room of her apartment another horror waited. Davina's body crumpled in a heap on the floor, a gaping wound in her throat.

Arphaxad cracked the door open and peeked through. Then he grabbed Eliana's hand and pulled her into the corridor. Shouts sounded in the distance, and a sudden loud crash much nearer.

"Hurry."

They'd run almost the length of the temple when Arphaxad stopped and took a key from within his tunic. He unlocked a door Eliana had seen many times but never been through, and they entered a dark storage room. He led her through boxes and crates piled up toward the ceiling. In the back corner, he tugged on a rope that protruded from a crack where the wall met the floor. The wall moved outward, and before she could fully take in the presence of the secret tunnel, he jerked her into it.

"Is this the secret tunnel the soldiers came through?" She dared not raise her voice above a whisper.

"No. They came in through the Eternal Fires and the Chamber."

At the end of a long tunnel, he opened another door and pulled Eliana through. They emerged into a dim light, and after a moment Eliana realized they faced a thick tapestry. Now her sense of direction snapped into place. An old, tattered tapestry hung on the wall of a storage room in the rider shed. She'd always thought it an odd place for a wall hanging.

They slipped out from behind the tapestry. Arphaxad grabbed two heavy energy cartridges and shoved them toward her without a word. She tossed her gown over her shoulder and grabbed one in each hand. Arphaxad held his weapon at ready before him, though Eliana devoutly hoped he would not have to use it again.

No one was in sight. His two-person vehicle was parked near the shed doors, and they hurried there. Through the open door Eliana had a clear view of the temple and several windows. Was anyone watching from those windows?

Eliana climbed into the rider while Arphaxad connected one of the cartridges. She stored the spare at her feet and secured the safety straps. When he finished, he started to climb in beside her.

A movement behind him drew Eliana's gaze. A shriek escaped her throat. Two Manessite soldiers rounded the side of the shed, their weapons held ready. Arphaxad whirled and swung his into position. All three fired at the same moment, but the soldiers' aim was better than Arphaxad's. One soldier was thrown backward, but to Eliana's horror Arphaxad's body was thrown with such force against the side of the rider that the vehicle jolted. She screamed, struggling to unfasten her straps to help him. To her amazement Arphaxad stood up.

"Don't worry." Pain wracked his voice. "Shoulder wound. Not serious."

As he climbed into the pilot's seat, she saw the torn flesh of his shoulder. His arm hung useless at his side.

"Hold on." He nodded toward the open shed door, where five more soldiers approached at a run. He shoved the lever to the high notch. The rider hit the shed door at the same time the side panel started to close, and splinters of wood showered her as they crashed through. Arphaxad hissed. The pain must be excruciating.

The door was still descending when one of the soldiers fired at them. It exploded into large chunks of metal. A piece dangled in the breeze as they gained velocity, careening westward toward the forest.

She turned in her seat. The soldiers looked their way, but none moved to follow.

"I think they've given us up," she said

He nodded, but did not slow their pace until they were inside the cover of the trees. Her gaze returned again and again to his wounded shoulder. Blood seeped from the wound to saturate his tunic.

Time crawled, though Eliana had no way to judge its passing besides the rapid beating of her own heart. After an eternity, the rider slowed, and Arphaxad guided the vehicle off the path, under the cover of trees. When he seemed satisfied with their location, he stopped.

Eliana unbuckled the safety straps and climbed out. She turned, expecting him to follow her, but he did not move. The amount of blood covering his chest sent waves of shock rippling through her. Panic bloomed at the sight, but she fought it down. She wouldn't be of any help at all if she fell apart.

"Let me help you." She leaned in and unstrapped his safety harness. He did not protest as she pulled his legs around toward her, then slipped his good arm over her shoulders. She heaved, staggering beneath his weight. He gained his balance and pulled away from her, but collapsed against the side of the rider and slid to the ground.

Swallowing fear, she retrieved the medic kit from the storage compartment.

"You rest a bit," she told him, kneeling in the grass beside him. "Then we'll go to the farm of Noah de Lamech. He'll help us."

Arphaxad struggled to push words from a breathless chest. "No use."

"Don't say that." Eliana pulled a wad of gauze and a bottle of clear water from the kit. "I'll clean you up, and then you'll feel better."

As carefully as she could, she pulled the shredded fabric away from the wound. Fear rose at the sight that met her. His shoulder was shattered, all the way down the arm and even part of his chest. Fresh water flushed away stray pieces of flesh and splintered bone, but no matter how many times she pressed cotton against the wound, blood continued to flow. She reached for another, and another, her fear growing. She could not stop the flow.

Arphaxad spoke, his voice low. "Have to talk."

He reached up with his right hand and pushed her away. The blood flow increased with even that feeble movement, and she stopped.

"What do you want to talk about?" Her voice caught on lump of pain.

"You. Me. Your mother." His eyes fixed on her face.

"My mother? What about her?"

"I...loved her, once. She didn't love me, but...I did. She...needed me." He closed his eyes, wincing against a wave of pain. "Ashbel couldn't...father. So I did."

Numbness stole over her. She stared down at Arphaxad as the truth became clear. "Liadan was the woman you loved? The one you told me about?" Arphaxad nodded. "Then that means you're..." She swallowed. "You're my father."

Arphaxad nodded again, and a faint smile appeared on his lips. "My greatest joy."

Everything fell into place. Liadan's sneers against her parentage, comments about being 'ill-bred,' her disregard for her offspring and heir. Of course Liadan, in her conceit, would have been horrified to find it necessary to search for someone else to father her heir. That embarrassment would have transferred to the child, especially if that child had inherited a mild manner instead of Liadan's aggressive nature. Even some of Arphaxad's comments over the years made more sense now, such as the one about Eliana's having an outside influence Liadan never had. And she'd thought he meant Girta.

Arphaxad was struggling to say more. "My bloodline...yours too...of Seth's line."

Joy crept into the deep recesses of her soul. "I'm descended from Seth." Not so odd, then, that she had been drawn to the One God after all. Like Liadan said, blood always tells.

Arphaxad nodded, though his head barely moved. "And Cain. A child of both. The best of both."

Eliana would have argued that had she not been so concerned for him. How could anything good come from Cain, the first murderer? She switched the bloody gauze pad, shushing him. "Thank you for telling me, *adame*." This time her use of the title was both a great joy and a bitter agony as she stared down at his pain-racked face. "Now it's even more important that you get better. Let me get you to Noah de Lamech. They can help."

His words were so soft she had to stoop down and place her ear next to his lips. "Remember...the One God loved Cain too...gave him protection. All children are His."

His eyelids closed.

"Hush." Tears blurred her vision and spilled down her cheeks. She grasped his hand and squeezed. "We'll rest here a bit, that's all. And then we'll go on, and Noah de Lamech will take care of you."

Soothing words poured out of her, though she hardly knew what she said. As she watched, the strength ebbed out of him. The skin of his face sagged before her eyes. His breath became shallow, and Eliana's tears flowed so freely she could not see his chest move at all. She ran out of words and fell silent, holding his hand as he died.

At the end, with one great effort, he opened his eyes and lifted them to her face.

"My greatest joy." A smile that belied his weakness lit his features. Then his head fell forward and Arphaxad breathed no more.

Chapter 30

Shem gripped Samson's sides with his legs as they galloped along the rough path. Though the horse was more accustomed to pulling a cart, he seemed to sense Shem's urgency and surged forward without balking.

Shem let him have his head, his mind full. How would he approach Eliana when he arrived at the temple? The manner of their last parting could hardly be considered friendly.

He was so preoccupied with his own thoughts he missed the first path through the forest, the one he customarily took. That one came upon Cainlan from the north, and was the more traveled. He almost turned around, but decided to go on to the second path, the more secluded one. It would lead to the south side of Cainlan, the side nearest the temple.

Though the sun would not set for several hours, and the dense forest wrapped this trail in green darkness. Shem caught sight of a rider ahead of them, stopped on the side of the trail. His first instinct was to guide Samson around. But what if there had been an accident? What if someone were hurt?

As he drew near, he knew he'd been right. The door panel was missing, and the metal on this side was charred and blackened as though by fire. He drew alongside, and slowed Samson to a halt.

A movement on the other side of the rider drew his gaze. The sound of a soft sob reached him, and his heart lurched. He dismounted and rounded the rider.

Two people sat on the ground, surrounded by a pile of bloody cotton. A man lay prone, his chest covered in blood, his head in the lap of a woman. It was her sob he'd heard. Her head bowed over his, a curtain of dark hair falling across his face. She did not move, but her pose conveyed a depth of anguish.

Sympathy twisted his stomach, and the memory of his pain after Mara's death stabbed at him again. A strangled noise came from his own throat. The woman turned at the sound.

Shem gasped.

Eliana raised her face to his, her eyes tortured. "We were coming to you," she said. "I hoped your family would help us."

The pain in her voice wrenched his heart. Love swelled inside him, mingled with purpose. Whatever he could do to soothe her pain, he would.

"The One God sent me."

She nodded, as though this was no surprise to her. Her hand smoothed the hair of the dead man. "This is my father. My friend. His name was Arphaxad."

A million questions came to mind, but he couldn't ask them now. Instead, he knelt beside her and took her hand. It was cold. Her eyes were black bowls, their lids puffy and red from crying.

"What can I do to help you?"

She drew a shuddering breath. "He was of your bloodline. The bloodline of Seth. Girta told me the custom of her family was to lay their dead in tombs." Her gaze circled the trees around them. "But there are no caves here."

Shem put an arm around her and pulled her close. She seemed so frail, so tiny, yet her grief so large. He pressed his lips to her forehead. "When we have no tomb, we make one instead."

A little way into the forest they found a creek with a stony bed. They excavated stones until they had a huge pile, and then they returned to the rider for Arphaxad's body.

"I'll move him," Shem told her.

She looked at him with huge, dark eyes, and nodded. "I must do one thing, and then I'll join you."

She ducked into the rider. Shem slipped his arms beneath Arphaxad's and pulled the man through the forest to their makeshift tomb.

A moment later, Eliana appeared wearing a brown gown. A grief gown, of the kind the people of Cainlan wore to mourn the passing of a loved one.

A hand smoothed the fabric. "I couldn't bear to wear it before." She looked at Arphaxad's body. "It seems right now."

Shem arranged the man's remains on a bed of rock, then they worked together to cover him. By the time their task was finished, the sun had dipped low, and long shadows filled the forest.

They stood side by side, gazing down at the mound of rock.

"He worshiped your God, the God of his fathers." Her quiet voice held a suppressed sob.

Shem took her hand. "We believe that the One God gathers His children to Him, taking them to heaven to be with Him forever. Death is a time of rejoicing for followers of the One God."

Eliana looked up at him with a skeptical expression, and Shem shrugged. "For the one who dies, anyway."

"I don't know the right words," she said, "but I

want to say something."

Shem squeezed her hand. "God hears your heart in your words. Say what seems right."

Her throat moved as she swallowed, then lifted her eyes toward the darkening sky. "True God of Heaven, I commit the soul of Arphaxad de Mahalaleel to You, for Your safekeeping. He was a good man, God of Adam, a son of your son Seth, and worthy of that bloodline. His life was not perfect, but he loved well and he served well and he was well loved. Let him rest with his fathers, One God."

"That was perfect," he whispered.

They stood a while longer, and the darkness grew. There was so much to say Shem didn't know where to begin. Dazed, numb from shock and grief, she needed a place to recover, to feel secure for a while.

He knew just the place.

Eliana stood on the porch while Shem unlocked the cabin door. He had sent his horse home alone and piloted Arphaxad's landrider. It traveled faster, which they may need if any from the Manessite army tried to follow her. During the ride to this place, she'd told him the events of the day. The tale left her exhausted.

Stars glittered overhead, and the moon cast a white light over this mountaintop clearing. So this was the cabin of the oldest man in the world. She touched a rough wood log. How she wished she could have met him.

"There." He pushed the door open. "You'll have everything you need here. The bed linens are even clean."

She entered the single room. A narrow pallet in one corner beckoned, and she longed to sink onto it.

Shem rummaged in a chest and drew out a stack of linens. "I'll be outside if you need anything. Tomorrow, after you've rested, we'll make plans."

His words startled her. Where was he going? "Is

there another cabin?"

"No, I'll make my bed beneath the stars." He smiled. "Don't worry, I've done it often."

He crossed toward the door, but stopped when he neared. His presence sent her blood racing through her veins. A memory rushed back to her, of the first time they'd met. She'd thought him the most handsome man she'd ever seen. She still thought so.

"It seems you've saved my life again. First from bandits, and now from..." She gestured in the vague direction of Cainlan. "Everything."

"Maybe that's why the One God brought us together." Though the room was dark, she saw the flash of white teeth as he grinned. "So I could come to your rescue."

Another memory surfaced, this one bringing with it a hot flush of embarrassment. She dropped her gaze to the floor. "I'm sorry about, you know. My request. It was wrong of me to even ask. I was thinking only of myself, without a thought for you." A painful lump swelled in her throat. "Or your wife."

He said nothing for a long moment. Then he raised a hand and placed a warm finger beneath her chin. She tilted her head back. His eyes were shrouded in shadow.

"I need to tell you something." His voice dropped to a whisper. "Mara was killed a few weeks ago."

A wave of sorrow washed through her. Coming so freshly upon her own loss, she felt the pain of his more deeply.

Then the import of his words struck her mind. He had no wife.

"Sleep well, Eliana."

The door closed behind him. Numb, Eliana sank onto the pallet.

Chapter 31

Two days passed. Shem showed Eliana how to find ripe fruit for their meals, and took her on the trails he'd followed as a boy while visiting Grandfather Methuselah. As he watched, this mountain sanctuary worked its healing on her. Her eyes lost the haunted look, and her skin grew rosy with long days in the sun.

They did not discuss Mara, or Governor Caphtor. But at night, as Shem lay beneath the stars, he opened his heart to the One God.

What do I say? How do I convince her that my love is real? She's been hurt. She's vulnerable. I don't want to take advantage of her.

But with each hour that passed, a sense of urgency grew inside him. The air took on a heavy quality, unlike any he'd ever felt. The forest animals seemed skittish, as though they sensed a coming danger they could not identify.

Shem could. The floods were coming. Everything in

him shouted that they must hurry to the ark.

Finally, he could wait no longer.

He found her at mid-day, sitting before Grandfather Methuselah's tomb. Upon seeing him, a smile broke free on her face, and his heart swelled in response.

This is *your plan, isn't it? Surely love like this isn't possible without you.*

She patted the ground next to her. "Tell me another story of Grandfather Methuselah."

Instead of sitting, Shem paced to the boulders that sealed the tomb. A sudden attack of nerves made it impossible to stand still. He'd rehearsed his speech a dozen times, reciting it to the stars and the birds roosting in the trees around the cabin. But as he looked into her expectant face, different words flew out of his mouth.

"Eliana, I want you to be my wife."

Her lips parted, and her eyes went round.

He rushed forward to stand before her. "Normally I would wait a long time before I took another wife. But I don't think we have much time. The farm is swarming with animals, ready to enter the ark. The One God has set the day for the flood, and I believe it's not far off."

She stood abruptly and walked a few steps away to stand with her back to him. His stomach sank. He'd offended her by being too abrupt.

One God, give me the words to convince her.

He approached quietly to stand behind her, close enough to feel heat from her body without touching her. He had to tell her the rest, and then she could make her decision.

"One more thing you should know. The day your note arrived, something happened. Something wonderful. An angel appeared to me. He told me to come and get you, that the One God had made us for each other. He urged me to hurry. That's when I found you in the forest." She still did not move. "I know this is unseemly. But please believe me when I tell you that I love

you. I want to be with you always. To share in your
future, and have you share in mine. Please, Eliana,
will you be my wife?"

She turned, her face tilted toward his. Sunlight
sparkled in the tears that streamed down her face.
When she spoke her voice wavered. "I want to be your
wife more than anything."

Late afternoon, and the sun still shone on the
mountaintop. Eliana's stomach fluttered as she stood
beside Shem at the altar his grandfather had long
used to worship his God. She smiled. Her God.

Brilliant sunrays shone on a flat stone. From its
charred and blackened surface Eliana knew this was
an altar, and the One God had accepted many offerings here. As He had accepted her own, five years ago.

I asked you to give me a man like Shem. She lifted a
smile toward the heavens. *Thank you.*

Shem's arm crept up to her waist, pulling her near.
"Are you sure?"

So many things floated through Eliana's mind that
for a moment she didn't know how to reply. How could
he ask that? Didn't he know how she had loved him
from their very first meeting? Didn't he realize how often she had thought of him since?

"If you were not your father's son, but some other
man without prospect or future or even the means to
make a living, I would marry you. If it meant that tomorrow I would die, I would do so just to spend one
night as your wife."

The joy that lit his face poured over her like water
on a wilted flower. His arms stole around her and drew
her near. She placed her head against his neck, feeling
his pulse throb in her cheek, and breathed deeply of
his scent. If the world ended at that moment, Eliana
would die happy.

Shem backed away, and stood looking down at her.

"If we were celebrating our marriage in front of our families, there would be vows and offerings. The ceremony would go on all day." A tender smile tugged at his lips. "Though it's selfish of me, I am glad I have you to myself."

Eliana's mind wandered back to her alliance celebration. She suppressed a shudder. "I don't want anyone here but you."

Shem lifted his head to the sky. "True God of Heaven, we are yours. Your people. Children of your children. We offer ourselves to you, and to each other. Husband and wife. Male and female, as you created us. Join us together, flesh and soul."

From beneath his tunic, he withdrew a length of rope. He took her hand in his, their elbows bent and their skin touching the length of their forearms. With his left hand he wrapped the rope around them.

"My covenant is with you and yours with me, from this time forward. I will honor you with my thoughts, my actions and my life. I will give my love and my children only to you. My vow is made before the True God of Heaven, to whom I am accountable." He nodded to her. "Your turn."

Heart in her throat, Eliana repeated the vow, and then they knelt together.

Joy rang in his voice. "As our hands are joined by this rope, so also now are our lives joined by the vows we have spoken. Our witness is the True God of Heaven, whose blessings we ask on our union."

They rose together, their arms bound. Shem dropped their hands to his side, and pulled her close with his other one. She raised her face to his, and he kissed her with a tenderness that made her want to laugh and cry at the same time.

When he lifted his head, he grinned. "Now is when all the people would cheer."

"My heart is cheering loud enough for a multitude." She pulled him to her for another kiss.

The short walk back to the cabin felt like a dream.

When they stepped through the doorway, her heart thundered. She was the wife of Shem de Noah.

He gathered her in his arms and his breath warmed her lips. Her body pressed against him, their hearts beating with a shared rhythm that filled her senses and made her head swim. Shem kissed her again, this time with a rising passion that snatched her breath. And then she was lost in the whirlwind of her husband's love.

Chapter 32

Eliana woke late in the morning, when Shem slipped out of her arms. She stretched and smiled up at him.

A noise startled them both, like a distant explosion that vibrated the air. They both ran for the door, and then froze, stunned at the sight that greeted them.

A large, grey mass that looked like thick smoke covered the sky, its edges billowing upward in huge puffs. The sun was above the mass, but as Eliana watched the greyness expanded upward, covering the entire eastern sky. At the rate the mass was growing it would catch up with the sun within a few hours, and by then it would also have reached them. She clutched Shem's arm.

"What is it?" Filled with a dreadful apprehension, she could not pry her eyes away from the sky. "Is it the war?"

"I don't think so." Shem's attention was riveted

eastward. "We need to leave, now. We must get to the ark before the waters come."

Her stomach tightened into a knot. With one more fearful glance toward the threatening sky, she whirled. She grabbed the few clothes she possessed, robes worn by Grandfather Methuselah, and his trousers that she kept on with a rope at the waist, and finally her grief gown. She had nothing else.

As she followed Shem out the door, he halted and spun to face her. The kiss he gave her was full of the urgency she felt, and also passion. It filled her with comfort.

"We'll be fine." His smile, though urgent, held confidence. "We began a new life last night as husband and wife. Today we make another beginning, and the One God will guide us as He has promised."

Eliana returned his smile, pouring all the confidence she could into it. Then Shem was out the door, pulling her along with him.

The rider flew down the mountain. She clutched the safety harness and could not stop looking up at the dark, threatening mass above them. Her stomach clenched with urgency. Though she did believe Shem's words concerning the One God's promise, the sight of that sky terrified her.

It seemed like days before they reached the forest at the mountain's foot. Shem pushed the lever forward, and the rider shot down a narrow path.

Time slowed to a halt. Above the treetops the grey smoky mass expanded, and seemed intent on pursuit. The air around them snapped with an eerie energy unlike anything she'd ever felt. Did the gray sky have something to do with this prickly feeling in the air?

The landscape grew familiar. Eliana had piloted this very rider here once before, when she visited Shem's home.

"We're almost there." Shem told her without taking his eyes off the path in front.

The sunlight disappeared. One moment they were

gliding through the greenish light of the forest and in the next instant they sank into a darkness almost as deep as night. Eliana couldn't help a shrill cry of alarm. Shem's hand tightened on the acceleration lever.

They emerged from the wooded area into a plain on the other side. Now they could see the full effect of the gray mass. It stretched across the sky as far as she could see, and it seemed close, so much closer than the sun. Her thumping heart threatened to bruise her ribs from the inside.

And then another sight snatched her breath. They had arrived at the farm. The ark rose huge and awesome into the sky, taller than the temple, taller than anything Eliana had ever seen. Five years before she'd gotten an idea of the ark's size, but completed it was so much more imposing. Covering the ground on all sides of the ark were animals, more animals than Eliana ever dreamed existed

Shem pointed the rider toward the ark, directly across a spent field. His family stood clustered at the bottom of the ramp, looking their way. There was Noah, now her father, in front of the others. Shem's brothers stood behind him, each with an arm around a woman. Eliana recognized Abiri, so the other must be Ham's wife. The woman standing nearby would be Shem's mother.

Now they were close enough for the people to recognize Shem in the pilot's seat of the small rider, and also to see Eliana beside him. The rider stopped with a jerk, and Shem himself unstrapped in an instant. Eliana did the same, while he leapt out and turned to take her bundle and her hand.

"It's all right. You're my wife. You're family now."

She looked into those wonderful eyes and saw love brimming there. Her fear fled and an unspoken prayer rose toward heaven. *One God, thank you for giving me this man.*

Then Shem turned, pulling her close to his side

with an arm around her waist. He approached his father. Eliana thought she saw a twinkle in the old man's eyes, and there was no mistaking the smile on his lined face.

"Ah, our guest returns," Noah said by way of greeting. "It seems you have news for us, my son?"

He turned expectant eyes on Shem, who stood straight and addressed his entire family.

"I have taken a wife," he announced without ceremony. "This is Eliana. We were married at Grandfather Methuselah's cabin last night at sunset."

Noah's smile broke into a wide grin and he came forward to take Eliana's shoulders in both hands. "My child, when I met you I knew the True God of Heaven had special plans for you. I didn't see how they could be involved with ours, but God is mighty enough to bring to pass all things in His own way and His own time. Welcome, daughter, into our home."

Tears stung her eyes while she returned his embrace. Then he grabbed her by the hand and pulled her away from Shem, taking the three steps toward the others.

"This is our new daughter," he announced to his wife. "And this is your new mother, my wife Midian."

Shem's mother looked at her a long moment. Her gaze slid to Shem, and then back again. Then she smiled as deeply as her husband and pulled Eliana into an embrace. With her lips close to Eliana's ear, she whispered. "I see in my son's face a joy I've never seen, and I already love you if for nothing more than that." She straightened, and released Eliana. "Daughter, you are welcome a thousand times."

The rest gathered around her, and took turns embracing her.

Soon Father Noah interrupted the greetings. "In normal times we would welcome you properly, but these are not normal times. The True God of Heaven has chosen His time. We must enter the ark."

Shem's gaze swept the animals. "How will we get

them inside?"

Noah smiled. "God will send them in."

Ham stepped forward. "We'll form a line inside and steer them into the stalls." He glanced at the blackened sky. "But I think we'd better hurry."

Japheth and Abiri were first into the ark, followed by Ham and Timna with Mother Midian. They went up the ramp, each person turning for one last look at their home before they stepped inside.

Eliana drew close to Shem, and he put his arm around her once again. Together they ascended the ramp, and they too stopped at the top. Turning, they gazed at the farm, and the surrounding forest, and the blackened sky.

"I've dreaded this moment for so long." Shem spoke so softly she wouldn't have heard had she not been standing in the shelter of his arm. "I never would have guessed that I could face it with such hope for the future." He pulled her closer with the arm he had around her. "That's because of you, my new wife."

Eliana dropped her bundle and threw both arms around his neck. "It's been so long since I even had a future to look forward to." She hugged him close. "How did I ever survive a day without you?"

"Come, children." Father Noah followed them up the ramp. "The animals are ready."

Indeed they were. The animals moved toward them, forming a line that began at the foot of the ramp. Eliana and Shem, with one last look in the direction of the city where they had met, picked up their bundles and entered the ark.

Noah stood at the top of the ramp and looked out over the fields he had farmed, now filled with the animals God had chosen to replenish the earth. He stretched his gaze toward the peak of the mountain where Grandfather Methuselah had lived. It was wrapped in the gloom of the darkened sky.

"One more use for that cabin." Chuckling, he shook his head. "You are truly a God of mysteries."

Two by two the animals passed by him on their way into the ark.

And Noah entered the ark, him and his wife and his sons and his sons' wives...and God closed him in.

Genesis 7:7,16b

Author's Note

When I was a girl my mother had a dream about a young woman named Eliana, the wife of Shem and daughter-in-law of Noah. She started writing a story about the daughter of a pagan priestess who was destined to become the many-times-great-grandmother of Jesus. For various reasons she never finished the book, but she read the unfinished chapters to me and the characters came alive in my imagination. We all know how any story about Noah's ark ends, but oh, how I wanted to discover how that ending came about for Eliana and Shem!

Many years later after I embarked upon my own writing career, Mom gave me an incredible gift—her partially written manuscript. She said, "The story is yours. Finish it." I read what she had written and again, the setting and characters became alive in my mind's eye. By then I'd developed my own writing style, so I put those pages aside and started over. The book you've just read is the result. I am so grateful to my mom, Amy Barkman, for giving her story to me and allowing me to make it my own. She has since gone on to write other books, including one of my favorite mysteries, *Murder at Tapestry Court.*

Over the years many people have seen this story in various stages of completion, and have helped me craft and polish it. I'm so grateful for their input, and for their enthusiasm for the story. Among them are Susie Smith, Beth Marlowe, Lisa Thomas, Tambra Rasmussen, Wendy Lawton, Susan J. Kroupa, Anna Zogg, and Sharon Hinck. Thank you, thank you, ladies!

Mostly, thanks to the One God for providing a

modern-day Ark to rescue us from the devastating re-
sults of sin—His own Son, Jesus.

I'd love to hear your thoughts about *The Days of
Noah*. You can write to me through my website,
www.virginiasmith.org, or at P.O. Box 70271, West
Valley City, UT 84170.

Virginia Smith

About the Author

Bestselling author **VIRGINIA SMITH,** or Ginny to her friends, is an avid reader with eclectic tastes in fiction. She writes stories in a variety of styles, from light-hearted romance to breath-snatching suspense. Her books have received many awards, including two Holt Medallion Awards of Merit.

When she isn't writing, Ginny enjoys exploring the extremes of nature—riding her motorcycle (a Triumph Bonneville T100 named Vickie), snow skiing, and scuba diving.

Learn more about Ginny and her books at
www.VirginiaSmith.org.

Books by Virginia Smith

Mystery and Romantic Suspense

Murder by Mushroom
Bluegrass Peril
Into the Deep
A Deadly Game
Horse and Burglary
Triple Layer Treachery

Classical Trio Series
A Taste of Murder
Murder at Eagle Summit
Scent of Murder

Falsely Accused Series
Dangerous Impostor
Bullseye
Prime Suspect

Contemporary and Romance

*Lost Melody**
A Daughter's Legacy
The Amish Widower

Incredible Mayla Strong series
Just As I Am
Sincerely, Mayla

Sister-to-Sister series
Stuck in the Middle
Age before Beauty
Third Time's a Charm

Tales from the Goose Creek B&B
Dr. Horatio vs. the Six-Toed Cat
The Most Famous Illegal Goose Creek Parade
Renovating the Richardsons
The Room with the Second-Best View
A Goose Creek Christmas

Historical Romance

Amish of Apple Grove series
The Heart's Frontier*
A Plain and Simple Heart*
A Cowboy at Heart*

Seattle Brides series
A Bride for Noah*
Rainy Day Dreams*

Children's Picture Book

The Last Christmas Cookie

* co-authored with Lori Copeland

Printed in Great Britain
by Amazon

57236967R00208